# P.S. DROP DEAD

Lance Colbert Smith

Neat Publishing

Published in Australia by Neat Publishing, Queensland

http://www.neatpublishing.com.au

Editing by Gail Tagarro Accredited Editor (AE) & Tyrone Couch

www.editors4you.com.au

Cover design by Mindy and Patrick at the Petridish

First Edition July 2022

Disclaimer :

Neat Publishing is proud to offer this book to readers. The story is entirely the author's creation.

This is a work of fiction. Any semblance between original characters and real persons, living or dead, is coincidental. A number of known people are referred to by name – not as characters, for the sole purpose of adding context to the story, the author does not speak for or represent these people. The author in no way represents the companies, corporations, or brands mentioned in this book. The author has endeavoured to ensure accuracy in such references, but offers no assurance that all references are entirely factual.

All opinions expressed in this book are the author's, or fictional.

# Dedication

I dedicate this book to two people who have been a major influence on my life: my fearless fire brigade mate for the past sixty years, Dave Holden, one of nature's true gentlemen and a terrific role model; and our very own angel, Sister Christine Marrinan, who took so many unwell children along one of life's toughest roads and gave them a soft landing, as well as a truckload of love and laughs along the way. You are both incredible human beings. Helen and I are privileged to be a part of your lives. I have used my perception of your personas and wisdom in telling this story.

# Comments

**Comments from industry leaders who evaluated the first draft of P.S. Drop Dead:**

"I loved it. The complexity of the interaction, the characterisation and their relation to the plot. Gripping and an exciting read." – *Pembo Press*

"Exceptional literary talent. I loved the frequency and intensity of the incidents, the theatrical flirtations around the margins of credibility." – *Book Review Team*

"I finished it at 3.45am as I couldn't put it down. Congratulations. A fabulous read." – *Skimming Post*

"I am not a great reader but, if I keep choosing stories like this, I may find a new hobby. I honestly couldn't put it down. It is an intriguing story that gets you in and keeps your attention." – *First Up Critiques*

# Prologue

How does an eight-year-old brain process murder?

Death has no boundaries—no particular time or place, and no common cause. Death can visit anyone, anytime, anywhere.

Take this balmy night, with trees swaying in the gentle breeze outside a Queenscliff family home. A young girl hears her dad's two gruff friends downstairs start to argue. Voices rise to a scream, and then gunshots echo through the house.

She looks down from the first-floor balcony and sees Mum and Dad, lying in a pool of blood. Her older sister runs for her life up the stairs, only to be gunned down by that horrible, scar-faced man. She watches in slow motion as the gun is wheeled around and pointed at her.

Fear. Pure terror. She turns and runs, and runs, and runs. She dives out the window, clambers down the drainpipe, crashes into the bushes below and takes off into the darkness.

Now, ten years later, that scar-faced man is a senior policeman, still looking for the only witness to his horrific crime.

*Beware of the dogs.*

# Chapter One

D etective Superintendent Tina Samuels and her sidekick Inspector Mike Broadfinger raced to the airport under siren and boarded the first available flight to Sydney out of the Gold Coast. They'd only just finished burying their friend when the news broke: a massive bomb had exploded at Parramatta Police Headquarters hours earlier, with many killed and injured.

Tina was working with the New South Wales Police Missing Persons Bureau, as well as heading various special task forces. Tall, with short blonde hair, a piercing stare and a huge reputation for her success fighting police and mob corruption, she was a force to be reckoned with, and very popular with the good guys in the ranks.

Her sorrows were twofold today.

The first of her troubles was the loss of long-time friend and fellow cancer sufferer Catie Lanyon, who'd died at the age of thirty-eight—far too young for such a talented and brilliant investigative journalist. Tina was so thankful their paths had crossed again at Dr. Emslie's surgery, where she too had first been diagnosed with cancer. Their reunion had led to Catie introducing her to a group of amazing people and, as a result of their combined efforts, worldwide headlines for busting major international drug cartels and illegal arms dealers. The New South Wales Police and Australian Federal Police profiles were at an all-time high, and Tina was getting the kudos. They'd produced some incredible results, some of which extended beyond her policing duties.

Catie's extensive list of influential contacts had been invaluable to the investigation. The information they were able to supply Tina, at great risk to themselves, led to the arrest and gaoling of many drug lords, mobsters, crooked cops and politicians worldwide. Catie's legacy would last forever.

*Great lives never go out; they just go on,* thought Tina.

Despite the overwhelming success of the operation, Tina still carried a nagging self-doubt. So many people had been killed on her watch—good ones, like Anita, the girlfriend of mob boss 'Wipeout' Tony Moribito. At least her little girl had survived the raids. Nick 'The Greek' Pashalidis, a vegetable stall boss from the Sydney markets, was another of the casualties. A decent and wonderful man, Nick had worked with Tina on mob corruption and criminal matters in the markets for years. Both were killed for giving invaluable information.

Then, of course, there was Catie's demise.

Tina was grateful that Catie had won the top Walkley Award and thus been appropriately recognised for her efforts before leaving this life. A lot of bad people were off the streets because of Catie's efforts, including some of Tina's colleagues. Many of them had died, and Tina was acutely aware that even they had mums, dads, children or siblings who loved them no matter what. The burden weighed on her heavily.

Her second sadness was about this morning's bomb blast at Parramatta Police Headquarters. Her close colleague, Inspector Derek Sward, was thought to be amongst the dead. Derek had been her backbone, confidant and mentor over the past few months, and she considered him responsible for much of her success.

Details about the attack were sketchy at best. There were no immediate leads to confirm if it was mob payback, terrorism or just a disgruntled citizen with a grudge against police.

Tina and Mike were to be met by another member of the special task force at Sydney Airport, Detective Sergeant Georgia McHenry-Holder, who'd been recalled from her honeymoon that morning to support the operation. Already on the job, Georgia was to brief them on the latest developments.

Tina rested her eyes as they approached Sydney airspace. It seemed so long ago that they'd solved the Riley Sampson missing persons case, yet it was only three months ago. The Cobama gang had abducted eight-year-old Riley for ransom. Riley's dad was a real estate agent who'd fallen into the claws of the Cobama gang through his large gambling losses. The gang had abducted eight-year-old Riley from his school camp at Narrabeen, cut off his finger and sent it to his petrified dad along with their demand for money. Rick Sampson had then begged from all his friends and associates, had a fire sale of his most valuable assets and misappropriated some of his clients' trust funds to repay the mob and get his son back.

It was good police work by Detective McHenry-Holder that had solved the case. There'd been a shootout at Riley's handover that resulted in the death of one of the mobsters and injuries to others, including one of the police task force. The good news was that

Riley had been kept safe and was returned home to his very relieved and thankful mum, Jan. Tina wondered if that mob might be responsible for the Parramatta attack.

It was a bleak day in Sydney as the jet flew under low clouds on the approach to Kingsford Smith Airport, the rain over Botany Bay skidding across the small cabin windows. The whitecaps on the ocean below looked like the peaks of a thousand snow-capped mountains. Several fishing trawlers on the water retreated to their moorings, seeking shelter from the howling wind and rising seas.

As soon as the plane landed, Tina turned on her phone and saw two missed calls from Police Commissioner John Palmer. She immediately called him back while Mike hauled down their cabin bags. They were in seats 1A and 1B, positioned to be the first off the plane.

"Hi Tina," the commissioner answered.

"Commissioner," said Tina. "What's the situation?"

"I don't know how much you know, so I'll just start talking," said Palmer. "The bomb was massive, and a real pro job. There were many civilian and police casualties, including Derek Sward, who is in a critical condition in ICU at Westmead. I'm on site now. I understand you're coming over from the airport, so I'll wait for your arrival."

"Where do you want me on this one?" she asked.

"I'm putting you in charge, because I suspect you'll have the best idea of what led up to the bombing. It looks to me like some sort of payback for recent events, but whether it's a local mob or international, we have yet to sort out."

"My thoughts exactly. Hard to imagine it's just coincidence."

"I've stationed extra police at all airports, railway stations and shipping departures to monitor anyone trying to get out. There are extra highway patrols carefully checking all vehicles. If they're on the road, we'll find them."

"Okay, commissioner. See you soon."

Tina signed off.

Her first sense was one of relief that Derek Sward was alive. She would keep her fingers crossed that he remained that way. She passed on the details of their conversation to Mike as they walked up the aerobridge and into the terminal.

Detective Sergeant Georgia McHenry-Holder waved as they exited and immediately briefed Tina and Mike as the trio walked down to the baggage collection area. Their two bags were amongst the first out, so they headed out of the terminal to the waiting police transport. It was a Wednesday, so the traffic was heavy.

Mike looked around as they drove out and frowned.

"Boss, a black SUV just pulled out behind us. Looks like it's following us," he said. "I'll get Pol Air to do a check straight away."

Meanwhile, Georgia reported that the explosion had not originated from a vehicle outside the Police HQ, as they'd first thought. It had been planted inside the station behind security and detonated from somewhere nearby.

"So that means whoever planted it had security access to the area," she added. "That narrows the field of inquiry."

"I've requested any surviving CCTV footage from the station, as well as various businesses and buildings on Charles Street," said Tina. "Parra Council also have some pole-mounted footage. What else do we know?"

"There was mass confusion after the bomb went off," said Georgia. "At the moment, we have fourteen confirmed dead; six civilians, and eight police and station staff. Some thirty to thirty-five were injured and have been sent to various hospitals, a number of them critical. Amongst those are Inspector Sward and his assistant, Sergeant Garry Townsend, who were both in the interview room near where the device was planted."

"Bastards," said Mike. "How is the recovery effort going?"

"Rescuers are expecting to find more buried under the debris. Sergeant Joe Hudson from Parra car twenty-eight, who I'm sure you remember from the Cobama bust, was soon on the scene. Terry Smythe and Charlie Wake also happened to be nearby with a special dog squad car. Those three, and some others, did a great job getting people out and to safety amongst fears that a second device might go off.

"I've asked Blacktown to give us a team to deliver the sad news to all the families of those who have died and are injured," the detective added. "Brian Carey went out to Barbara Sward himself. Says she was devastated. He's on his way to Garry Townsend's home at Chipping Norton now."

By the time they arrived at the scene, Georgia had relayed all the known facts to Tina and Mike, but they still had only a very rough picture of events.

The two were surprised at the extent of the destruction. Smoke was still spurting out from a number of areas in the ruins.

"God, how could anyone have survived?" said Mike, speaking for all of them.

There were still many ambulances, fire engines and special units working at the site. The rescue teams painstakingly sifted through the broken and twisted rubble. Cranes lifted large, broken slabs of concrete and tortured metal away into waiting trucks. Forensic teams were everywhere, taking notes and photos and placing evidence in sealed containers.

Tina could hear a dog barking somewhere nearby.

Then, a loudhailer announced, "Quiet on the site. Quiet on the site."

Suddenly, an eerie silence descended on the scene as everything ground to a halt.

Rescuers with specialised locator devices pointed, checked screens and listened on earphones. Everyone looked on as a team of four galvanised into action around a crumbling mess of debris in the far western corner.

One of the men spoke into the rocks in a deep, reassuring voice.

"We hear you. Stay still. We're nearly there. Can you hear me?"

There must've been a response from under the rubble, as the team leader appeared to be talking to someone. Tina, Mike and Georgia looked on as the team burrowed further into the destruction.

After what seemed an eternity, but was no more than a few minutes, excited cries and claps rang out as two people were hauled carefully out of the devastation and placed onto stretchers. One man was in a uniform which, by now, was hardly recognisable. The other person appeared to be a youngster. Both were covered in debris, dust and obvious injuries. Surrounded by rescuers, they began the risky trek through the crumbling wreckage. Then, the rescue noises started all over again as the pair were loaded into two of the waiting ambulances.

Tina felt a shiver go down her spine.

"What sort of animal would do this?" she asked, looking to Mike for answers.

He had none to offer.

Georgia had wandered off and returned with three men, one of whom was in uniform.

"Superintendent, this is Sergeant Joe Hudson and Detectives Terry Smythe and Charlie Wake," she said. "They were the first on the scene and did a great job mobilising the rescue effort."

Tina had met 'Smokin'' Joe Hudson at the Riley Sampson handover shooting, and she knew Charlie Wake from previous task forces. She remembered him as a good cop with a brother in the force. With the surname Wake, their nicknames were 'I'ma' and 'Wida'. She couldn't remember which was which.

"Have you all given statements?" asked Tina.

All three nodded.

"Okay. I'll go over them back at my office. You look buggered," she said. "As soon as you can, go home, clean up and rest. Thanks for your efforts. It sounds like a good few people owe their lives to you three. I'd like to see you in my Chatswood office at 9 tomorrow morning. I should be ready to move forward by then—unless there's anything you think we need to do sooner?"

Nothing was forthcoming. The three men wandered off in a trance-like manner. They'd had a long and tough day.

"Mike, you stay here and keep me posted on any developments," said Tina. "Georgia, you and I are going back to Chatswood to get started. But first, I'd like to call in at the hospital to check on Derek, Garry and the others."

They headed back into Charles Street, which was full of curious onlookers, anxious relatives, media and rescue teams, as well as a group of uniformed police trying to maintain some sort of order. They avoided the media scrum and left quickly.

As they drove west along Hawkesbury Road on the approach to Westmead Hospital, Tina directed Georgia to park outside the main entrance.

"We won't be here long," she said. "I just want to set up a line of communication and find out how everyone is. I'm feeling a bit uneasy about all of this. Call HQ and get twenty-four-hour police security set up wherever the victims are, hospitals or otherwise. I should be back soon."

Tina strode into the main entry and presented at the reception desk. She told them who she was and was asked to wait.

Shortly after, a well-dressed man in his late forties came up to her.

"Good afternoon, Superintendent," said the man. "I'm Richard Doyle, CEO of Westmead. Whatever you need, we will provide to the best of our ability. Like so many others, I am saddened to hear all the dreadful news."

After a fruitful five-minute discussion, Tina bid farewell to the CEO, who'd informed her that Derek and Garry were both in deep comas with multiple injuries. He'd said their conditions were extremely serious, but assured her they were in the best of hands, promising to call as soon as anything developed.

Tina was deep in thought as they drove north along the M4 heading towards Chatswood. Nearing the city, she wondered how Brad and the 4G Team were coping after Catie's funeral. She hoped the wake had gone well.

*This was her 'other side',* she thought, shivering at the notion.

Peak-hour traffic was starting to build on the southbound lanes. An ambulance made slow progress, weaving amongst those trying to move out of its path.

"Oh God, Georgia, I forgot to ask," said Tina. "Forgive me. How was the honeymoon?"

"No worries, Super. Totally understandable," she said. "It was wonderful. We spent the first week on Daydream Island. The Whitsunday weather was fabulous. We snorkelled, scuba-dived and cruised. We even took out a sailing boat. Dave is no sailor, and I'm even worse, but we had a ball. Daydream Island has an amazing underwater observation area. Sensational. We came home for the last week to do some work on the house. Dave had to go back to work today, and I was called in this morning. A sad end to two great weeks."

Tina nodded solemnly, then chuckled.

"The wedding was beautiful, and so were you ... but that little flower girl upstaged you all. She was priceless."

"That's my niece, Carley," Georgia laughed. "My sister Fiona's little girl. She really is a hoot."

They talked more about the wedding for a time, then got back to the case at hand. Tina made a call to Commissioner John Palmer from the car, outlining her plan to form a new task force and set up a special working room at Chatswood. She agreed to go into Day Street Police HQ the next day after her meetings, and then signed off.

"This bloody COVID," Tina sighed. "The commissioner is saying we have to cut down on numbers because so many are on pandemic patrol. What a waste of resources."

"Why can't people wake up and obey simple restrictions without bringing the boys in blue and the defence force in? What a crazy country," Georgia replied.

Neither of them saw the black SUV coming up behind them in the adjacent lane. Georgia was first to realise they had a problem when she saw through her rear vision mirror the gun barrel poking out of a window. She took instant evasive action, swinging straight into the left shoulder lane and jamming on the brakes as the shooting started.

Tina and Georgia felt a huge impact. There was a crunching sound as the police car crashed into a stationary van and crumpled, followed by a deathly silence as they both fell unconscious.

# Chapter Two

J ane sat bolt upright in the chilly pre-dawn air, still hearing
the terrified screams. Her crumpled bedding and clothes were
damp from the nightmare sweats, her heart racing from the fear.

*It's okay, breathe slowly, relax,* she told herself.

They were the same mental images that had haunted her for the
past ten years. The pain never seemed to ease. She prised herself out
of the narrow wooden bed, realising further sleep was impossible.

*At least I'll be first in the shower and have hot water,* she thought.

She shuffled down the sparsely-furnished hallway towards the
cold bathroom, floorboards creaking.

Jane had hated Weatherall Cottage from the moment she was
first taken there by the National Park Rangers all those years before. She'd been pushed up the stairs and into the reception area
like an unloved orphan, still grubby, with matted curly hair and
torn clothing hanging off her skinny frame.

The three adults who'd questioned her were angered by her
silence. She still remembered the stern dressing-down she'd
been given about her attitude as one of the supervising nuns
half-dragged her up the steep wooden stairs to her new home. For
over two years, she didn't utter one word to anyone. Unable to

identify her, they'd marked her file 'Jane Doe', which changed to 'Jane Dee' after a while.

Her arrival at the cottage was ten years ago now. Jane had survived and learnt to cope since then, though she still dreamed of a life in a place far away, anywhere but here.

Now eighteen, she desperately wanted a way out—a chance for some happiness and some sort of normality, free from all the draconian rules and regulations of the orphanage. Maybe she could even solve her own personal mystery.

Weatherall Cottage was a group of cold, dreary buildings of stone, with leaking pipes and rattling windows throughout. Rough gravel pathways meandered through the barren, poorly-kept gardens and patchy lawns to the bare cobblestone exercise yard. The complex was a leftover from the old Camperdown Children's Hospital days, founded in the latter part of the twentieth century, now just over two acres and surrounded by an eight-foot-high motley clay brick fence, the tops covered with jagged broken bottles set in concrete.

The constant rumbling of the early morning winter traffic along Pyrmont Bridge Road reverberated through the ageing complex as Jane dressed into some loose-fitting work clothes and slip-on shoes in readiness for another day in hell.

At any one time, there were usually around thirty girls aged between eight and twenty resident in the shelter—or 'the founding home for abandoned young ladies', as the Sisters of Saint Bernard referred to it.

Jane was now an 'elder' in the place, having survived the tough regime for over a decade. She'd seen many girls come and go over that time, adopted, fostered out, employed or otherwise deemed able to handle the outside world by the cottage board at their monthly meetings.

She was disappointed that some of those girls she'd got on well with had never contacted her, or even sent cards, after they left, though she fully understood their desire to break ties.

Jane's name rarely came up for consideration in the adoption parades, held regularly in the downstairs common room for potential parents.

Jane's file showed she was 'unidentified, moody, known to display unusual behaviours and afflicted by deep-seated fears', and thus inappropriate for release. The chairman of the board, Brian McGarry, made her skin crawl; he often sat on his own in the common room, just watching the girls.

Weatherall Cottage was a state government institution, but was also supported by several influential private philanthropists. The shelter prided itself on a number of awards under the 'Early Childhood Education and Care' industry banner. The centre had been declared a participant of the 2020 national redress scheme, a government apology to children who'd experienced state-run institutional care or abuse.

Behind this caring façade, however, was a very different and challenging environment. Many of the 'misfits' and mixed-up kids in the system were incarcerated by circumstance, through no fault of their own. This institution was for those assessed to be 'unmanageable' despite the best efforts of a hard-working and well-meaning team—for the most part.

Thursdays, like this one, weren't too bad for Jane. After her breakfast duties, daily chores and morning schooling, she had her weekly one-on-one session to look forward to.

Dr. David Holder, the shelter's clinical psychologist, was one of the few people who brought a little warmth to her existence. He'd been working on her case for just over two years. Jane much preferred the one-on-one appointment to the regular group sessions, which usually ended in an angry slur-fest with multiple walkouts. Dr. Holder was the one person who seemed to understand her and genuinely care about her situation.

*Not that it makes any difference,* she thought.

"Hey, schizo! What's for breakfast?"

Roxy burst into the kitchen, her rasping voice bringing Jane out of her trance.

"Help yourself, barge arse. You know the drill," Jane quipped.

Roxanne Jenkins was another long-time resident; a short, solid, no-nonsense angry tomboy who barked at everyone and tried to rule the roost. Roxy had been admitted to the shelter after her father received a life sentence for beating her mother to death in front of her and her little brother. That was eleven years ago, when she was only nine years old.

She'd been classified as uncontrollable, separated from her younger brother and made a ward of the state, placed into the care of Weatherall Cottage. Her ripped, faded jeans and checked flannel top with torn, rolled-up sleeves made her look tough.

Years ago, Jane had been frightened by Roxy, but not now. Her brashness had become just another part of their everyday life. Jane had a soft spot for Roxy, depending on what mood she was in. There was a glimmer of hope that one day, Roxy would find and be reunited with her little brother and rise above this hellish life. She wasn't all that bad, and had come to Jane's defence many times in the past.

"Did I hear you talking to the ghosts again?"

"They're not ghosts, they're spirits," Jane replied coolly.

Local folklore held that Weatherall Cottage was haunted by two ghosts: one, a kindly nursing sister who'd died in a hospital fire years before in the so-called 'library'; the other, a young orphan girl found dead in the kitchen. Many of the resident girls and the staff were spooked by the frequently reported sightings.

Jane had never seen the young girl, but had encountered the spirit of the nurse on a number of occasions, and was able to communicate with her.

"How come you didn't help the ambos last night?" demanded Roxy.

"What ambos? What happened?"

"Your best mate, Crazy Cate, cut herself again. Might have succeeded this time. They'll probably make us clean up the mess. Stupid bitch."

Roxy headed for the pantry.

"I didn't hear anything. I had my headphones in," Jane answered.

Jane loved cutting out the noise of the world at night with audiobooks and podcasts. It was her way of drifting off to sleep.

"Don't tell me you're still listening to that friggin' crap! What good does studying do for a loose cannon like you?"

"You might find out someday. You never know."

"And pigs might fly," mumbled Roxy as she helped herself to a large bowl of cereal.

"Is Cate okay?" Jane enquired.

"Who cares? It happened well after lights out. No one has said anything to us."

Roxy's prediction came true. Sister Victoria came into the kitchen just as a number of girls were finishing up.

"Roxy, Jane and Amber. No school for you three today. When you are finished here, I want you to clean up Catherine's room. She's in hospital, seriously ill, and may be away for a while."

That was it. Nothing more was said; just 'do it'.

Cate's room was indeed a mess, and Jane was instantly very concerned. There was blood all over the bedding, walls and floor. It looked like a cyclone had gone through it.

"She even smashed her mum's photo," said Amber, pointing to the broken glass and frame, now crumpled up on the floor. "That was the only thing she liked."

There was one other photo in the room, featuring Cate and Jane, taken on a rare trip to Luna Park. Cate was very pretty, and her smile could light up any room. Jane picked it up and put it in her pocket.

Amber was younger than the other two, just fifteen years old. She'd come from a broken home in nearby Redfern and had been an ice addict for some years. The rumour was that she'd been held on a murder charge, accused of pushing a man off a balcony in their high-rise government flat.

Dark-skinned with sharp, piercing green eyes and intelligent features, Amber was quick-witted and popular amongst the other girls. She was very attractive when she smiled, but that wasn't very often.

She'd been trying to get the others involved in learning about indigenous culture, but with little success. Amber obviously had deep personal convictions and a good foundation of knowledge in that area. She often talked of her early years on country in the

Northern Territory, where the tribal elders had taught her their abundant bush skills and language.

Sadly, like the other two, Amber had never had a visitor in her three years at Weatherall Cottage.

She suddenly stiffened.

"Look, under the pillow!"

She pointed, then picked up a mustard-coloured envelope.

"It's addressed to you," she said, handing the hand-written note to Jane, who slipped it straight into her pocket.

"Why don't you read it now?" demanded Roxy.

"It can wait," said Jane. "It won't change anything now. Both of you, keep quiet about it."

"Bossy bitch," mumbled Roxy.

# Chapter Three

After Amber, Jane and Roxy had scrubbed, cleaned and made up Cate's room to a presentable standard, they were called to a special assembly in the common room.

"Mirrors wants to talk to us all," came the message.

Just after 12.30pm, the senior nurse, Graham Larkin, came into the room, shabbily dressed and looking stern as usual. The girls called him 'Mirrors' because every time they came to him with a problem, he'd say, 'I'll look into it', but never did.

"As you all know, Catherine is gravely ill and in hospital from what looks to be a self-inflicted injury," said Graham. "This is a very disappointing outcome for Weatherall Cottage, as we work hard with *all* of you to offer a safe and friendly environment."

He went on in his usual disinterested tone. The girls had heard it all before.

"If any of you have personal issues you want to discuss, my door is always open."

*"And so is your fly,"* Amber said quietly.

The senior nurse had made many suggestive, threatening remarks to her in the past, but she always simply stared him down with those angry eyes of hers.

Thirty long minutes later, the lecture was over, and the girls headed into the kitchen to grab a bite to eat.

Jane made a sandwich and took a bottle of orange juice before heading upstairs to the privacy of her room. She was keen to read Catie's note.

The room was basic. There were no personal photos or trophies; just two team centrefolds of her beloved Manly Sea Eagles rugby league team stuck proudly on the wall beside her bed and a small, round mirror balanced on her wooden dresser. Jane rarely glanced into it, thinking herself very plain-looking. She hated her freckles, crooked teeth and pale skin.

The only other item in the room was a beautiful, multicoloured crystal hummingbird hanging from the window frame between the drab curtains. The breeze allowed the reflection of the sun's rays to project its many colours—sparkling reds, yellows, greens and blues—all dancing around the walls and ceiling. It reminded her of the fairies she saw in the secret garden at National Park.

Jane had seen the crystal at the Glebe markets on one of their rare outings and pleaded with the stallholder to hold it for her. She'd saved all her meagre pocket money for months while others squandered theirs on cakes, chocolates and lollies. She loved that pretty bird.

"I hope you get lots of enjoyment from it," the stallholder had said, seeing the joy in her eyes when she'd made the final payment.

Jane took another bite of her sandwich, sipped her juice and opened the sealed envelope.

*Dear Jane,*

*By the time you get this, I'll be dead.*

*You're the only thing I'll miss about this life. You taught me so much. I'm sorry to do this, but it is for the best. Thank you for being my best friend.*

*When I was thirteen, my drunk father got me pregnant. I never told anyone at the cottage—not even you. It was too much for my beautiful mum, and she ended up topping herself too.*

*They took my baby away before I even saw it, then sent me straight to this hellhole.*

*I would've been a real good mother, I reckon. My gran said we could live with her, but they wouldn't allow it.*

*At least now I'll be with Mum and in a better place.*

*I was on the adoption parade this morning and allocated to those two creeps who keep showing up to parade. I know this is a better outcome for me.*

*I hope you get out soon, and you and your sister really do well in life.*

*You deserve that and more. Goodbye, my friend.*

*Love, Cate. XX*

A tear ran down Jane's cheek; a rare thing.

*What a shit life. Poor bugger*, she thought. *God, I hope she's okay.*

Jane and Cate had had many discussions after lights out, often well into the morning. They snuck into each other's rooms between the nun's patrols, and had never been caught.

Cate had learnt little about life before coming to the cottage. Her father had been an alcoholic, and hardly ever worked. He'd often beat her mother in a drunken rage. She'd been absent from school a lot, preferring instead to stay at home, helping her mum make beautiful clothes to be sold at the local markets. She'd loved listening to Jane's stories and adventures.

She once asked, "Where did you learn all this?"

Jane had told her that her sister Darlene 'could see things', and would pass them onto her.

That was one of the few things that kept Jane's sanity intact. Even though she hadn't seen her sister physically for ten years, Darlene came to her in her room and other places when Jane was alone, and they had many robust conversations. She could feel her presence and hear her loud and clear.

"Jane? Doc Holder is here."

The booming voice of Sister Chrissy Marion, Jane's favourite nun, jolted her back to the present. She quickly finished the sandwich, grabbed her shoulder bag and descended the stairs to the interview room.

She slumped into a chair opposite the psychologist.

"Hi Jane," said Dr. Holder. "How's it going?"

Her reply came instantly, accompanied by a cold stare.

"Upta. Life's crap in this rat-infested place."

"Well, my job is to get you out of here, ready to enjoy the best of the outside world ... but you haven't made it easy over the past couple of years, young lady."

The departmental authorities had no idea who Jane was, or anything about her life before she'd been found in the dense bush on Manly's North Head. No child had been reported missing, and there was no trace of Jane's family. Her DNA and photos were shown and matched to every family with a missing child, but without a match. Jane was still petrified that if she was identified, the scar-faced killer cop would find her.

"Listen, kiddo. You and I have always got on pretty well," said the doctor. "I know that behind those sad eyes is a wonderful and intelligent human being, capable of great things. But this therapy thing? It's a two-way street, and you have to play your part."

Dr. Dave looked Jane dead in the eye.

"Let me ask you one simple question. Do you want to get out of here and live a happy life? Yes, or no?"

Jane's shoulders slumped forward. She shuffled uncomfortably in her chair.

After a long pause, she returned his gaze.

"Yes," she said firmly.

"Great. Then let's both get to work and give it a go," he said. "I spent last weekend going over your file and everyone's notes, trying to make sense of all the conflicting reports. It's obvious that you experience good days and bad, sometimes in the extreme. That isn't unusual; we all get a bit like that sometimes. But in your case, you seem to have locked away a whole lot of your life inside your head. I would love for us to unlock that door and start releasing some of the pain that hides behind it. I know that, between us, we can do it—but I really need you to trust me. Am I making sense?"

Jane didn't respond.

Her mind started to race backwards again. The session was going down the road she hated most—past all the garbage she never wanted to think about. She said nothing, simply staring at the floor.

The doctor ploughed on.

"Let's go back to before you came here. I'm happy to offer you one hundred per cent confidentiality. Nothing goes into your file without your approval. Whatever it takes," he assured her. "We both know you'll never be able to move forward until you exorcise those demons of yours. I'm not worried about who you've been or what you've done; I'm not here to judge. I'm here to work with you through whatever it is. There are no mistakes, only lessons. Learn from yesterday, live for today and hope for tomorrow."

Jane remained silent, but was clearly thinking.

"You were brought here some ten years ago under circumstances that are still a complete mystery. You were only eight years old, and yet you refused to give us a name or any family history. You didn't speak a word for over two years, so it can't have been your run-of-the-mill trauma. I know you can win out over whatever caused it, and I think you do too. I can help.

"What we *do* know is that somehow, you'd been surviving in the bush around Manly's North Head and the National Park for months, and no one knows how or why. Reports of a feral child being sighted in the area had been circulating for some time. My question is, why did you give up so easily when you were found?"

Jane closed her eyes, remembering the many cold, miserable, lonely months looking in bins for scraps, digging up yams and eating them raw. Running and hiding every time she heard human noises, terrified 'they' would find and kill her, the last witness.

She could still clearly see, hear and feel the rain, wind and lightning. She smiled to herself, remembering her beautiful fairy gardens by the sea. She'd become close to a large family of long-nosed bandicoots, who eventually walked and played with her for hours at a time, totally at ease. They'd taught Jane to dig up the yams and snuggled into her nest of old rags and newspapers, sleeping with her every night. They were family. She wondered if they missed her—particularly Brokenfoot, the young bandicoot with the mangled leg she'd become so close to.

She thought of the rare cold showers she took in the old quarantine block when no one was around, then finally looked up, straight into Dave's eyes.

"Because I was starving," she said flatly. "What would you have done?"

The psychologist was taken aback. This was the first time that Jane had acknowledged her past in any way.

He continued quickly.

"Why didn't you ask the police for help?"

"Because coppers are killers," she blurted out.

"Jane," Dave said gently. "I am married to a wonderful copper. She's kind, fair, caring and a credit to the police force. What do you think about that?"

There was another pause, but this time, she jumped up suddenly.

"Drop dead!" Jane spat loudly.

She jerked up her shoulder bag and stormed out, slamming the door as she went.

Dave's jaw dropped. He hadn't been expecting that reaction.

"This is going to be a rough ride," he said to himself. "But at last, we have a starting point."

He reflected on the last part of the conversation for a few minutes, then wrote a short note to Jane and handed it to Sister Chrissy on his way out.

"Don't give it to her until she calms down," he suggested. "Maybe tomorrow."

Sister Chrissy nodded understandingly.

She waved goodbye to Dr. Holder as she slipped the note for Jane into her cassock pocket. The kindly nun liked Dr. Dave, as did many of the other staff and resident girls. He came across as kind and genuine, and had achieved some great outcomes over the past few years. She thought they were lucky to have him at Weatherall Cottage.

She knew Jane's was a tough case, but thought that if anyone could get through to her, it would be Dr. Holder. She hoped so, at least, because Jane was one of her favourites, and in real need of someone to trust. Though she wondered what had caused Jane to storm out of his office, she was not surprised by the outburst. She could be volatile at times.

Though Jane's behaviour was nothing out of the ordinary, Sister Chrissy felt that not all at the cottage was as it seemed. She'd been wary of Chairman McGarry and the CEO, Mrs. Mary O'Brien, from day one, and now that some of her concerns were being validated, she didn't know who to turn to. She considered confiding in the psychologist, Dr. Holder, but still didn't have enough to go on.

Dr. Dave's first day since returning from his honeymoon had been long, and he was happy to be heading home to his new bride. He was halfway to the car when his mobile started vibrating. Glancing at the screen, he did not recognise the number as he answered.

"Dr. Holder, this is Sergeant Brad Henderson from Chatswood Police Headquarters," said the voice on the other line. "I'm one of Georgia's colleagues. I am ringing to let you know your wife has been injured in a car accident and is on her way to Royal Prince Alfred Hospital by ambulance. We have no further details at the moment, but thought you should know straight away. I'm sorry."

Dave froze.

Sister Chrissy watched from the window as the doctor approached his car. She saw him answer his mobile phone, exchange a few words and then slump against his car, distraught. She ran down the stairs and across the car park just in time to see Dave recovering his composure, searching for his car keys.

"Are you alright, Dr. Holder?" she asked.

"My wife has had some sort of car accident," he said, flustered. "She's at the Prince Alfred. I don't understand. She was decorating our lounge today."

He practically fell into the car.

"Are you okay to drive?"

"I'll be fine. The hospital is just along Missenden Road. I'll be there in five minutes."

He fumbled with his keys before finding the ignition.

"Please call me if any of us can be of any help. May God be with you both," she offered as he pulled out of the car park.

She went back into the cottage and looked at the clock. It was almost time to head back to the monastery, where she would stand for the evening prayer session. There would be no kneeling for this ageing nun. Religion and arthritis didn't mix.

# Chapter Four

The two ambulances were fairly close together as they sped under siren, lights flashing along Missenden Road towards the Royal Prince Alfred. Their police escort had cleared a lot of traffic, and they'd made good time. A third, unmarked police car had turned off Parramatta Road and was close behind as they approached the hospital.

Both trolleys were quickly unloaded at the emergency entrance. Tina and Georgia were rushed into the ICU, where medical teams waited and immediately went to work.

As reported by the paramedics, both police officers were in a serious but stable condition, having been knocked unconscious as the police car smashed into the broken-down van. Had it not been for the deployment of both airbags, things could have been a lot worse.

Police Commissioner Palmer, who'd followed right behind the ambulances, walked with the trolleys inside, standing well back as the medical teams got to work. After placing the two other police teams on watch, he went to the nurses' station and asked for the person in charge.

The lady at the desk looked up.

"That would be me, Sir. Sister Debbie Carter. What can I do for you?"

John Palmer introduced himself and told the nurse that shots had been fired from a passing vehicle immediately prior to the accident, and that as a matter of precaution, he would be stationing police in the hospital ward and corridors until the matter was investigated further.

"Is there somewhere I can wait until I can talk to the two officers?" he asked.

Sister Carter took him into her office.

"There is a phone, pads and pens. Make yourself at home while I check on the team's progress," she said. "Let me know if you need to access the computer."

The commissioner was soon at work organising surveillance teams and getting reports from the scene. Some fifteen minutes later, he looked up as Sister Carter came back into the office.

"Reasonable news from both patients," she said. "They were severely knocked about, but both have regained consciousness. Their injuries are not considered life-threatening, and they should be okay to talk to you within the hour.

"You'll need to take it easy with both of them," she added. "They may not remember much about the accident itself, and will tire easily. The medication will keep them sleepy, so their concentration will lapse quickly."

"Thank you, Sister," said Palmer.

"One last thing. The husband of one of the ladies has already arrived, as has another senior police officer. I've got them both in the main foyer."

The commissioner nodded and asked to be called as soon as he could talk to the patients. Sister Carter then took him to the main foyer and suggested he wait in the coffee shop.

As they arrived, the commissioner recognised Inspector Mike Broadfinger talking to a well-dressed gent. He assumed this must be Georgia's husband, as he knew David Samuels, Tina's husband, quite well, and that certainly wasn't him.

"Commissioner," Mike acknowledged as they approached. "This is Dr. Dave Holder, Detective Sergeant McHenry-Holder's husband of two weeks. He was nearby in Camperdown when the word came through. Any news?"

"Yes, and it's not too bad." He shook Dave's hand. "Hello, Dave. Commissioner John Palmer. This is Sister Debbie Carter. The medical team have just told us both the girls have regained consciousness, but are very groggy. The good news is, there are no apparent life-threatening injuries. Having said that, it was still quite an ordeal. I'm hoping to be able to talk to them shortly."

After advising that police surveillance crews were on their way as a precaution, he asked Mike to join him in the coffee shop to discuss the case. He promised Dave that he would be called into Georgia's room as soon as possible.

The pair sat in a quiet corner of the coffee shop with a hot cappuccino apiece.

"Something's not right, chief," said Mike. "When we left the airport this afternoon, I called for a Pol Air report on a black SUV that looked like it was following us. In all the happenings at Parramatta, I forgot about it—right up until I heard that a black SUV was used to shoot up the girls' car on the M4."

"I have a feeling you still haven't got to the bad news," said Palmer.

"I'm afraid not. It appears the Pol Air request was intercepted, and somehow 'lost' in the system without notifying me. We ran the request again as soon as we found out, and it turns out the vehicle was hired by two men who'd flown into the international terminal from Colombia on Sunday morning. I've asked for a red flag priority on their identities and put out an all-points bulletin on the vehicle. If I'd known this earlier, things could've been different. I have no idea who intercepted the original report."

The commissioner cursed.

"Mike, it may well be that we still have more bad eggs in the ranks—maybe even high up," he said. "It looks like they're quite concerned about our recent successes. Has anyone spoken to David Samuels yet?"

"Brad Henderson rang him, as well as Georgia's husband," said Mike. "He's on his way from Epping."

"Okay. You head back to Chatswood and ring Deputy Commissioner Hardcastle. Tell him to get 'task force clean-out' together tomorrow—3pm, at the usual. We have to get ahead of these bastards. I'll stay here and call you as soon as I see some progress. I may need to see you before the task force meets tomorrow."

Mike nodded and rose from his seat.

Just then, his mobile buzzed and he answered it.

"Henderson? Calm down. What's wrong?"

As the call continued, the colour drained from Mike's face. He fell back into his seat.

"What is it?" the police commissioner asked.

"Someone got to Westmead Hospital before our security team," he said. "Inspector Sward has been murdered."

# Chapter Five

Tina's vision was foggy, as was her mind. The room swayed from side to side as she wondered where she was and struggled to comprehend what was happening. Why was her face covered in plastic? Why were the tubes from the drip bags hanging from the pipe tree? She tried to shift her body, but pain caused it to seize. She moaned softly, her mind flashing.

"Ah, you're awake. Welcome back to the land of the living," said a voice. "I'll do the talking, you do the listening. I'm Sister Fran McBremner, and you, Tina, have had a nasty car accident. You're in the Royal Prince Alfred Hospital. The good news is, you're going to be okay, but it'll take a wee while before you get there."

Tina could only make out a blurry image of a person, but the Scottish brogue of the nurse was a comforting sound, and soon had Tina thinking furiously. She remembered the sound of shooting and some sort of collision before she blacked out.

*Georgia.*

She tried to ask, but only a gargled sound came out.

"Now you just relax. Everything will be okay, but you have to let yourself heal. You've been through a lot," said Sister McBremner, as if she were chiding a youngster. "Your friend Georgia is okay.

She, too, has a lot of healing to do, but the good news is you'll both come through this."

Tina tried hard to piece together what had happened, but her head was hurting. Thoughts were difficult to marshal, and kept coming in and out of focus. Above all, she knew she had to get up and get to work.

She realised the nurse was giving her some kind of injection, then relaxed and drifted off to sleep.

When Tina next came to, she could see the nurse more clearly this time, but her head was still hurting. She tried to turn it to see more of her surroundings and breathed in sharply, causing her to make a gargling sound.

"Hello again, lassie," the nurse smiled at her. "Your vital signs are on the improve. You're doing very well. Just relax, breathe deeply and let mother nature do what she does best."

Tina was worried.

*David. Does he know?*

She was thinking fast.

*What happened to my gun? Who has it?* Typically, a police officer's first thought.

Then she remembered her two mobile phones.

*Oh God. I've got to get them.*

She panicked as she remembered her second phone and the explosive material it contained. She wondered if Brad and the 4G Team—the people from her other life—knew about this yet.

*What a mess.*

She tried to untangle all the thoughts in her head and make sense of it all.

"Tina, this is Dr. Humphreys," said Sister McBremner. "He has been looking after you since your admission. Doing a bonnie job, if you ask me."

Tina saw the doctor come into her space and tried to say something, but it sounded like no more than a mumble.

"Hi, Tina. You've been to hell and back, but all the signs are good. No major broken bones or organ damage. We've run a number of scans, and all the reports are better than expected. You are one lucky girl," said the doctor.

Tina thought he sounded English; either that, or a posh Kiwi.

"You have a mild concussion, a couple of black eyes, a lot of bruises and a few stitches here and there ... but all in all, you've come out of it very well," he continued. "Are you up for a bit of company? The commissioner is here, as is your husband. I can let them in briefly to say hello, but you need rest above all else. What do you think?"

Tina nodded and closed her eyes.

A few minutes later, she sensed someone was nearby and looked up.

Commissioner Palmer sat in the chair next to her bed, looking very sombre.

"Hello, Tina. The doctor tells me I have to do all the talking, and be quick about it, so here goes," he said. "David is waiting outside, so I just want to put you in the picture before I hand over to him. We're organising task force clean-out to reconvene tomorrow, and I'm going to ask Mike to join us until you're back on deck.

"Georgia is okay; about the same damage as you. The accident was a good bit of luck, as it happens. After the shooting started, the sudden stop probably saved your lives. The shooters' car kept going and sped off. Don't worry—we've got some leads. The SUV was hired by a couple of Colombians who flew into Oz on Sunday. Mike is following that up. Speaking of Mike, he has all your things from the car in a bag, including your gun. Everything is under control, so please rest up and get well soon."

Tina closed her eyes again.

*Colombians. Shit! I've gotta get the news to Bernardo!*

Her mind started to panic, but her body was unable to resist drifting off as the commissioner left the room.

# Chapter Six

L ater that same evening, Brad Spruce, the six-foot-seven, fit and ruggedly handsome former soldier and Victoria Cross winner was an imposing sight as he raised his glass to propose a toast. He looked out across the sand and the calm waters of the Broadwater, where the moon's rays reflected and danced between the myriad of luxury craft moored at the prestigious Southport Yacht Club marina.

"Here's to Catie, the beautiful girl we buried today," Brad said solemnly. "To a better world, and to what the 4G Team has achieved."

He wished Tina was here with them, as they had a lot to celebrate and reflect on. He thought of the remarkable chain of events that had brought them together.

Tina had collaborated with Catie and Colombian undercover contact Bernardo Sarmiento to blow open a huge, organised crime mob operating at home and around the world. After that, she'd placed the two of them into witness protection on the Gold Coast. Later, Catie had met Brad and his fellow commando Bert Hunter through some investigative work on potential war crimes in Afghanistan. That was the best thing that had happened to the two men in years, as it had enabled them to process some long-held trauma.

Catie had also introduced them to Garth Peterson, an old acquaintance of hers from the Gold Coast radiation clinic, where he too underwent treatment for cancer. He was a highly-respected corporate giant and well-known philanthropist, and they'd previously worked together on corporate crime matters with great success. He'd been only too happy to join the team.

The six raised their glasses and drank a toast. There was a moment of silence as each reflected on their remarkable journey over the past few months. They thought back to the barbecue at Garth and Meg's penthouse, where they'd instantly bonded.

Bernardo clinked glasses with Bert. He was very pleased with their progress to date. After a number of dinners where they'd told their stories, Bernardo had seen that the others all had demons of their own. Catie, Tina and Garth were all wrestling with the prospect of life-threatening cancer prognoses, and Brad and Bert had witnessed the same death and atrocities in Afghanistan as he had back home. He'd wanted to set the record straight, and recognised that they all wanted to make the world a better place with whatever time they had left. And so, he'd challenged them to pool their knowledge and resources and take some direct action.

After some deep soul-searching, they'd all agreed; they would go after some of the untouchable crime bosses, mobsters, crooked cops and politicians they knew who'd cleverly avoided detection. Even Tina, one of Australia's straightest senior police, joined the cause. She knew her time was borrowed, and was eager to right wrongs that had resulted in the deaths of some very decent people.

Garth had organised the purchase of a large factory and sales complex at Molendinar, where the *4G Guild for Gigs, Gadgets, Gigabytes and Gizmos* was established. It had quickly become a successful IT sales and repairs operation, and the rest of the staff remained totally oblivious to the team's after-hours activities fighting crime and corruption.

Catie's death from cancer had been a terrible blow, as had the murders of their informants Anita and Nick along the way. Those left behind became even more determined to push on and finish the job they'd started.

After finishing their delicious meals, the six of them headed to the yacht club car park. Garth and Meg drove home, while Brad dropped Jane at their apartment. After that, he, Bert and Bernardo proceeded to the 4G Factory to prepare for their next clandestine operation.

"I'd better call Tina and let her know about the wake," said Brad. "She'll still be up."

He dialled her private mobile.

A male voice answered.

"Superintendent Samuels' phone."

Brad was taken aback.

"May I speak to Tina, please?"

"Who's calling?"

"Just a friend. I'm returning her call."

"I'm sorry. She's not available," the voice said flatly before ending the call.

Brad looked at the others. He felt a chill going down his spine.

"Something's wrong."

# Chapter Seven

Detective Inspector Mike Broadfinger was still reeling from the events of the past twenty-four hours. Catie had been a great friend to all of them, and her funeral had taken a toll. Almost as distressing was the news of the bomb blast at Parramatta, and the devastation he'd witnessed when he and Superintendent Samuels visited the bomb site. Then came the news of Tina and Georgia's accident, the shooting and their injuries—and on top of it all, Superintendent Derek Sward's assassination in his hospital bed only an hour before the police surveillance team had taken up their positions.

*Who would ever choose to be a cop?* he thought.

Before he'd had a chance to process any of this, Mike was appointed temporary commander of the new special task force until Tina was back on the job. It was a huge responsibility, and almost too much for him to handle as things stood. He hoped he was up to it.

But that was half an hour earlier. Mike now sat bolt upright in his Chatswood office, eyes open wide and jaw sagging.

"Holy Toledo," he said. "What next?"

He'd just taken a phone call from Detective Graham James, who was at Westmead Hospital.

"Mike, are you sitting down?" Detective James had said. "The hospital mixed up the admission information. The killers only *think* they murdered Derek Sward. His file had him in Ward 2E, but the medicos put him in the wrong room. They killed Garry Townsend by mistake."

"You can't be serious," said Mike.

"Deadly. A bearded guy with a doctor's ID injected him with a lethal cocktail. Knocked a nurse over as he raced out of the room. He got away, but we have a few good descriptions and clear CCTV images. No one knows the bloke, but I'll get back to you as soon as I have something. For now, I've doubled the team inside and outside Derek's ward, and we're double-checking anyone who tries to come in."

Mike wanted to pinch himself to make sure it wasn't all a bad dream. He suddenly remembered the police were heading back to Derek's wife right now with the original bad news. He grabbed his phone and dialled.

"Detective Carey speaking," came the response.

"Brian, it's Mike. Are you at Derek's?"

"About a minute away, Inspector. I'm not looking forward to it. Barbara was shattered when I told her about his injuries a couple of hours ago, and now this? It won't be pretty."

"Brian, there was a mix-up at the hospital. We've just found out that it was Garry Townsend in room 2E, not Derek. They got Garry by mistake."

There was a long pause with no response.

"Did you get that, Brian?" said Mike. "Derek is still alive."

Another pause.

"Got it. Sorry, Mike. Had to pull over," said Brian. "Shit. I don't know what to think. Poor Garry. He was a great bloke, but I'm happy the Super is okay. Thank God you got me before I got to Barbara. I don't think she can take anymore."

"Sorry, Brian, but I've got to ask you to go back to Garry's and break the bad news before the bloody media knocks their door down. Is that okay?"

"Jesus, Mike," he sighed. "I only left there an hour ago! Alright. I'm on the way. Somebody better tell Barbara about the mix-up and warn her that the media might misreport it. Sounds like some sort of surveillance is required at the Sward residence. Whatever these bastards want, they must want it real bad."

"I'm on it. Can you come back to Chatswood when you've finished at Garry's? I need all the help I can get," said Mike. "But before all that, are you up to speed on Tina and Georgia's accident?"

"What accident? I've been off the air for the past hour or so. Christ, Mike, what is going on?"

The inspector filled the detective in with as much as he knew, then walked to the kitchen. He needed a strong, hot coffee. Back in his office, Mike grabbed a pad and pen and began writing out a list of bullet points. It was going to be a long night.

The next morning, the lights were on very early at Chatswood Police HQ. Mike had gone home just before midnight, and was back before 5am. The office cleaners had just started their rounds as the team began to drift in. Many of them held takeaway cappuccinos from the coffee shop in the downstairs foyer, *The Cell*, which operated twenty-four seven. The cleaners were used to this, and simply worked around them.

At around 8.45am, Police Commissioner John Palmer arrived and was ushered upstairs to Tina's office, Mike's temporary base.

The full team then assembled in the new control room, which had been set up overnight. Mike walked in with the commissioner right on 9 and looked around to see who was there. There were nine others in the room. Tina and Georgia were absent, still in the RPA. The news from the hospital that morning had been encouraging; their vitals were good, and visitation was now open to close family.

The remnants of the old missing persons team were there: Detectives Brad Henderson, Brian Carey, Bruno Campbell and Graham James were keen to be back together. Graham was now back on full duties after his recent gunshot wounds, which were on the mend. Sergeant Elwyn Bell, from the Sampson kidnapping, was also present, a happy-go-lucky last-minute inclusion. The sarge was a real showman, and very popular at the Pennant Hills Police precinct. Next to Sergeant Bell was Senior Constable Alison Hanagan from the commissioner's handpicked team. Tall, blonde and slim, Alison had transferred from Western Australia to special duties in the Day Street Headquarters. She was happy to be in Sydney, as her ageing mum was being cared for in a beautiful facility in affluent Wahroonga.

The final three, Sergeant Joe Hudson and dog squad detectives Terry Smythe and Charlie Wake, were all from Parramatta. Joe had been very helpful in the Riley Sampson handover saga and, along with the other two, had been heavily involved in the Parra bombing rescue efforts and subsequent investigations.

Mike formally welcomed everyone, then did the introductions before handing the floor over to the commissioner.

"Good morning, everyone," said Palmer. "I'm sure I don't have to tell you that the tumultuous events of the past twenty-four hours indicate strongly that our recent successes against organised crime mobs, illegal arms dealers and drug cartels around the world may have set off alarm bells with some of the 'Mr. Bigs' that we've thus far been unable to identify. Given the Parra bombing, subsequent murders and attempted murders, it seems they are keen to put an end to our investigation early. This team will have a large target on its back, so be very careful.

"The old saying 'loose lips sink ships' is very apt in this case," he continued. "It may well be that some of the rats are in our very own midst. I ask that you keep our investigations totally in-house, and do not discuss them with anyone, be they spouses, best friends, trusted associates or anyone at all outside of this team. The consequences could be fatal for both you and your families, so watch out."

He went on to give an encouraging report on both Tina and Georgia, but advised that Superintendent Sward's condition was still critical. He explained the hospital mix-up that had resulted in Garry Townsend's murder.

The commissioner spent the next half an hour or so going over all the snippets of information they'd collated, including some new revelations from overnight. One of these was that they'd identified one of the Colombians involved in the shooting, who'd flown into Sydney via Dubai on a forged passport the previous Sunday. He pointed out that, with reduced flights due to COVID, getting out of the country would not be easy for them, particularly now that they had facial recognition for both men. All departure airports around the country would now be screening everyone attempting to leave Australia.

He also spoke of Mike's concern about the Pol Air inquiry results going 'missing', advising that the special operations team responsible for the success of the previous busts was re-forming and would meet later that day. He also noted that they were awaiting further information from their Colombian contacts.

The new task force members were then allocated their various individual roles and responsibilities, to be reviewed at a daily 9am meeting in the control room under Inspector Broadfinger.

"In conclusion, I must stress that the only ace up our sleeve at the moment is they believe Derek has been silenced," said the commissioner. "That must remain secret for as long as possible. We need to find out why they want our key people taken out so badly."

They all filed out of the room in a sombre mood, sensing they were only at the very beginning of a long campaign. The three Parramatta detectives jumped in the lift and descended to *The Cell* coffee shop.

When they sat, Joe Turner said, "Why did they put that bitch Alison from the commissioner's office on the squad? I hear she's poison. Probably there to spy on the rest of us."

"She'll get on well with that dickhead Bruno Campbell," said Terry Smythe.

They went on talking about the mix-up with Superintendent Sward.

Before he left Chatswood, the commissioner sat with Mike and advised him he would not only be filling in for Tina in the new task force leadership, but also on the secret operations team. They were due to meet at the Eastern Suburbs Rugby Leagues Club boardroom at 3pm that day.

"As I did with Tina, I am forewarning you that some in attendance may surprise you," said Palmer. "You'll just have to trust me."

The commissioner drove out from the underground car park just after 10am. Mike then rang the RPA Hospital and spoke to the sister in charge of the ICU, requesting permission to visit Tina. She introduced herself as Sister Penny Button.

"The doctor will be back later this morning," she said. "I'll pass on your request, and he'll discuss it with the patient. I'll get back to you as soon as I know."

He gave the ICU manager his direct mobile phone number and hung up. Then he rang Tina's husband David, who must have recognised the number.

"Hi Mike. I was just about to call you. I'm still here at the RPA, in the coffee shop. I'll be going back in to see Tina when she wakes up again, hopefully within the hour. It's difficult to communicate with her at the moment with the sedation and the masks, but she did tell me she needs to see you ASAP."

"I just spoke to the head sister in ICU about coming," said Mike. "She tells me that the medicos will talk to Tina and she'll get back to me later."

"That would be Dr. Humphreys," said David. "He's in charge of both girls. Seems to be a thorough and competent fellow. I'll tell him that Tina wants to see you in particular. Dave Holder is here, too. He's in with Georgia right now. She seems to be perking up well."

"Good to hear. David, we're concerned that someone has it in for Tina and the others. Please keep your eyes open. We have people at the hospital, but your observations could help."

"Yeah, there are police everywhere. I just hope none of them tell Tina about Derek Sward's murder. It'll freak her out more than is needed right now."

Mike decided not to tell David about the mix-up, just in case.

He went back to his notes and the commissioner's spreadsheets, looking for something they might have missed or a link they might've overlooked.

Mike was still making notes when the hospital called back just before noon.

"Inspector Broadfinger, the patient is apparently very keen to speak with you," said Sister Button. "She's managed to digest some soft foods this morning and seems to be gaining strength. The doctor wants her to have another long rest before you visit. Is late this afternoon okay?"

"Thanks, Sister. Yes, that's fine. I plan to leave Bondi after 4, and will be there around 5-ish. Does that work?"

"Perfect. The sister in charge will be Joan Moloney. She'll be expecting you."

Mike sent a text to David Samuels and suggested they meet up in the coffee shop later.

He arrived at the Leagues Club early, signed in and waited in the foyer. The commissioner arrived with Deputy Commissioner Warren Hardcastle just before 3—no surprises there. Mike knew him well as the commissioner's go-to man. The three of them took the lift to the executive level, where they were ushered into the boardroom.

Mike immediately recognised the two others already seated. One was Alan McDonald, the new commissioner of the Australian Federal Police and a well-respected senior law-enforcement officer. The other one threw Mike a little. Rusty Nolan was a flamboyant and well-known character from the rugby league and eastern sub-urbs circles who'd come under a fair bit of police scrutiny over the years. He was a board member of this club, which explained the meeting venue.

The commissioner introduced Mike to the other two and they all sat down. As they went over the investigation, it soon became clear that Rusty Nolan played a key role in this team, and that surprised him even more.

The commissioner once again expressed his grave concerns about both the safety of a number of the police and the possibility they could be dealing with a bad egg 'very high up'—in police, politics or even an overseas organisation.

They broke up just before 4, with the commissioner urging them to communicate only by their secure phones. He told Mike he'd have a phone delivered to Chatswood within the hour.

Driving back along Lang Road, skirting around Centennial Park, Mike turned his police radio off, allowing him to think about all the possibilities and challenges ahead. By the time he navigated his way to Newtown and onto Missenden Road, he'd arranged the questions he would ask Tina in priority order. There were many of them, after all, and he wasn't sure how long he'd be allowed to stay, or even if he'd be able to communicate with her.

As the police car passed Carrilon Avenue, Mike's heart missed a beat. The area in front of the emergency entry was cordoned off, with people running and emergency vehicles everywhere.

Mike went cold.

# Chapter Eight

The next morning, Sister Chrissy went looking for Jane and found her in the kitchen with a few of the other girls.

"Before you go to school, Jane, I would like to see you in my room. Is that okay?" she asked.

Jane simply nodded.

The night before had been long, with not much sleep. Jane had felt sick and started shaking when Dr. Holder had told her he was married to a cop, but after calming down, she'd felt sorry that she'd yelled at him and left the way she did.

She hadn't gone to dinner that night. She was too wound up. She kept thinking of her last night at her home in Queenscliff, and the blond-headed, plain-clothed cop with a scar over his right eye. He'd been to the house many times before that night, and Jane had never liked him. He'd always called her 'Freckles'.

She could still easily picture her Mum and Dad lying grotesquely on the floor.

Jane was haunted by the cold stare in the blond cop's eyes as he'd turned the corner, looked up and took aim at her sister. After she'd yelped involuntarily, he'd turned those heartless eyes on her.

\*

"Where are you, you little slut!" he shouted, breathing heavily. "Stop wherever you are and come out!"

He was puffing by the time he reached the landing, but Jane was long gone. She'd bolted to her bedroom, locked the door and then climbed out of her window onto the garage roof—something she'd done many times before. She jumped, hurting her ankle as she landed in the garden bed, then quickly bounced up and raced into the bushes beside the house, avoiding the streetlights on Lumsdane Drive. She could still hear him and the other man yelling, the eerie reflection of their torch beams at her back as they began searching the undergrowth for her.

Unluckily for them, this was her territory. Jane knew every track through the bush. She ran for what seemed like an hour, covering herself in cuts from bushes and overhanging branches. Her escape took her through Duke Kahanamoku Park towards Queenscliff Bay, where she cut across Freshwater View Reserve to the walkway towards North Steyne.

Only eight years old and very frightened, she sobbed as she ran, tears running down her cheeks. Her ankle hurt, but she kept running. As she skirted behind the houses, a large Doberman bounded over a fence, snarling and barking at her. In the dark, she grabbed a large piece of deadwood just as the dog caught her, biting the back of her leg. She brought the branch down hard on the dog's head, causing it to let go and whimper away into the darkness. She decided the stick would come in handy, both as a crutch and protection. If nothing else, it made her feel a little better.

By the time she reached Manly Beach, Jane was totally spent. She hid under the stairs coming up from the beach, hugging her knees and breathing deeply between sobs.

She tried desperately to work out what had happened. Why had the man started shooting? Were Mum, Dad and Darlene okay? She didn't think so.

That awful copper. He'd still be looking for her. Jane remembered him well, as he often came to the barbecues at her house. She called him 'Scarface', and he and her dad had been doing some sort of work together. She doubted it was police work, because Dad hated coppers.

*They're all crooks,* he'd say.

Hours later, Jane was still hiding under the stairs, resting her sore ankle as the predawn light started breaking. The sea was fairly calm that morning. She made her way slowly along Manly Beach, past the Far West Children's Shelter, just as the golden sun's rays began to peek out and shimmer off the blue waters. She walked towards Shelly Beach, heading for the National Park, where she knew every trail backwards.

Jane was surprised how many people were out so early, jogging and walking. She avoided all of them.

In a way, that was the beginning of her long nightmare.

*

"Hello? Hello! Is anybody home?"

Amber was shaking her shoulders.

"Are you okay?" she asked.

"Yeah. I was a million miles away, on a beach holiday."

Jane tried to make light of her memories as the girls finished cleaning and left the kitchen. She walked through the empty common room to Sister Chrissy's cubbyhole and knocked on the old wooden door.

The nun invited her inside and asked her to sit.

"Jane, I don't know what upset you so much yesterday," said the sister, "but I do want you to know that Dr. Holder may be the one person who can get you back on track. He is totally on your side, and I know he would never deliberately upset you. He's one of those rare souls who you just know you can trust, and he won't let you down."

Jane stared at the floor, unflinching.

"The doctor left you a note," Sister Chrissy continued. "I'll leave you alone to read it. Please stay here until I get back."

As the nun handed over the envelope and left, Jane breathed in deeply, broke the seal and slowly took out the note.

*Jane,*

*I have no idea what caused your reaction this afternoon, but please know it was not in any way intentional.*

*I'm assuming I opened the door to your traumatic past in some way. I know it will always hurt, whatever it is, but we need to open that door and walk through it together.*

*Life is precious, Jane, like your crystal hummingbird. But there will always be a few bits of broken glass along the way. You, too, are precious, and I want us to work as a team. I know we can both do it.*

*Jane, I am one hundred per cent on your side, and I hope you can come to realise that.*

*I look forward to seeing you next Thursday as usual. Perhaps we can even put a smile back on your dial!*

*Yours sincerely,*

*Dr. David Holder*

Jane smiled to herself, relieved.

*At least he's still talking to me,* she thought.

She knew the doctor was right, and that Sister Chrissy probably was too—it was very likely that he was the only one who could get her out of this foul place.

*But he's married to a cop! What if he tells her about me? What if she tells the ugly blond copper? They could trace me here!*

She was still terrified, all these years later.

*I'm still the only witness.*

She hated going back over her past life and revisiting all of the unanswered questions there, but even she couldn't deny that she had begun to open the door—and so far, so good.

Sister Chrissy came back into the room and sat at her desk across from a composed-looking Jane.

"Jane," she said, "I, like Dr. Holder, would love to see whatever burden you carry start to lessen, even if only a little. Is there anything you want to ask me?"

She gave no response.

Sister Chrissy tried a different approach.

"Jane, I need your help. There are a few things happening in the cottage that just don't seem right to me. Tell me, did you ever hear from that bubbly Barbara or Angie Murray after they left? You were very pally with both those girls, and I'd have assumed they'd keep in touch."

"Haven't heard a thing," Jane responded sourly. "They probably want to forget all about this rat house."

Admittedly, she'd thought it was strange that the girls hadn't sent a card or any messages to say they were doing okay.

"That surprises me. I got on very well with those two, as well as some others, yet I haven't received so much as a Christmas card from any of them. It's a little disappointing."

The ageing nun furrowed her brow.

"If you do hear anything, please let me know," she added. "Oh, and by the way ... Dr. Holder received a phone call just as he was leaving yesterday. His wife was in a serious car accident and was taken to hospital. Please be kind to him in your next session. He doesn't deserve this sort of thing."

With that, the nun dismissed her, and Jane left to join the others in class. She wondered how the doctor was handling that news.

As the door closed behind Jane, Sister Chrissy made up her mind. She would talk to David about it when he was next in the office.

She picked up her old Bible and started to read.

# Chapter Nine

D etective Inspector Mike Broadfinger pulled his car up right next to the police control van outside the RPA Hospital, concerned about the mayhem outside and fearing for the girls. People scurried about everywhere amongst a large pack of media representatives and general chaos.

Mike recognised one of the officers standing near the front door.

"Hey, Ron," he asked nervously. "What's going on?"

"Bloody protesters, Mike. A horde of COVID anti-vaxxers stormed the hospital about an hour ago. Took a while to sort it out, but we're on top of it now. How come they sent you?" asked the sergeant.

"We've got two of our team here in ICU from a car accident yesterday. I've come to check on them."

"Yeah, heard about that. Someone shot them up? Your mob have certainly put the wind-up on some of these bad bastards. Well done."

Mike entered the foyer and introduced himself to the receptionist.

"I've been told to ask for Sister Joan Moloney in ICU," he said.

Shortly after, he was ushered down the corridor towards the unit.

"You can see both patients, but you only have five minutes with each of them," said Sister Moloney. "They're both much improved but they still have a long way to go."

Tina was still a mess with her masks, tubes and drips. Mike had not expected it to be so bad. Tina tried to talk, but it was difficult to understand her.

"Listen, boss. The good news is that both you and Georgia are on the mend, and we're getting ourselves organised for your return."

He went on to tell Tina everything that had transpired over the last twenty-four hours, including the make-up of the new task force and their investigation. He told her of his surprise meeting with Rusty Nolan alongside the commissioner at Easts Leagues Club.

That brought a smile to Tina's face. She nodded her understanding.

"By the way, boss, I've taken care of all your incoming emails and phone calls. I'll give you a list of them later. The only one I can't work out came in on your red iPhone. Bruno reported a fellow named Brad; said he was returning your call. Is that the big bloke from Catie's funeral? Do you want me to give him a message?"

Tina shook her head and indicated it could wait. For a moment, Mike thought she looked concerned, but it was hard to tell.

The five minutes went by very quickly, and Mike took his leave. Tina had managed to thank him for coming and tell him that her husband was there in the coffee shop, so he promised to catch up with him after he met with Georgia.

When he got to Georgia's room, he found she was a lot chirpier than Tina. She was more concerned about Tina and Derek than she was about herself. Mike decided not to say anything about Derek, Garry Townsend and the hospital mix-up, instead assuring her that all was under control.

They talked about the accident and subsequent events for a few minutes, and then Mike took his leave.

David Samuels saw Mike walking into the coffee shop and waved. Over a frothy cappuccino, the boys talked about the ongoing security precautions, including the planned twenty-four-hour stake-out at their home after Tina was discharged.

"This will be the norm until we get on top of things," said Mike.

"I'm hoping we can spend time down at our south coast holiday home to allow Tina to get back into shape," he said. "I know she'll be a pain and want to come back to work straight away, but I'm sure Doc Humphreys will put a stop to that."

David and Mike had always got on well. The conversation drifted off to other things, including that day's COVID protest.

Mike looked around at the many odd-shaped tables and assortment of clientele in the coffee shop and suddenly breathed in sharply. His eyes locked with a man sitting on his own in the far corner. Mike immediately recognised Alan Trundle, the small-time crim from the Riley Sampson kidnapping and the raid on the Cobama gang's headquarters. He'd thought Trundle was in gaol. Trundle looked very uncomfortable and quickly left his half-eaten lunch and the coffee shop.

David Samuels saw the look on Mike's face, then looked over in time to see Trundle making a hasty getaway. Mike was on the phone to organise a tail straight away, rising from his seat to follow Trundle outside.

*Could this be the link?* he wondered. *Is the Cobama mob involved in this after all?*

He saw Trundle disappear through the main entrance doors towards the car park.

He looked around, trying to see if he recognised anyone else.

*This could spell trouble.*

# Chapter Ten

B rad Spruce had not slept well, and Jane was worried. Over
breakfast, he'd told her about the man, whose voice he didn't
recognise, who had answered Tina's private phone.

"Why don't you phone David?" said Jane.

Brad was annoyed with himself—he'd forgotten he had David's
number in his contacts. He made the call and then stiffened as
David related the news of the bombing, the shooting and the
accident.

"I'm sorry, Brad. I should've rung you earlier, but I've been
really out of sorts. I don't think the force has many leads at this
point," said David. "I was told they had information about some
Colombian gangsters flying into Oz last weekend, but that's about
it."

Brad's mouth was dry. He sipped some water as he dialled
Bernardo and relayed the news, particularly around the possible
Colombian connection. They arranged a meeting at the 4G Fac-
tory. Brad promised to get the third member of the team there too,
Bert Hunter. He also said he'd alert Garth, their financier, just to
'keep him in the loop'.

Brad's mind was racing.

*Have we been found out?*

He started to think back over possible leaks or mistakes they might've made over the past few weeks.

Bernardo was already at the factory when Brad and Bert arrived. Brad closed the office door so they could talk in private. The clear glass walls allowed them to see what was going on outside.

Brad brought them up to date with what little he knew about the current happenings in Sydney and his discussions with Tina's husband.

"As far as I know, there's no link to us," he said. "It seems to be some sort of vendetta by the mobs against police success. Maybe they're trying to silence the cops and shut down the investigation. It's happened before."

"I think we owe it to Tina and Catie to keep going with our plan," said Bernardo. "I'm sure those Colombian men have me in their sights. The drug lords over there would love to see me silenced—murdered, just like many of my family has been. Retribution, Colombian style."

Their decision made, they got down to work. Some time ago, Tina had uncovered the story of a Supreme Court judge, Judge James Latta, living a highflying life in his waterfront mansion at Darling Point. Through her underground contacts, she'd established he'd been paid by unknown sources to pervert the course of justice many times. At the big end of town, it was known that 'Judge Jim' was the man for doling out lenient sentences and overturning convictions, and had done so for a number of convicted, well-connected malingerers.

Last month, Judge Jim had let one of Sydney's most notorious drug dealers out on bail, despite the protests of the prosecutors.

They'd made a very strong case, with over three hundred million dollars in drugs seized and the perpetrator a clear flight risk from his previous convictions and abscondment from bail. Judge Latta had insisted the ankle brace would keep him in check. The next day, to huge public outcry, the ankle brace had been found cut free, with no trace of the career criminal.

There'd been another media outcry the year before, when the son of a well-known politician had been sentenced to twelve months' house arrest after killing a three-year-old girl playing in her front yard at Rose Bay. She'd been slain by a random shot from the boy's unlicensed pistol, and 'Judge Jim' had found that it wasn't his fault, as he was under the influence of drugs. These had allegedly been placed unknowingly into his drink at a high-society party in Woollahra, and therefore the boy had diminished responsibility for his actions.

The judge had been reported to the law society on numerous occasions, but to that day, no action had been taken. Tina had told them he was being protected at the highest level, and the team had decided to do something about it.

They learnt that the judge had a remote luxury holiday home hidden in the rainforest valleys near Bellingen on the mid-north coast, where he spent most weekends. He'd fly up to Coffs Harbour in his private jet, where his spare red Porsche was always parked. He'd then drive himself for about half an hour to his valley lodge, nestled in the lush green forest.

Over the past few weeks, Bert and Bernardo had spent a number of nights hidden on the property, camouflaged in the dense rainforest up in the hills overlooking the mansion and adjacent flowing stream and waterfalls, observing the judge's habits. It was clear he enjoyed fishing from his small runabout.

They'd also been there mid-week, whereby they'd been able to disarm the judge's security system and gain access. This was second nature to Bert, given his military training in such systems.

Bernardo was very impressed with the whole area, and loved the drives along Waterfalls Way. Sometimes they drove the long way home through Dorrigo and north to Grafton alongside the picturesque Nymboida River and its cascading rapids. On their second trip, Bert had taken Bernardo on a white-water rafting adventure, and he'd loved it.

After today's meeting, the final decisions were made. The operation was to be carried out this weekend, and plans were well underway.

On Thursday night, the last of the required equipment was loaded into the Mitsubishi Outlander, including wetsuits. The final item was a sturdy green river canoe and paddles lashed securely to the roof racks.

They drove out of the factory mid-morning on Friday for the four-hour run south, anticipating a mid-afternoon arrival—well before the judge was due to arrive.

"Are you off on holidays?" said Kim Knott, one of the initial 4G employees.

"Sort of," said Brad. "Bernardo and I are spending the weekend on the Sunshine Coast, hoping to get amongst the flathead near Bribie Island."

Everyone knew Bernardo was a keen fisherman.

"Sounds like a blast. Have fun!"

After watching the boys drive out, Kim walked into the reception area and turned to his fellow worker and good friend, Shane Caddy, another 4G original.

"Have you sensed a change in the air this week?" said Kim. "Brad has been moody, which is quite unusual, and Bert and Bernardo seem on edge."

"Well, I've just finished last month's business reports, and whatever it is, it sure isn't a problem with 4G," Shane responded. "We've had our best month ever. I think they're just struggling with Catie's death. It's never easy to process something like that."

"I suppose you're right," ventured Kim, still a bit vexed. "They said they were heading to the Sunshine Coast, but they turned south out of the car park."

"Probably gone to get bait at Southport."

Kim nodded, shrugged and went back to work.

The boys drove south in silence for quite some time, listening to the *Tania Kernaghan* CDs that Bert loved. They stopped for fuel and a bite to eat at the Halfway Creek Roadhouse, just north of Coffs Harbour, before the short drive south to turn onto Waterfalls Way towards Bellingen.

Later, they arrived at a dirt road just west of the judge's lodge and drove in to their selected spot. They unloaded all the gear and took it up the hill overlooking the house, set up their camp, stowed the gear and sat down to wait. They would not be lighting fires or giving away their location to anyone.

Just before dark, the judge's Porsche came winding along the road up from Waterfalls Way, with parking lights on as the golden sun set over the majestic mountains. Twilight was fast approaching, and they basked in the beautiful time of the day.

"Welcome, Judge," whispered Bernardo. "I hope you enjoy your swim."

The two men climbed into their wetsuits and then sat in silence for a long while. Just before midnight, they made their move. They picked up the canoe and set out down the hill towards the lodge. They made no noise as they navigated the winding pathways through the lush forest, approaching the house in total darkness. It appeared that all lights were out.

Bernardo and Bert looked at each other.

"Let's do it," Bert said quietly.

They crept towards the house.

# Chapter Eleven

S ydney had turned on a magnificent, sunny, cloudless Tuesday morning with just a hint of a cool breeze as Dr. Dave Holder left RPA Hospital in a relaxed, buoyant mood. Both his new bride Georgia and her boss, Tina, had made great progress over the past few days.

Acting on advice from Inspector Broadfinger, Dave had installed CCTV cameras, security lighting and deadlocks to their duplex house, and he had to admit he felt safer for it. He hadn't thought of that sort of thing prior to their wedding last month, but he was learning fast.

*Just in case,* he told himself.

The city was nothing like his old hometown, Nabiac. The only night lights Dave had seen were the porch lights left on by his folks when he or his brother came home late from the oyster farm on Jimmy's Island at Tuncurry. Life had been very different then.

Dave had become quite close to David Samuels, Tina's husband, over the past week. They'd had many discussions about ongoing safety issues—particularly around Tina, as they all assumed she was the target. There were still police everywhere at the hospital, and the boys realised the force was putting a lot of resources into this case. It seemed they were expecting it to turn into something very big.

Dr. Holder was right on time for his 10am group session at Weatherall Cottage. He was expecting seven or eight of the girls to be there, but wasn't sure whether Jane would be back after last week's volatile consultation. He certainly hoped so.

Jogging up the stairs, Dave saw Sister Chrissy hovering near the front door.

"Good morning, Dr. Holder," she said warmly. "I've been thinking of you these past few days. How's your wife? I do hope she's recovering well."

"She is, Sister Chrissy. The improvement over the weekend suggests she just might be coming home at the end of the week. Fingers crossed."

"Must have been my prayers," the old nun smiled cheekily. "You'll no doubt be pleased to hear that young Jane has been settled for the past few days and will be present at your gathering this morning. Whatever your note to her said, she seemed very relieved to get it. I really hope you have a win with her. I can only imagine what she's been through. It must've been horrible."

Dave was pleased to hear this. It made his day all the better—but he knew that, dealing with these young girls and their serious challenges, anything could happen at any time.

"David," the sister said tentatively, "is it possible for you and I to have a talk in private? Somewhere away from the cottage? I hope I'm not asking too much. I just need some advice."

Dave wondered what could be wrong. He knew she was a real favourite with the girls, and deservedly so. She was the textbook nun; smart, caring and non-judgemental. He was happy to agree.

They arranged a meeting at the RPA coffee shop at around 5pm, since he'd be there visiting Georgia anyway and it wasn't far for the nun, who often visited patients there as part of her volunteer work.

Jane and Roxy were the last two to arrive in the room. David observed Jane carefully, and was pleased to find that she seemed genuinely relaxed.

The doctor welcomed them all as they took up their seats.

"Good morning, everyone."

Amber settled into her favourite beanbag and made herself comfortable. She, too, enjoyed these sessions.

"Today, I want to talk about decision-making. Following last week's get-together, a few of you alluded to the fact that making big calls, or even little ones, can be a difficult process—especially here, where there are so many rules and regulations.

"Life is all about making decisions; especially those important ones about you and your future, your circle of acquaintances and your lifestyle. Remember this: the decisions you make don't necessarily define you. It's how you face up to the consequences of those decisions that does."

For the next hour, they discussed individual decisions, good and bad, and how they'd affected everyone there. Some knew all too well the consequences of bad decisions.

Amber suggested that many decisions had been forced upon them, and they'd been given no real options. She related this to the story that she'd pushed a drug peddler off a balcony.

"I was nowhere near the place, but they still made the decision to put me in here. I didn't even get the chance to defend myself."

One of the new girls, Trish Collins, created a great deal of discussion when she confided that she didn't know whether her running away from home at thirteen had been a good or bad decision.

"It had to be bad, dickshit. You ended up here," Roxy said pointedly.

"Maybe," said Trish, brushing her long, dark hair. "But I think I'm probably better off."

"That's crap," said Amber. "Even hell would be better than this ratshit place!"

Dr. Holder saw the discussion was getting animated, and asked Trish why she'd left home in the first place.

Trish took a while to answer, and finally told them that her uncle had been molesting her for years, and when she couldn't stand it anymore, she'd taken it to her mother.

"And what was your mother's reaction?" asked the psychologist.

"She called me a liar and slapped me around. She said that whatever had happened, it was my fault anyway."

"She'd be right there," said Roxy. "You're a loser."

"Not so. At least, not in the way Roxy is implying," said Dr. Holder.

The psychologist was quick to counter that such a decision was not an easy one to make for anyone, let alone a thirteen-year-old kid.

"Sometimes, you're a loser either way, and circumstances can make that a given. In this case, Trish, that decision was all but out of your hands. It's your next ones that are really important, and yours alone to make. As Danny Kaye once said: 'Life is a big canvas. Throw all the paint on it you can.' There is a terrific world waiting for you outside of these walls, and your next few decisions can allow you to get out there and enjoy it."

"Who the hell is Danny Kaye?"

This was Jane's first contribution to the discussion.

"Probably one of the old ghosts you talk to," giggled Roxy.

"Far from it, Roxy," Dave chimed in. "He's an old American actor and singer. The line came from one of his great movies, *Hans Christian Andersen*. I should bring in the DVD. You'd love it."

And so the discussion continued.

The lunch bell went at 12.30, and Dave took the cue to call the session to a close. All in all, he was quite pleased—no walkouts, no tantrums, and all eight girls ended up contributing in one way or another. It had been a productive session and had finished on a positive note, with quite a few of them expressing a desire to get out and make something of their life.

Dave casually approached Jane as they walked through the common room towards the kitchen.

"Did you get my note on Thursday?"

"Yeah. Sorry I spat the dummy."

The words came out slowly. Jane was not used to saying sorry—in fact, she couldn't remember ever having said it, but she felt better now that she had.

"Not necessary. It just took me by surprise. I guess I opened the dungeon door," said Dave. "Look, Jane. What we were talking about today ... there's a fabulous world out there, and you could make a great life for yourself. Whatever the past may have been, we can put together a plan for your future—not only to survive, but to thrive. The question is, are you up for it? It could be a rough road."

Jane had been anticipating something like this, and had thought long and hard over the past few days. She'd already made up her mind.

It was now or never. She had to trust someone, somewhere, sometime.

"I am," she said. "How's your wife doing?"

That threw Dave.

"How did you know?" he asked

Then, the penny dropped.

"Of course. Sister Chrissy. I should have known. She couldn't help herself, God love her." He smiled. "Actually, Georgia is coming on really well. She's just up the road at the RPA and may well be home soon. See you Thursday."

Jane left to head into the kitchen, and Dave went into the city for a meeting.

Later that afternoon, back at the RPA, Dave confirmed with Georgia that she was to be discharged on Thursday morning if everything kept going the way it had been.

"Are you okay to pick me up?" she asked.

Dave assured her he would make it work. Georgia told him that Tina's mask had been removed.

"She's breathing on her own now, and even eating solids."

Georgia still blamed herself for the accident, but nobody else did. She went on to tell Dave that Dr. Humphreys had indicated Tina could be allowed into rehab in another week or so.

Just before five, Dave bid farewell to Georgia and told her he was meeting Sister Chrissy in the hospital coffee shop.

He'd just sat down when he saw the black and white habit coming down the hallway. Dave sat Sister Chrissy down and brought coffee and cake back to the table.

"How long have you been at the cottage, Sister Chrissy?" he asked

"Just over twenty-two years now," she said, reminiscing. "Yet, in many ways, it seems like only yesterday."

"You must've seen many changes in that time."

"Yes, and not all of them good. We've had better results in years gone by, but we still have some excellent help—yourself included."

Dave brushed off the compliment tactfully.

"It seems that something is bothering you at the moment. Is it a personal thing, or something at the cottage?" he asked.

"Both, in a way, but I don't know where to turn. I was hoping you might give me some guidance."

"Well, I don't know a lot about shelter administration or their operational procedures, but I can give it my best shot," he promised. "Fresh eyes alone could help. They often do."

"The trouble is ... I don't know *what* it is, but something is happening. I can feel it," said Sister Chrissy. "When the latest chairman, Brian McGarry, was appointed six years ago, I instantly disliked him. I can say the same of Mrs. O'Brien, whom he appointed CEO about a year later. In my faith, such prejudice is unacceptable. Mr. McGarry often loiters around the cottage and says very little, and though it makes a number of us uneasy, it is hardly enough to accuse the man of any wrongdoing. My concern could be completely unfounded, and if so, I should be punished—but if it isn't ..."

"I think I know you well enough to say that there isn't a vindictive bone in your body," said the doctor, "and I'm sure I wouldn't be alone in saying so. Something else is obviously bothering you. What is it?"

"It's just that ... girls who have left the shelter often pop in to say hi, or at least send the occasional letter, to myself and some of the other staff. This practice has almost totally dried up, and I have no idea why. I'm still getting messages and gifts from girls we farewelled years ago, but not a single one from residents over the past few years. I've talked about it with some of the long-time staff, and they too are very concerned."

Dave pondered this for a while.

"Could the foster parents have been instructed that it was bad for the girls to stay in touch with their pasts? A new policy, perhaps?"

"If it were, then surely at least one of us would know about it," she said. "I can't help but worry that it's something more sinister. One of the things we've noticed is that a number of the same people are attending the adoption viewings. Originally, I thought it must've been people who kept missing out ... but for two years now, I've been taking note of who gets allocated to whom, and most of them have taken at least one girl, if not more. I know of one couple who have taken five. How can that be?"

Dave furrowed his brow, but could not come up with a positive answer. They exchanged mobile phone numbers.

"Give me a few days to think it over. Call me anytime," he said. "But before that, Sister Chrissy, I would ask your advice on another matter. Without giving away any confidentialities, I feel that Jane is getting close to opening up to me about her past. I'm almost there, but I need help."

"It's tragic to see her stuck here for over ten years now. She deserves better. How can we help?"

"Firstly, I need to know who her closest friends are. I've been toying with the idea of introducing some group challenges to build up her confidence, and there's a better chance of achieving that if it's done in good company."

Sister Chrissy didn't have to think hard.

"Her best friend is Catherine, or Cate, as the girls call her. She's a beautiful girl, lost as she may be. She's currently in hospital after harming herself. Jane is also close to Amber and Roxy. They spar a lot, but deep down, they get on well."

"That's exactly what I wanted to know. Thank you, Sister. By the way ... Roxy said something today about Jane talking to ghosts. Does that mean anything to you?"

The nun gave a little laugh.

"Well, yes, we are supposed to have two ghosts in residence."

She went on to explain the long-held superstition to Dave.

"Whether it's related or not," she continued, "Jane is often heard having conversations in her room when no one else is there."

"Tell me, Sister. Have you ever encountered these ghosts?"

Dave had posed the question very seriously.

The nun considered her answer.

"David, I do believe there are spirits in the cottage," she said. "And yes, I have felt their presence from time to time. To answer your question, however, I haven't had any direct communication with them."

She paused, and then went on.

"Jane is different. She has some sort of special power, or spiritual awareness. On more than one occasion, she has foretold things that have later come to pass exactly as she'd described. There's something unusual and very special about that young lady."

Dave's interest was thoroughly piqued.

Just then, a voice came from behind them.

"Can I interrupt, or is this a secret society?"

Dave looked over his shoulder and laughed.

"Who let you out?" he said, practically jumping up to help Georgia sit down.

"Sister Chrissy, this is my beautiful wife, Georgia. She must have bribed her way out."

"Escaped, is more like it," said Georgia, raising the takeaway coffee cup in her hand. "One more of these from the hospital trolley and I'd have been sick. I've arrested people for less."

"Dr. Holder, you didn't tell me your wife was such a character," said Sister Chrissy. "Why don't you bring her to the cottage to meet our girls? I don't have to tell you many of them have a jaundiced view of law enforcement, and a charming lady like Georgia could dispel a few negative thoughts."

"Great idea. I'll try to convince her." He chuckled. "I agree, it could be a culture shock for a few of the girls."

Eventually, Sister Chrissy left and Dave began to walk Georgia back to her ward.

"I don't normally bring my work home," said Dave, "but Sister Chrissy just gave me some information that could have major repercussions for the shelter. I'm hoping you can give me a way forward and help me decide who best to talk to."

He went on to explain the nun's concerns, and Georgia nodded gravely.

"I'm going to Tina's room later. Let me talk to her about it. I'm sure we can help."

Dave didn't sleep well that night. He got up early, had a shower and made himself two soft-boiled eggs with toast and tea. Afterwards, he settled down to write up all his notes from the day before.

Shortly after 9 o'clock, his phone pinged. It was a text message from Sister Chrissy:

*I've just been instructed to clean out Catherine's room, as she will not be returning. She is now the sixth child to be taken by that same strange couple. C.*

David poured himself another cup of tea.

*That seals it,* he thought.

# Chapter Twelve

M ike hadn't slept much over the past week. Bags had appeared under his eyes. He could feel his frustrations coming to the surface, and found them hard to control. He looked forward to Tina's return to the special task force, hoping it was no more than a couple of weeks away.

At the team briefing that morning, it felt like they were continually going over old ground. Some of the members were getting niggly until finally, towards the end, a new piece of information came from the senior constable out of the commissioner's office.

Alison informed them they'd been successful in identifying both of the Colombian gangsters suspected of being involved in the Parramatta bombing.

"Santiago Fernandez and Juan Pablo Cortez are members of the Black Tuna drug trafficking cartel operating out of Miami, Florida," she said. "The mob are well connected in Australia, reputed to have laundered hundreds of millions of dollars through Aussie casinos and real estate deals. The two are believed to be stranded here, unable to leave the country."

Detective Terry Smythe reported another concern.

"The two CCTV cameras located closest to the detonation point were destroyed in the blast, as we'd expected," said Smythe. "What we *didn't* expect was that they'd been tampered with well before the explosion. As such, we were unable to retrieve any footage."

Mike took the floor.

"It may well be that we're once again dealing with enemies both internal and external," he said, "which only makes our job that much more challenging and dangerous. Please be vigilant on both sides."

Mike was one of the few men in the room who knew that the information Alison had given them had come from the commissioner's secret operations team. He'd also been briefed on where the two Colombians were likely to be hiding, but was advised not to repeat it in hopes that it would lead to bigger fish—namely, any rats that might be hiding in their midst. He was starting to wonder who he could trust.

Just before 3pm, Mike rang the hospital to confirm that Tina was up and about and keen to see him at 4 as planned. She agreed, tasking him with grabbing a coffee from *The Cell*, and bringing with him the day's *Daily Telegraph* and her red mobile phone. Tina advised that Georgia was hoping to be discharged the next morning, and by the way she spoke, it was clear she was keen to get out and back to work. He wondered what her husband would think about that.

Mike entered the hospital hallway with his completed shopping list and case files in tow. He stopped to talk to the police security team before knocking on Tina's door and entering. Inside, he found her lying down but awake. The bruising and lacerations were still very evident, and she still had a drip in her arm.

"You sure look brighter without the mask and tubes," said Mike.

He handed over everything Tina had asked for—including the packet of chocolate Tim Tams she'd called back to add to the list at the last minute.

Tina immediately opened the newspaper and read the banner headline:

*SENIOR JUDGE FOUND DEAD*

She tried to look nonchalant, but was clearly engrossed in the story. The paper reported that prominent judge James Latta had been found dead, apparently drowned, at his North Coast property on Monday afternoon. The grounds staff had found his boat capsized and empty in a lagoon at the end of a small set of rapids, prompting a search and rescue mission. First responders from Coffs Harbour had found the judge's body snagged on a dead tree in the creek just on sunset.

Some of the police dive team had reported huge eels lurking in the deep water, where dark shadows were cast by the tall rainforest trees and ferns. At the time of reporting, there were no suspicious circumstances, as the judge was known to be a keen fisherman. The incident was assumed to have been caused by a medical episode, or the result of recent rains in the Dorrigo Mountains.

Alongside the particulars of Latta's demise was a spotlight on the judge's colourful career, and the many questions around his recent court rulings and light sentences. There were personal tributes and platitudes from a number of leading legal practitioners and prominent politicians from both sides, and Sydney's more conservative radio personalities were reportedly singing his praises and bemoaning his passing. The State Coroner had ordered an autopsy, and police were continuing their investigations.

Mike watched Tina reading the front page and raised an eyebrow.

"Do you know him?" he asked.

"No, but I've heard plenty about him," said Tina. "Nothing good, mind you."

"Likewise," said Mike. "Funny how the most questionable characters have the most allies in the top end of town, isn't it?"

Tina just smiled.

"Organise surveillance footage at his funeral," she said. "Just in case."

They spoke at length about the current task force investigation, including the special operations info on the Colombians. They were soon joined by Georgia, who looked much better and was walking unaided. She speculated that she would be back on light duties in another week or so.

"Speaking of duty," said Georgia, "I received a message from Rick Sampson, who is apparently out on bail. He expressed concern for both of us, and offered his services if we feel he could help."

"What do you think?" asked Tina.

"I think he is one very remorseful, *hopefully* former gambler who is keen to atone. His wife, Jan, is very supportive, but his in-laws certainly aren't. He may be able to help with information on the Alan Trundle lead. I'll follow it up as soon as I'm out and able."

\*

After Mike left, promising to return before the weekend, Tina and Georgia continued to talk about the task at hand and the apparent lack of progress.

"Here we go again," said Tina, sighing. "I'm worried about Mike. He looks so worn out."

"All the more reason to crack this thing," said Georgia.

After they'd exhausted all avenues of inquiry on the case, the conversation went elsewhere.

"About Weatherall Cottage," Georgia began slowly. "There have been some ... developments, and I'd like your support with opening a preliminary investigation."

"You're looking very serious all of a sudden," said Tina. "What is it?"

"I met with Sister Chrissy and Dave again this afternoon. Dave and I went over all the files since his practice was appointed at the cottage eight years ago, and nothing appeared to be *too* out of order ..."

"Except?"

"Except the reporting system implemented shortly after Mrs. O'Brien took over as CEO," said Georgia. "Most notably, the removal of the requirement for reports on the girls' progress once their cottage stay is at an end."

"Not much to go on by itself," said Tina.

"That's not all. One of the girls, Cate, was recently hospitalised for self-harm. Rather than returning to the cottage after discharge, she was sent straight to a new home and adoptive parents. That makes Cate the sixth of the girls these 'new' parents have taken in over the last two years."

Tina thought for a while.

"You're right," she said eventually. "That doesn't add up. Let's be careful about how we approach this. The nun suggested you go to one of Dave's sessions and talk to the girls, right? Why not accept the invitation? It's a good way for us to get better acquainted with the shelter without drawing attention to ourselves. You can put it down as part of your light duties in the community."

"Sounds like a plan," said Georgia. "Dave will be at the shelter tomorrow afternoon. I'll talk to him when he picks me up, and he can organise it with the nuns."

Georgia left to go back to her room.

As soon as the door closed behind her, Tina reached for the phone Mike had brought with him. She was concerned about Bernardo's safety, and wanted to find out more about the judge's demise.

She had to be careful what she said, even on the red phone.

She dialled and closed her eyes.

# Chapter Thirteen

D ave entered Weatherall Cottage and went looking for Sister Chrissy before his afternoon sessions. He knocked on her office door.

"Hello, Dr. Holder," greeted the nun. "Which one would you like to see first? Jane, or little Maggie?"

They'd agreed ahead of time not to speak of their concerns within the cottage walls.

"First up, I just want to talk to you briefly about your suggestion of my wife coming to talk to the girls," said Dave. "I took her home from hospital this morning, and she told me she's keen to come. She can make it next Tuesday, if that suits you?"

"That's wonderful news. Next Tuesday it is. How about 9am, after the breakfast clean-up?"

They talked about the content and purpose of Georgia's presentation and what they hoped to achieve.

"As I said before, most of the girls here don't like the police for one reason or another," said Sister Chrissy. "I'm certain your sweet Georgia will change their impression. It could be a very positive experience, and one that is much needed here."

With that organised, Dave elected to see Margaret first, followed by Jane. The first session went by without incident, and he prepared himself for his last one-on-one for the day.

By then, he'd gone over how he would approach Jane's demons a hundred times in his mind, and was primed and ready when she entered the room.

She slumped into the chair opposite him.

"Hi Jane," he said. "I'm going to try very hard not to cause you any heartache or trauma this week, but to make sure it doesn't happen, I need you to work with me. So, let's start where we left off last Thursday. I asked if you wanted to get out of this place and you answered with a definite yes, so let's go from there."

The doctor intentionally sidestepped their discussion around Jane's admission, hoping to help her to be comfortable talking first.

"What is it you don't like about the cottage?" he asked.

"Everything. It sucks. I hate it."

"You can do better than that. Is it the food? The rules? The staff? The routine? What are your major concerns?" Dave said evenly.

"I hate being cooped up," said Jane. "I hate not being able to make my own decisions. I hate feeling like I'm a useless piece of shit."

"Okay, let's address that last bit. First, we need to deal in facts. The fact is, you are far from useless. We know you have a great brain, are a very caring person and deserve a better life. We also know you're a keen learner. You've told us in the group sessions you like listening to podcasts and reading. Where did you learn to read?"

"Mostly here, from the nuns. I've had ten bloody years to learn it; not much else to do around here."

"Did you ever go to school before the cottage?"

Jane hesitated before answering.

"Sometimes. I went to primary school for a while."

*Bingo,* thought Dave.

He was ecstatic. This was her first direct reference to a memory from before the shelter.

"Do you remember your early teachers?"

"Some of them," said Jane, looking angry. "They were all the same. We were from the wrong side of town, and so were they, I suppose."

Dave wanted to sidetrack her before bringing her back.

"What about your teachers here? Do they treat you better?" he asked.

"Sister Chrissy and Mr. Drinnan are okay."

"What do you like learning about?"

"Mostly about birds, animals, the bush and food, I guess."

"Do you know anything about bush tucker?" he asked. "It's a favourite in our house."

"Only what I've learnt from Amber," said Jane. "She knows a lot of that stuff from when she was a kid."

"That makes sense. Is Amber a friend?"

Jane considered her response.

"I suppose so. You haven't got many choices in this rathole."

"Jane, there is an old saying that *the grass is greener on the other side,*" said Dave. "It means we often overlook what we already have in search of something more; some non-existent paradise where we're free from all of our problems. Problem is, even if we found somewhere like that, we'd inevitably find new things to be dissatisfied with. We must all learn to appreciate everything we have—especially our friends. Life is too short, and friends are too few. Who's your closest friend here?"

Jane was silent for a while.

"I guess it'd be Cate, but I don't even know if she's alive or dead. They won't tell us anything."

"I can tell you she is very much alive," he said. "I understand she's recovering well, and will be heading to a new home after she discharges."

Jane looked up quickly.

"Oh shit. Not those awful people from the parade?"

Dave took note that Jane, too, had some misgivings about the couple.

"Cate is a lovely girl with a lot of personal challenges. We're all hoping she does really well on the outside. Did she say anything about her new parents?"

Jane fidgeted in her chair uncomfortably.

"She ... did leave me a note. Said she didn't like them."

Jane talked more about Cate and what she knew of her past life. Suddenly, she produced her letter on impulse and gave it to him.

He read it through twice before responding.

"You know, Jane, just about every girl here has a tragic tale to tell," said Dave. "Life can sure be cruel, and everything about Cate's situation is a sad indictment on society. Far too often, kids like Cate and yourself are burdened with horrendous and unfair challenges."

Now, the boot was on the other foot. It was Dave's turn to trust.

He decided to go for it.

"Sister Chrissy has also expressed some concerns about that couple," he began. "I'm trying to help her, if I can. My wife, Georgia, is out of hospital today. She's coming here next Tuesday on the pretence of talking to the girls about life in the police force. In reality, she's using it as a means of getting a feel for the cottage and the people who run it. If there *is* something going on, we'll get to the bottom of it—together. Will you help us?"

Jane was stunned into silence.

"What could I possibly do to help?" she said finally. "I know stuff all."

"For starters, you could encourage the girls to listen to Georgia. Then, after Tuesday, you could ask the office to put you in touch with Cate, and we can see what comes of that."

They talked more about Cate and the week to come. Jane visibly warmed to the idea of helping her friend, heartened by the opportunity to give her a shot at a better life.

Dave decided to change tactics yet again.

"Jane, on Tuesday, Roxy said that you talk to ghosts," he said. "I know of some people who have had amazing experiences communicating with others who were not in the same room. Has that ever happened to you?"

After another long silence, she conceded.

"Sometimes," she said with cautious enthusiasm.

The doctor pressed on.

"There's a lot of talk about the spirit of a nurse who lingers in the cottage. Have you ever encountered her?"

"Yeah. She can go on a bit, but she's a nice old thing."

That opened Pandora's box. Jane went on to speak of the many conversations she'd had with the old nurse, and Dave let her continue until she was finished.

"Cate's note talked about your sister," he said. "Do you communicate with her?"

She looked at Dave with terribly sad eyes.

"Yeah," she said quietly. "She helps me a lot."

"That's not unusual. Sisters are often in tune with each other's thoughts, likes and dislikes. She probably knows you better than anyone else. Would that be a fair assumption?"

Jane warmed to the discussion, and a rare smile came over her face.

"Pretty much. She gets pissed when I don't take her advice, though."

Dave looked Jane straight in the eye.

"Kiddo, when you smile, your whole face lights up. You should do it way more often." He smiled himself, then was suddenly solemn. "Tell me, is your sister alive or dead?"

He knew he was heading into dangerous territory, but felt the time was right.

Jane's eye's dropped to the floor and her smile instantly faded.

"Darlene's dead."

"And what about your parents?"

Jane looked up at Dave, tears rolling down both cheeks.

"They're all dead. The coppers killed them all."

It was Dave's turn to breathe deeply before responding.

"Jane, I believe you. I am so, so sorry. Please believe me that I'll do everything in my power to keep you safe and right these horrible wrongs."

He could see her shoulders shaking.

"Are you okay?" he asked.

Jane nodded slowly, tears flowing.

"Do you think you could tell me your name?"

Jane stood up slowly and silently walked out of the room. No tantrums, no slamming of doors.

This time, the tears rolled down Dave's cheeks, falling onto the wooden floor below.

*We'll find them, kiddo*, he whispered to himself.

# Chapter Fourteen

Commissioner John Palmer opened the hastily-ordered special operations meeting, apologised for the late notice and introduced a new member.

"This is Superintendent Dick Sellis," said Palmer, acknowledging the room. "The rest of you know Dick. Mike, I'm not sure you've met."

"Inspector Mike Broadfinger," said Mike, extending a hand.

The two recalled having met briefly once or twice, but not for many years.

"Dick, Mike is standing in for Tina until she's back on deck," the commissioner explained.

"The sooner the better," was Mike's smiling response, though it was forced in the extreme.

The mood in the room was sombre. Everyone knew the reason for the sudden notice.

"I'll come straight to the point," said Palmer. "Last night, Judge Tiffany Wallace was assassinated, and it's a catastrophe in every sense of the word. Tiff was one of the straightest, most conscientious human beings I've ever known, and a wonderful lady all-round. As you all know, she'd been appointed to preside over a number of cases involving some of the leading figures in our recent illegal arms trade and international drug cartel successes.

"I'll have Dick tell us more about the murder in a minute," he said, "but first, I must establish context. After Judge Latta's widely reported fishing accident, Tiff is the second senior judge to die in the past ten days, and the media are having a field day trying to link the two. From where I sit, there's no connection at this stage ... but especially after the report I received from the coroner this morning, it cannot be ruled out.

"The report indicates that there was no water in Latta's lungs, which rules out drowning. Further, there's no evidence of any medical condition or organ failure. The man was dead before he hit the water. I'd rather not compare the two judges—Latta was a devious crook, in my opinion—but his death looks like foul play, so we have to take that into consideration. I will now ask Dick to give us a report on last night's murder."

"Thanks, John," said Dick, stepping forward. "Just after 6pm yesterday, Judge Wallace left the central courthouse in Liverpool Street in a taxi headed for Chinatown with three of her staff. They dropped one of the staff at the Sydney Meya Conservatory of Chinese Music in Sussex Street around 6.15pm for her regular tutorial, and the three remaining passengers arrived at the Red Dragon restaurant on George Street, opposite Saint Peters Catholic Church, around 6.25pm. They were soon joined by another five colleagues in celebrating one of their birthdays.

"Just after 7.30pm, two men in dark suits, overcoats, hats and sunglasses entered the restaurant, brushing right past the lass checking COVID vaccination certificates. Both men produced machine pistols and shot Judge Wallace seven times, wounding three others before shouting threats in broken English and firing into the ceiling as they made their getaway. They were last seen running through the grounds of St. Patrick's College on Campbell Street.

"Forensics have matched the shells from this shooting to those we found at the Samuels shooting on the M4 last week. Further, CCTV cameras place the SUV from the M4 shooting on Pitt Street at 7.51pm yesterday, travelling south immediately after the Wallace shooting. Lastly, facial recognition on the footage from Westmead Hospital has identified the man seen running from the ward after Inspector Townsend's murder as Juan Pablo Cortez, one of the Colombians who rented the SUV. If that were not conclusive enough, the SUV was captured by CCTV on Hawkesbury Road, showing its arrival just before 3.20pm and departure some twenty-five minutes later. Thus, we can conclude that all of these events are directly linked."

"Thanks, Dick," said the commissioner. "Two things. First, our leads on the whereabouts of the two Colombians have dried up for the moment. They somehow escaped undetected from their known hideout at Punchbowl sometime over the last two evenings. Sadly, this has had tragic consequences. Second, it's becoming clearer that we're looking for someone very high up in the food chain; someone capable of orchestrating all this without alerting us. Unfortunately, we have no idea who it is."

The commissioner was gutted. He realised that, had they moved in earlier, they might well have apprehended the Colombian gangsters, saving the life of his good friend Tiffany Wallace in the process.

His long-time associate and fellow team member, Rusty Nolan, was just as down. His underworld contacts had passed on the initial information about the Colombians, but had since closed ranks. This was unusual, and frightening besides.

The men spent a good hour going over every scant detail with a magnifying-glass approach. Tasks were issued by the commissioner, and they broke up just before 3pm.

Dick Sellis, Rusty Nolan and Alan McDonald headed to the bistro for a late lunch. The others left to drive back to their offices. Mike, however, decided to go via the RPA to give Tina an update and see if she had any ideas or suggestions.

Tina was saddened to hear the news about Judge Wallace. She'd known her reasonably well and had great respect for her fairness and intellect. Tina had been very pleased when the judge was appointed to her recent cases, but now recognised it for the death sentence that it had been. More fatalities on her watch.

She told Mike that she might be allowed out in a few days, but that Dr. Humphreys had insisted she spend at least a week recovering away from the stressors of work, so she and David were planning to hide away at their south coast holiday home for the time being. Though she was unhappy at the thought of not being able to steer the new task force at this important time, the thought of the beautiful Tomago River at Mossy Point, the crackling winter fire and the sound of the rolling surf in the distance had great appeal, and so Tina had agreed.

David Samuels arrived just before 5pm, and Mike took that as his cue to leave for his office in Chatswood.

*

Around the same time, Professor Doug Latimer and Dr. Tony Phillips were arriving at Sydney International Airport for their 8pm Qantas flight QF1 to Dubai. The two were looking forward to the top-level international climate change conference at the one hundred and sixty storey Burj Khalifa Hotel, grateful for the opportunity to present their findings to a distinguished group of the world's best scientists. Professor Latimer was honoured to have been invited to be their keynote speaker in recognition of their landmark research results.

Check-in through the shorter business class queue was relatively quick, and they soon found themselves with their boarding passes for seats 11A and B. After browsing the duty-free shops and newsagencies for a last-minute read, the pair sat in the carvery for their last meal and a final opportunity to go over their presentation papers.

They moved on to the departure lounge just before 7, again presenting their boarding passes and passports and taking a seat near the departure gate. Some ten minutes later, the loudspeaker announced their names, calling them to the airline desk.

As they approached the desk, two uniformed Australian Border Force officers strode up to them and advised that their immigration papers contained a technical error, insisting they go with them to sort it out.

Dr. Phillips protested that they couldn't afford to miss their flight, but the senior officer assured them all would be well, and the issue would only take a few minutes to rectify.

They followed the officers along the pedestrian concourse, noticing that the one in front had a pronounced limp. Suddenly, the officers stopped, asking both men to follow them through the doors into the restricted area. About twenty or so metres along the dark hallway, the two officers turned, drawing their guns in the same motion. No one heard the muffled shots through the silencers, emitting only a puff-like sound as both men fell to the floor, dead.

They were quickly dragged into a nearby cleaners' room and stuffed into a solid-looking storage cupboard. There would be no international climate change conference for these two great pioneers.

The killers removed their Border Force uniforms, revealing casual street clothes underneath. They threw their disguises into the cupboard on top of the two bodies, locked the storeroom door, pocketed the key and switched off the lights as they left.

"They won't find them for a week or so, when the stink starts," said the taller of the two as they walked towards the transit lounge shops.

Twenty minutes later, the passengers walking down the aerobridge towards the A380 jetliner took no notice of the two men in dark suits, overcoats, hats and sunglasses who entered halfway along the aerobridge via the tarmac stairwell. They joined the queue at the front door of the aircraft with an excess of hand luggage in tow, presenting boarding passes for business class seats 11A and B.

After being given hot towels and welcomed aboard by the cabin crew, they settled in for the flight to Dubai, where they would board a special flight to Colombia—but not before strapping a nasty surprise under their seats, with a timer set for the ongoing flight to the UK.

At least they wouldn't have as much hand luggage on their next flight.

# Chapter Fifteen

Jane sat in her room, staring blankly out of the small window overlooking the cottage car park and cobblestoned exercise yard, seeing nothing. The misty rain did its best to dampen her spirits. As she stared, she tried to work out why she hadn't been able to give Doc Holder her real name the previous Thursday. She couldn't bring herself to go back to the pain of all those years ago. She wasn't angry; she wasn't even upset. She just couldn't understand why she had to dig up her past at all. After all, she was only an eight-year-old kid at the time.

The last few days had been miserable. She felt very sorry for herself, but knew deep down that she had to come to terms with the past somehow if she wanted to make it to a future.

Darlene had said as much the night before. She'd come in the pitch-black dead of night, as she usually did. She'd told her to *grow up and deal with it*, as if it were that easy.

Jane didn't like it when Darlene talked about her dad drinking and beating up their mother. It hadn't happened all that often ... had it?

She was always sad when Darlene left.

She thought of her mum cradling her in her strong arms, singing lullabies to her.

*Go to sleep; go to sleep …*

Sometimes, she remembered the tears that came tumbling down her mum's swollen cheeks and over her split, bloodied lips.

Jane was confused. She didn't know what to think. Nothing was going right. Even her beautiful hummingbird refused to spread its rays of colourful reflections. Maybe some sunlight in the last part of the day would come along to save her.

Jane was still worried that if she told the doctor her secret, he would tell his wife, who might tell the bad cops where she was. They would still be looking for the only witness.

*The doc's wife is probably a good person*, she thought. *There must be some good coppers out there.*

In fact, she was kind of looking forward to meeting her the next morning.

Aimlessly wandering down the stairs to dinner, Jane was still not hungry but she knew she needed to eat something. In the kitchen, she found Roxy and Amber sitting on their own at the far end of the old wooden table. Many of the girls who'd come before had carved their names into the tabletop before they got out; it had become a must-do tradition. It was nice, but it made the table hard to clean and a hazard for drinks and small dishes.

Jane almost fell into the seat next to Amber.

"You look shit," said Roxy, without the usual barbs. "What's up?"

Normally, Jane would fire back with something rude and change the subject. Today, though, she felt different—even mellow.

"I'm facing up to some of my demons, and it isn't fun."

"Jeez," said Amber, half-laughing. "If I thought too deeply on *my* bloody past, I'd spiral into depression."

"It's the same for all of us here. We're all screwed up," Roxy offered. "It's always some other arsehole's fault, but it's us who end up carrying the can."

This was a rare moment. Gone was the usual bravado, the spiteful personal snipes and putdowns. The three girls were starting to open up, if only a little.

"Wish I knew back then what I know now," sighed Roxy.

"Don't we all," Amber responded. "Ain't hindsight easy!"

For the first time, Amber told the girls her story. She'd started out living an idyllic bush lifestyle in the vast wilderness of North Eastern Australia. Her family lived in a remote gully about half an hour's drive along a rugged bush track to the tiny town of Gulung Mardrulk, on the Central Arnhem Road in the Roper Gulf Region. The girls were amazed at how clearly Amber recalled the details.

She'd spoken only the traditional tongue with her grandma, whom she idolised. Gran, as she called her, used to spend hours with her every day, showing her the agricultural and aquacultural ways of the tribe, as well as their hunting skills.

Amber recounted her one and only road trip to the big town when she was around nine. They'd spent many hours driving along the dirt track through the outback over Beswick Creek to the Stuart Highway, and then north to Katherine, which was about three hundred kilometres south of Darwin. Amber had never seen anything like the shops, the service station, the church or the school. She'd peeked into a smoke-filled pub filled with men drinking piss and yapping noisily, all of which had been completely foreign concepts.

She recalled how shy she'd been at the Kintore clinic as the old indigenous nurse asked all her questions. Her favourite memory of all was her first ice cream, liberally sprinkled with hundreds and thousands on top.

"It was heaven," Amber said dreamily.

Jane couldn't make sense of it.

"Why'd you leave such a great life for this crap city?" she asked.

"Authorities," she said bitterly. "After my visit to the Katherine clinic, somebody read my life file and decided I had to go to a school. One day, two black four-wheel-drives loaded with cops and some departmental jerks came into our camp and grabbed three of us. I ended up living with an uncle in Redfern so that I could get to a school. It was that or an orphanage in Darwin."

"Bloody hell, they're deadshits," Roxy exploded. "What was your uncle like?"

"Put it this way; the most exercise I ever got was running away from him and his leering eyes. Whenever he was sober enough to walk, that is. The only thing he ever gave me was ice, and we know how that went."

"Did the arsehole ever catch you?" Jane asked.

Amber went quiet.

"Let's talk about something else, eh?"

They spoke of other things for a time, then returned to their rooms.

After lights out, Jane stared at the ceiling for hours before sleep finally came over her overheating brain.

The next morning, after the breakfast dishes were dried and put away, the usual eight took their places in the classroom, all talking noisily over one another.

A few minutes later, Sister Chrissy walked in with Dr. Holder and a bright-eyed, trim and fit-looking young lady, whose brown, curly locks fell onto her shoulders. She was dressed in a casual but classy aqua-blue top and denim jeans.

It was easy to see the scars and bruising under her light make-up, and her left hand was still bandaged. To Jane, she looked a little like an Egyptian goddess.

After everyone was settled, Dave stood up.

"Morning all," the doctor started brightly. "I've convinced my beautiful wife Georgia to come along and tell you a little about her life, and how she came to be where she is today. It's a good story, and you can ask her anything you like at the end. Take it easy on her, though; she's just come out of the RPA after a pretty nasty car accident."

Sister Chrissy sat amongst the girls, who either nodded to Georgia or mumbled some sort of greeting. They were not used to any speakers or guests in these sessions.

Georgia, however, looked very relaxed. She told them she was looking forward to the chat, but that it was also very new to her. As she spoke, she looked at each girl in the eyes and was pleasantly surprised when seven of the eight held her stare. Only one of the girls, Bridie, looked away.

Georgia spoke softly, but with a real strength of character, and she soon had everyone's interest. She told them she was born in Caringbah Hospital and lived out her childhood 'on struggle street in The Shire', living in a fibro house in nearby Gymea. Her dad had been a trier, but also a bit of a plodder, working for over forty-five years at the local supermarket-turned-IGA, where he served as manager for the last eighteen before retiring at sixty-five. She told them that, in his generation, it was not fashionable for mothers to work, so her mum stayed at home, but still did other people's washing and ironing to make ends meet. She admitted she hadn't been a good student at either primary or high school, but she had loved sport—particularly netball, for which she'd ended up captain of her school's team in year ten.

Georgia explained that, though she hadn't given it much thought at the time, she now realised how much her mum and dad had gone without to give her a shot at a good life. They'd allowed her to follow her heart and leave school early to go to TAFE (and later teachers' college) full time to realise her dream of becoming a physical education teacher.

Georgia recounted that it was around this time the wheels fell off for her. Towards the end of her third year at teachers' college, one of her professors started to make suggestive remarks every time they were alone. Eventually, he made it clear that he could influence her yearly results if she acted out of turn. Late one afternoon, when she was on her own in the dressing room, he tried to pin her on the bench and take her gear off. She fought 'like a cat', she said, biting his hand with great force until she felt the skin rip. He yelped and stepped backwards, giving Georgia the opportunity to jump up and kick him hard between the legs, leaving him screaming in agony on the floor as she ran off.

She was a mess when she got home, but didn't tell her folks. Now, she wished that she'd spoken up. The professor never spoke to her again but he failed her in the exams.

Georgia was devastated when the exam results were announced, and so she made the decision to tell the principal what had happened five weeks earlier. The result had been that the evidence was inconclusive, and so no action was taken. She was told that she had no proof and no witnesses, and should have spoken up at the time.

Georgia said that this was the turning point for her. She decided to join the police force so that she could get square with these types. Georgia loved the police academy at Goulburn, coming second in the group. She went on to do three years in uniform at Randwick before joining the Missing Persons Bureau at Chatswood as a detective constable, which was around the time she'd met Dave at the local gym.

She finished her story by letting the girls know that she'd worked on many cases involving teenagers and adolescents, and was highly conscious of the challenges they faced.

"What I can leave you with is my strong belief that, in most cases, right will eventually prevail," she said finally. "I do know, however, how tough that road can be. Even so, there *is* a light at the end of the proverbial tunnel, and I truly hope that you all find it. I'm happy to take any questions."

Georgia then sat down next to Dave.

"How'd you get hurt in the car accident?" asked little Maggie Durack.

Georgia explained their recent successes on the world crime-busting stage and told them of the attempted murder, the shooting and the collision with a broken-down van that probably saved her life, as well as the life of her boss, the superintendent.

This got all the girls interested.

"This super-whatever, did he get hurt?" asked Jodie, one of the recent arrivals. A feisty fourteen-year-old, she'd come from just north of Dubbo.

"Not a he, but a she," said Georgia. "Superintendent Samuels is a real force to be reckoned with. I almost feel sorry for the bad guys when she catches them."

She laughed softly and all the girls joined in.

"Are there bad people in the police force?" said Roxy.

Dave looked quickly at Georgia, who already knew of Jane's background. He wondered if the question had come from her.

"Great question, and sadly, the answer is yes. Wherever you go in life, there are always bad eggs. In education, religion, politics, police—even in kids' so-called safe houses like the scouts and guides. That's the bad news. The *good* news is that the rotten eggs are rare, and are increasingly getting caught and having to face the music.

"I'm lucky to be working with one of the greatest fighters of corruption Australia has ever turned out. My boss, Superintendent Tina Samuels, is hated by crooked cops. She's had tremendous success with rooting them out."

That seemed to impress the girls. Jane smiled at Roxy.

"Are you Egyptian?" Jane asked.

Georgia giggled.

"I don't think I'm brave enough to contact *ancestry.com*. I'm terrified of what I might find out," she laughed. "According to my birth certificate, I'm a descendent of both Scottish and Romanian heritage—a real mixture, but I'm a true-blue Aussie."

The light-hearted banter continued for another few minutes before Sister Chrissy stood up.

"Georgia, I was hoping for a good result today, but I never expected such an open and refreshing presentation. I think I speak for everyone here when I say you're a breath of fresh air," she said. "And that Dr. Holder is a very lucky man."

They all laughed, and Dave concurred.

"In all my years here, I've never seen such a good response," she added, bowing respectfully. "I thank you from the bottom of my heart. God bless you."

She invited Georgia to look around Weatherall Cottage and have a coffee while Dave continued with his group class. They left the room deep in conversation.

Dave was over the moon. The talk had gone over very well, and the girls were in a positive mood—the best he'd ever seen there.

After a short break, he reopened the session.

"One of the points Georgia made was that there are way more good people than bad in this world," he said. "It's also true that many of them are creative and talented people who rarely get the opportunity to show it. So today, I want us to start thinking of how we could develop some of those talents. Let's split into two groups and take away a project to work on. Do any of you have a hidden talent you could share with us? Music? Sport? Theatre?"

He looked around the girls. There was no ready response.

"Amber is a black tracker," said Roxy.

"Wow. That sounds different," said Dave. "What's she on about, Amber?"

Amber often tried to get the group interested in her culture, and so she seized the opportunity. She told them all of her grandma's teachings about finding bush food, tracking animals—even lost humans—and navigating by the sun and stars. The girls were amazed at Amber's knowledge of the bush and her survival skills.

"That was brilliant, Amber," said Dave. "Any other volunteers?"

He looked around the group.

"Roxy writes poetry," said Bridie. "I've heard her reading it."

Dave smiled at Roxy.

"Now that's unexpected," he said. "Come on, Roxy. How's about delivering one of your poems for us all?"

He was surprised when Roxy stood silently, looked around, breathed deeply and started speaking with emotion.

"*Escaping The Chill*, by Roxanne Jenkins.

Escaping the chill

Cold misty winds

Rushing by unchecked

Leaves falling freely

Winging to earth's bosom

Madly twisting and twirling

Born to be wild

Mesmerising a child

Tortured souls fleeing

Eyes wide with pain

Souls not believing

Fair weather all over again

Grim Reaper's singing

Flying wing to wing

Fortunes are far away

Show me the path

Chase ere the light

Fades from belief

Keeping fireflies bright

Dreams held aloft in

Skies clear and blue

Seasons come seasons go

Please let me fly

Before calling to die."

Roxy quietly sat down. There was stunned silence.

Dave looked at the girls and saw tears.

"Roxy ... that was beautifully crafted. You are a truly amazing and gifted soul. Do you have any more?"

Roxy smiled. "Plenty, but that's enough for now."

She looked very pleased with herself. It seemed she'd wanted to air her poems for a long while, but had never been game.

Dave's mind was spinning.

*What next?* he wondered.

He would soon find out.

# Chapter Sixteen

Detective Inspector Mike Broadfinger was in his office with senior task force operatives Detectives Brad Henderson and Brian Carey, door shut. He'd instructed the others that there were to be no phone calls or interruptions until the meeting was finished. Because of this, he was surprised when his phone suddenly buzzed.

Looking at the screen, he saw it was Commissioner John Palmer. This was an unusual time for him to ring, so he reached out to pick up.

"Good evening, Sir. How's—"

"Mike, drop everything," the commissioner interrupted. "Get into your car, grab some offsiders, take your secure phone and head to the international airport—now. It's big. I'll brief you on the way. Move!"

*Click.*

Mike jumped up.

"Come on you two," he said. "Grab your guns. Quickly!"

The three of them raced to the lifts and down to the car park.

Brad took the wheel, having been a well-known and successful sprint car champion from the old Parramatta Speedway. Brian was with him in the front and Mike was in the back. Mike briefed them with what little he knew on the way, pad and pen ready to take notes. Headlights flashing and sirens blaring, the unmarked car speeded down the hill towards the harbour and into the airport tunnel.

As they wove through light evening traffic, the commissioner's next call came through.

"You're on speaker, Sir," said Mike. "Go ahead."

"Okay. This is what we've got," Palmer started. "About an hour ago, just after 8 tonight, a Qantas desk attendant witnessed a pair of Border Force officers escorting two of her passengers into a restricted area. When the passengers didn't return before boarding, she became concerned—and even more so when their A380 bound for Dubai departed on time with all passengers accounted for."

"I don't like where this is heading," said Henderson.

"Nor did security," the commissioner continued. "When they searched the area, they found faint traces of blood in the hallway and followed the trail into a cleaners' store. They broke into the cupboard and found two bodies, both shot, along with Border Force uniforms.

"Long story short, it looks like that flight has two stowaways on board. They've been in the air for just over an hour now, and we need to make some big decisions very soon. Border Force will meet you on the top deck at the terminal. Get back to me as soon as you have anything concrete."

The commissioner signed off.

"Jesus, Mike. This could be our two Colombians," said Carey. "Sounds like the way they operate. Those two are real pros."

"Could be," said Mike, writing down a few questions in his notepad. "Let's keep an open mind until we get the full story."

They kept the siren on as they skirted the airport perimeter road on approach to the international precinct. Both men had faith in Brad's driving, even at this speed.

As they approached, they saw the Border Force team, a number of AFP officers and New South Wales police waiting by the roadside and pulled in beside them. Mike immediately recognised Sergeant Glenn Smith, a good mate of his from way back. Glenn was a former Queenslander, now based at the airport.

Glenn introduced Mike to the two senior Border Force team members, who reported that they'd already preliminarily identified the two bodies as Professor Doug Latimer and Dr. Tony Phillips, researchers who'd been travelling together to Dubai. The aircraft chief pilot also confirmed that there were two bearded passengers sitting in seats 11A and 11B, those previously allocated to the dead men.

While they were talking, another Border Force agent arrived with a report from the professor's office, which identified that the victims had been en route to a major climate change conference in Dubai. The event was to be attended by Prince Charles and many eminent scientists from around the globe.

This news really set the alarm bells ringing.

Mike went with the group to the area where the bodies were discovered, and then to the departure lounge and aerobridge to try to figure out how it had all happened.

Just before 10pm, Mike rang the commissioner.

"Sir, I think we have some answers," he said. "The airport team are currently looking at all the CCTV footage in the areas both prior to and after boarding. We also did a series of quick re-en-actments of the various possibilities, and we're fairly convinced that after the researchers were murdered, their killers exited the airport. At the same time, it looks like our stowaways entered the aerobridge via the tarmac and boarded with duplicate boarding passes. If that's the case, it would've taken a lot of planning and internal contacts within the system to get that far. We're dealing with a well-organised mob here."

"That fits closely with the scenario we've reconstructed," said Palmer. "Mike, I'm told that the aircraft is now north of the Queensland border, past Cunnamulla. We've got less than three hours to figure out a plan to get that big bird out of the sky at Darwin without panicking the two stowaways. Knowing those dopey bastards, they'd rather become martyrs than prisoners, and we can assume that they're armed. If they kill the pilot, that could be the end for everyone. The A380 carries over five hundred passengers, not to mention the crew. We have to avoid the worst-case scenario, and we don't have much time."

"Okay, chief. The team here at the airport seems very compe-tent," said Mike. "It'll be easier for us to have direct contact with the pilot. Give us a chance to look at our options and come up with a plan. I'll get back to you within thirty minutes with the best we can manage."

"Sounds good. We'll do likewise here and compare notes. Good luck. Time is not on our side."

Mike then spoke quickly with Border Force officer Jim McIntire and his 2IC, Barbara Martin. Barbara suggested they get the Qan-tas team involved immediately, as they knew the aircraft layout and crew procedures backwards.

Less than five minutes later, eight people sat around the table in the Qantas Club Captains' Lounge.

The Qantas team consisted of Chief Operations Engineer Ted Maynard and Airport Manager Samantha Edwards. They confirmed there were five hundred and seventeen passengers and crew on board. The engineer pointed out that row eleven, where the stowaways were seated, was the first seat in the upstairs business class lounge, a window and aisle seat combination. He also said that business class on the flight was almost full; only five of the ninety-two available seats were vacant.

"And by now, the other passengers will have spread into those," he added.

He advised that the aircraft cabin upstairs was forty-five metres long and six metres wide.

Mike told them about the big picture—namely, the climate change conference and Prince Charles' attendance. He also advised them that the police were fairly confident they knew the identity of the two stowaways, both Colombian gangsters, who would certainly be armed.

"They've been on a horrific killing spree in Sydney over this past week," he pointed out. "My first question is, do you have an undercover marshal on board this flight?"

Both members of the Qantas team looked at each other.

"I'm sorry, Inspector, but that's classified information we're not at liberty to discuss," said the manager. "You're aware of those protocols, I'm sure."

"Let's cut the bullshit, Samantha," Mike responded tersely. "There is no space for bureaucracy here. We have over five hundred lives in our hands, and the only real chance we have is to take out those two killers before they bring down the whole aircraft. A trained undercover marshal would be one hell of a good start."

Samantha thought for a second and nodded.

"I suppose there are times when rules have to be broken. Yes, we do have a marshal on board, though he's downstairs in economy."

"That's great news. Thank you," said Mike. "Now, all that remains is to come up with an excuse to land the aircraft in Darwin and send a team on board without alarming the two killers. We have fifteen minutes to invent a miracle."

Some ten minutes later, they'd formulated a plan that gave them a real chance of success. Both the Qantas team and the Border Force chiefs had some excellent ideas, and all of them contributed. The plan felt plausible. They'd agreed to 'think outside the square', and all shared a healthy degree of optimism.

Mike went over the details one more time before ringing the commissioner.

After explaining the plan, Mike waited for his response.

"Mike, we too had some ideas, but yours is a great plan and we'll go along with that. I'll alert the local law enforcement in Darwin and await your instructions. Good luck, and please keep me regularly informed."

With that, the commissioner hung up.

Mike felt sick.

"It's up to us now, and the stakes are huge," he told the others.

With the time they had left, they proceeded to emulate previous strategies and scenarios from similar challenges worldwide until it was time to put their plan into action.

Everyone knew the consequences if they got it wrong.

# Chapter Seventeen

Bernardo hauled a nice flathead from the canal. Still officially in the police witness protection scheme, he enjoyed fishing off the jetty just behind his rented unit on the Gold Coast, particularly on balmy twilit nights like this one. With the tide turning and darkness fast approaching, this was the perfect time to fish.

As he sat, Bernardo dreamed of returning to Colombia when the trials were over and reuniting with his wife Olga and his two children, now teenagers. He was well aware that he was very much a target for the major drug cartels, especially with the recent arrests of so many drug lords, for which he was largely responsible.

He toyed with the idea of regrowing his beard so that his ageing mother would recognise him, but Tina had asked him to wait.

He thought about the superintendent lying in hospital following an assassination attempt by two of his fellow countrymen, and couldn't help but feel responsible. He was glad, at least, that both she and her detective colleague Georgia were recovering well.

He could never thank Tina enough for what she'd done for him. His life had turned around completely once his old market boss, Nick the Greek, had introduced them. He'd been able to pass on all his information about the Colombian gangs' Australian operations, which had assisted greatly with the worldwide arrests of many mob bosses. Nick had been murdered for his role in the arrests, which weighed heavily on Bernardo.

Bernardo turned his thoughts towards his efforts in bringing the 4G Team together, and was pleased with what they'd accomplished. The world was now a much safer place, thanks to them. Though their actions were not legal under Australian laws, he knew full well that if not for them, the lowlifes they'd taken off the streets would still be out there, untouchable, pushing their poisons onto children and silencing those brave enough to stand up to them. He felt totally at ease with what they had done.

He thought about the final look of terror on the crooked judge's face the week before. Bert had shone a big army torch in his eyes as he woke, but it was far too late for him. All traces of the chemical they then injected him with would disappear from his body within twelve hours. They'd carried his limp form down to the stream and loaded it into his canoe, navigating it through the slow-moving waters down to the first rapids. There, they'd capsized it and snagged his body on a dead tree, knowing it would be found by his staff on Monday. The boys had then returned to their own canoe, to the far bank and up the hill to their vehicle, where they took off their boot covers, gloves and plastic gowns.

Bernardo wondered if the judge had realised two of his hard drives had gone missing. He and Bert had taken them from his home office during their reconnoitre the previous week. They'd found thousands of sickening images of young boys and girls being raped and brutalised. They were now in safekeeping at the 4G Factory, complemented by the diaries Bert found that night. Brad and Tina would find a way to get the intelligence into the police system, and hopefully lead to the identities and arrests of those on the dark web who were responsible.

Tonight, Bernardo and Bert were to revisit the 4G Factory after hours to finish making the bombs and detonators required for their new target: a mob of crime bosses meeting in Sydney's Kings Cross that weekend.

The boys had decided to push on with the project despite Tina being in hospital. They had all the info they needed to keep going. Tina's intelligence had pinpointed the exact time, date and venue for the mobs' joint meeting, which had been called to stop other gangs from infiltrating their territory. Bert had found the perfect room not far from the venue for them to use as a base during the operation.

Brad and Bert had been on surveillance duty in Sydney for the past two days, planting tiny hidden cameras, camouflaged cables and listening devices. Once again, their old military skills had proven invaluable.

Suddenly, Bernardo was on high alert. He sat bolt upright.

Something—or someone—had just moved under the jetty.

# Chapter Eighteen

D
ave was just starting to pack what he needed for the day's regular one-on-ones at Weatherall Cottage when his personal assistant rushed into his office.

"Dr. B wants to see you ASAP."

He furrowed his brow, wondering what this was about. "Sounds important," he said. "I'll see him before I head out."

Dave had worked at the practice for over seven years now, and was very pleased with his progress to date. His good reputation was spreading; he'd built up a very healthy list of new patients, and his contribution to the clinic's bottom line was well above average. He secretly harboured the hope that he would one day be offered a partnership.

Coming through university, he'd been concerned that a lot of newly qualified psychologists languished on the scrapheap for a long time, with few career opportunities. He knew he'd been lucky when one of his tutors, old Professor Chambers, had recommended him to his close friend, Dr. Brinsmead. The rest fell into place quickly and he'd soon settled in well.

Dave took all his gear and walked down to the doctor's office on his way out, where he expected to find him having a healthy lunch in his rooms.

"Hi, Dr. B. You wanted to see me?"

Dave had always got on well with the senior partner, so he was surprised at the hard look on his face.

"Sit down, Dave."

He did as he was asked.

"I've had a phone call from the CEO at Weatherall Cottage this morning telling me that you brought police into the shelter unannounced yesterday," said the doctor. "Mrs. O'Brien is very unhappy, and concerned that we would do that without her prior knowledge or approval. She left me with the strong impression she's considering cancelling our contract because of this breach of trust."

This took Dave's breath away.

"Whoa, hold on, now," said Dave. "Firstly, I didn't bring 'the police', as such. One of the nuns thought a talk from Georgia might inspire some of the girls to lighten their anti-police sentiments, or even give them some incentive to take on a new career. She did it at my request as a civilian, and as part of her voluntary community work. What's more, it worked a treat. All eight of the girls responded very positively. The nuns were ecstatic."

"I know Georgia quite well by now, and such a lovely lady would win over any group with that sort of presentation," said Dr. Brinsmead. "However, the client's wishes must always come first, so I'm afraid I must insist that this sort of thing never happens again."

Dave thought for a while before responding, but decided not to enlighten the doctor about the possibility that something sinister was going on at the cottage.

He bit his lip.

"Fine by me. Anything else?"

Dr. Brinsmead could see his young colleague was not impressed, but stood his ground.

"No, nothing else. All I ask is that you play by whatever the rules are at the shelter. I'd hate to lose that account."

Dave nodded and got up to leave.

"For what it's worth," said Dr. B, "I'm sure Georgia's presentation was exactly what those girls needed. Unfortunately, our hands are tied on this one. My best to Georgia."

As he drove to the cottage, Dave started to wonder if Georgia's presence alone had been enough to spook the shelter's hierarchy and threaten whatever it was they were doing. He decided that as the CEO had made the first move, he'd endeavour to explain the innocence of Georgia's presentation as a civilian and demonstrate the huge success of the idea.

Arriving at the shelter, he made a beeline for the CEO's office.

She greeted him with an icy glare.

"Mrs. O'Brien," he began, "as I'm sure you know, I was counselled by our senior partner today, whereby I was admonished for bringing my wife in unannounced to talk to the girls. Approval or no, Georgia attended in the capacity of a civilian, and it was clear to all present that her talk had an overwhelmingly positive impact on the girls. That being the case, I cannot make sense of the cottage's reaction."

"Dr. Holder, there are many devious people out there who would love to get access to our girls and this shelter for one reason or another," said Mary. "I cannot make rules for some and bend them for others, no matter how beneficial it may be. No one comes into this establishment without my prior approval. If it happens again, I will have no option than to cancel your clinic's contract. You are dismissed."

Dave left the room, where he was met by Sister Chrissy.

The look on her face told Dave that she too had been put through the wringer. He decided not to go into it and proceeded to start his sessions as normal.

As with the week before, he left Jane until last. The moment she entered his office, he could see that she was in a much happier mood and more relaxed than ever.

She expressed that she'd been looking forward to the session since Tuesday's meeting with Georgia. Like the other girls, she seemed to have been won over by the couple, and appeared to be at peace with her decision to open up to him.

"Afternoon, young Jane," Dave said brightly. "Please, take a seat."

"My name is Jamie, but please don't tell anyone."

She almost became tongue-tied as the words flew out of her mouth.

Dave concealed his surprise.

"Pretty name for a pretty girl," he said quickly. "Would you rather I call you Jamie or Jane?"

"Better stick with Jane," she said. "I don't want others to know."

"Okay, Jane it is. Now, let's go over this once more. My sole aim is to get you out of here, give you a great life and help you find some closure. Please know that Georgia and I want only to see the bright, bubbly girl we know is inside you. If you work with us, I know we can right some of the wrongs of the past. Are you up for it?"

"I think so. Your wife's a nice person."

"I was hoping you'd think so. She sure is. Not only that, but Georgia is in the perfect position to be an intrinsic part of our team."

"What do you mean?" asked Jane.

"I mean the three of us together could be a formidable force," he said. "We could work as one to make the world a better place, and find out what happened to your family."

For the next half-hour, Dave talked carefully around Jane's childhood and her nightmares. She told him the harrowing tale in bits and pieces.

"Dad was often away for long periods as I was growing up," said Jane. "Darlene says he was in gaol, but neither of us knows why. We lived in an old, run-down timber house on a big, bushy block of land in the middle of Queenscliff. Must've been the original farmhouse in the area. Went to shit without anyone looking after it."

"What about your mum?" he asked.

"Mum was beautiful. Tried really hard to keep a clean house and food on the table, looking back. She often went without so we didn't have to. We had fuck-all, but that didn't stop Dad from putting on those bloody barbecues. There were always cops. Especially that blond cop, Scarface. He ..."

Dave listened carefully as Jane told the story of her family's murder, interjecting only when necessary so as not to interrupt her train of thought.

The story continued into her time on the run in the National Park at North Head, and her lifestyle at that time. Dave wrote down the main points on his pad, which was filling fast.

Eventually, Jane slowed down and slumped into her chair.

Dave took up the running.

"That is an amazing story, Jane. You're a remarkable young lady, and a survivor in every sense of the word. One in a million," he said emphatically. "You *are* going to come through this. Let me ask you a few specific questions, and then let's both get to work on a plan to get square with these lowlifes."

Jane nodded.

"What's your family name?"

"Bennet ... with one 't'."

"What about your mum's name?"

"Elizabeth, I think. But everyone called her Betty, or BB."

"And your father?"

"Len."

"What sort of work did he do?"

"I don't know. Mum always told me he was away working, but I don't remember where or what he did. He fixed cars at home a lot. Maybe he was a mechanic or something."

Dave decided to delve a little deeper.

"You've already told me a little about Darlene. You mentioned that you still talk to her regularly," he said gently. "Have you ... any idea how that's possible?"

Jane looked confused. She shifted around uncomfortably in her chair before answering.

"Her spirit is alive. She never left me."

"Of course," he said, changing tack. "Jane, about your friend Cate. We're still hoping you could ask the office here to put you in touch with her. We need to find out how she's going."

"She's sad," she said easily. "She hates it there."

"How do you know? Has Cate been in touch with you?"

"No, Darlene told me. She talks to her."

Dave recalled Sister Chrissy's assertions that Jane regularly predicted things that happened exactly as she'd described.

Suspending his disbelief for a moment, he decided to ask.

"Did Darlene tell you where she is?"

"Yeah. She's in a building in the bush, south of Sydney somewhere. I think she said the Highlands, or something like that?"

A shiver went down Dave's spine. This was new territory.

"That must be the Southern Highlands," he said calmly. "A beautiful place, but very cold in winter. Jane, how do you feel about talking to Georgia, and her boss Tina, if I can swing it? You remember Georgia telling you about Tina. She's a wonderful person, and really good at making the baddies face up. It won't be easy to organise, but I can try."

Jane nodded.

"Okay."

Dave thanked her and hurried off.

# Chapter Nineteen

S everal hours earlier, the twenty-one crew members set to board the 8pm service to London's Heathrow Airport via Dubai assembled in the crew sign-on area on the air side of customs at Sydney Airport. Chief Pilot Warwick Taunton and Customer Service Manager Ash Brown— 'Cinders' to his many friends—gave the flight briefing. Just before 7, they all filed out of the lounge knowing they had a near-full deck, including three of Australia's top athletes en route to the World Athletics Championships in London.

By the time they boarded the A380, all catering had been stowed, engineering checks were complete and the cleaners were just leaving the aircraft.

The crew set about preparing the cabin for boarding. The Customer Service Manager and Customer Service Supervisor took up their posts at their respective doors just before 7.30pm, starting to greet all passengers and handle all the normal pre-flight queries and complaints.

The crew were well aware of the need to get the passengers on board, hand luggage stowed and everyone seated on time to avoid the potential penalties for late departure, not least of which could include the loss of their take-off slot. The company frowned deeply on such occasions.

At 7.55pm, the aircraft doors were closed and locked. All passengers were counted and all seatbelts checked. The CSM completed the safety briefing as they taxied to the take-off area.

QF1 was third in the queue and before long, they were in the air, turning out over Botany Bay towards the Tasman Sea. From there, they tracked to cross central Australia and on to Dubai.

Chief Pilot Taunton handed over controls to the first officer as they began their climb to thirty-five thousand feet in a cloudless sky. The reflections of the city lights on the harbour were spectacular. Two ferries could be seen cruising across to Manly.

Once the seatbelt signs went off, the crew got to work preparing to serve dinner and beverages before the cabin lights were dimmed.

About an hour into the flight, the CSM's secure phone buzzed. He looked at the screen and saw it was the captain.

"Hi, Warwick. All well here," he reported.

"Ash, we could have a problem. Sydney are reporting that two of our pax have been found murdered at the airport, but we've confirmed all four hundred and ninety-six passengers are on board, as per the manifest. They're saying that the two people murdered were to be seated in business class in seats 11A and B. Without giving the game away, can you do a walk-past and get a look at the two in those seats while I await further instructions from Sydney?"

The CSM walked out of first class and casually through the business class section, stopping occasionally to chat or pick up dropped articles. A few minutes later, he returned to his office and called the skipper.

"Two bearded blokes of South American appearance. I'd say about thirty-five to forty years old. There are two vacant seats not far from them, 14C and 15B, if we need them. Next to them is a lady with two young kids in the centre section."

"Okay. I'll get back to you as soon as I have anything."

The CSM then called his 2IC downstairs, CSS David 'The Voice' Mosley, and briefed him.

"Say nothing at this stage. I'll keep you up to date."

"Thanks, Cinders," he replied.

The two had flown together many times over the years. David was well known for his karaoke bar performances and had been nicknamed 'The Voice' for years.

All was quiet in the cockpit until finally, the phone rang.

"Captain? It's Sydney. They need to speak to you," the first officer said over his shoulder.

Captain Taunton listened for some time to instructions from Chief Engineer Maynard, his friend of over twenty years.

"Okay, got that, Ted. We'll do our best," said the captain. "ETA at Darwin will be around 0115 local time. I'll need instructions on where to taxi and park, plus a full briefing on what to expect from them on arrival. I presume it'll be the manual staircase, so we'll use the main centre doors to avert suspicion."

He immediately rang the CSM.

"Ash, we have an air marshal on board in 63C travelling under the name of Rogers. Give him the code words 'bad apples' and take him into your office for a briefing. Then, get him into seat 14C while there's a lot of traffic in the aisles, after dinner and before the cabin lights are dimmed." The captain then briefed the

CSM about the Sydney plan. "Come up to the flight deck in thirty minutes."

Ash then called the CSS.

"David, our Air Marshall is in 63C, one Mr. Rogers. Quietly give him the codeword 'bad apples' and bring him up here via the rear stairs to avoid business class. I'll meet you there."

"Wilco. On it now."

The last of the dinners were still being cleared when the CSS approached seat 63C.

"Mr. Rogers?" he asked quietly.

The young man looked like the proverbial gym junkie.

"That's me," he replied.

"I do apologise about the bad apples earlier. If you'll follow me to the rear galley, we can arrange for an alternative."

"Sure can."

And with that, passenger Rogers pulled his briefcase up from under his feet and followed the CSS towards the rear stairwell.

Ash and David touched elbows in greeting as they arrived at the top of the stairs. The three of them sat down on their own so they could get a full briefing on what had happened in Sydney, the probable suspects and the fact that they were thought to be armed. Ash quietly told them of the plan to create a medical emergency on board about half an hour out of Darwin to necessitate them having to divert there. A commando team dressed in medical uniforms would then come aboard. They planned to put the marshal into 14C and hand-pick crew to take up positions in the galley after lights out.

All were nervous, including the marshal. They were well aware of the extreme danger they faced if shots were fired in the pressurised cabin, or worse. They discussed various scenarios, including the possibility of a bomb vest, as the men had not come through security before boarding.

David Mosley left first to check the seat was clear. The marshal followed one minute later, weaving his way past the cabin crew and trolleys on the opposite aisle before doubling back to sit unnoticed in 14C. As he walked, the captain came over the speakers, reporting a clear night with a slight headwind and advising everyone that the cabin lights would soon be dimmed. Lights were dimmed, reading lights came on in some seats and most passengers settled into watching the in-flight entertainment as semi-darkness enveloped the cabin.

As soon as lights were lowered, there was some quiet movement in seats 11A and 11B. No one noticed the window seat life jacket being removed from under the seat. The passenger in 11A placed a device neatly into the life jacket cavity and taped the bomb and detonator securely, just as he'd practised.

The timer was switched on and set to go off in sixteen hours. If the aircraft departed on time from Dubai, it would detonate over the Mediterranean Sea, north of Egypt. If it was late, then it could be over Europe. Either way, it would be long after they'd left the plane. This would destroy any trace of their presence. They'd be heroes back home, and well rewarded. Happy with their work, both men settled down for the remaining ten hours of flight time to Dubai.

Some fifty minutes later, QF1 flew over Mt. Isa, treating those awake on the eastern side to a good view of the city and the mining lights.

Suddenly, the captain made an unexpected announcement.

"Attention, passengers. If there is a doctor on board, please make yourself known to the crew immediately."

The passengers in business class heard a couple of 'pings' in the distance, either upstairs or downstairs—the familiar crew call button.

Shortly after, lights came on in the rear of the aircraft, which burst into activity. Some ten minutes later, the captain again came on the air just as all the cabin lights were turned up.

"Ladies and gentlemen, this is the captain speaking. We have a medical emergency on board, requiring us to divert from our course and land at Darwin. One of our passengers upstairs requires hospitalisation immediately. Sadly, this is a common occurrence on these long-haul flights. We estimate our arrival in Darwin at around 0115 hours local time—that is, in about forty-five minutes. The plane will meet an ambulance at the end of the runway, as it has many times before, and there will be no need to disembark. After the passenger has been safely evacuated from the aircraft, we will immediately return to the air and be on our way to Dubai.

"I'll keep you updated as our new arrival time comes to light, but I can say that we're expecting tailwinds when we cross over the Indian Ocean, meaning we'll be able to make up for some lost time. We'll begin our descent in about twenty minutes. When the seatbelt signs come on, all seatbelts must be fastened. We do apologise for this delay, and will do all in our power to minimise the disruption."

With that, the captain signed off.

The two Colombians in 11A and B looked at each other and began talking quietly but animatedly.

The passenger in seat 11B then stood up and moved slowly towards the rear toilets.

# Chapter Twenty

S ydney had never looked better than it did earlier that day. Glassy, calm blue waters shimmered under a cloudless sky as people fished along the shores, from jetties, the wharves at the Opera House and along the Parramatta River. Others enjoyed a clifftop bushwalk around the picturesque, tree-lined lookouts and vantage points above this spectacular, world-famous waterway. Pleasure craft plied the waters like spiders spinning silk along their webs.

By all accounts, it was a perfect Saturday morning as Dave and the three girls boarded the small ferry at the end of Wattle Street in Glebe, not far from the Sydney Fish Markets in Blackwattle Bay. They were bound for Circular Quay, where they'd board the much bigger Manly ferry to cruise past Taronga Park Zoo and the gentle swell of the harbour mouth. It had only been a ten-minute walk from the cottage to the ferry terminal.

Amber pointed out all the colourful fish near the wharf. The water was very clean, and they could clearly see the bottom. Numerous small creatures and craggy seaweed swung to and fro from the pylons as the water ebbed and flowed freely.

"Can we go fishing?" Amber almost begged Dave.

He chuckled. "No, not today. We've got a full day planned. We're meeting Georgia at the Manly Corso, then going up to Jane's old stomping grounds around the National Park and North Head. You'll love it."

Jane had said she was quite nervous about going back to where it had all started, but that despite herself, she was also looking forward to it.

Dave and Georgia had spent much of the past few days organising this trip. After leaving Weatherall Cottage on Thursday, Dave had met with Sister Chrissy at the RPA Hospital's coffee shop. The nun had told Dave of the trouble she was in for 'aiding and abetting' him by allowing Georgia into the shelter, and he'd responded with the flow-on effect of Jane opening up about her previous life that day. He also mentioned the information she'd imparted about Cate's whereabouts.

"It's not uncommon in schizophrenia for the patient to present with any number of personalities, like a sister who has passed living on inside one's mind," he'd said. "What *is* uncommon, if it truly occurs at all, is for that patient to see into the past or future. There are many who claim that genuine clairvoyants are real, just rare."

Sister Chrissy had reminded Dave that Jane had been able to predict things correctly in the past. Though not quite as convinced as she was, he did his best to open his mind to the possibilities. And so, together, they'd hatched a plan.

The nun had noted there were no management or admin staff present at the cottage over the weekend, leaving her in charge to authorise any outings. They'd agreed that Jane, Roxy and Amber would leave the ward with the doctor this Saturday under the auspices of learning bush skills from Amber in preparation for a proposed garden landscaping project.

Dave had sat down with Georgia that night and told her the full story of Jane's family, including her 'visits' from Darlene. Georgia had gone into the RPA early the next day to brief Tina before she was discharged and headed south to her riverfront holiday home near Batemans Bay. Especially after hearing Jane's story, Tina was eager to remain in Sydney and work on the case, but knew that she couldn't.

They'd agreed that Jane would go into Georgia's work that day to chase up whatever police history there was for Jane's family, and that Tina would be kept informed, as she was keen to do some work on the phone from down south.

Georgia had soon dug up the full computer files on one Len Bennet, a small-time petty thief who'd done three short stretches in Long Bay for car theft and re-birthing, but nothing major. He'd been wanted on minor drug peddling charges, but the warrants had never been served, and Bennet had disappeared off the face of the earth from his last known address in Queenscliff some ten years earlier. It all fitted with Jane's description.

Georgia had carefully looked over the file, taking note of police officers past and present who'd been involved in his various cases. She'd readily agreed to Dave and Sister Chrissy's idea of a special project outing on Saturday, which would give her a chance to find out more about Jane's family from her directly and an opportunity to ask Roxy and Amber about things at the cottage.

Now, Georgia stood waiting for the others at the end of the wharf at Manly.

Dave arrived with fresh doughnuts, coffee, milkshakes and the girls in tow. The five of them sat by the water for a time, laughing and watching as children dived into the water, chasing the money thrown in by passers-by. After walking for five minutes along the water's edge, they all loaded into Dave and Georgia's car for the trip up the hill, past the old St. Patrick's College and along Darley Road to North Head.

Dave drove through the old stone archway, then slowly along the North Head scenic drive before going downhill through the scrub to Wharf Street and Cannae Point. He parked the car just past the old quarantine complex. As they got out, he noticed Jane had gone very quiet and was standing a little away from the others, looking tentatively around the area.

He walked over to her.

"Penny for your thoughts?" he said.

"What? Oh. Just remembering all that time I spent hiding around here years ago. I don't remember it being this beautiful. I think I must've only come out at night," she laughed.

The five of them walked off on the bush tracks towards the near-by remote harbour side. As they went, Jane pointed out unusual landmarks to the group and started to open up a little about her time there. The others listened with interest as they went, trying to picture an eight-year-old girl living here all alone, fending for herself in all weather. Other than Jane herself, only Amber could imagine it.

As they came around one corner in the thick bushland, Jane stopped, carefully examining the ground.

She grinned.

"Come. I'll show you my secret fairy garden."

She pushed her way into the dense undergrowth. There were no obvious traces or tracks, but Jane seemed to know where she was going. A couple of minutes later, they walked out into a small, secluded clearing. There were pretty butterflies everywhere, with colourful wildflowers bursting from vibrant green bushes. Jane motioned for everyone to sit down, and they all found stumps and rocks to rest on while they took in the ambience. It was so peaceful that all five sat in silence, breathing it in.

Suddenly, Jane started making a clicking, guttural sound. They all looked at her inquisitively.

A rustling came from the undergrowth and they watched, spellbound, as an old, long-nosed bandicoot emerged from a thick clump of weeds, slowly limping across the clearing towards Jane. It crawled up the side of her jeans and sat in her lap. She picked the creature up and kissed it.

"Brokenfoot! You're alive!" she whispered.

Tears rolled down her cheeks, finally reunited with her ageing friend.

They must've sat there talking for over an hour. The bandicoot didn't leave Jane's side for a moment as she pointed out all the butterfly species and different flowers, telling stories about the bandicoot family from way back then. Jane picked up a few large white feathers to take home as a memento.

"This is the perfect backdrop," said Dave, "for Roxy to regale us with another of her fantastic poems. How's about it, young lady?"

"Why not?" she said happily. "The one about getting out of that rotten prison seems fitting."

Roxy stood on the stump she'd been sitting on, clasped her hands together in front of her and spoke strongly.

"*The Way Out*, by Roxanne Jenkins.

Shadows fly by

Through rays of sunshine lit

Reflections abound

In life's wonderful light

Footsteps treading lightly

On crusty, dusty soil

Sandy trails of knowledge

For others trying to toil

Time stands still

Bathing in silence

Hearts to fulfil

Stretching in wonder

How brave the sky

Eagles soaring

Flying so high

Spirits unbroken

Preparing to flee

Releasing the loneliness

Listening for the sea

The pathway to Paradise

Points east from our cottage

To a new life out there."

When she finished, there was a long pause before Georgia broke the silence.

"Roxy," she said, "Dave said you were gifted, and I agree. You are very talented to be sure. Thank you."

Everyone agreed.

Roxy beamed, and even the bandicoot joined her on the stump as if to show appreciation.

After Jane and Amber succeeded in digging up some fresh yams and hand-feeding them to Brokenfoot, it was time to say goodbye. The group then walked slowly back to the built-up area and car park before Dave drove them up to North Head Lookout, taking in the scenic view of South Head. The rolling waves and the wide entry into the harbour were truly a sight to behold.

"The only time I ever see this is on Boxing Day at the start of the Sydney-Hobart yacht race," said Roxy, sighing. " I'd love to go sailing on the high seas. I watch the start of the race on TV every year. Close as I'll ever get, I suppose."

Jane and Georgia walked over to some shaded benches, where they sat and began to talk. Georgia was pleasantly surprised by how detailed Jane's memory was, as well as her willingness to tell her everything of her tragic tale. She asked if she wanted to know about her father's record, and she did.

Jane wasn't surprised by anything she had to say. She informed Georgia that it was consistent with what Darlene had told her, then gave her a good description of the blond copper, 'Scarface', and his mates.

Dave decided to talk to Roxy and Amber about his concerns that something might be wrong at the cottage. He quickly realised that he, Jane and Sister Chrissy weren't the only ones worried.

Once everyone had reunited, it was apparent that the three girls were more than willing to work with Georgia on the investigation. They agreed upon a series of things to look out for and to report any of their findings.

"Whatever happens, say nothing of this to the other girls," said Dave. "With something like this, you just don't know who you can trust. As far as anyone else is concerned, only me and you three have been out here learning bushcraft and landscaping ideas from Amber. Whatever you do, do *not* mention that Georgia was here."

They all agreed.

It was late afternoon when Dave and the three girls walked uphill from the Blackwattle Bay Ferry terminal along Wattle Street, satisfied after a wonderful day out.

As they walked onto Pyrmont Bridge Road, only blocks away from home, the fire engines and ambulances outside Weatherall Cottage came into view.

They instantly broke into a run.

# Chapter Twenty-One

Things were hotting up in the special operations room at Sydney Airport. Inspector Mike Broadfinger was part of the team of five endeavouring to bring about a happy ending to this quasi-hostage situation, charged with bringing the A380 aircraft and its five-hundred-plus passengers safely to the ground.

In the past hour, there'd been two significant arrests at the airport. One was a ground control supervisor downstairs, who'd broken his collarbone in his efforts to escape when Border Force moved in on him. He'd been picked up on a hidden CCTV camera guiding the two men into the stairwell under the aerobridge while the QF1 passengers were boarding. He'd already admitted to knowing one of the gangsters, and was still being interviewed.

The other arrest was a long-serving Qantas reservations manager who'd married into a Muslim family three years before and since converted to Islam. She'd been under surveillance for a time, having raised a few red flags with immigration some months earlier. They'd already been monitoring her computer, so it had been simple enough to trace the duplicate boarding passes back to her.

The investigation had already established that both men came into the airport precinct driving delivery trucks, presenting what appeared to be the correct ID and paperwork at the two security gates. Both vehicles had been located downstairs and were currently being searched for evidence, prints and possible explosive devices.

The bodies of the two murdered men had now been removed, and both families informed. There was still a total media blackout to ensure there was no contact from outsiders to those on board the A380.

Earlier, Mike had caught up with Tina over the phone to bring her up to date on everything that had happened since he'd left her at the RPA a few hours earlier. Already, it had seemed like a week ago. Tina had advised him to call the commissioner straight away if they needed urgent and accurate info on the Colombians, as both Rusty Nolan and Alan McDonald from the AFP had excellent contacts. Mike also asked her to hurry up and get better, as he was far happier being the 2IC.

Qantas Chief Operations Engineer Ted Maynard walked into the room and sat with the other four.

"I've just spoken with the A380," said Maynard. "Captain Warwick is the one person I'd have in this situation; he has a quick, sharp mind and is utterly unflappable. He tells me they're about to commence descent, and will be on the ground in Darwin in just under thirty-five minutes. So far, the plan is working well. The air marshal has been planted in seat 14C successfully, just three rows behind the two gangsters, with a clear view from the other side of the aisle. He's equipped with the very latest in space technology and US Armed Forces pistols, the same sort used by the Red Beret commandos in confined areas. The soft, snub-nosed bullets are deadly for humans, but will not penetrate the aircraft fuselage if shots are fired. Regrettably, the same is not likely for the Colombians' firearms.

"The captain has followed our script to the letter, calling over the cabin speakers for any doctors on board. It turns out there were two of them, who were quickly briefed on the situation and are playing their roles to perfection. They're currently treating the 'sick' passenger on the top deck of the aircraft. The surrounding passengers have full confidence that it's a real emergency, especially after witnessing the crew member collapse earlier. Warwick tells me he's going to recommend the doctors and crew involved for Oscars."

Samantha then spoke of the operations at Darwin Airport. They planned to deploy two ambulances, as well as an airport security car and a set of mobile stairs—just enough to be credible without causing concern on board the aircraft.

"There are a total of nine special service troops in various paramedic and security uniforms," she said. "Five will board the A380 with the fold-up medevac rolling bed and make their move on the killers just as the 'sick' passenger is about to be lifted by the cabin crew."

The CSS, David, had dropped a full briefing note onto the lap of the air marshal in 14C to let him know what was going on. As far as air traffic control and Qantas operations were aware, it was a genuine medical emergency, and all procedures and protocols were being followed as per the manual. Those involved with the ruse were just hoping and praying that the mobsters had bought the whole medical emergency setup.

Meanwhile, back on the QF1 top deck, Juan Pablo Cortez had made his way towards the rear of the A380. He stopped in the semi-darkness outside the toilet cubicles, observing what was oc-curring in the next cabin. He could see what he assumed was a lady doctor giving orders to the crew and propping up a man's head with extra pillows. Another lady, possibly the patient's wife, was quite distraught. The doctor looked like she was using some sort of portable defibrillator on the patient.

After watching for a few minutes, he returned to row eleven, took his seat and reported to his compatriot. By then, the youngest of the two children in the centre seats was crying. Cortez glared at the flustered mother as he tried to describe to his accomplice what was happening up the back. They were both reasonably convinced that the emergency was real and presented no threat to their plans.

Still, Fernandez felt uneasy. He didn't like it when things didn't go according to the script. He told Cortez to keep a vigilant eye out for anything that appeared out of place. As a precaution, both men held their Colt M1911 pistols under the airline blankets on their laps. Cortez liked the M1911; the semiautomatic had fewer chances of misfiring or jamming than most, and the seven-round box magazine could be reloaded in less than a second. Very efficient and reliable. They were deadly, accurate killers, and easy to hide at just 8.5cm long.

Three rows behind them, the air marshal, too, felt around in his briefcase, making sure his new Glock was within easy reach. He switched off the safety catch to be ready in an instant, and was watching the two Colombians like a hawk.

Starting to get jumpy, not even he was immune to the distraction of the crying baby. After two and a half years on the job, this was his first major challenge. He'd rehearsed scenarios such as this in many training roles, but the real McCoy left a knot in his stomach.

He'd watched as one of the men walked past him, presumably to check on the commotion in the rear cabin, and felt relieved when he returned and sat back down. The marshal checked his watch—under nineteen minutes to go. He couldn't see anything outside from his seat, as all the window blinds were pulled down so that the passengers could still sleep when daylight came.

Upfront in the cockpit, the lights of Darwin were in full view. Captain Taunton had already gone over the last-minute preparations with CSM Ash Brown, who'd donned one of the three bullet-proof vests stowed on board for just such an emergency. The captain was now on the phone to Sydney, doing one last recap.

When he finished, he turned to the CSM.

"It's up to us now, Ash. So far, so good. Let's hope it stays that way."

They both looked up at the ceiling and beyond, hoping for all the help they could get. Then, looking at each other, they shared a firm handshake as Ash got up to leave and return to the galley, positioning himself near the two killers. CSS Moseley was already there hiding, vest on.

"Eight minutes to touchdown," were the last words Ash heard as he left the cockpit after one last look at the Darwin city lights.

He carefully locked the door behind him.

*Let's get this big bird out of the sky safely,* he said to himself.

# Chapter Twenty-Two

B rad Spruce, the mountain man ex-commando, had been out of sorts for the past week since Tina's accident. He'd been thinking about what might happen to his beautiful wife, Jane, if they were ever found out. One half of his conscience was listing all the great things they were doing for the world, but the other kept reminding him that the gaolhouse beckoned if they were caught, and that he'd be in for the long haul. Still, he knew the judge's fate was well deserved and was pleased with the success of the operation, which had revealed more than they'd expected.

It had been a fairly quiet road trip to Sydney. Bernardo was still angry with Bert for creeping up on him the previous Tuesday evening at the jetty, frightening the life out of him. Bert had thought it was hilarious, and was still laughing about it.

The day before, Tina had phoned Brad to tell him that her week of rehab on the south coast had just begun, and that her informant had confirmed the meeting of the top mobsters that Saturday was going ahead. This left only tonight to finish the fit-out of the old building. She'd also told Brad that her colleague, Georgia, was working on an interesting case involving a children's shelter, which they'd discuss later.

Brad was angry. He felt that the courts, the police and the justice system should have brought the lowlifes they were now dealing with to justice long before it had come to this. Instead, there they all were, flouting the law in Ferraris and Lamborghinis, cruising in big luxury yachts, flying in private planes and living the high life, thinking they were untouchable. They had a network of protectors in lawyers, law enforcement and politics while the kids they used for their operations were dying, or defenceless or their lives ruined, as they made these mobs millions. He hoped that tonight's work would take out a few of these 'Mr. Bigs' and put those crooked pollies, lawyers and cops on notice.

He smiled, thinking Catie would have been pleased with the venue for tonight's operation—upstairs, behind a strip club in Kings Cross, only a few metres down the road from where her hero Juanita Nielsen was last seen alive all those years ago. He imagined that she had probably been killed by offshoots of the same mobs they would be dealing with shortly.

Both Brad and Bert were in awe of Tina's contacts and her ability to get unbelievable things done. They trusted her completely. Last weekend, as she'd told them they would be, the entry doors off the laneway had been left unlocked, and no one was inside. They'd only had a few hours to set everything up and get out without leaving a trace, but it had been enough. All they needed to do tonight was place the charges, wire up the detonators to receive the radio signal and run the last of the leads for the cameras and eavesdropping bugs. They also had to set up their room on the other side of Barncleuth Lane off Roslyn Street, overlooking the strip club. Tina had also organised the room and paid an exorbitant amount of money to the occupant for the two weeks' minimum rent, no questions asked. Bert knew the lady as Jess, who looked like she'd been working around the Cross for many years. He'd thought that even the best dentists and plastic surgeons would have a challenge with her.

The room was very basic; a made-up three-quarter bed, two chairs, a small desk, a wash basin and a tiny cupboard with hinges coming adrift, revealing four old wire coat hangers inside. The showers and toilets were at the end of the old hallway, but this wouldn't worry the lads too much—they wouldn't be staying overnight.

The boys had brought with them a fold-up card table with solid legs and a foldaway director's chair, as well as two desk lamps to augment the single lightbulb that hung sadly from the sagging ceiling. They spent the later afternoon setting up leads and the listening and recording desk until the light faded.

Tina had been very clear that the upstairs meeting room area in the club and the back stairs would start getting busy around 8pm, and they'd need to be clear of the area well before then.

Just after dark, Brad and Bert quietly crossed the laneway carrying two bulky hand luggage bags, slipping into the back stairwell unnoticed. Because of their military experience and their preparatory work earlier in the week, they were all finished and back into Barncleuth Lane in under twenty minutes. Bernardo was waiting for them by the door, having cleaned and then locked up. He'd set hidden threads around the entrance to ensure that no one had been in the room without their knowledge.

They didn't need disguises, as Bert had taken care of the only CCTV camera in the area, up near the square. The three of them walked the other way and turned east down Roslyn Street to a nearby hotel on Bayswater Road, where they'd be spending the night. Before retiring, they enjoyed a quiet dinner at a kebab stop in nearby Rushcutters Bay before walking back to the hotel for an early night. Naturally, they paid in cash wherever they went.

Saturday morning was wet. Traffic splashed dirty water up onto the footpath as people walked busily to and from work. The only ones happy about the weather, it seemed, were the ducks quacking away in Rushcutters Bay.

The three men decided not to eat breakfast at the hotel, opting for a brunch on the waterfront along New Beach Road. They reminisced about one of the recent jobs they'd successfully carried out in the nearby marina a few weeks before.

Most of the afternoon was spent back at their hotel. Bernardo played his favourite online game, *Fortnite*, with people from all over the world. Brad and Bert talked about Tina and what was happening at the 4G Factory. They both enjoyed the fact that the business itself was doing very well, and its bottom line was unexpectedly healthy. Kim, Shane and KT had been excellent appointments at the very beginning of the venture, and now only seven months later, they had five full-time staff, plus three casuals. The only foreseeable challenge was squaring away their taxes.

Around 4pm, Bert left for their Barncleuth Lane room. Brad had decided that, as it was still daylight, they should arrive separately and from different routes.

As each of them arrived, they took their plastic overclothes out of their backpacks in the hallway and, after pulling them on over their street clothes and slipping on skin-tight gloves, they entered the room. There was plenty to do.

First up, Bert switched on the listening desk. There was no sound at all, but that was expected, as the meeting was a pre-dinner get-together, not due to start until 6pm. They were expecting eight men to turn up; two from each of the main eastern mobs, one from a south-east Asian gang, another from the Red Baron outlaw motorcycle gang and a key figure of a Middle Eastern gang. Between them, they were responsible for the majority of drug trafficking, contract killings, racketeering, ram raids, car thefts and drive-by shootings in Sydney.

Around 5.30pm, the first noises came from the room. There were no voices as yet; just sounds of shuffling and the room being set up. Bert decided not to record or film yet.

The first of the meeting's delegates entered right on 5.50pm. There were four of them, and they sounded like they'd been drinking in the downstairs bar. Bert switched on the recording gear and cameras. He was pleased with the audio and the images, which were remarkably clear.

Two more came in just before 6. Then, five minutes later, a girl in her mid-thirties with dark sunglasses and a hijab entered the room. It was clear from the others' reactions that her presence was not expected. She explained that her brother and his colleague had gone into hiding after the recent Hazmal family shootings, and so she was attending in their place. There were dissenting comments around the room and various sledges between rivals, but eventually they settled and commenced the meeting in earnest.

For the next ninety minutes, the group discussed the threat of the Melbourne gangs coming north into their territory—particularly the Pettigrew family and associates of Joe Wray, the controversial Melbourne businessman. They also expressed concern over the rise of rivals in Sydney, such as the Azmadaez family and the Brothers in Arms gangs. Combined, they were starting to make a dent in the Sydney mobs' operations and revenue, and they needed to put a stop to it.

The three boys exchanged the occasional look of awe at some of the intel they were gaining. It went well above what they'd expected; names, locations and systems that were surely closely-guarded secrets. Brad didn't know what Tina would do with it all, but knew she would be very, very pleased.

As they listened, the three men carefully cleaned the room, wiping and removing all traces of their presence. When Brad thought they had enough footage, he and Bernardo stopped filming, packed all their gear into their kit bags and made ready to leave. They carried out a last-minute check before switching off the lights, leaving the key on the table and disappearing downstairs into the pitch-black laneway.

Bert had left earlier to retrieve their car from the hotel, where all accounts had been settled. They told reception they were heading to Canberra early in the morning and didn't want any hold-ups.

Brad and Bernardo waited for Bert to bring the car around into the darkest part of Ward Avenue. As he pulled in, they quickly threw their bags into the back seat and took off along Barncleuth Square, turning left onto Darlinghurst Road. As they drove past Roslyn Street, Brad took out his pre-programmed mobile phone and dialled. A split second after he pressed send, an enormous blast went up from directly behind them. Bert could see the dust pouring into the street as he turned right into William Street towards the city, then right again into Palmer Street to join the westbound lanes of the Eastern Distributor. They crossed the Cahill Expressway northbound on the main deck of the world-famous Sydney Harbour Bridge.

Not much was said as they drove through North Sydney. The only stop they made was in a dark section of the highway near Lane Cove, where they swapped out their false number plates for the correct ones.

They still had a ten-hour drive ahead of them.

# Chapter Twenty-Three

D etective Inspector Mike Broadfinger felt nauseated. The knot in his belly had grown very big, and very tight. There was less than ten minutes until the QF1 touched down in Darwin, and Commissioner John Palmer had just informed him that Juan Pablo Cortez's brother had been martyred two years before in a suicide vest bomb blast in Kabul, which had killed sixty-three people. He'd decided not to tell the others—they had their own immediate challenges without the extra worry, and it was too late to change course now.

Samantha was on a call with Darwin Airport while Ted Maynard gave last-minute instructions to the chief pilot. On the ground, the occupants of two ambulances, a set of mobile stairs and an airport security car were watching the A380 headlights as they approached the runway.

Seven men and two women quietly checked their equipment, going over the plan for the final time. They were parked on the southern taxiway, close to the far end of the main runway. Darwin Airport is a joint-use facility between the Department of Defence and the civilian airport authorities, who control eighty-five percent of the combined area. Fortunately, the two agencies regularly worked together and this time, their coordination was crucial.

Things were very tense aboard the QF1. In the cockpit, Captain Warwick Taunton had broken out into a sweat. He could feel beads of water travelling down the right side of his neck and pooling under both armpits. Just moments before, he'd given the passengers a casual 'all systems normal' briefing, all the while knowing that the air marshal and the chosen crew were in position, ready for whatever happened.

In the business class area, the two children in row eleven must've been experiencing barotrauma, as they were both crying. Their mother tried to shush them, giving the eldest a handful of chewy snake lollies in hopes that it would quieten or at least distract him.

In seats 11A and B, both men were sweating. Fernandez lifted the blind and nervously watched the lights of Darwin approaching. Both he and Cortez had been looking around the cabin for any sign of trouble, their fingers itchy on their colt pistols, ready to throw the blanket and start firing if anything happened. Fernandez was acutely aware of the red button on the bomb detonator, and was happy to use it if necessary. He would be martyred for his cause, and his family well rewarded. If they survived, however, the rewards would be even greater.

About ten feet away, Ash Brown and CSS David stood quietly in the darkened galley with dry throats, holding on in preparation for landing. When the five 'medical' team members entered the aircraft, they were to wait until they heard the order to 'lift', which would be the signal for the special operations team and the air marshal to act.

Ash had carefully pulled the curtain between the two cabin sections as normal so there was no visual contact between first class and business. The same had been done at the rear of the business class cabin.

They all waited, hardly breathing.

Those on the ground watched as the A380 grew larger, descending from the black night sky into the airfield lights. It was about to touch down on runway thirty-six, as cleared by the air traffic controllers, who'd already alerted Darwin Hospital to expect a passenger suffering from cardiac arrest.

Captain Warwick tensed as the wheels hit the tarmac right on 0115 hours; a textbook landing. Ash and David braced grimly against the bulkhead as the sound of the engines reversing thrust filled the air.

The children in row eleven were still crying, which was pushing Fernandez to his limit, his eyes searching wildly for unexpected activity on the airfield. He could see three vehicles parked up ahead at the end of the taxi runway, lights flashing, but no other movement.

Fernandez watched closely as they neared the end of the runway. He could make out two ambulances and one other vehicle with flashing yellow lights, plus a set of mobile stairs ready to drive against the aircraft. He counted eight or nine people in all on the ground. There were two men driving the stairway into position and he could see two security people, one female, and four paramedics, three men and a woman. He nodded quietly to Cortez, and both men relaxed just a little. Fernandez continued to watch what was happening outside.

As the stairs were chocked and the cabin doors opened, the captain's voice came over the loudspeaker.

"Ladies and gentlemen, this is your captain speaking. We have now arrived safely on the ground here at Darwin, and are about to evacuate our sick passenger. Please leave all seatbelts fastened and do not move around the cabin, as we hope to return to the air in just a few minutes. There will be no service or use of toilet facilities for a short time. We apologise for the delay, but rest assured we'll be on our way again shortly."

As he spoke, three of the 'paramedics' came up the stairs carrying an ambulance stretcher, plus some first aid equipment. Fernandez was not worried at all when the men tasked with affixing the stairs came up to open the A380 doors and attached them to the lugs. Nor did he hear the air marshal three seats behind him silently unbuckle his seatbelt, drawing his Glock pistol and concealing it under his lap blanket, ready for anything.

Time seemed to stand still. The Darwin team came noisily up the rear staircase to the upper deck to attend to the 'sick' passenger.

Meanwhile, the two stair handlers and two of the 'medical' team were quickly and quietly making their way up the front stairwell into first class to wait for the 'lift' command from the rear.

The remaining 'paramedic' nodded to those grouped around the would-be patient and was about to give the order when suddenly, a terrifying scream came from somewhere up the front of the A380.

A female passenger in first class had seen one of the commandos dressed in black, gun drawn, moving silently down the aisle at speed in the semi-darkness, and immediately thought it was a terrorist hijack. Her piercing cry instantly sent terror through the aircraft. Fernandez and Cortez quickly rose from their seats, guns in hand, just as Ash whipped the curtains open to allow the commandos through. The air marshal was already out of his seat, about to move forward.

Pandemonium and shrieking filled the cabin. Suddenly, shots fired. Both Cortez and the air marshal were hit simultaneously. After firing blindly, Fernandez quickly sat in his seat, his right arm seeking the red detonator button underneath. Before he had a chance to press it, the commando at the fore put a bullet through his neck. Fernandez fell lifelessly to the floor. Wounded, the commando collapsed on top of him.

Though the threat had passed, it was too late to stop the panic on board the A380. On hearing the first shots, many passengers immediately bolted towards the downstairs exit doors and stairwells from the upper deck, oblivious to anyone else's safety.

Some fell and were either trampled on or tumbled down the stairs. The cabin was full of screaming passengers; others just sat frozen in their seats. No one knew what was happening.

The remaining three people on the ground had run up the stairs as the noise of gunfire and screaming broke out, but were unable to manoeuvre around the horde trying desperately to escape.

Across the airfield, previously hidden police, security and emergency vehicles raced towards the stricken A380, lights flashing and sirens blaring, all personnel with their hearts in their mouths.

The crew in the air traffic control tower were open-mouthed, taken off-guard by the sudden chaos. One immediately pressed the alarm button to shut down the airport and call for backup.

Too late, it seemed; the first officer on QF1 yelled over the speakers for calm, and the remainder of the crew tried to stop the panic. Captain Taunton had raced out of the cockpit and headed for the business class as soon as the shooting erupted, but it was all over by the time he approached the curtain. He was greeted by a number of bodies in the seats and in the aisle, including CSM Ash Brown, lying on the galley floor in a pool of blood. CSS Mosley sat by his side, trying to make him comfortable.

In Sydney, the Special Ops room was deadly silent as they listened to the cockpit microphone, the captain reporting a safe landing to the panic and gunfire.

It was five long minutes before a breathless captain made a report to Chief Engineer Ted Maynard, with all the others listening on speaker. He confirmed there were a number of casualties and several injured from gunshot wounds, plus numerous broken bones and serious lacerations from the ensuing stampede and panic. He went on to report that both Colombians were deceased, and that the bomb squad had successfully located and disarmed a large explosive that had been set in the lifejacket pocket under the seat.

It was some time before anyone in the room spoke. They were all experiencing mixed emotions—part relief, part sadness.

A lot had happened in five and a half hours.

# Chapter Twenty-Four

D r. Holder and the three girls were out of breath as they ran past the fire engines and ambulance then up the front stairs into Weatherall Cottage, despite the best efforts of a lone policeman trying to stop them. The smell of smoke was very thick.

The first thing they saw were the paramedics treating Sister Chrissy and one of the nurses who was half-sitting, half-lying on the old lounge in the common room. She appeared out of sorts, but otherwise okay.

The nun soon told them that the fire had started in the kitchen and spread quickly. According to the girls, the new girl, four-teen-year-old Trish Collins, had been playing with matches and set fire to the old curtains, which had quickly engulfed the whole corner before they could put it out.

By the time the fire brigade arrived, Sister Chrissy and two of the staff had taken up garden hoses in an effort to put out the flames, one from inside the shelter and another through the kitchen win-dow. The fireys soon got to work with a hose reel and put out what was left of the blaze. There was extensive heat and smoke damage and some superficial paint scorching, but aside from the old curtains, there was little permanent damage.

Sister Chrissy and one of the other staff had been overcome by the smoke and steam, but both were okay, save for a few minor abrasions. The nun was more concerned about the welfare and the whereabouts of the young girl responsible. She'd run away as soon as the alarm was raised, and no one had seen her since.

"The poor child has a troubled past, and would be terrified of facing punishment," said Sister Chrissy. "I'm worried. I have no idea where she'd go."

"She's down at Johnsons Creek, near that Jubilee Oval," Jane said quietly. "She's okay."

"How would you know that, ya dork?" rubbished Roxy.

"I just know," Jane said flatly.

Remembering the nun's assertions that Jane 'saw things', Dave thought it was time to put it to the proof. He glanced at Sister Chrissy, and they shared a nod.

"Great news, Jane. Can you take us there?" he asked.

"I think so."

The nun heard this and smiled at the doctor.

Dave, Jane and Amber half-walked, half-ran along Booth Street to the roundabout, turning right onto Wigram Road. Jane led them down a dirt track onto a pathway next to Johnson Creek, and they walked along the canal reserve for some five minutes where the bush started to thicken.

"I think she's just past the next bridge," Jane told them as they approached Dalgai Way.

Amber soon spotted a yellow ribbon caught up in the bush at about shoulder height.

"I think that's Trish's," she said. "She always ties her hair up in one just like that."

The three of them pushed on down the side track, and it wasn't long before they came into an open area. There, they saw Trish sitting at a picnic table on her own. She was crying when she looked up, but didn't try to run.

"G'day Trish," said Dave. "Thank God you're okay. Sister Chrissy is worried about you. Looks like things got a little out of hand back there, huh? We've all done something like that. The important thing is that we learn from it. Everything is fine at the cottage, by the way; not much damage, all in all."

"I didn't think it'd burn so quick," Trish sobbed. "I'm sorry. What will they do to me now?"

"Not much, if anything," said Dave. "These things happen, and we all move on."

"How did you find me?" asked Trish.

Amber looked at Jane to see what she'd say, but the doctor spoke up instead.

"A lucky guess. We followed our noses until Amber saw your hair ribbon stuck in the bushes."

The four of them talked for a while before setting out to walk back to the cottage. Dave phoned back in advance to report that Trish had been located and all was well.

By the time they got back, the fire brigade and the ambulance had left, but the smoky smell still hung heavily in the air. Sister Chrissy, who was waiting by the door, made the appropriate fuss over Trish as she assured her she was not in trouble, and that her welfare was most important.

Dave took Jane aside to sit in the corner of the common room.

"If I wasn't convinced before, I certainly am now," he said. "Jane, you have a gift. I don't know what it is, and I can't even begin to explain it, but it's incredibly special, and you must guard it well. It's as if you are able to simply 'know' things when the situation calls for it."

Jane looked straight into Dave's eyes.

"There are some things I'd rather not know."

She left it at that but looked happy that the doctor understood.

She went to her room and took some photos of Cate and some of the other missing girls from her drawer. She brought them downstairs and gave them to Dave.

"These are for Georgia. I've written the names of the girls on the back of each one."

Later, Dave called for a meeting with Sister Chrissy. Once they were alone in her office, he showed her the photos Jane had given him.

"I'm fairly sure that Jane has some form of mild schizophrenia," he began, "but am equally convinced that she has some sort of genuine clairvoyant ability. I can't wait to tell Georgia about this. Do you remember when Jane spoke of Cate and her current whereabouts? I think we might actually be able to use that to track her down and find out what's really been happening around here."

The nun nodded gravely.

"Let's just hope we're not too late."

# Chapter Twenty-Five

By all accounts, Tina should have been totally relaxed. Here she was with hubby David, sipping a delicious 'boat shed' latte at the Mossy Point boat ramp on a magnificent, sky-blue day with just a hint of a cool breeze. A young lady in shorts and a t-shirt was standing knee-deep in the crystal-clear waters of the clean, sandy creek about ten feet from them, talking to three massive wild stingrays swimming around her feet. On the edge of the circle, pelicans and cormorants chattered noisily, eyeing up the nearby fish and picking off dining tables, waiting for scraps from the nearby flotilla or the next inbound pleasure craft.

It was a daily routine here that kept the locals and tourists alike well entertained.

In spite of it all, she couldn't help but feel tense.

David watched her carefully, well aware of her inner turmoil. Even though Tina was recovering tremendously from her physical injuries, he knew that mentally, it was another story.

He was not surprised when Tina turned to him, eyes resolute.

"We're going back tomorrow. Please, no arguments."

David said nothing.

"Mike, Georgia and the team have challenges coming at them from every direction. Now, more than ever, they need all hands on deck, and here I am, sipping on lattes. Even besides all that, Brad and the boys need me to discuss forward planning options."

"That's that, then," said David with a smile. "Decision made."

David was the only outsider who knew Tina's secret. Police Commissioner John Palmer, Detective Inspector Mike Broadfinger and Detective Sergeant Georgia McHenry-Holder certainly didn't. They only knew the side of Tina that was an exceptionally talented detective superintendent with contacts in many areas; the fierce police corruption fighter and scourge of organised crime worldwide. As far as they knew, Tina was as straight as one could get. They knew nothing of Brad, Bert, Bernardo, Garth or the poor late Catie. The 4G Team took on the seedy side of life alongside Tina their own way, so far undetected, and very successfully.

Nevertheless, alternating between the two hats was wearing on Tina, and David could see it clearly. When he considered that she also had the threat of cancer hanging over her head, he was amazed that she was able to carry it all and continue functioning, let alone as efficiently as she did. He knew, however, that it couldn't last.

For the past week, Tina had been on the phone to Mike, Georgia and Brad constantly, and she and David had stayed glued to the TV screen as the QF1 hostage drama unfolded. The news channels forgot all about COVID for a few days in the wake of the murder of two preeminent scientists at Sydney Airport, as well as the Colombian stowaways who had taken their place on the ill-fated flight bound for Dubai. The emergency landing at Darwin, the shootout aboard the aircraft, the ensuing panic and the civilians injured in the fallout served only to prolong the coverage.

She'd heard directly from the team that the two Colombian mobsters had been confirmed dead, and though the air marshal and the CSM had both been wounded, they'd been saved from more serious injury by their bullet-proof vests. Not so lucky was the Special Service commando, who'd been shot in the face at close range and was still in a serious condition in Darwin's intensive care unit.

Over five hundred passengers and crew had been evacuated alive and transported from the scene in buses, to be accommodated all over Darwin while the A380 aircraft was taken out of service for a full check-over. The best news of all was that the operations team had taken out one of the mobsters right before they'd detonated a huge bomb strapped under the seat.

Many people bought a lottery ticket in Darwin next day. The city had not seen so much media in town since Cyclone Tracy the previous century.

Of course, there was also the news of the massive explosion in a Kings Cross strip club. Again, the media were having a field day jumping to conclusions, bandying about various accusations about inter-gang warfare. So far, there had been nine bodies removed from the wreckage; eight men, and one woman. One 'exclusive' front page report held that senior members of a Middle Eastern gang were supposed to be in attendance but had sent a representative in their stead, giving rise to the suspicion that they'd organised the bloodbath and sacrificed one of their own in the process.

The majority of the media outlets predicted that this would be the start of all-out, open gang warfare across Sydney, and might even extend into the other states. As Tina listened to all their baseless assumptions, she was pleased to hear not one voice pointing to the 4G vigilantes. Brad had given her a blow-by-blow report on the operation, and the boys were all safely back in Queensland, with no evidence of a border crossing at any of the COVID checkpoints.

Tina paid close attention to Mike's face as he spoke at the many press conferences and media scrums being televised. He looked sad and worn out as he tried to cover all these major cases, all the while hard at work trying to solve them. She felt very sorry for him, and that she was letting him down by not being there to ease the burden.

On top of all this were the conflicting reports of the assassination of Judge Tiffany Wallace, and the unexplained death of another senior judge, James Latta. It felt like Sydney was now the red-hot crime capital of the world, and many were concerned that the police weren't coping with this influx of crime—or worse, that they were involved.

There was so much going on that the news had almost forgotten the Parramatta Police Station bombing and the attempted murder of the two senior police officers investigating the case only two weeks before.

Tina was at the heart of it all, and was eager to get back in the driver's seat. She owed it to all sides.

Early the next morning, she and David drove out of *Paradise Lost* and alongside all the beaches to Batemans Bay, then west up the Clyde Mountain, waving to 'Pooh Bear' on the ascent, which had been a tradition for years.

They stopped at the Braidwood bakery for a compulsory pie, plus a take-home fresh, roll-top loaf of hot bread and an apricot pie, with no more stops until they arrived back home at their unit in Epping.

While David was out shopping for dinner and supplies, Tina was on the phone to Mike, Georgia and the police commissioner respectively, organising briefing meetings for 8.30am, 10am at Chatswood, then midday at Day Street Police Headquarters.

She then rang Brad and organised for him to fly to Sydney in two days to allow her time to get on top of her police duties before she met up with him.

Tina knew she was breaking Dr. Humphreys' explicit instructions, but she was far too happy to be back to care.

# Chapter Twenty-Six

Police Commissioner John Palmer was in his casual civilian clothes as he showed his membership badge at the huge Eastern Suburbs Rugby Leagues Club. The receptionist smiled. She didn't need to check it; the commissioner was a regular.

As he made his way to the lifts and then up to the boardroom, he thought of his long-time friend Rusty Nolan and the journey they'd been on together over the years. They'd met playing junior rugby union in the Judd Cup in the late seventies, then later again in the South Sydney district rugby ranks, better known now as South Juniors. At the time, John was a rookie cop fresh out of the Goulburn Police Academy, and Rusty was an aspiring top-grade league player. The two boys were great mates, even living together in a Bondi unit for a few years, loving life in the surf.

As time went on, their lives began to take them in different directions. John got married and rose up the ranks in the police force, while Rusty started acquainting himself with some colourful characters in the eastern suburbs, many of them associated with local gangs. He played first grade for Easts, and was popular with the players and supporters alike. After retiring from football, he went on to become a board member and later president of the thriving Eastern Suburbs Leagues Club, where they were set to meet that day.

Despite their differences, the two of them had remained very close over those forty or so years. Rusty was still closely associated with and trusted by many of the movers and shakers in Kings Cross and the eastern suburbs. He played hard but fair in all his dealings—and above all else, he knew right from wrong. Rusty had been very happy working closely with John Palmer, providing valuable intelligence about the many mobsters who'd done little to earn his respect. Together, they'd been a formidable combination, unseen by the outside world.

The two sat talking casually in Rusty's office as sandwiches and coffee were brought in. Rusty enquired as to how Tina was going. The two had got on quite well while working in John's small team of trustees, and he'd been happy to help Tina out on more than a few occasions.

"I've talked to her a bit over the past week," said Palmer. "She and David are down on the south coast. She's on the mend, but desperate to get back to her desk. A touch early, by my estimation, but you know Tina. I'll be seeing her tomorrow."

"From what I'm hearing, they could use her on the front lines."

"Rusty, we've been mates for a long time, and I don't mind telling you I've never been so unsure of what's going on around me," said Palmer, stone-faced. "I'm worried. My gut feeling is that we're getting close to someone very big, but for whatever reason, Tina's not giving anything away. I think the world of her, but someone, somewhere, wants her dead by any means necessary, as well as those close to her. Those Colombians in the Qantas drama were proof of that. I just wish she'd open up to me. She's pulled some unbelievable strings of late, and you and I both know that can't happen unless you're very well connected."

"Whatever it is, John, I know her well enough to say that she is hellbent on making this world a better, safer place," said Rusty. "But I share your concern. She's pushing it real hard."

"More than you know. This is not for anyone else's ears ... but Tina has some real health challenges going on. She's on chemo, and it's taking its toll. I have the feeling she thinks she's on borrowed time and so she's trying too hard to fix the world before she goes. She was very close to Catie Lanyon, that journalist who died of cancer. The girl was one of her best sources, and a great contributor to her success ... but I can't help but think there's more to it."

The two men continued talking about current events, including the two dead judges, swapping opinions and theories until it was time to head to the boardroom for the 2pm task force meeting.

Alan McDonald had flown in from Canberra that morning, while Mike had arrived with Deputy Commissioner Warren Hardcastle. Dick Sellis was unable to attend due to pressing work commitments, but sent his regards.

The commissioner welcomed everybody, then officially opened the meeting.

"First things first," he said. "Mike, what's the latest on Tina?"

"Health-wise, she is on the improve. She called this morning to say that she and her husband are returning to Sydney today, and she'll be present at our next meeting."

"Sounds positive. Here's hoping it isn't too soon. Next up, Mike, we need to congratulate you and those responsible for the QF1 result. You had little time and scant information, and what you all pulled together in five hours was a credit to you. The slightest misstep could easily have resulted in a disaster."

Mike humbly received the accolades and went on to give a full report on the QF1 operation. Eventually, the discussion turned to the latest on the two dead judges and the Kings Cross explosion, amongst other things.

"Gentlemen," said the commissioner, "I don't know how yet, but somehow I think that all of this is linked. There's something, or someone, we are missing. Our job is to pull the jigsaw together and solve it. Of course, this is easier said than done."

They deliberated further until just before 4.30 and then broke up, having given Mike plenty to discuss at the next day's follow-up meeting.

Both Alan and Rusty shook Mike's hand and said goodbye, pleased that Tina would be returning to the fold.

Mike and Warren left the club to drive back to Day Street Headquarters, where Mike had left his car. They drove towards the city, discussing various angles that might connect the cases.

"If Tina is back on deck, I suppose Georgia will be too?" said Warren.

"Yep. She's doing some community work on light duties at the moment, and it sounds like it's going well."

"Do you know anything about her new husband?"

"Dave," said Mike. "I've met him a few times. Seems like a really nice guy. He's a psychologist and has been doing some great departmental work, from what I'm hearing. Do you know him?"

"No, we've never met."

Just then, the police radioed them and directed them to go immediately to the Kings Cross bombsite. They reported that investigators had located a flat on the laneway across from the explosion that might have been used by those responsible.

Siren on, they headed for Darlinghurst Road.

# Chapter Twenty-Seven

Weatherall Cottage CEO Mrs. O'Brien was in a bad mood. She picked up the phone and dialled the private mobile of Chairman Brian McGarry.

"Good morning, Mary," he answered.

"Not here it's not," she said tersely. "I've finished the report on the fire damage. We need to talk about what sort of penalty we can issue to the Collins girl."

"I'm planning to be in just after lunch. We can discuss it then," McGarry offered.

"There's more to it. That psychologist, Dr. Holder, is involved again. Somehow, he and three of our girls were cleared for a day excursion by the old nun, Sister Marion. I'm told they returned after the fire, and yet they knew where the girl was hiding. I don't know what's going on, but I don't like it. He may want to involve the police again."

"There's no need for law enforcement," said Brian. "This is a simple in-house matter, and we'll deal with it ourselves. Is that your only cause for concern?"

"That, and the fact that someone has placed a large, white quill feather on my desk pad, either dipped in iodine or blood," she said.

"What's that mean?"

"It either represents cowardice, or it means that angels are near. Take your pick."

"Good God, Mary. What's going on over there?"

"I wish I knew," she responded.

"Okay. I'll be there in an hour, but I need to make a couple of calls first. Keep your ears and eyes open. We don't need anything going wrong now. See you soon."

McGarry then dialled another number and took the phone off speaker.

"This is Brian McGarry. I would like to speak with Chief Justice Larucci, please."

The voice on the other end responded.

"Thank you. Would you please ask him to call me on my mobile as soon as he gets back?"

He hung up the phone.

Some forty-five minutes later, McGarry entered Mrs. O'Brien's office holding up a white quill feather, also dipped in something dark reddish-brown.

"This was on my chair in my office," he said. "No one other than you has keys to it."

"And the emergency key's in the safe," she corrected, "but no one can get to that without you or me knowing about it, and it certainly wasn't me. Here's mine."

Mrs. O'Brien lifted up her feather. They were an exact match.

"Whatever is going on here, we need to nip it in the bud," said McGarry. "Which girls went with the psychologist?"

"Jane Dee, the freckle-faced girl we haven't identified; Roxanne Jenkins, the large, butch-looking one; and Amber Newbould, the aboriginal."

"Well, for starters, put the coloured girl into the next parade. She's pretty and she'll be a good fit for the studio. After that, it's time to do something about that old nun."

"Leave it to me," said Mrs. O'Brien. "I'll take her little excursion up with her superiors at the monthly meeting next week. I think it's also time we cancelled the psychologist clinic's contract, but let's wait until the nun is out of the way. With both of them gone, we can be certain we've put a stop to whatever they're up to. I can watch the others."

"What sort of punishment do you propose for the girl who started the fire?" asked McGarry.

"Put her in solitary for a week or so until the others are gone, then have her on next month's adoption list. It's just a shame we can't put two on this month without risking the authorities getting suspicious."

McGarry's mobile began to vibrate. He looked at the dial.

"This is important," he said hastily, turning to leave. "Come up to my office in an hour or so."

After he left her office, he answered the phone.

"Hello, Nat. Just give me a second. I'm on the way to my office now."

He was puffing as he reached the top of the stairs, walked into his office and shut the door.

"Nat," he said finally, "we may have a problem."

# Chapter Twenty-Eight

D etective Superintendent Tina Samuels hit the ground running on Thursday morning. She was still not cleared to drive, so she boarded the 6.15am metro train from Epping for the short run to Chatswood. She wanted to be early. Tina walked slowly along Victoria Street, doing her best to conceal her limp. She'd scoffed when David had suggested she use a walking stick throughout their holiday, but imagined she'd be better off right now if she had.

By the time she reached Police HQ, she was in considerable pain. She opted for the longer wheelchair ramp as her ingress, as she didn't think she could face the stairs. She hoped that no one saw her.

Injuries and indignities aside, it felt good to be walking back into the station. She smiled and nodded to the desk sergeant in the foyer and used her security pass to gain access to the lobby. *The Cell* coffee shop was open, as always, so she treated herself to a large, long black— takeaway, very hot, with two sugars—then entered the lift and rode it up to her office.

Stepping into the all-too-familiar space, Tina sat down slowly behind her desk. She smiled when she saw the neat piles of separate tasks laid out before her, all marked in sequence and ready for actioning. Mike was a wonderful 2IC and knew exactly what she needed. The office was spotless; even her favourite pens and pads were ready to go. A bright, colourful bunch of flowers had appeared on her desk, which she loved.

Mike came in early, just after 7.15, but by then, Tina was already on her fourth page of notes, full of questions to ask various individuals.

"Morning, boss. Welcome home," he chirped. "Goes without saying, but I am so, so pleased to see you back."

Tina chuckled.

"Thanks for the flowers, Mike. Grab whatever notes you have and we can go over the day ahead."

Mike was back in less than thirty seconds. He'd prepared for this long before he left the office the night before just before 10.

"Okay. First up, congrats—you did spectacularly well in my absence. If you wouldn't mind doing it one last time, I'd like you to conduct today's briefing. I just want to sit up the back, look and listen before I address the team."

Mike nodded firmly—again, he'd been expecting this. Tina continued.

"I think Georgia will be there as well. She can sit with me up the back, as she hasn't been fully briefed yet either. So tell me, what do you think of the team?"

Mike thought carefully about his response.

"I've worked with a happier bunch. I think it's a mixture of frustration, short staffing and personalities. Having said that, they're all keen, and doing a great job under the circumstances. There still hasn't been a lot of substance to work on."

"I can well imagine all that," said Tina. "Remember the early days on the Riley Sampson case? Tell me about the personalities."

"Well, the ones from our old team are fine, and will be even happier with you two back. The Penno sergeant, Elwyn, is fitting in well too. Senior Constable Hanagan keeps to herself and doesn't mix much, but I'm glad she's with us for two reasons: for one, she is very sharp and savvy; and secondly, she has direct access to the commissioner's intelligence and assets, which is nothing but good for us. The three guys from Parra seem to have some sort of issue with both Bruno and Alison, but I have no idea what it is. I reckon they'll perk up when Derek eventually rejoins us."

Tina just nodded.

"Speaking of Derek, last I heard, he was off the ventilator and out of ICU. Has there been any other news?" she asked.

"I saw him yesterday. He's pretty banged up—a total of nine major broken bones. His fractured skull and jaw make it hard for him to talk. He's on liquids through a straw only. It'll be a good while before we see him out and about, I'd say."

Tina shook her head sadly.

"How did he take the news that Garry was killed by mistake?"

"He took it real bad, but I actually reckon it's done him some good," said Mike, smiling faintly. "He's so keen to get even, I think it'll speed up his recovery."

Tina smiled.

"Sounds like Derek. I'll see him tomorrow."

Mike went on to give Tina a detailed account of everything he'd been working on.

Georgia popped her head in the door shortly after 8.

"Morning, chief. Welcome back. Love the flowers," she said. "Morning, Mike. Present and accounted for. See you both at the briefing."

With that, she went to her office to prepare.

Before sitting up the back, Tina introduced herself to the two Parra dog squad detectives, who she'd met only once previously, and said hello to everyone else, who she knew reasonably well.

Mike opened the session and called for any updates or new evidence on any part of the investigations. For the next hour, the task force revisited all they knew about the Parramatta bombing, the attempted murder of Tina and Georgia, the death of the two judges, the QF1 flight, the Colombian mobsters and the Kings Cross bombing. There had been a huge effort from the force in sifting through a long list of leads across cases, trying to find anything to link them. Their efforts had led to more arrests at the airport, plus the identification of the seven gang members and two staff members killed at Kings Cross. The SUV used in the bombing, Judge Tiffany Wallace's murder, the Westmead Hospital murder and the M4 shooting had also been located, though it had been burnt out and was of little help. Further, Judge Latta's death had been determined a homicide, with CCTV evidence across the board producing many leads to follow up.

Tina took notes through the session, though she was already across most of it—until Detective Brian Carey spoke up towards the end.

"A small-time brothel operator and an old informant of mine, Jess Yurong, happens to operate out of Barncleuth Lane, just opposite the strip club where the bomb went off," said Carey. "To hear her tell it, a man rented a room for two weeks just days before the event, and wasn't seen again afterward. Says she saw three men in the room over that time; two of them tall and fit like fighters, and the third relatively average, South American in appearance and accent. Yurong doesn't put up just anyone; the room was arranged by a friend of hers, a barman at the Eastern Suburbs Leagues Club. We're set to interview him at 3pm today. We've done a thorough forensic on the room, but they were thorough. They were seen crossing the lane into the back of the strip joint on a few occasions, so it's highly likely that these are our men."

Tina felt a chill go down her spine. Descriptions of Brad, Bert and Bernardo and a link to Rusty Nolan.

Mike wrapped up the meeting soon after 9.30 and gave the floor to Tina.

"Thanks Mike, and thanks to the rest of you for a job well done during my absence. I'm well aware of everyone's frustration at the lack of troops and the sheer amount of legwork to be done. We've been here before, and we won't let it get the better of us. Over the next couple of days, I'd like to have a one-on-one with you all to get a better idea of where everyone is at. Brad Henderson will contact each one of you to make a time to suit. In the meantime, I will be enjoying being back at my desk and hoping we continue the run of successes we've had recently.

"I cannot stress enough how proud you should be of your efforts on the QF1 incident. Congratulations to all concerned. If we haven't already, make sure that Qantas recognises the desk attendant who raised the alarm in the first instance. The A380 crew, the Darwin Airport team and the air marshal are equally deserving of commendation—without any one of them, we would have two escaped killers and over five hundred dead civilians on our hands."

The briefing came to an end naturally, and Tina asked Alison to be the first to catch up with her.

Back at Tina's office, they went through a number of issues and questions from the commissioner, culminating in an arranged meeting with him the next day.

Right on 10am, Georgia appeared at Tina's door.

"My turn?" she asked.

"Not until we get a coffee refill."

Tina was already feeling the effects of being back at work too early.

Georgia gave Tina a complete update on Weatherall Cottage, their day at North Head, the fire and the runaway girl. She told of Dave's belief in Jane's clairvoyance, his diagnosis of her schizophrenia and the terrible events surrounding the presumed murder of her entire family, with potential police involvement.

"Plus, I've unearthed some worrying facts through the cottage's files and the Department of Communities and Justice," Georgia continued. "There have been no records or follow-ups on any of the cottage girls fostered out or adopted for the last five years. Prior to that, it was standard procedure to monitor the children until they turned twenty-one."

"You mentioned as much when you first brought me the case," said Tina. "That look on your face tells me there's more."

"Much more. There are a number of reports of missing children that have gone unresolved for years now, yet the records clearly show them being taken into Weatherall Cottage and then adopted or fostered out, with no notification to the parents—single mothers or women in domestic violence situations, mostly. I've uncovered the names of eleven girls over the past five years who've simply vanished. I've put their names and photos into the system, but no luck so far.

"There's also the issue of Len Bennet, Jane's father. His rap sheet shows that he was arrested and convicted twice by the same officer, who went on to become his parole supervisor on both occasions. I believe you're quite familiar with him."

"Who was it?" asked Tina.

"Jim Hegarty."

Tina breathed in sharply. Hegarty was a crooked cop she'd exposed some time ago. He'd been killed in a house explosion in Surry Hills a few months earlier, and though the cause had never been established, she knew more about it than most.

Tina happily agreed to meet with Jane and the girls at the weekend under the guidance of Sister Chrissy. She asked Georgia to bring a photo of Hegarty, preferably his mugshot.

After Georgia left her office, Tina rang Brad on her secure phone and advised him of the less-than-welcome news from the morning's task force meeting. They arranged to meet in Sydney the next morning to discuss their next move.

"I've got a few surprises of my own," said Brad. "Wait 'til you see the judge's hard drive material. See you tomorrow."

Tina was exhausted. She closed her eyes and let her thoughts take her.

# Chapter Twenty-Nine

D r. Holder was hosting a second group session with Roxy, Amber and Jane, and though they were confined to the cottage this time, he was still on a roll. He was pleasantly surprised at the change in their attitudes in such a short time.

"Afternoon, ladies. I've been going over my notes from the past few months, and particularly the last two weeks. I think we can all agree that we've made a lot of progress."

He looked at all three girls and saw no objections, which was a good sign.

"So today, I want to explore a quote from the great Pablo Picasso, the famous Spanish painter and philosopher. It goes like this: *The meaning of life is to find your gift. The purpose of life is to give it away.*"

He let that sink in for a few seconds.

"Let's start with *finding* your gift," he continued. "Amber, you have the extraordinary gift of understanding the bush, tracking, hunting, bush tucker—everything about Mother Nature and our extreme climatic changes. This has been passed on to you by your ancestors with a lot of help from your gran, who obviously adores you. That's a real gift."

Amber smiled, and it lit up the room.

"Roxy," he went on, "your poetry demonstrates an ability to look at life from above and outside the square. You express yourself in such a sensitive, dramatic and imaginative way. You had no training in this; it's a natural literary gift.

"And Jane, your connection to the spiritual realm is an incredible gift. Your ability to observe the world, past, present and future, is truly awesome. You've all come through so much tragedy and trauma, and yet you have these amazing gifts and talents. So, if the purpose of life is to give those gifts away—share them, as Amber's gran did with her—have you any ideas how you might go about sharing your respective talents?"

Roxy was the first to comment.

"I dunno, but I do know that if you set your hopes up too high, you set yourself up to fail."

"Not necessarily," replied Dave. "In fact, the greater danger is setting your hopes so low that you believe your goal is impossible, so you never try hard enough to succeed."

"You're just an optimist," said Jane.

"An optimist is wrong just as often as a pessimist, but they have lots more fun," he countered with a smile.

"How are we supposed to have fun in this rathole?" Amber asked sadly.

"Whether you live here or in the biggest mansion on the Watsons Bay harbourfront, you can be as happy or as miserable as you like. It's all up to you, and no one else. So there's no fun here, huh? Then let's use your gifts to change that. You've all told me how drab the grounds are, in one colourful way or another. Amber, with your knowledge of nature, you could design a bush garden that'll put some colour into the place and bring in all the pretty birds and butterflies."

"Right, and who's gonna pay for that?" she scoffed softly.

"I'll secure a sponsorship to cover the costs. There's a start. Now, Roxanne," he continued. "Bring me in some of your beautiful poetry on Thursday—say, a selection of three to start with. A good friend of mine is a professor at New South Wales Uni, and also the editor of its magazine. They have a poets' corner, and it'd be lovely to share your gift with the outside world from there."

This bought a rare smile to Roxy's face.

"Jane, you can use your gift to help us with our concerns here at the cottage," said Dave, conscious of his surroundings. "We'll talk more about that later."

Jane gave a firm nod.

By the time the session had finished, all three girls were looking forward. Amber was already drawing various bushes and listing which birds liked what blossoms. Roxy told Jane that she'd write a new poem about her, which Jane claimed would be boring, but she'd insisted. She then asked Amber for some more ochre powder for her drawing.

Dave told the girls he was hoping Sister Chrissy could authorise another day out on either Saturday or Sunday, but to keep that to themselves. Amber promised she'd ask Mrs. O'Brien for Cate's contact details on the pretence that she didn't get to see her before she left, to gauge the CEO's response.

Before leaving the cottage, Dave called in to Sister Chrissy's office to tell her about the group's new project to upgrade the gardens and open areas under Amber's guidance.

"They're all very keen," he said. "Is it possible to organise another outing for this weekend? I'd like to take them to a few of the big nurseries to keep their enthusiasm going."

Dave noticed some apprehension in the nun's eyes. She looked over Dave's shoulder to make sure no one was around. She kept her voice very low.

"I can, but there's a problem," she said. "The names for next week's adoption parade have just come through, and Amber's is one of them. I haven't told her yet."

Dave's breath caught in his chest. This spelt trouble.

# Chapter Thirty

Less than an hour after landing at Sydney Airport, former commando Brad Spruce stepped off the small ferry onto Hayle Street Wharf at Neutral Bay. Tina's directions said to get off the boat, walk up the ramp and take the first door on the right into a café called *Thelma and Louise*. He'd seen the tables overlooking the water through the window as the ferry had approached the wharf.

Tina had arrived by taxi and was already seated, waving as Brad walked up the gangway from the jetty. They said little, ordering from the counter then returning to their table, looking over the edge of the rails at schools of fish picking at the weeds growing on the rocks and pylons below.

"Great spot," said Brad. "Had no idea it existed. You're looking a lot better than I thought you'd be, or is it just a cover-up?"

Tina laughed softly.

"I couldn't run a marathon yet, but I'm getting stronger every day. How are things in Queensland?"

"Well, since Amnesia Paddleduck opened the borders to you pox-ridden southerners, things are on the up and up. We're finally getting some of your hard-earned money and paying our bills. Life's good."

"I meant at the 4G Factory," she said.

This time, it was Brad's turn to smile.

"Oh, us? We're making more money than we ever thought possible. The whole team is doing well, but we sure miss Catie."

Brad reported quietly on their last two operations—Judge Latta at his Bellingen hideaway, and the mobsters' meeting at Kings Cross. He said that they'd both gone to plan, and the world was better off.

"We're far more worried about you and your colleagues," he said. "How are they all going? What's happening down here?"

Tina quickly updated Brad on Georgia, Derek and her own progress, as well as the death of Garry Townsend in a case of mistaken identity.

"But never mind all that. There are some things you should know," said Tina. "Judge Latta's death is now considered a homicide, but the police are aware that he and his associates were rotten eggs, and they aren't looking much further than his associates. The Cross, however, is a very different matter. The madame who rented you the room on Barncleuth Lane was an informant for one of our detectives, and gave a solid description of you three, as well as an uncomfortable amount of detail about your movements."

"Ah, that would be our Jess, I presume. Bert told me she wasn't the classiest girl he'd ever met."

"Luckily for us, our team are still convinced it's gang warfare. The Middle Eastern mob happened to send a junior in their stead, and the others are convinced they did it themselves and used her as collateral damage. Fingers crossed it stays that way. I'll stay on top of it. Now, what did you find out from the meeting?"

"More than any of us could have hoped, but all of it is an afterthought in the wake of what we found on the judge's hard drive."

Tina blanched.

"What is it?"

"It's kids, Tina. Some of the things he and his cronies have done ... suffice to say we are *very* glad to have taken him out." He handed her a disc. "I don't know how you'll get it into your system without giving up where you got it, but you've gotta make it happen."

"Leave it to me," she said, tucking the disc away. She took a breath. "You said you had a *few* surprises for me. Can't be any worse than that one. What else have you got?"

"The judge had two files and a notebook on his bedside table next to the computer, plus some handwritten notes. It looks like some of his mates were leaning on him for favours and threatening blackmail, and he'd had a gutful. Seems he was thinking turnabout was fair play, and was making some big plans."

Brad handed the paperwork to Tina, and she began to scan through the files.

"Oh my God. Brad, this is dynamite," she said, looking at some of the names and faces that featured. "Who'd have guessed?"

Her heart missed a beat when she saw a reference to Weatherall Cottage.

"Frightening, isn't it? They go right to the top," said Brad.

"More untouchables."

Tina was amazed at the full extent of this new information.

"Here. We also found his two mobile phones. I reckon they'll tell you a story or two."

Tina took the phones, documents and footage of the Kings Cross meeting and placed it all into her briefcase.

"I'll need an army to follow up on all this," said Tina. She looked directly at Brad. "Thanks. I'd venture there are some very big, very nervous players wondering what the judge's death means for them right now, so I think it's best if the 4G Team lies low for a while. You three stay out of sight—go and do some fishing, or focus on the legitimate side of the business for a change."

"It's not my first choice, but I have to agree," he said. "What'll you do?"

"I have four major investigations underway right now, and I get the feeling they're all connected in some way. Seeing as the police are the ones with the resources to flush these bastards out, my first instinct is to leave it in their hands ... but we have rats in our ranks, and we need to tread carefully."

They talked more about the 4G 'family', and even had a tasty danish with their second coffee. Tina promised to go up to the Gold Coast with David as soon as she could see daylight. They parted ways, and Brad boarded the next ferry back to Circular Quay. Tina waved goodbye and then walked back up Hale Street to the taxi rank.

On the way to Chatswood, her head was almost exploding at the thought of the people she'd just seen implicated in the worst crimes imaginable. She didn't really know where to start. Some of Sydney's best known corporate, radio and TV personalities were named, and there were a number of references to 'The Chief.' If this referred to the NSW Chief Justice, a deputy police commissioner she *thought* she knew well, then it was a worst-case scenario. John Palmer had full confidence in this man, so he would have a direct line into everything they were doing. She thought hard on how she could gather enough evidence and witnesses to convict them without tipping these monsters off. On top of getting the vital Kings Cross meeting evidence into the police system without giving away the 4G Team, she had her work cut out for her.

Arriving back at Chatswood HQ, Tina took the lift to the lobby, bought a potent long black from *The Cell* and then took the lift to her floor. As she stepped out onto the floor, white as a sheet, she saw Georgia and Mike deep in conversation.

"Crikey, boss. Are you okay?" asked a worried Mike. "You look like you've seen a ghost."

"Give me five minutes, then both of you come to my office," was all Tina said as she brushed past.

Mike went to speak, but Georgia motioned him to silence. They shared a look.

"Whatever that's about, I hope it's not worse than what we've got to say," said Mike.

Georgia nodded grimly.

Five minutes later, the two of them walked into Tina's office and took their seats.

"I'm not sure what's happened, but we have news and it's not going to improve your day," said Mike, getting in first. "About fifteen minutes ago, Westmead Hospital rang to advise that Derek Sward had passed away a few minutes earlier. We tried to call you. It appears he had some sort of massive stroke as a result of his injuries, and they were unable to revive him."

Tina just looked at Mike blankly, tears rolling down her cheeks.

"Derek Sward. A great man—such a dedicated crime fighter. How could this happen?" She closed her eyes, feeling very weak.

"What an awful world we live in. Poor Barbara. And those two beautiful girls ... I'd better get over there. Has anyone told them?"

"Yeah. Brian Carey drew the short straw," said Georgia. "He should be there about now."

"Could this day get any worse?" Tina sighed.

Head in her hands, she dismissed them.

The moment they left the room, she wept.

# Chapter Thirty-One

B ack at her and David's unit in Epping, Tina toyed with her dinner. David was very concerned and already sorry they'd come back from Mossy Point early.

"Is there anything I can do?" he asked. "Any way I can help?"

"Oh, David," she said, "I've never been this gutted. There's a price on my head, Derek and Tiffany are dead, the 4G boys are at risk, and now those poor children ... I just feel so sick; so helpless. On top of it all, someone in my own team is covering for those scumbags, so I can't even get help without tipping them off."

"Sounds like you need to go back to square one," said David. "Who can you trust to start building a strong, clean team?"

"It's not that easy. Even if it were, this is my mess. I got us into it by joining the 4G Team." She sighed deeply. "I've got an 11am tomorrow with the commissioner, the CPU Super, Mike and Georgia. If I gave them everything I've got, they could nail these bastards to the wall ... but it would expose Brad, Bert, Bernardo, Garth and myself in the process. They don't deserve it, and neither do I. If I withhold anything I can't source, those deviants and killers will continue on their merry way, maiming kids and murdering countless innocents. What do I do?"

David weighed his answer carefully.

"T, I know you well enough to know you're not going to let those pigs get away with this, no matter what," he said eventually. "You gave me two options just now, but does it really have to be one or the other? Is there nothing even halfway credible that might explain how you came by the evidence without it leading back to the five of you?"

"God, if only it were that simple," said Tina. "If any of it is going to stick, the source of the evidence needs to be completely airtight. I don't know any of the northern state team well enough to ask them to cover for us. If necessary, I can sit on the Kings Cross info for a while, but this Latta intel needs to get out *now*."

David paused.

"He died near his Bellingen hideaway, right? I'm sure they've searched *that* top to bottom, but what about his mansion at Darling Point?"

"Anywhere even halfway related to Latta has been torn apart since they started suspecting foul play," said Tina.

"Well, why don't you give them a reason to look again?"

Tina blinked and immediately brightened up.

"Why not indeed. Shit, David. You should have my job. All I have to do is work out what it is. I know we can do it. Even if I put myself at risk, I don't have to expose the others." She was feeling better already. "Pour me a red while I think it over."

Tina ate a little more and finished the wine.

"I'm going to have a long, hot shower," she said. "I know I'll think better after that."

After drying off, Tina dressed into comfy PJs then returned to the lounge and poured herself another wine.

"Decision made. It was easier than I thought," she said to David brightly. He looked relieved to see her relaxed.

"What brilliance have you concocted?" he teased.

"Every now and again, you have to back your own judgement. Earlier this year, I asked the commissioner's best and most trusted underground contact, Rusty Nolan, to help me out. I knew he was batting for both sides and walking a tightrope, so I told him I was as well, without giving anything away. He then gave me some invaluable intelligence and never told a soul—not even his best mate, John Palmer. I'm happy to take a chance on him again."

She picked up her secure mobile and speed-dialled Rusty.

"Hi, Rusty. Sorry to call so late. I'm in a jam. Can we do breakfast in the morning?" Then she left the room to have the rest of the conversation in private.

She soon re-entered, still on the phone.

"Great. Is 7am okay? Great. Yes, that's a perfect spot. I'll see you there. Thanks."

David looked up and saw Tina smiling as she hung up.

"That'll work. I know it. Problem solved," she said, beaming at him. "Thanks, Dick Tracy."

She lay down on the lounge, closed her eyes and immediately fell asleep. David picked her up like a ragdoll and carried her into bed.

Against all odds, Tina slept well that night.

*

The next morning, Tina took a taxi to Chatswood HQ and walked into her office just after 9am. The meeting with Rusty at The Rocks Waterfront had gone very well, and she felt comfortable they could meet the challenge ahead if it arose. Rusty had organised a fake, anonymous informant for Tina who, if identified, would testify that they'd tipped her off to the location of the Latta hard drives and files at a 'hidden' location at the judge's Darling Point mansion. It wasn't airtight, but it got the evidence into the right hands without putting anyone other than her at risk, which was more than enough. Rusty also promised to find a solution for the Kings Cross film and tapes too, if asked.

The other task force members could sense that something big was happening. Tina had called Georgia and Mike into her office and locked the door without a word to anyone.

"What's this about, Tina?" asked Mike, nervous.

"One of our special contacts has just led me to some very sensitive information regarding the death of Judge Latta," said Tina. "We have evidence that he was part of a well-connected paedophile ring."

"Jesus, that's awful. The sick bastard," said Georgia. "Why all the secrecy though?"

"What we have implicates some very big names, many of whom will be difficult to prosecute. I'll give you more on them later. For now, don't breathe a word of this to anyone, as one of them is disturbingly close to us."

Georgia and Mike looked at each other as Tina removed a disc from her briefcase.

"These are images from the judge's computer. We also have a list of his associates and more, but I've yet to see what's on here with my own eyes."

She loaded the disc into her computer.

"I've called the commissioner and asked him and the officer in charge of the Child Protection Unit to join the three of us for a meeting at 11," she said. "I have total trust in John Palmer, and I know he has that with Superintendent Max Logan. Now, let's get this over with. Are you ready?"

The two of them nodded with grim resolve. Tina opened the disc.

The three of them watched in horror as one by one, revolting images of children being brutalised and tortured filled the screen. Brad had been right—they all felt nauseated.

Suddenly, Georgia yelped.

"Stop! Oh my God. Wait here."

She raced out of the room, returning seconds later with a photo clutched in her hand.

"Go back a few images," she said.

Tina did.

"There," said Georgia. "That girl."

The image showed a pretty girl, around fifteen, being tortured with red-hot iron rods.

Georgia held up a clear photo of two girls. One of them was Jane, and the other was on screen right in front of them.

"That's Cate. The last girl to be adopted from Weatherall Cottage."

They all sat there, stunned.

*

At around 10.45am, Tina and Georgia left the office and joined Mike in the basement. He'd just picked up five 'extra hot' takeaway coffees, which rested on his lap as Georgia drove them out of the car park and down Fullers Road to the secluded Blue Gum Reserve.

They pulled up a few minutes before 11, right next to the commissioner's unmarked car, where he and Superintendent Max Logan were waiting. The five of them chatted brightly in greeting as they walked over to a shaded picnic table, away from prying ears. To any observers, they would look like five office staff having a smoko in the park.

Commissioner John Palmer didn't know what was coming, but he knew he wasn't going to like it.

"First up, let me say how sorry I am to hear about Derek. I know how close you two were," he said. "Now forgive me for forging ahead, but Tina, the last time you called a meeting like this, I had a knot in my belly for weeks. What are we dealing with here?"

"Sadly, Sir, the three of us are already experiencing that," said Tina. "I'm just sorry we have to share it."

She went on to explain the full Weatherall Cottage story, including Georgia's relationship to Dr. Dave; his request for Georgia to look into the nun's concerns; the unusual number of adoptions by one couple; the likelihood of police involvement in the murder of Jane's parents; and the CEO and senior director's resistance to any cooperation.

After that, she showed the commissioner and superintendent the disc full of sickening images, stopping when they arrived at Cate's situation.

"That is Cate Maynard," she said, "a fifteen-year-old who was 'adopted' from the cottage two weeks ago."

The commissioner and Max Logan had seen this sort of thing before, but both of them still looked sick.

Tina then pulled out a written brief and gave a copy to the four others.

"I've gone through the letters, notes and files I recovered personally from Latta's Darling Point home, and this is a list of his associates and accomplices."

She watched their faces as they read.

John Palmer was first to react.

"No," he said, incredulous. "Tina, this *cannot* be real, surely?"

"I'm afraid it is, Sir," she said with absolute conviction. "I've checked the tapes, emails and calls firsthand. There's no mistake. We also have access to Latta's encrypted phone, which contains a staggering amount of evidence."

She turned to the superintendent.

"Max, I'm hoping you can get us more from your team on the dark web. There's just one party we haven't been able to identify; a man consistently referred to as 'The Chief'. I'm not even sure he's in Australia. As you'll see from the rest of the brief, we've identified a number of ringleaders around the globe. Gentlemen, I'd venture that this is the break we've been looking for for quite some time."

The commissioner and superintendent agreed, though both seemed shocked. Mike and Georgia were also seeing the brief for the first time, and were devastated by some of the names on the list.

After thinking for quite a while, Commissioner Palmer laid out his plan.

"Tina, you and the task force work on the shelter issue and the missing children," he began. "Look into the murder of the Jane Doe's family too, but do it quietly. This is on top of the Kings Cross bombing, Derek and Tiffany's murders and everything else you're currently working on. I realise you'll need more troops and will work on that today.

"Max, you'll need to make a start on this apparently global paedophile ring and work down the briefing list. I imagine you'll need to get phone taps and devices in all sorts of places, as well as the dark web. How are you placed?"

"Let me go back and talk it over with my key team," said Max. "I'll get back to you today. I'll need the hard drive and the photos to get to work."

Tina handed them over.

"Okay," he said. "Now, both of you, no raids or arrests until I get my head around this. Clearly, I can't call our special task force back together until we've worked out a plan. I'd like both of you in my office at 8 tomorrow morning. I'll organise breakfast. Any questions?"

"More of an observation, Sir," said Tina. "I get the feeling that some of my task force know some of what we've discussed today for all the wrong reasons. I need to be very careful about what I say, and to who."

"Good thinking," said the commissioner. "Max, you'd best be on your guard too. It's going to be tough to stop the word getting out to these lowlifes. I'll see you both tomorrow. Meantime, I'll phone if I need anything."

With that, they broke up and headed back to their respective vehicles.

Once inside his car, the commissioner looked over to Max.

"Superintendent, sometimes I wish I'd never signed up for the force, and today is one of those days," he confessed. He looked long and hard out the window. "Warren Hardcastle has been a close friend of mine for over thirty years, and my deputy commissioner has been my most trusted ally for the past five. Who would've thought?"

They drove off in silence, both thinking of a long day ahead.

# Chapter Thirty-Two

Dave was entering uncharted territory. This was the first time he'd ever gone to Georgia's office, and also his first foray into detective work. When the call had come in from Sister Chrissy late Friday night to warn him that the excursion they'd planned for Sunday had been cancelled courtesy of the CEO, they knew something bad was happening. The three girls had been looking forward to their trip to the nurseries and Botanical Gardens, completely unaware of the situation with Cate.

Georgia had insisted they needed a plan to get Amber out of the cottage before Tuesday's parade without spooking the CEO or chairman. She and Dave had met Tina and David for lunch on Sunday, since they'd already set that time aside to meet the girls at the Botanical Gardens. Dave had rung Sister Chrissy later that night and told her of their plan for the next day. The nun had been quite worried. She'd never been involved in something like this before.

Driving out from under Chatswood Police Headquarters, Dave went straight towards Camperdown and Weatherall Cottage for his meeting with Sister Chrissy. This was deliberately to be held in the main lobby, in full view of all the others.

As Dave entered the cottage lobby, he found the senior nun talking to a group of girls.

"Ah, Doctor Holder," she said. "Thanks for bringing in that information on those nurseries. The girls are keen to get working on the project today."

Dave handed over the books, pamphlets and a small buff envelope with the letter 'A' on the front.

"The pleasure is mine, Sister Chrissy. I was passing by here anyway. Tell them I'll see them for the group session tomorrow as usual, and that I hope they'll have a plan ready for the gardens."

With that, he turned and left, pleased with his acting skills as he drove out to his clinical appointments.

Sister Chrissy finished talking to her group, then went off in search of the three girls. She found Amber, Roxy and Jane with the other girls in the kitchen and advised them that Dr. Holder had dropped off the information they needed for tomorrow's project meeting.

She then slipped the envelope into Amber's hand, indicating for her not to react. Amber was surprised but she carried it off well and soon left to return to her room. A little while later, she came back downstairs for lunch and sat with Jane.

Right on noon, two unmarked cars pulled up in the car park right in front of the stairs. A man and a woman from the Department of Child Services and two detectives from Chatswood Station alighted from their vehicles and onto the front stairs.

Once in reception, the four asked for the CEO, Mary O'Brien, who soon came out of her office. She stared coldly at the group, recognising Libby Anderson from the department.

"Mrs. O'Brien," Libby announced brightly. "We meet again. We need to see you in private, if that's okay."

It was plainly not a welcome visit for Mrs. O'Brien, and it showed as she ushered them into her office.

"I need to get two more chairs," said the CEO, moving for the door.

"That won't be necessary, ma'am. We won't be long."

Looking out the window, the CEO saw a police paddy wagon pulling into the car park.

"What's going on?" she blurted. "This is going to unsettle our girls. I won't stand for it."

Libby Anderson introduced her colleague Stanley Bolitho and the two detectives, Brad Henderson and Graham James.

"We're here about one of your residents, Amber Newbould," said Libby. "Her file will have shown there was an investigation into the death of a young man at her apartment in Redfern just before we placed her in your care. New evidence has come to light, and the New South Wales police are now ready to press charges. We're here to take her into custody for an interview."

The CEO visibly relaxed, her demeanour lightening up considerably.

"I understand. I believe she's in the kitchen. I'll have her brought in."

One of the detectives and the departmental officer went out to stand by the door and block any escape attempts as the CEO went with Libby Anderson towards the kitchen. They returned a few minutes later with a very frightened Amber in tow.

"What crap is this?" she raved. "What've I done?"

She was pushed into the seat at the CEO's desk.

"Amber, this is Detective Henderson," said Libby. "The police have requested that you be taken into custody for questioning in relation to the death of a young man in Redfern some three years ago."

"That's bullshit! I went through all this already. It's got nothing to do with me," Amber protested. "Ask the shitheads he owed money to. I wasn't even there."

Brad Henderson spoke sternly.

"You'll have every opportunity to prove yourself, but in the meantime, you're under arrest and will be coming with us."

As he spoke, he quickly placed handcuffs over Amber's wrists. She tried to pull back and make a run for it, but the detective had been through this many times and soon had them fastened, with Amber secure in his grip.

By the time they left the office, about a dozen girls and some staff had gathered in the lobby, wondering what was going on. They started calling out to Amber.

"The pigs are taking me to gaol!" she yelled. "It's all bullshit!"

Roxy became very agitated and moved towards them.

"Fucking pigs! Get out of here! Leave her alone!" she screamed. Others rallied behind her, advancing on the group.

The two uniformed police arrived in the lobby and joined with the detectives and Child Services officer. Together, amid a chorus of abuse from the girls as the nuns tried to calm them down, they soon had Amber down the front stairs and bundled into the back of the paddy wagon.

Jane saw Roxy about to pick up a brick. She grabbed her arm firmly and hissed, "It's okay! It's okay," she reassured her.

"What, another one of your stupid fuckin' visions?" said Roxy. "That's crap. They're taking Amber away!"

The three cars drove out of the cottage grounds and disappeared towards the city. As they turned onto Glebe Point Road, all three vehicles pulled over. Brad and Graham came to the back of the paddy wagon as the uniformed police opened the door.

Brad smiled.

"Move over, Debra Mailman. We've got a better actor. Well done, Amber."

She looked at him sheepishly.

"I was shit-scared the whole time," she said as they removed her handcuffs. "Didn't have to do much acting for that."

"Good luck, Amber," Libby said kindly. "You're in the best of hands. We'll see you when all this is sorted. I know it'll work out for you."

With that, Amber got into the police car with Brad and Graham, and they drove away.

Back at the cottage, a very relieved nun had gone into the CEO's office.

"Mrs. O'Brien, can I ask what that was all about, please?" said Sister Chrissy, looking anxious. "All of the girls are extremely upset."

"It had nothing to do with us," she said. "The police took her away to question her about a murder. I understand they'll be charging her later today. In my opinion, we're better off without her."

She dismissed Sister Chrissy with a smirk and ordered her to shut her office door behind her. Once she was gone, she picked up her phone and dialled Brian McGarry.

Meanwhile, Jane had taken Roxy upstairs to calm her down. When they were alone in her room, she told Roxy that Amber had been put on the next day's adoption parade, and that Georgia and her boss had put on the whole show to fix it. She told her about Amber's note that morning, which laid out what was happening.

"Well, you could've at least told me, arsehole. I was gonna kill those cops."

"I didn't have a chance, or I would've," she said. "You sure made it look real, though."

The two of them giggled and agreed to meet in Roxy's room after lights out.

When Brian McGarry took the CEO's call, she expressed her relief.

"That could be why that policewoman was here a week ago," she said. "I think her husband, the psychologist, was trying to get information from the girl."

"I'm not so sure. It could be, but I think we should still get rid of the old nun and cancel the clinic's contract, just to be sure," said McGarry, still jumpy about the feathers. "Whatever the case, the coloured girl won't be in tomorrow's parade, and I've promised the studio another girl. Who was it you suggested for the following month?"

"Trish Collins, the girl who started the fire. I was going to put her in solitary today."

"Well, don't. Send me some photos of her and put her on tomorrow's list," he said. "I'll be in early, in case the other board members have any questions. We don't need any of them to start delving. Did the Child Services lady ask about anything else?"

"No, nothing," said Mrs. O'Brien.

"Good. I'll see you tomorrow."

He hung up and immediately rang the Chief Justice's office.

CEO Mary O'Brien rang Sister Chrissy and instructed her to have Trish Collins ready for the parade the next day.

The nun was immediately depressed. She liked young Trish and was confident she would eventually do well in life. Now, her life was in mortal danger.

She left her office and went looking for Trish so she could break the news.

# Chapter Thirty-Three

Alarms blasted out over the internal speakers as dozens of people evacuated the Blacktown Police Station in an orderly fashion. Superintendent Max Logan was annoyed. Every minute mattered, and the fire drill right before his top-level meeting could not have come at a worse time.

The Child Abuse and Sex Crimes Squad, known as the CASCS, was normally based at Parramatta. Because of the bomb blast, they'd temporarily relocated to Blacktown, which was already overcrowded. Max had been in charge of the squad for the past 11 years, and was very well respected across the board. Two of his team had been badly injured in the Parra blast, even though they'd been on the floor above. Max was also a long-time friend of both Derek Sward and Garry Townsend, and was keen to see their killers brought to justice. He'd been the best man at Derek's wedding to Barbara over twenty years before.

Max and the two men he'd been set to meet with walked down the stairs with the others onto Kildare Street, then around the corner to the assembly point on Balmoral Street, where their names were marked off the attendance sheet. He considered asking them to take the meeting across to the nearby *Coffee Club* café in Westpoint Shopping Mall, but there were too many ears, and it was too close by. The three men simply stood with the rest, waiting for the signal to return to the station.

His two compatriots were trusted, long-time members of his special unit. The first was Detective Sergeant 'Mo' Mario Savalis, the OIC of the Child Protection Registry. A tall, bald and very fit officer, he trained daily for his triathlon racing. He'd only recently been given the nickname 'Mo' as his blond locks had receded to the point of shaving, resulting in a resemblance to Peter Garrett of Midnight Oil. The other officer was Detective Sergeant 'Stretch' Steve Butler, another very tall, likeable larrikin who'd been with Max since the start. He was OIC of the Child Exploitation's Internet Unit and was an IT wiz. Both men were aware that the superintendent was tense, and they were concerned about whatever this latest case was.

After some fifteen minutes, the throng was advised they could return to the police station and resume their normal duties. Stretch voiced concern over how many 000 emergency calls they'd missed in the past half-hour, wondering at the value of such drills versus the time it took away from responding to real emergencies.

The three men sat back down in meeting room two, and Max started them off.

"What I'm about to tell you may well be the break we've been seeking for years," he began. "I've known both of you for a long time, and I must warn you, as the commissioner warned me, we have rats in our ranks. We have to be extremely careful who we share this information with. We cannot alert the top dogs that we're onto them. This may be our big chance."

Both Mario and Steve paid careful attention.

The super went on to explain about the death of Judge Latta and the shocking images found on his computer, as well as the diaries and notebooks he kept that identified the worldwide paedophile ring.

"I'll show you those in a minute," said Max. "Our real break came from Superintendent Samuels' Chatswood team, who've been investigating a string of suspicious adoptions from the Weatherall Cottage Children's Shelter at Camperdown. One of the images from Latta's hard drive shows a fifteen-year-old girl being brutally tortured, and Tina's team identified her as the most recent child to be adopted from there. Last I heard, an indigenous girl from the shelter was due to be taken in, and Tina's team had planned to extricate her this morning. I can only hope it went well."

Max Logan then handed the two men the complete written brief on the judge's diaries and notebooks. Both detectives' eyes were wide open as they read the 'who's who' list and absorbed the information in front of them. They made a number of involuntary remarks such as 'no way', 'wow' and 'who would believe' as they read through the volumes of evidence.

"It seems the judge was very thorough in his efforts to save his own skin," said Max. "Stretch, the images I'm about to show you will be a good start for your dark web team. We need to work fast—*without* giving away any names. For now, we just need to know where these are circulating and build up a case. The commissioner doesn't wany any raids or arrests that might jeopardise the big picture until the time is right. Mo, I need you to go through the registry worldwide and see if you can find any matches. This should also identify anyone who's managed to fly under the radar so far."

Max turned his screen to face the others and began to scroll through the images, allowing them to see the shocking abuse for themselves of young girls and boys, some as young as five or six.

He stopped when he had a clear picture of Cate.

"This is Cate Maynard, the fifteen-year-old girl who was adopted from the shelter a few weeks ago. Sickening stuff." He pulled a picture out of the file. "Here's a recent photo of Cate with another resident of the shelter for reference. Mo, can you start with these as you run through the system?"

Max handed the photo to Savalis, who'd gone very quiet. He noticed that the scar over Mo's right eye had begun to twitch. He'd never seen it move before.

The meeting broke up just after 1pm, and they all left the room with purpose.

Mario Savalis returned to his office and grabbed his secure phone, a briefcase from his safe and some papers from his bottom drawer, then headed outside. He'd long suspected that his office might be bugged, as many others had.

*You can't be too careful*, he thought.

Savalis walked back out onto Kildare Road and crossed. As he turned the corner, he dialled his direct line to the chief justice.

"Nat, it's Mario," he whispered urgently. "We need to meet *now*. Drop everything and be at *The Forum* in twenty minutes. Big trouble. Ring Warren and get him ready to go."

He hung up and headed for the car.

NSW Chief Justice Nat Larucci was sweating. That was the second emergency call he'd received in a matter of minutes. Brian

McGarry had just rung about the police arrest at the cottage, and now Savalis had a crisis on his hands. He told his PA to cancel his afternoon appointments, saying that he was unwell and was going to the doctor's.

He quickly rang the deputy police commissioner, then ran to his car. It was raining as he drove towards Leichhardt, without his usual chauffeur and entourage.

# Chapter Thirty-Four

F or the second time ever, Dave Holder walked into Chatswood Police HQ. The first time had been only six hours earlier. He was cleared by the same desk sergeant and escorted to level three.

Georgia was waiting by the lift, all smiles.

"Like clockwork," she said. "Brad Henderson says you'd better teach the girls some less colourful language. Apparently, they didn't hold back as the team escorted Amber out. It sure sounds like they believed it was the real deal, so hopefully management did the same. They should be here in ten minutes or so—less, if siren-happy Graham has his way."

They made their way to Tina's room. Dave saw straight away that what Georgia had said this morning was one hundred per cent correct; Tina looked completely washed out, but at least she was doing what she loved best. She'd just hung up the phone after a discussion with Alison from the commissioner's office and welcomed them both.

Dave began to fill them in on Amber's background when the phone rang. Brad Henderson was on the other end, advising that the team had arrived.

"Ask them to go into the task force control room," said Tina. "I'll be there in a jiffy."

She asked Mike to join them as they walked past his office along the passage, then asked Georgia to organise tea, coffee and something to eat for them all.

"There's no way Amber had lunch at the cottage," she said. "She would've been too nervous. Put it on my departmental account and sign for it."

Tina was right; none of them had eaten, and she saw how nervous Amber still was as soon as she came in. Georgia introduced Amber to Tina and Mike, then asked for everyone's food and drink preferences. Amber ordered a milkshake and a sandwich, while the others asked for teas and coffees and an assortment of finger food.

Dave wanted to put Amber at ease before they got down to business, so they talked about their excursion to North Head National Park. Amber described in detail Jane's 'secret fairy garden' with the butterflies, the pretty wildflowers and, best of all, Brokenfoot and the bandicoots. She brought a laugh out of everyone when she tried to mimic Jane's bandicoot call.

"Actually, that was really close," Georgia laughed. "Now, tell me. Did Sister Chrissy get our note to you this morning? Did it make sense? We didn't know if you'd been told about the adoption parade, but we couldn't wait any longer."

"Sister Chrissy handed me the note when she gave us Dr. Holder's nursery pamphlets and landscaping magazines. She'd already told me about the parade at breakfast, and I didn't know what to do. I'd talked to Jane about running away, but the note came before I had a chance. I understood it; I just hoped it worked."

Tina chimed in, "By all reports, everyone thought it was very real. Your friends were not very complimentary." She smiled.

Amber laughed.

"I nearly joined them. When this guy brought up the Redfern death," she said, indicating Brad Henderson, "he sounded way too convincing."

Tina smiled again, and asked Amber to tell them about her life in the Northern Territory. By the time she'd finished and answered a few questions from everyone there, she felt comfortable and at ease.

They talked more about the cottage and Jane's unusual powers. Tina told Amber she would be staying with Dave and Georgia temporarily until they worked out a plan. She told her about the break in the case and mentioned Cate without going into too much detail.

"That's why we had to get you out today," she said.

"Our place is nothing flash," Georgia explained, "but this way, we can keep you out of sight and also in the loop. We think we're going to need you on the team."

Amber looked quite pleased with that.

"I can help out around the place, too. I can cook … but I haven't got any money to buy food."

"Don't worry about that," said Tina. "You're now in what we call a witness protection program, so all costs are covered. Georgia has brought you some more botanical books, pads and pencils so you can continue with your garden designing."

"Thank you," said Amber. "What about you? What happens now?"

"Mike and I are heading out to an unscheduled meeting called by the commissioner's special team. I hope to be back here after 7. I'll see most of you tomorrow," she said. "Dave, we need to show Jane that photo of Hegarty. Georgia tells me you're at the cottage tomorrow. Can you show it to her?"

Dave nodded.

Just as they were about to disperse, his phone buzzed. He looked at the message, and his face fell.

"They've put young Trish Collins into tomorrow's parade," he relayed softly.

*

Mike and Tina were about five minutes late but they had phoned ahead, arriving at the Leagues Club just after 4pm. Walking into the room, Tina was welcomed warmly by all.

"You look like I felt after playing my last grand final," Rusty chuckled.

They all joined in, including Tina. She was glad to be back.

"Okay, let's get to it," said the commissioner, taking charge. "Welcome back, Tina. It's good to see you're on the mend—and we all know Mike is a much happier man now that you're back on the job. Thanks again to everybody for making the time at short notice. Especially you, Alan. Your flight must've only just arrived.

"Now, onto business. We have some serious breaking news, and I didn't want to pass it on by phone. I'll now ask Tina to brief you on the latest from the Judge Latta case, which will also explain Warren's absence."

Tina gave them a full rundown on what she'd shown the commissioner and Superintendent Logan. She also gave the latest on Weatherall Cottage, including Jane and Amber's stories and Amber's rescue from the shelter that morning. She handed out copies of the written brief on Latta's contacts and notes.

The room was silent for a few minutes as everyone digested the latest intelligence.

John Palmer was the first to speak.

"I don't know how many more kicks in the guts I can take. I would've sworn on a stack of bibles that Warren was a good cop," he said.

He sighed deeply, then straightened his back.

"Regrettable though it may be, Warren doesn't know that we're onto him, and we can use that to our advantage. The goal of today's meeting is to come up with a plan to have him lead us to the top, wherever that may take us. Max Logan met with his 'A Team' earlier today, and they'll be working on this too. Whatever we're doing, we need to be doing it now. Time is running out on the children's centre outcome too, and we need a resolution before tomorrow's adoption parade at the shelter."

They discussed a number of options before deciding to call another special meeting first thing the next day, which was to include the deputy commissioner.

"Alan and Mike, you two are needed elsewhere, so no need for you to come in for this," said Palmer. "Rusty, Tina, Dick and I will be okay to set it up. I need to talk to Max and see what they've come up with."

Just as they were leaving, Tina's phone vibrated. She opened it to check the message, and the blood drained from her face.

"It's from Alison at the commissioner's office," she said. "The deputy commissioner just rushed out in the middle of an important meeting looking 'angry and surprised'. I've organised a tail ... but if this is anything to go on, we might be too late."

The commissioner swore.

"How could they have known? Only our most trusted are across this."

They all sat back down.

# Chapter Thirty-Five

The Italian Forum shopping mall at Leichhardt was vibrant and noisy, bustling with late-afternoon shoppers and corporate types. The brochure said it all: *Stroll in from Norton Street along our gallery walkways and be magically transported into a beautiful slice of Italy, with touches of Tuscan architecture.*

There were a variety of lights and colours, though burnt reds and tans dominated the spectrum, showing off the upmarket boutique shops and the very latest in European fashions. All of this overlooked the stunning outdoor Piazza, ringed by a slew of busy cafés and restaurants spilling out into the square, trattoria style.

Paying no heed to the classical Roman ambience, three men arrived within minutes of each other, each making their way hastily upstairs to the professional suites.

The receptionist at the International Immigration Advocates' Office, a young woman named Lisa, was mentally preparing to leave for the day. She had just over an hour left on her shift, and business was as quiet as ever. Complacent as she was, she nearly leapt out of her seat when one of the directors, Mr. Larucci, pushed through the door and barked at her.

"Are the others here yet?"

Lisa had no idea what he was talking about.

"No one is here," she said, flustered.

He didn't even hear her as he brushed past into the boardroom.

Not far away, the deputy police commissioner had entered *The Forum*'s car park from Balmain Road, still in uniform. The third member would arrive last, having had to come from Blacktown down the M7 and M4 towards the city.

Warren Hardcastle soon joined the chief justice, hurrying into the room.

"What the fuck's going on, Nat?" Warren asked angrily.

"Your guess is as good as mine," came the terse reply. "Savalis rang and said we had big trouble, and to warn you to be ready to go immediately. He said nothing else."

Just then, Mario Savalis burst through the door, out of breath, carrying bags and a briefcase.

He sat straight down at the table.

"Listen closely," he said flatly. "In a nutshell, that piss-weak queer Jim Latta dropped you two right in the shit. The cops have found pictures, diaries, contact lists and notes identifying each and every one of you in detail. I reckon he was gearing up to blackmail the both of you if you put any more pressure on him. I always warned you he was the weak link.

"On top of that, the bitch from Chatswood—Warren here's best mate—has been on another case, investigating missing girls from Weatherall Cottage. They found pictures on Latta's hard drive of the last girl we took to the studio, so now they've gone and linked the investigations."

"Jesus, Mo," said Nat. "We have to move fast."

"I'm not finished," Savalis growled. "As if it couldn't get any worse, Len Bennet's daughter has turned up at the kids' home. You may remember him as that low bastard we knocked off about ten years ago for pinching our hash and on-selling it. They haven't identified her yet, so they don't know the story, but it's only a matter of time. We've got to get to her before she fingers Joe and I. Thank God Hegarty is dead, or we'd really be up shit creek."

"Ring McGarry and have the girl taken away now," said Larucci.

"No dice. McGarry and that stupid O'Brien woman have fucked up royally. The coppers have set them up big-time, and they'll sing like larks as soon as they're picked up if it saves their own dirty arses. We've got to take them out first. Smokin' and I will get the girl ourselves tonight."

"What the hell do we do now?" asked Hardcastle.

"You both need to get straight down to the studio. That's the only place they haven't figured out yet," said Savalis. "Thank Christ Latta didn't know where it was. I don't know if McGarry or O'Brien were ever brought in, but it's the safest bet we have, and we have to do this now. I'll have Sluggo and Spud take McGarry and O'Brien on a one-way trip into West Head National Park, and Hudson and I will get the girl from Camperdown so she can't put any more fucking spanners in the works. I'll ring the studio and have rooms organised for the two of you. Smokin' and I aren't on any of these lists, so we'll stay and cover."

"Shit, Mo," said Larucci. "We're stuffed. What comes after the studio?"

"We figure out a way to get you two to the safe house in Majorca. No matter how you look at it, you two are rooted if you stay here. You'll be locked up for life—or worse, if the whole puzzle gets solved, and they're well on their way. That fucking judge has sunk the ship. Max Logan has Stretch moving into the dark web with Latta's images, and that'll blow the lid off everything. I'll come down to the Southern Highlands tomorrow to help take care of the movie stars and organ donors. No room for sentiment; we have to clean house. All our arses are on the line."

Hardcastle and Larucci both looked uncomfortable.

"We're just going to kill them all? Surely the kids don't know any of us. We don't have to take them out," said Hardcastle.

"Maybe not, but the staff have gotta go," said Mo. "Now, enough talk. You two need to get out of town now. They'll be looking for your cars, so head to the Budget Hire on Glebe Point Road. I know the guy there. All you need are the false IDs and passports from the safe. Warren, there's a selection of civvy clothes in the back room. Get changed, and get moving—fast."

The two of them stood around anxiously as Savalis organised the hire car over the phone and then rang his accomplice, Smokin' Joe Hudson. He instructed Joe to bring a 'hot' car and some ties and gags, advising him to avoid any of his task force mates for the time being.

"Has anyone told The Chief?" asked Larucci.

"He's on his own, and still at the yearling sales," said Savalis. "So far, there's nothing to connect him that I've seen. I'll get word through to him tonight, supposing the bloody media doesn't get wind of it first."

By 9 o'clock, Larucci and Hardcastle were heading south on the Hume Highway, trying to sort out a way forward. The surveillance team that had been waiting for the deputy commissioner's car to leave had taken no notice of the red hire car departing in the rain.

"Maybe if we took out Savalis and his mate, it'd take the heat off of us," said the chief justice as they drove through Campbelltown.

"Not likely," responded Hardcastle. "They've already got all of Latta's info. We're gone."

Larucci went quiet.

"What happens when our families find out?"

Warren didn't respond.

Just before 10pm that night, Mario Savalis switched off the office lights, locked up and left *The Forum* car park with Smokin' Joe Hudson, each of them taking separate cars. They soon pulled up around the corner and got into the stolen car that Joe had prepared earlier.

They drove through the rain on the short run to Weatherall Cottage at Camperdown. Their hit men, Sluggo and Spud, had rung an hour before. They had Mary O'Brien and Brian McGarry in their SUV, all trussed up and headed for the bush. The CEO had gone straight to water when questioned, describing in detail where Jane's room was, the code to get after-hours access and the internal directions.

Things were about to get messy, but Savalis was pleased that he was finally about to silence the last witness to the Queenscliff killings after all those years.

He smiled as he drove, but the scar above his eye was still twitching.

# Chapter Thirty-Six

D r. Dave Holder guided his latest patient, a former fireman, out of his office. The man had been experiencing mild PTSD since being unable to save two young children from a fire, but they were making good progress.

His receptionist waved him down as he passed.

"Dr. Holder," she said with urgency, "Dr. B would like to see you immediately."

Dave turned to his next patient and assured them he wouldn't be much longer. He was already running fifteen minutes behind, and wasn't happy with the further delay.

Walking in to Dr. B's office, he saw the look on the senior partner's face and knew the news was not good. As he sat down, Dr. B thrust a sheet of paper at him.

"Read it," he said simply. "It was just delivered by courier."

Dave picked up the letter.

*Dear Doctor Brinsmead,*

*The Board Of Weatherall Cottage has been concerned about the close personal relationships your assigned psychologist, Dr. Holder, has been developing with our impressionable young girls for some time. We fear that his involvement verges on the inappropriate, and are very worried for our residents, some of whom are aged as young as fourteen.*

*As we are duty-bound to protect the welfare of our girls here at the cottage, our board members have unanimously decided to cancel your clinic's contract with us, effective immediately.*

*Yours sincerely,*

*Mrs. Mary O'Brien*

*Chief Executive Officer*

Dave read the letter a second time, but could make no more sense of it than the first.

"I'm very disappointed that it's come to this," said Dr. Brinsmead. "Consider yourself forewarned that I'll be calling a special meeting of the partners to discuss the matter tomorrow morning."

Meanwhile, back at Weatherall Cottage, senior nun Sister Chrissy Marion sat in her office with tears rolling softly down her cheeks. Her long-time friend and workmate Alice had just told her of the letter she'd been asked to transcribe and have couriered to Dr. Holder's clinic. Alice had also overheard Mrs. O'Brien talking on the phone to the Mother Superior at the convent, insisting that Sister Chrissy was too old to perform her duties and requesting that she be retired by the end of the week.

Alice was terribly upset. Like most who worked there, she loved both Sister Chrissy and Dr. Dave, and would hate to see them go.

After a few minutes, the nun composed herself, wiped away the tears and went looking for Jane and Roxy. She found them upstairs talking to Trish Collins. They all looked up as she entered the room, seeing her sad eyes and expecting the worst.

The nun quietly told the girls the news about herself and Dr. Holder, sharing her fears for after they were gone. She told them she'd get in touch with Dave and Georgia to see if anything could be done before the adoption parade the following day.

"We were just talking about that," said Roxy. "We reckon it'll be safer if Trish bolts tonight. She has an aunty at Surry Hills she can hide out with."

The thought of a lone fourteen-year-old girl wandering the city in the dark did not thrill Sister Chrissy, but she knew these kids were survivors, and agreed that it could be the best option in the short term.

"Whatever you decide, may God bless you," said the nun as she made her exit and went back downstairs.

Trish, Jane and Roxy decided to meet around 9pm in Roxy's room, as it was close to the fire escape. They thought midnight would be a good time for Trish to make her way out, as she'd be less likely to be seen and they'd be able to use the old wooden gate in the bush at the bottom of the exercise yard. The girls had used it for many unauthorised outings and knew how to open it easily.

Dinner that night was a quiet affair. A sombre mood filled the kitchen. Word had spread about Dr. Holder and Sister Chrissy, and some of the girls had seen the CEO storming out just before five. Mrs. O'Brien had looked like she was on a mission, and they were all worried about what that might mean for them.

Around 9.30pm, Jane and Trish crept along the dark hallway to Roxy's room. Trish had already filled her backpack and left it with Roxy. When they arrived, they went over the plan again, just to be sure. They'd decided to bring Trish's departure forward to 11.15pm so that she could catch the 11.35 bus from Glebe Point Road. Both Jane and Roxy gave her some extra money for the trip.

The girls talked quietly about their lives and their futures, planning where they'd meet up after they got out and how they'd communicate. Trish stood at Roxy's window, looking out idly as they talked.

Suddenly, she gasped.

"Shit. What's this?"

The girls all crammed into the small window space and watched as a red car moved slowly into the cottage car park without headlights on. When it came to a silent halt, two men in dark suits got out and walked quickly towards the locked front doors. The girls saw the men readying balaclavas to pull over their heads just as they came into the light, and as they came into view, Jane stiffened.

Even without his blond hair, she could never forget that face.

"Look, that scar," she hissed. "That's Scarface. Fuck, I'm dead. He's a killer. He's finally come for me."

There was no time to ring Georgia or to dial 000, so the girls decided they would all get out, together, now.

Sneaking along the hall, they quietly unlatched the bolt on the emergency exit. Just then, they heard the front door opening downstairs. They quietly locked the exit door, descended the fire stairs and raced across the exercise yard towards the bush and the old gate.

"Look!" said Jane, who'd glanced back towards the cottage.

The light in her room had just been turned on. For a second, it was very quiet, then all hell broke loose. Lights went on all through the cottage, and girls started screaming. Jane, Roxy and Trish raced through the old gate and took off, running as fast as they could.

Jane led the girls down a shortcut through the dark lanes towards Wattle Street. Dogs barked madly at them as they ran, invoking bad memories of Jane's escape nearly ten years earlier.

"I think there's a late ferry from the fish market to Circular Quay," Jane wheezed breathlessly as they slowed for the first time since they'd left. Even then, they kept walking fast, avoiding the street lights.

On arrival at the market, they found that Jane had been right. They approached the dock, purchased tickets from the vending machine and waited in the shadows. As the ferry pulled in, they walked slowly through the barriers. They only had to wait ten minutes for the ferry to arrive, but it seemed like an hour to the girls. It felt like even longer before the crew untied the ropes and pulled away from the dock, cruising out towards the harbour and relative safety.

As the laughing face of the Luna Park clown came into view on the north side, Jane told the two girls about 'Scarface' and the death of her family in detail.

Once again, she was on the run and fearing for her life—but this time, she had help.

This time, she wasn't alone.

# Chapter Thirty-Seven

Troops ran about everywhere, and Police Commissioner John Palmer was in a foul mood. This was out of character for him; normally placid in all situations, he felt that things were getting away from them, and he was struggling to keep a level head. His prime suspects had escaped, there were young girls in danger and all of this had been preventable.

The commissioner had entered the station at 3am, furious with the Leichhardt Italian Forum surveillance team. They'd allowed both the chief justice and the deputy commissioner to escape without a trace, with no leads as to how they had managed their getaway or any idea where they'd gone. Only after sitting in the rain at both exits for hours had the police realised that the car park closed at midnight, and a stroll through the basement revealed that only two cars remained. As expected, one was the deputy commissioner's car and the other the official car of the New South Wales chief justice, who they hadn't even known was there. He'd subsequently been reported missing by his family around 2am.

Following abrupt orders from the commissioner, they were now scanning through hours of CCTV footage, trying hard to trace all vehicles in and out. Considering that the car park only had capacity for ninety-six cars, they knew it could've been worse.

Teams went from door to door in The Forum shopping mall looking for information, but what little they turned up seemed too late and too unreliable. The commissioner knew the men had left, but where had they gone? Who'd helped them escape? Had they even been in the centre in the first place?

Before he'd even had a chance to be angry about all of this, Tina Samuels woke him up at 2am to tell him there'd been some sort of raid at the children's shelter. Reports held that two assailants had terrified the residents and the nun on duty with balaclavas on and guns drawn, but ultimately left without their mark, who was amongst three girls currently missing. A large local search had yet to locate the girls or the gunmen; everyone assumed they were either in hiding near the cottage or had escaped. Police had gone looking for the cottage's CEO and chairman to make inquiries, but they too had vanished and were soon reported missing by their respective families.

With incompetence and unresolved leads all around him, the commissioner was far from happy. Tina, too, felt washed out and frustrated by these turns of events.

Tina had received a call from Georgia just after midnight reporting the violent raid and the missing girls, and had been trying to coordinate a search from Chatswood since 1.30am. Georgia had brought a distraught and fearful Sister Chrissy from her monastery home into Chatswood at around 3am. The nun had reported that the cottage CEO had stormed out just before 5 in the evening, and that she herself had left shortly after. Police inquiries had revealed that the CEO had not made it home, and the chairman had also been reported missing around 5am. Georgia and Sister Chrissy had also discussed Dave's reprimand at work, the cancelled contract and the fact that the sister had been forced into retirement and was not welcome back at the shelter.

Tina approached the commissioner, but he was still angry and in no mood to talk. He did, however, take a moment to reiterate his displeasure over the handling of the Italian Forum surveillance.

Tina decided that, if they were going to get anywhere, they had to regroup. She pushed the task force meeting back until noon and rang Mike and Georgia, arranging to have breakfast with them at *The Cell* café downstairs instead. As the core of the team, the three of them needed to go over everything in detail and give themselves some time before the meeting to put everything into perspective. There, Tina made it a point not to mention Jane's telepathy or the Southern Highlands lead to anyone until they were sure of who they could trust.

Meanwhile, Dave and Sister Chrissy had just arrived at the Macquarie Street Clinic after dropping Amber off at Chatswood Police Station. Dave had been asked to give his version of events to the four partners, and Sister Chrissy had insisted on accompanying him to serve as a character witness. Georgia had wanted to provide further support, but decided that confirming the whereabouts and safety of the three young girls should take precedence.

Dave entered the boardroom just after 9.30am, where he was met with a frosty reception. Sister Chrissy trailed in behind him. The partners had clearly not been expecting her. Between them, they took some thirty minutes to tell the partners the whole story and the ongoing investigation.

Back at Chatswood, right on 10am, a brief came through from the commissioner, calling for a 5pm meeting at the Easts Leagues Club with Tina, Max Logan, Dick Sellis and Rusty Nolan. The brief stated that the national media had got wind of a leak—likely from within the police—hinting that something big was happening, and some prominent names were involved. Apparently, the New South Wales police minister was en route to police headquarters and making life hell for the commissioner, demanding a briefing. Palmer requested a complete update on the missing girls, the disappearances of the CEO and chairman of Weatherall Cottage, the escape of Larucci and Hardcastle, the death of Judge Tiffany, the ongoing QF1 arrests, the Parramatta bombing and the Kings Cross mob deaths, making it clear that he expected some concrete progress.

Just after 10.30, Dave and Sister Chrissy arrived at Weatherall Cottage. Dave couldn't thank her enough for her support in the meeting. She'd shed tears on his behalf and told the partners how Dave and Georgia had been instrumental in bringing her concerns to a head, claiming that as horrible as the situation was right now, it would've been far worse for all concerned if not for their support. She'd also told them of the wonderful progress the girls had made thanks to the good doctor, and the high regard in which he was held by all, staff and children alike. In the end, Dr. B had apologised to Dave for doubting him, and the partners all agreed that he should return to the cottage to help sort out the mess.

As Dave and the nun arrived at the top of the cottage stairs, they realised that things were still a long way from returning to normal. Police remained there, searching for the missing girls, while the remaining six board members debated endlessly, trying to make sense of everything. The girls and the rest of the staff, including some who'd come in on their day off, wandered around the grounds and inside the cottage.

Sister Chrissy found the strength to take charge of the situation, asking Dave to assemble all the girls in the classroom for an update. She also called on Alice, and Detective Brian Carey who was in charge of the police presence, to join them.

Once all had assembled, she addressed the board, the staff, the girls and the detective and reported everything she knew, including the cancellation of Dr. Holder's contract and her own sacking, leaving no stone unturned. She also said that the CEO and chairman might not be the only ones involved in the incident, asking that anyone who had concerns to share them with Detective Carey. This caused some consternation amongst both the staff and board members, but the nun felt it needed to be said.

When Sister Chrissy finished, Brian Carey asked a few questions and the meeting dispersed. Father John Shepherd, one of the longest-serving board members, asked the other five to join him in the upstairs meeting room for a discussion. The rest of the staff went back to their duties. Brian Carey spoke with the nun for a short time, telling her he was confident the girls were not in the cottage or nearby and must've got away safely. He said there'd been reports of people running down the back lanes late the night before, and a homeless man had seen three girls near the jetty well before midnight. The nun told Brian of Trish's plan to run away to her aunty's place in Surry Hills and he promised he'd follow that up, going on to ask for the files on all three girls to present at the next task force meeting. Alice soon found the files and handed them over to Brian, who then left for the police station.

In the meantime, Tina and Georgia were putting together some last-minute information for the task force meeting.

Suddenly, Mike came running into the room.

"Boss, a call, just in," he said. "Trail bike riders found two bodies on a track just off West Head Road at Terry Hills, near the ranger station. Sounds like they're from Weatherall Cottage. It looks like they were murdered, and recently."

Georgia's heart sank.

"The girls?" she almost croaked.

"No, a woman around fifty and an older man. Sounds like the CEO and chairman."

Tina and Georgia breathed a collective sigh of relief.

"Georgia, grab Bruno and get over there now," said Tina. "And take Amber with you, if you think she's up to it. She can do an immediate identification."

"These kids have had to be tough, sadly," Georgia responded. "We're on it."

She left quickly, grabbing Bruno and Amber and heading straight for the car park.

They were driving north along Mona Vale Road when a call came over the radio. A local officer reported that a capsized dinghy had been found in Blackwattle Bay, and though no bodies had been found, it might be related to the girls' disappearance.

Georgia's heart missed another beat. She so wanted to go there, but decided to continue to the murder scene. She made a frantic call to Tina asking for extra water police to get involved, then hung up the phone.

"This might not be a good time," Amber said from the back seat, "but Roxy can't swim."

That was the last thing Georgia needed.

# Chapter Thirty-Eight

L unch was about to be served at Weatherall Cottage. All twenty-one girls had been rounded up and sat at the table, ready to eat. The room was noisy; it seemed everyone wanted to talk. Everyone had an opinion about who that night's raiders were, and what they were after. Sister Chrissy, Dave and two nurses were also in the dining room, trying to keep the peace. Unexpectedly, Father Shepherd entered the room and asked the nun to join the board at their meeting upstairs.

Sister Chrissy's mind raced as she reached the first-floor landing. She could only imagine the grilling she was about to receive.

Father Shepherd asked her to sit and then took his place at the head of the table. Sister Chrissy saw the looks on the board members' faces and knew they must've been having a very heavy discussion.

"Sister Marion," began Father Shepherd. "At the outset, let me tell you how devastated we all are with the goings-on here at the cottage. We wish unanimously to apologise to you, the girls and the staff for our failure to see what was happening. We truly had no idea, and are sickened to have let you all down so badly."

This was not what Sister Chrissy was expecting.

He went on.

"Looking forward, we want to do everything we can to right the ship. The board has elected me as the new chairman, and we will be asking Mr. McGarry for his resignation pending whatever other legal proceedings are to follow. I'm deeply honoured by the trust they've placed in me, and will do all in my power to make our cottage the safe haven we've been telling the world we offer. The board has also voted unanimously to reinstate Dr. Holder and his clinic's contract immediately, in addition to increasing hours and sessions. We recognise the progress that Dr. Holder has made with all of our girls, and the genuine respect they and the staff have for him. We were completely unaware of the CEO's cancellation of the clinic's contract, and had certainly never discussed it at board level."

This was very welcome news. The nun smiled in agreement.

"Finally," said Father Shepherd, "the board would like to ask you to accept the position of CEO here at the cottage. Not an acting, temporary position, but a confirmed, full-time appointment. Whatever happens with Mrs. O'Brien, we will be terminating her appointment forthwith when she returns or contacts us."

Sister Chrissy had to take a good, long moment to compose herself.

"Before you respond, all six of us are happy to commit to working hard in support of your efforts and are keen to take your advice," the father continued. "Like Dr. Holder, we know that all of our residents and staff here hold you in the highest esteem, and we're confident that with you in the role, we will deliver only the best outcomes."

"Thank you, Father John," said an elated Sister Chrissy. "The cottage and the girls here have been a huge part of my life for many years, and I'd be honoured to be a bigger part of our efforts to give these children a well-deserved chance at a wonderful life. I share your belief that together, we can do it, and gladly accept your offer."

The board members brightened and began to smile for the first time that day.

They discussed the way forward for some time before heading downstairs, where the staff, Dr. Holder and all the girls were asked to gather in the common room.

When everyone was settled, Father John stood up and called for quiet.

"I'd like to start with a heartfelt apology from myself and the board for not recognising the indignities that all of you have suffered over the past few years," said the father. "We've made some major decisions today that we'd like to share with you all. Firstly, Mrs. O'Brien and Mr. McGarry's positions here have been terminated, effective immediately."

Murmurs and grins broke out around the room, showing the immediate relief everyone felt.

"Next, we give thanks to Sister Marion, who has agreed to take up the role of full-time CEO for Weatherall Cottage."

The instant clapping and yells of encouragement said it all. Even Dave was on his feet, cheering. He knew what this must mean to Sister Chrissy, and also knew that she was up to the challenge.

"Our final piece of news is that not only is Dr. Holder's contract reinstated, but we are offering him a position on our board and will be asking his clinic for more of his involvement."

Another rousing round of cheers and clapping put a huge smile on Dave's face. He went red.

Everyone in the room could feel the confidence that Father Shepherd's announcements had instilled in the staff and residents alike. Sister Chrissy received hugs from a number of the girls and staff.

Just then, Dave felt his phone vibrate. Hoping it was the clinic so that he could pass on the good news, he looked at the screen and saw it was a text from Georgia.

*The CEO and chairman's bodies have been positively identified at Mt. Ku-ring-gai Chase National Park. I'll call you soon. G.*

He blanched. Sister Chrissy saw the look on Dave's face.

"Are you alright, Dr. Holder?"

Dave asked to see her and Father John outside.

In the lobby, he turned and gave the news to the new CEO and chairman.

\*

Georgia, Bruno and Amber arrived at the crime scene, climbing under chequered police tape to where two bodies lay under tarps next to the track. While the forensic detectives' team collected evidence from the surrounding bush, the tarps were partially pulled back at Georgia's request, revealing that both victims had been shot multiple times. Amber immediately confirmed their identities, and the tarps were replaced.

Georgia and Bruno spoke with the head of the forensic team.

"This doesn't look like the work of professionals," said the detective. "The murders took place at the site, shells have been recovered and it appears they did little to hide the bodies. They seem to have been in a real hurry."

Amber, who'd been walking around the area, approached Georgia.

"There were two men, and one of them has a bad limp," she said matter-of-factly.

The three detectives all looked a bit taken aback. Georgia explained Amber's childhood and cultural hunting and tracking skills.

"Can you help us see what you see?" Georgia asked.

Amber took them over to the tracks.

"They were parked here," she said, indicating tyre tracks. She then pointed to two sets of footprints leading away from them. "Both prints were made by men's shoes. On this set, you can see that the imprint of the right foot is at a constant angle, which means the right leg was bent."

She went on to explain the difference in walking styles, then pointed to a small tree close by.

"You see those scrape marks? They're fresh. You can see the sap starting to ooze out. They must've backed into it when turning. You can also see flecks of dark-green paint on the edges."

The head forensic detective whistled and laughed.

"I wish you'd brought this young lady to our last job. She could've saved us a lot of work." He looked straight into Amber's eyes. "You're good. Thanks for that, young lady. You've made our work here a lot easier."

Amber grinned, looking very pleased with herself.

She followed Georgia as she spoke with the other detectives, trying to reconstruct the events around the murder.

Georgia turned to her.

"So? What have we missed?" she asked, half joking.

Amber pointed out that the man with the limp had walked into a bush nearby.

"The guy took a leak over there," she concluded. "Not sure if you can use it, but if you take those leaves and some of the soil underneath, you'll have his DNA."

The forensic detectives shook their heads in amazement. They started putting the leaves and sandy soil scrapings into plastic bags.

The afternoon sun was halfway to the horizon, and a southerly breeze had taken some of the sticky heat out of the day. Having achieved all they had set out to, Georgia, Bruno and Amber walked back to the car. Georgia was on the phone to Dave, asking if he had any news on Jane, Roxy and Trish. She told him what she knew about O'Brien and McGarry, and he filled her in on all of the changes at Weatherall Cottage, as well as the partners' meeting earlier in the day. This brought a smile to Georgia's face.

After she ended the call, she told Amber the news about the cottage.

"Wow. That's cool," she said. "I reckon the girls'll be happy."

"It certainly sounds like it. Sadly, there's been no news about the three girls on the run. The aunty at Surry Hills hasn't heard from Trish. Tell me, Amber," she asked on a hunch, "if you were that frightened, where would you go? Would you go back to Redfern, and familiar territory?"

"No way. That's where the crooks would go." She thought for a while and then said, "I'd go to where I thought *you* would look—to the bush at North Head, where we had that day out. She trusts you."

Georgia opened and shut her mouth twice.

"Christ, why didn't I think of that? Let's go!"

Bruno was totally confused but he followed Georgia's lead.

Siren on, they headed south along Pittwater Road. Georgia told Bruno the story of their excursion that day, and Jane's story about her family's murder. She also rang Chatswood and gave Mike an update on the Weatherall Cottage murders. As they approached Manly and turned left up Darley Road, she turned off the siren.

The sun was beginning to set over the Quarantine Station parklands, the picturesque Sydney Harbour waters reflecting the afternoon's golden colour. It was a spectacular sight.

Parking just off Wharf Street near Cannae Point, they followed Amber along the bush track. Bruno was bemused; he couldn't imagine a good result. It was like looking for the proverbial needle in the haystack.

Amber motioned for silence as she turned and walked into the dense scrub, followed closely by Georgia and Bruno. A little further on, Amber motioned for them to stop, then gave Georgia the thumbs up and nodded. There was a real twinkle in her eye.

Jane, Roxy and Trish jumped up and yelped as three bodies suddenly appeared from the bush at the edge of the clearing. This quickly turned to squeals of delight when the girls realised it was Amber and Georgia. Amber saw Brokenfoot disappear into the bush behind Jane and laughed.

They hugged and all tried to talk at once. Eventually, Georgia calmed things down and the girls began to tell the story of their escape. After catching the 1am ferry to Manly from Wharf Two at Circular Quay, they'd walked up to North Head with hamburgers and hot chips they'd bought from the twenty-four-hour takeaway on the Corso.

"We spent all day here. Haven't been game enough to poke our heads out," said Roxy. "Jane reckoned you'd know where we were."

"Well, I didn't," said Georgia. "Luckily, Amber's a lot smarter than I am."

Georgia then went on to tell the girls about the grisly discovery at West Head National Park, and the murders of Mrs. O'Brien and McGarry. She told them of their trip along the northern beaches to Jane's fairy garden on Amber's hunch. She then told them all the good news from Weatherall Cottage, and the three girls were delighted.

"Maybe it won't stay such a shithole forever!" said Roxy.

Georgia rang Mike and gave him the good news that all three girls were safe and well.

The police car was overcrowded, but the mood inside was bright and bubbly as they drove into the underground car park at Chatswood Police Station. Roxy and Trish were apprehensive until Georgia took them all to *The Cell*, where she produced milkshakes and mixed sandwiches that the hungry girls soon devoured.

Upstairs, Georgia took them on a tour of the task force operations room. There, she found out that Tina had gone to the commissioner's task force meeting and would be back later in the evening. Georgia introduced the girls to Brad and Alison, who were the only two still there. She filled them in with the latest from the task force investigation.

"As for you three," said Georgia, directing herself to the girls, "we have some leads on the men who raided the cottage."

Jane shuddered at the thought.

"Still, it's not enough of a sure thing to leave anyone in harm's way. Roxy and Trish, no one is on the lookout for you, so you're fine to return to the cottage. You two, on the other hand," she said, indicating Jane and Amber, "are totally safe with us. I propose we all go back to the cottage, say hi to everyone, pick up some clothes for Jane and Amber, then come back here to see Superintendent Samuels. We'll keep you both out of sight until we know for sure that you're safe."

Before they left, Georgia rang Dave at the clinic to tell him all the good news. He immediately passed this on to Dr. B and the others, then headed for the cottage to help Sister Chrissy settle into her new role. Georgia had told him they'd be there soon, but asked him not to tell Sister Chrissy or the other girls to preserve the surprise.

As they drove over the Harbour Bridge, all four girls were very excited about catching up with Sister Chrissy and the others about all the news.

The resident girls were still in the dining room with Sister Chrissy, Dave and one of the nurses when the doors burst open, revealing Jane, Amber, Roxy and Trish.

Pandemonium broke out. Georgia gave Dave a big hug, and then saw tears of joy rolling down Sister Chrissy's face. She went straight over and gave her a huge bear hug. Jane soon joined them.

Eventually, calm was restored. Georgia took Sister Chrissy aside and gave her an update on the murders and the investigation. She told her they'd be keeping Amber and Jane out of sight until they were sure of their safety, confiding in her that it was mostly for Jane's sake, but that Amber would be good company and her talents might come in handy. She told Sister Chrissy of Amber's contribution to the forensic team that day and they shared in a moment of pride.

"They'll both be staying with Dave and I," said Georgia, "but that's for your ears only."

After things started to calm down, Georgia left with the two girls to return to Chatswood Station, having told Dave that she expected to be home with both girls in a couple of hours.

# Chapter Thirty-Nine

E arlier that morning, Superintendent Samuels had left the San Hospital at Normanhurst with husband David behind the wheel, heading east along the leafy Comenarra Parkway towards Chatswood. She still hadn't been cleared to drive following her accident, and the two murders that morning were the last things she needed right now.

Her visit to eminent oncologist Dr. Marie Emslie had not gone well.

"She says I can't blame the accident for low platelet readings and slow growth," Tina explained. "She's putting that down to workload, saying that if I want to continue being a good detective, I have to start delegating immediately. Either way, I'm back on weekly sessions."

She knew the doctor was right. Not only was Marie Emslie an excellent specialist, she was also a long-time friend of hers and was genuinely worried about Tina's cancer.

David was relieved. Stubborn Tina rarely took good health advice on board but since Catie's death, she'd been more accepting.

Once back in the office, Tina called in Detective Inspector Broadfinger. As Mike entered her office, he saw a mixture of despair, tiredness and anger in her eyes. Not a good sign.

"I'll be blunt," said Tina. "I'm not travelling too well health-wise, and I need you to take the reins for a while. I'll sit up the back of the room, so to speak. Any word from Georgia?"

He'd been expecting something like this.

"No worries, boss. Georgia's leaving the murder scene now. We should have her report within the hour. Will you be heading down to Mossy Point? We can Zoom every day."

"Sounds good, but not just yet. We'll be going away for a couple of days, but I'll be at home more often than not, and in here from time to time. The doctor needs to see me a bit more regularly."

She detailed her commitments to Mike, who would take over the task force once more and sit on the commissioner's special panel in her place. Just as Mike was leaving Tina's office, her desk phone rang.

"The taxi for Ms. Proud is here," reported the desk sergeant, who knew that Tina never ordered a taxi under her own name.

As the taxi drove towards North Sydney and her rendezvous in Blues Street, Tina thought about Rusty's phone call earlier in the day, intrigued by his request to meet her 'a.s.a.p.'. The taxi pulled up right outside the *Devon Cafe* on Blues Street, and as Tina was first to arrive, she ordered coffee and her favourite Croissant Saint Denis.

Rusty arrived soon after and sat down after ordering. They shared some general banter before he got down to business.

"Tina, you and I have never discussed our clandestine pursuits, and we still have no need to," he began. "What I do know is that we're both keen to see good triumph over evil. As you know, I'm very well connected as well as trusted by some highly questionable characters. I've used that to the police force's advantage many times over the years, and I don't need to tell you the risk."

Tina nodded, well aware that Rusty's intelligence had been an invaluable part of their recent major successes worldwide. She was in awe of his results, and knew full well how dangerous this was for Rusty.

He handed her a large, buff-coloured envelope.

"These photos are doing the rounds of some of Sydney's most sophisticated organised crime bosses," he said. "These cretins play for keeps."

Tina took out the two photographs and reacted instantly.

"Oh shit!" was all she could muster, looking at the clear black and white images.

The first showed Brad, Bert, Bernardo and Tina leaving Catie's burial plot, and the second depicted Brad handing over Judge Latta's hard drive to her at the *Thelma and Louise* café the week before.

"Jesus, Rusty. I don't need this," Tina blurted, trying to remember who'd been in the café.

"They've identified the three boys as the ones in the Barncleuth Lane room at Kings Cross, courtesy of the brothel manager, Jess Yurong. At the very least, they don't know who or where they are. The mobs suspect they're from one of the emerging gangs. But they *do* know that they're in contact with you and think there's some sort of police protection at play."

"What next?" said Tina, tiring fast. "Where do we go from here?"

"The only thing we can do is try to bust these big mobs before they get to you," Rusty offered. "I'm happy to work with you and John to make that happen, but I don't want the others to know. You might have to get your other team to mop up some of the loose ends and take out some of the untouchables. Your call."

Tina shivered and looked into Rusty's eyes.

"I hate these bastards with a passion," she said. "They've ruined the lives of, if not outright murdered, many good people—too many of whom I knew personally. I'll do whatever it takes. I'm just glad you're on our side."

She updated him on the cottage girl's plight and the murder of the CEO and chairman.

After making plans to meet with the commissioner, Tina called a cab and left, looking around to see if there were any suspicious types in the café. She half laughed when she thought they all could've been. After what she'd just seen, she couldn't help but be jumpy.

Back at Chatswood, Mike came in from a task force meeting just as she was finishing her list.

"In a nutshell, boss, not a lot of progress or new leads," he said. "Brian Carey says the lead at the Easts Leagues Club came to nothing. The barman only remembered a casual customer asking his advice, and gave a very vague description. Brad followed up the black SUV rego inquiry. Records show it was sent to me through the Blacktown switchboard at 11.52am, but it ended up with someone else. Brad's still looking into it.

"There *is* some interesting news on the forensic front," he added. "They've found identical DNA at both the Bellingen murder and the Kings Cross room, which links the two events. Looks like it's gang-related after all, but we've no leads yet."

Tina stiffened, but said nothing.

"We've also heard from Alison via Graham James at the Italian Forum. They've located the shopfront being used by the paedophile ring and are interviewing the receptionist right now. The CCTV footage shows the chief justice and Hardcastle arriving within minutes of each other, but that's not the interesting bit—one of our own CPU cars drove in just after them and stayed 'til late."

Mike updated Tina on Georgia's findings from the murder scene at West Head, then left to return to his ever-increasing list of duties.

Tina phoned Superintendent Max Logan and gave him the details of the Child Protection Unit car seen at the Italian Forum. He promised to look into it.

"I visited Derek Sward's home earlier," said Max. "Barbara's still a mess. Can you drop in one day?"

"Of course," she said sadly. "It's already well overdue."

"By the way, Stretch has identified another six of your cottage girls on the dark web. I'll send the details through. What a bunch of sick mongrels we're dealing with."

Tina finished her notes, updated her files and organised to be driven home. As she was leaving, Mike ran out of his office.

"Georgia just called in. They found the three girls, all safe and well. They'll be here in twenty minutes," he said, smiling from ear to ear. "I'll bring them in."

Tina also smiled, for the first time that day.

*Finally, some good news,* she thought.

# Chapter Forty

Superintendent Max Logan felt miserable as he waited outside the commissioner's office. His head kept telling him things his heart didn't want to accept. The commissioner's long-time PA, Meryl, brought him out of his trance with a smile and some clicks of her fingers.

"Hello? *Hello?* Anyone home?" she chided gently. "The commissioner's ready for you."

The superintendent entered the office.

"Sorry, Max. I'd had that call booked for a week so I had to take it," said Palmer. "You sounded worried. What's the problem?"

"One of my CPU cars was seen on CCTV footage at the Italian Forum at the same time as the chief justice and the DC made their getaway," he said. "I checked our records and found that Mario Savalis was the rostered driver. He's one of my two most trusted men, and I've kept him in the loop from day one. I can't believe he's mixed up in this. His record of convictions is second to none, but ... I'm nervous."

The commissioner was stone-faced.

"I'm listening."

"I showed Mario and Stretch Butler Tina's brief on the Latta evidence the day after you and I met with her. It was around lunchtime, after we'd all been held up by a bloody fire drill," said Max. "Anyway ... the chief justice and Warren Hardcastle's disappearance happened only a couple of hours later. I checked Mario's day sheets, and they're almost blank; just our meeting, a few mundane calls and normal procedures. I asked him casually yesterday arvo if he was at the Italian Forum that day, and his answer was evasive. Something along the lines of, 'I often grab a pizza at Johnny Gio's or meet people at the Capriccio Osteria and bar, so it's possible.' The final straw was that he didn't turn up for our exec meeting today, and there's no sign of him at home. John, if he's a dud, then the bastards have everything we've got, and I'm a bad judge of character."

"Tell me," said Palmer. "Does Savalis spend any time with Joe Hudson from the Parra Ds?"

"Yeah. They work together a lot, and mix socially too. Why?"

"They were both identified by The Forum's receptionist. Those are our men."

The commissioner pressed a button.

"Meryl. Have Alison come in here now, if she's still in the building."

"She's left for Chatswood Station for her task force meeting," Meryl responded.

"Of course. Get her on the phone a.s.a.p. and ask her to call me."

He hung up and dialled another number.

"Morning, commissioner," came Mike Broadfinger's reply. "What can I do for you?"

"Mike, what time is your task force meeting?"

"In about twenty minutes. I'm just about to head in there. Is there a problem?"

"Could be," said Palmer. "Alison gave me some information concerning Joe Hudson earlier this morning, and I've just had something else come in. Whatever you do, don't pass on anything new or sensitive to Hudson until I've had time to sort it out. Ask Alison to ring me when she gets there."

"Okay, Chief. Will do," said Mike, taken aback.

"Sorry, Max. Had to do that. Alison came in earlier after a chance conversation with a colleague and long-time friend from Parra station," the commissioner explained. "CCTV places Hudson's work car two hundred metres down the road just as the bomb went off. If that weren't enough, the missing message on Mike's SUV rego request was logged under Hudson's name. It looks like we could have double trouble, as Hudson is privy to all of the task force intel. Where do these bloody rotten apples in our ranks end? Let's go over to Chatswood now and see what we can dig up."

Halfway across the Harbour Bridge, the commissioner's car phone rang. He answered.

"Hi, Chief. Mike B here. Hudson didn't turn up for the task force briefing. I've followed it up, and it seems he's disappeared into thin air—not at home or at work. Totally out of character."

"Thanks, Mike. No surprises there. Sit tight; Superintendent Logan and I are north of the bridge. We'll be there in five. Keep Alison with you. Get an 'all points' ready to go out on Savalis and Hudson, but don't action it until we get there."

"Okay, Chief. See you soon."

John Palmer did a rare thing; he turned on his siren and flashing blue lights and put his foot down hard on the accelerator, hoping to save precious minutes.

By the time the two men arrived, Mike had caught up with Alison and prepared the paperwork for the arrest warrants. They sent downstairs for coffee and sandwiches as the four of them sat around the table.

"Let's go over everything we have. Mike, you first. I presume Tina has given you the full brief?"

"Sure has," said Mike. "Okay. Across all the linked jobs, here's what we have in point form."

Mike had been ready for this. He passed around a single-page brief that read as follows:

*T Squad Current Cases Discussion Sheet*

*1. The bombing of Parramatta Police Station – deaths and injuries*

*2. The attempted murder of Superintendent Samuels and Detective Sergeant McHenry-Holder on the M4*

*3. The murder of Detective Sergeant Garry Townsend at Westmead Hospital*

*4. The death of Judge Latta, now a homicide investigation*

*5. The murders of the two scientists on the QF1 flight and subsequent hostage drama*

*6. The assassination of Judge Tiffany Wallace*

*7. Long-term reports of missing girls from the Weatherall Cottage Children's Shelter*

*8. The murders of the cottage CEO and chairman*

*9. The raid by unknown parties on the cottage and the disappearance of three more girls, since confirmed safe*

*10. The bombing at the Kings Cross strip joint. Deaths and injuries of senior mob / gang bosses*

*11. The disappearance of the Chief Justice Nat Larucci and Deputy Commissioner Hardcastle*

*Links:*

*Two, three, five and six are linked by the two Colombian hitmen, later killed on board QF1 at Darwin*

*Questions:*

*{A} Who were they working for?*

*{B} Was Derek Sward the intended target at Westmead?*

*Four, seven, eight, nine, ten and eleven are linked back to the Latta hard drive and images, plus matching DNA found at both four and ten.*

*There are three main trails:*

*(i.) The mobs: One, two, three, five, six and ten. With society's insatiable appetite for illicit drugs, generating billions of illegal dollars in profits, there seems to be some internal warfare developing between the established gangs and emerging mobs from interstate and overseas. Judge Wallace was taken out because she was about to handle all the mobs' trials and convictions and, by reputation, she was too straight*

*(ii.) The Weatherall Cottage Children's Shelter saga*

*(iii.) The worldwide paedophile ring*

*There are strong links between two and three, and probable links with one. CPU have mounting dark web intelligence*

*Questions:*

*{A} Who is the mastermind?*

*{B} Where are the missing girls being held?*

*{C} Where are they working from?*

While they were all reading the brief, Mike took the floor.

"I know things are moving fast, and both Alison and the commissioner have things to add," he said, "but before anything else, we need to address the leak from within the task force. The media has already linked items one, five and six, and the coroner's verdict on Latta is due out on Friday. This will really bring the ghouls out, along with all their questions. The Weatherall Cottage murders will be front page tomorrow, and some of the material they're quoting should not have left this room. We need to be vigilant and root out whoever's responsible."

The commissioner took over.

"When word gets out about Larucci and Hardcastle, my job becomes almost untenable. I'd love to wrap it up before the pressure gets too high. We have an international paedophile ring on our hands, with material being filmed and distributed from Australia and our own chief justice and deputy police commissioner up to their necks in it. On top of that, we have Savalis and Hudson. We need to mount extra airport and coastal security to stop them from leaving the country, and we have no option but to issue arrest warrants for the four of them today. The media will have a field day, and we don't know anywhere near enough, but there's no putting it off."

He went on to explain the new evidence on Savalis and Hudson, then issued tasks to everyone, with a special request to Max Logan to find the missing link—the 'needle in the haystack'.

"Before we go," said Palmer, "I don't have anything to prove it yet, but I'm starting to think that some sort of vigilante group could be at work here. Between Latta, the Kings Cross bombing and recent cases such as the Joe Iminez explosion and the deaths of Hegarty and his mates, we have a growing list of dead scumbags with leads that go nowhere. Normally, our underground network has at least *some* insight into what's happening, but they've had nothing to say about any of it. By all accounts, they're as mystified as we are. Keep your eyes peeled. Mark my words, something is different about these cases."

At the same time as the Chatswood meeting broke up, a stolen Porsche coupe with false numberplates drove south towards Berrima and Bowral in the Southern Highlands. It was tulip season, and magnificent blooms and colourful spring gardens dotted the landscape all over the region. The view of the fields was spectacular as the sun sank over the western ranges, but the two men in the car took no notice. Dark sunglasses hid their nervous, searching eyes—especially those of the man whose scar was still twitching.

Savalis and Hudson were almost at 'the studio'. They'd been told that a green light would clear them to traverse the mile-long bush driveway to the mansion, where they'd be safe until they could plan their next move.

# Chapter Forty-One

Australian Federal Police Commissioner Alan McDonald had booked security room four at the Canberra headquarters, a quadrant-shaped conference centre in the Edmund Barton building on the edge of the parliamentary triangle. The room had a commanding view over Lake Burley Griffin, the Kings Avenue Bridge to Grevillea Park and one of Alan's favourite eateries, *The Boathouse*. A perfect, cloudless day overlooked the famous man-made lake, a gentle breeze propelling a number of trailer yachts across its waters.

McDonald was joined by Superintendent Dick Sellis, his long-time friend from the New South Wales Police Special Task Force and Special Constable Jessica Jones, an officer from a unit within the AFP.

"Thank you for joining me," said Alan. "Dick, I heard you were on leave in Lakes Entrance, so thanks to you in particular for dropping everything to be here. This is only a hunch, but there are a number of synergy indicators raising red flags and I thought we should throw it around sooner rather than later."

Jessica nodded.

"Seconded on all counts," she said. "Dick, if you didn't know, I lead a team that investigates the illegal organ trade worldwide. Right now, we're following up a lead on a potential network in Australia exporting body parts to Saudi Arabia, Israel, Colombia, Kosovo and China."

Alan said, "We're starting to link a number of distressing stories in the background of this insidious trade. Jessica here recently gave us some worrying intelligence about transplant organs leaving Australia without being registered on either the domestic or international authorities' systems. It seems those responsible have been exploiting a loophole where registration can be bypassed if the donor and recipient are deemed to be close relatives. The practice has become known as 'transplant tourism'."

He asked Jessica to elaborate.

"In today's economy, a body with all its organs, skin, joints and tissue stripped down and dissected can sell for up to $4.5 million. A complete, recently deceased and frozen body can attract around $3 million, and that can be broken down into things like a heart—particularly now that the OCS' 'Heart in a Box' system is available for around $1 million. The most traded organs of all, the kidneys, go for about $250,000 each. Even an eyeball can fetch well over $1,000. The younger the donor, the higher the price of the organ," Jessica explained. "All this is to quote ethical operation charges, mind you. The black market is somewhat cheaper, but unfortunately, the demand far exceeds the supply. This is keeping prices up, despite science's best attempts to increase the production and availability of 3D bioprinting.

"We've been following papers from those attempting to address the problem, from the World Health Organization through to the likes of our own Dr. Dominique Martin from Deakin University. From what we can establish, up to ten per cent of all transplants worldwide involve illegal organ trafficking," she added. "Many of these have fatal consequences due to botched surgeries, mismatched organs and serious post-op infection. We estimate there were over ten thousand illegal kidney transplants last year alone."

Dick Sellis was intrigued by these figures.

"How does the whole scheme work?" he asked. "Given what's involved, there must be qualified medical practitioners and safe, fast and secure transport systems involved."

"We've identified a number of what we call 'mobile nephrology surgeons' who operate in unregistered rooms," said Jessica. "They work with brokers, or self-styled 'matchmakers', who compare tissue and blood types from organ requests around the world—mainly from richer, more developed nations. They are robust, resilient, exceedingly mobile, and generally one step ahead of authorities."

Alan McDonald chimed in.

"The first thing I saw about all this was a list of regular organ transport mules who'd been taking body parts overseas," he said. "Two of the names near the top of the list were Santiago Fernandez and Juan Pablo Cortez, the two Colombians killed in the QF1 drama last week. They were responsible for several attempted—and successful—murders the week before, and who knows what else."

"Those are two of the four names we've seen making regular deliveries to both Dubai and Bogotá," Jessica added. "They were both registered as accredited couriers."

"Can you tell Dick about the red flag from Mittagong?" McDonald asked.

"I can, but it needs to be said that this information is as confidential as it gets," said Jones. "About two weeks ago, we received copies of documentation approving transport of the cadaver of a young Muslim woman, whose body was to be flown to Riyadh in Saudi Arabia. The woman, Haifaa Al Shafal, was a listed as a twenty-seven-year-old student, reportedly killed in a car accident. Her family are apparently connected to royalty, and the request received expedited diplomatic approval.

"One of our Sydney team noted that the request was very similar to one that had been processed a few months ago, which prompted them to check the paperwork more thoroughly. They found no reports of her accident or death in the Wollondilly area—what's more, Mittagong Hospital were entirely unaware of the request, even though they were the ones who'd supposedly made it. There were also no records of that name registered on any student roll. On further inspection, both of these cases were found to have been approved by New South Wales Chief Justice Nat Larucci, and granted by Judge James Latta."

Dick Sellis whistled under his breath.

"If you'd told me that a week ago, I wouldn't have believed it."

"Thank goodness our team flagged the anomaly and took photos of the body," Jessica continued, producing a photo. "Firstly, there are not many blonde Saudi women, and secondly, the images showed no signs of injury that would have resulted in death, much less anything to indicate she'd been in a car accident. We processed the photos to see if we could uncover any erroneous information or identification and found a one hundred per cent match. The body was positively identified as one Angela Murray, a twenty-seven-year-old Scottish Australian fostered out from Weatherall Cottage Children's Shelter five years ago and not seen or heard from since."

Dick Sellis was at a loss for words.

"This is dynamite," was all he could manage.

Alan McDonald nodded and suggested, "We'd better get Tina and Max's teams onto this."

# Chapter Forty-Two

D avid Samuels was so glad he'd called his sister Elspeth three days before. They hadn't seen each other much since she and her engineer husband, Damien, had moved to Melbourne over two years previously after being offered a partnership in an award-winning design group. David had told his sister that Tina was on the mend from the accident, but was not coping well with stress. Elspeth had insisted they use their Kirra beachfront unit on the fourteenth floor of the five-star *Nirvana By The Sea* resort apartment complex on the Gold Coast to take some time to rest and recover.

After dropping Tina at Chatswood Police HQ following her next visit to the oncologist, David went into Flight Centre on impulse and organised air tickets to Coolangatta that night, with open returns. Tina had told him recently that she needed to catch up with Brad and the 4G Team, and he'd used that as his draw card. They'd flown out on the last flight at 9 that night.

Now, here they were, covered in sand some fourteen hours later, out of breath and laughing like a couple of teenagers. They'd just raced out of the surf after a shark alarm raised by a reported drone sighting.

David couldn't believe the improvement in Tina in just that short time.

*Sun and surf is a great cure-all,* he thought to himself

Twenty minutes later, they were dining in *Café All Sorts* on the ground floor of their building, having ordered coffees and a light lunch. David introduced himself to their host, Cameron, who'd just recognised this as their second visit for the day.

Back on the fourteenth floor, they sat on the spacious balcony and soaked up the panoramic view of the ocean and the Surfers Paradise skyline.

After they were showered and refreshed, Tina called a taxi to take them to the 4G Factory in Molendinar for a look over the complex. David had never seen it before, and Tina had only been there at night with Catie when Brad, Bert and Bernardo had been working on their 'after-hours projects'.

Brad had been delighted when Tina phoned that morning to say that they were already on the coast.

"Perfect timing," he'd said. "We're cutting a cake to celebrate our first six months' success this afternoon at 4. Garth and Meg will be here, and Jane will get here around 4.30."

Tina was amazed to see the car park nearly full, and a vibrant atmosphere in the busy reception and sales foyer. For something that had started as a front for their other activities, it had become an instant success in its own right. They'd already doubled their original number of staff.

After a look around the well-appointed training facilities, sales rooms, administration area and the factory itself, Brad led David and Tina back to the boardroom. There, Bert and Bernardo were already seated alongside their greatest supporters, Garth and Meg Peterson. A delicious spread was laid out before them.

Brad left the room and came back with the three original 'outside' staff, Kim Knott, Katrina Tee and Shane Caddy.

"Tina and David, I'd like you to meet our engine room," he said. "Kim and Shane, two of the smartest geeks in Oz, and the lovely KT, who charms the socks off anyone who phones in or walks through the door."

They all laughed as KT and Kim served teas and coffees, everyone grazing on the sumptuous food on offer. Brad's better half, Jane, arrived at around 4.30, and the cake was cut in celebration.

"I know it's only the six-month mark," announced Garth, "but thanks to this team and its excellent reputation, we've drawn in over twelve months' worth of our original budgeted income already. In a way, it's kind of like our first birthday. Congratulations to you all."

Kim, KT and Shane knew only that Tina and David had been close friends of Catie. KT spoke quietly to Tina, telling her how much Catie was missed. The three staff had no idea that the others were involved in all sorts of clandestine activities behind the scenes, making the world a better place by night.

Brad took the floor and spoke about some proposed expansions. Tina felt her secure phone vibrate, and upon seeing that Mike was calling, she quickly excused herself and went outside to take the call. She was stunned to hear the news of the organ-harvesting operation involving Weatherall Cottage and that the Colombian killers had been involved in the illegal organ trade.

"Christ, Mike. What next? What have we stumbled onto here?" she said, horrified. "Have you told Georgia?"

"Yep. She and Dave are at the cottage right now. They're both coming in here at 11am tomorrow with whatever records they can find," said Mike. "Commissioner Palmer has authorised five new hands to help sift through all the leads and paperwork. Georgia said they have some sort of lead on a possible hideout down south. They're going to talk to one of the girls at the cottage to get something more precise."

"Okay. Sounds good. David will kill me, but I'll be there at 11."

Tina signed off and rang Georgia immediately.

"Mike just filled me in," she said. "Whatever happens, say nothing to anyone about Jane's predictions. We can't take the risk. I'll be there tomorrow morning and we can both work with Jane once we have the full picture. We must make sure that whoever we're dealing with here doesn't get wind that we're onto them."

Joining the others back in the boardroom, Tina returned just in time to say goodbye to Shane, KT and Kim. Then she settled back into a comfortable chair to talk about old times with the others.

Later, with everyone gone and the business locked up, Tina updated the 4G Team on Judge Latta's death.

"We knew he was a lowlife, but no one expected we'd unearth an international paedophile ring when we went after him," she said. "We certainly didn't expect the state's chief justice or my own deputy police commissioner to be implicated in the process. You are all to be congratulated. Latta's death was a great thing for society.

"However," Tina continued, "There's something I need to tell you. I have no idea how, but the Sydney mobs have come into possession of photos of you three fellows with me at Catie's funeral, as well as one of Brad handing over Latta's hard drive to me at last week's meeting in Neutral Bay."

This made everyone take careful notice.

"At the moment, my information says that the mobs think you're an emerging gang, and that I'm giving you some sort of protection. Let's hope it stays that way, but in the meantime, you must lie low and stay out of sight. Having said that, I may have to call upon you for a dangerous raid into the Southern Highlands to save some children in dire trouble. There are crooked cops involved, and we need to make sure they don't forewarn the creeps."

"Whatever you need," Brad assured her. "The only thing we're working on at the moment is making limpet mines to sink an Iranian oil tanker with a huge drug haul on board. Do you want us to put that on hold?"

"No, keep at it. That must be at least a few weeks away, and we could be clear by then," she said.

She then told them about the eleven children who'd gone missing from the cottage, the murders of the CEO and chairman, the discovery of the Murray girl's corpse and the illegal organ trade.

"We know for sure now that at least one of the children missing from the shelter has been murdered, so we need to move fast to save whoever we can."

Garth asked Tina for more information on the cottage. She told them the whole story about Sister Chrissy's suspicions, Georgia and Dave's efforts, Jane's tragic family story and all that had been going on underneath the surface.

"That's exactly the sort of thing we're in this to set right," he said.

Tina promised to talk to Georgia about how they could help and get back to them, as she knew the cottage was working on some new projects with the girls.

Just after 7pm, the team began to disperse and make their way out towards the car park. As Bert went to leave through the workshop, he stopped suddenly, noticing that some lights had been left on. He went towards them and to his surprise, he found that two of the staff had stayed behind, determined to finish repairs on some computers due for pickup in the morning. He called out to farewell the others, then settled in to help the boys finish the job.

David was disappointed, but not surprised, to be told they were flying back in the morning. Tina was cautiously optimistic, feeling that they were tightening the screws and finally getting somewhere.

*Here's hoping Jane has the superpowers that Georgia believes she has,* she thought.

# Chapter Forty-Three

After all of the turmoil at Weatherall Cottage—the fire, the raid, the murders, the return of the three missing girls and the drastic changes in management—things were finally starting to quieten down.

The new CEO, Sister Chrissy, was feeling the good vibes. The staff had been smiling a lot more readily and seemed much happier with their world. The girls, too, all laughed and chatted at breakfast, which continued into the morning. They even seemed to be enjoying their menial tasks and lessons.

These changes for the better were felt by all the board members when they came in for their special meeting that Tuesday. Father John opened the meeting by welcoming Dr. Holder to the board, then gave a full account of the police's murder investigation at Mt. Ku-ring-gai Chase National Park. He gave a progress report on the late-night raid; most notably, the fact that the police had positively identified both of the men involved and issued warrants for their arrest. Sister Chrissy outlined her short-term goals and modus operandi, advising that she would be contacting the agency for a shortlist of potential new staff and beginning the recruitment process. She noted that senior nurse Graham Larkin had failed to show up for three rostered shifts in a row, and they had not been able to contact him.

The chairman then led a lengthy discussion on possible changes, ongoing sponsorship challenges and budgetary constraints. He advised Sister Chrissy that things were already tightening up, and that recent events were not going to help their cause.

Despite all the gloom, there was a real sense of optimism as the meeting broke up just before lunch. The entire board took the unusual step of dining with the rest of the girls and staff, and the high spirits in the room were palpable.

When Dr. Holder arrived mid-afternoon for his normal sessions, Sister Chrissy greeted him.

"I'm expecting Georgia anytime now," she said. "We'll be going over recent records and diary entries. Only one couple of the expected four turned up for this morning's adoption parade, and we're planning to go over all that as well, including the previous prospective parents. I'm proposing a completely new way of handling adoptions and fostering, which I'll bring to the attention of the board for approval in due course."

Dave asked for permission for Roxy and Trish to join Jane and Amber on an excursion on Thursday to visit some nurseries and get some landscaping ideas for the proposed garden design. The CEO agreed, but warned Dave that budgets were very challenging and not to get his hopes up or to be too extravagant with his plans.

By the time Georgia arrived, Dave was in one of his regularly scheduled group sessions. She went straight into the CEO's office, ready to get to work.

Sister Chrissy expressed her joy around the renewed sense of purpose in the cottage and the positive signs for the future. Unfortunately, Georgia's news was far less heartening. Sister Chrissy's smile faded when Georgia told her of the grim discovery of Angie Murray's corpse, and she finally disclosed the contents of the dead judge's hard drive. Sister Chrissy was white by the time Georgia finished telling her about the worldwide organ trading ring, the chief justice and the deputy police commissioner.

"Lastly, we've identified both of the men involved in last week's late-night raid," said Georgia. "Unfortunately, they're both policemen, in league with the criminals. The good news is, we know who they are and what they were after. The bad news is that we don't know where any of these new players are. It's as if they've vanished. We have plenty of people at airports and seaports who are very vigilant and will prevent them from getting out of the country, but there's been no sign of any of them. I'm hoping to go through the previous CEO and chairman's files to see if we've missed anything."

"Of course," said Sister Chrissy, struggling to digest these revelations. She shook her head, distraught.

"Poor Angie. She was a funny, impish girl. She had a ready laugh, and a wicked Scottish sense of humour. This is just awful."

Georgia attempted to cheer her up, suggesting that they redirect their energy towards catching those responsible. Together, they went through all the missing girls' files and reports in search of anything that might aid them in their search.

"You should come with me to Chatswood tomorrow," said Georgia. "You can work with us at the coalface, and see Jane and Amber at the same time."

Sister Chrissy smiled. "I'd like that."

Meanwhile, David mentored eleven of the girls, who all seemed to have a new lease of enthusiasm. He addressed the long-held perspective that cottage residents, in the main, had low self-esteem and were different from others.

"All people should be unapologetically themselves," he said. "No two people are the same, and nor should they aspire to be. Our individual differences, beliefs, experiences, self-expressions and talents are the collective sum of who we are. They're what enables us to live out our true purpose and values. We should never feel shame about them."

Looking around, he was pleased to see general acceptance and agreement—a pleasant change from the norm.

He split the girls into three groups and issued them the challenge of working amongst themselves to identify their future career paths. He asked them all to think about it over the weekend and to relay their answers the following Wednesday.

Dave wrapped up the session a few minutes early, as he'd been requested to attend a meeting at the clinic at 5pm. It had come at short notice, and he'd yet to be told what it was about. Before he left, he went to say goodbye to Sister Chrissy and found her in tears, sitting alone in her office. Georgia had left a few minutes earlier, and the nun couldn't hold back any longer.

"Dr. Holder, we may have sent all those girls to their deaths," she sobbed. "This is unforgivable."

He shook his head.

"Sister Chrissy, the cottage boasts many good and reliable people, staff and residents alike. Yes, there were some really rotten apples," he conceded, "but they're gone now, and we owe it to all of the girls, past and present, to deliver the best results we can. Beyond that, all we can do is pray that the authorities find the missing girls in one piece and bring those responsible to justice."

Sister Chrissy nodded.

Pressed for time, Dave made his way back to the clinic. He arrived just before the meeting was due to start. On his way in, he asked the receptionist if she knew what the meeting was about.

"I have no idea, but all the partners are here. The bank manager Mr. Ambrose and our motorbike-riding solicitor Ed Byrne are here too," she said. "It must be about the budgets. There's been a fair bit of noise about them lately."

This intrigued Dave.

He received his summons right on 5pm.

As he entered the meeting room, he instantly recognised a much different mood to his last encounter with the partners.

"Dave. Please, have a seat," Dr. Brinsmead directed him. "Thanks for coming back early. We've had a long afternoon and I must say, I much prefer working with our patients than I do our financiers and legal team. Way less challenging."

There were smiles and laughter all round.

"But I digress. Dr. Holder, you joined us fresh out of university eight years ago, and have since been a great contributor to our success and fellowship over that time. The board has unanimously decided to offer you a full partnership as our way of saying thanks for a job well done. Should you accept, you will be the youngest partner ever to be instated."

Dave was stunned. Partnership was something he'd always aspired to, but he'd thought it much farther in the future, if at all.

"Thank you, Dr. B. Thank you all," he said. "I will do my best to honour your faith in me."

"You've more than earned it," said Dr. Brinsmead. "You'll also be pleased to hear that we've decided to part with some of our hard-earned money to become sponsors of Weatherall Cottage. I'm sure Sister Marion and her new team will find a good cause for us to support."

Dave was over the moon. He knew how much this would mean to Sister Chrissy and her team, and how much good it would do for the girls.

"Congratulations on your appointment to their board," he continued. "We're well aware of the challenges that lie ahead, and want to support your efforts in any way we can. We look forward to being a part of your ongoing success."

Dave left the meeting room with a satisfied smile. He couldn't wait to get home and tell Georgia all the good news.

# Chapter Forty-Four

B reakfast at the Holder residence was a mixed bag of emotions. Jane and Amber were shattered to hear the news about Angie Murray's body and were worried for Cate and the other girls. Despite this, they were looking forward to seeing the cottage and their friends that morning before going to Chatswood Police Station with Sister Chrissy, where they would continue helping the detectives on the case.

After breakfast, Dave, Georgia and the two girls drove towards Camperdown, discussing the design of the garden. 'Cheap and colourful' had been his initial advice, but since his clinic's offer to sponsor special projects at the cottage, he was happy to tell them they could think a little bigger.

Georgia wanted to be at Chatswood well before the 11am meeting with Mike and Tina. She'd been concerned for Tina when Mike had told her she was cutting her rehab short and would be back in the office today, but couldn't deny she'd be very glad to have her there. She could just imagine David's eyes rolling at the news.

When they arrived at the cottage, Jane and Amber soon found Roxy and Trish, then took off together to wander the grounds and discuss their new design and plans. Dave and Georgia helped Sister Chrissy carry all the files and load them into the boot. When everyone regrouped, Dave told Roxy and Trish that their adventure to the nurseries and gardens was back on and would go ahead the following Thursday.

They said their goodbyes and squeezed into Georgia's car for the twenty-five-minute run to Chatswood, arriving just after 10.30 and heading straight to *The Cell* café for takeaway milkshakes and cappuccinos.

Both girls became noticeably quieter as they entered the task force control room and saw all the activity, whiteboards, picture walls and files strewn around the room. When Amber saw their own photos on the wall, she laughed and pointed them out to Jane. They were soon introduced to Mike and, a few minutes later, Tina. Both of them instantly made a good impression on the two girls. Mike then introduced Tina to three of the new task force team members who'd arrived to start that morning.

Sister Chrissy, Dave and the two girls followed Georgia to meeting room three, where they all sat around the table.

"Now Jane," said Dave, trying to lighten the mood, "Superintendent Samuels is on your side, so please don't tell her to 'drop dead'."

Jane smiled sheepishly and nodded.

Tina entered the room and sat at the head of the table, addressing the room.

"I'd like to welcome you all here and thank you for everything you've contributed to date. Let me say at the outset that we're aware of much of the sadness and horror that has brought us to this point, and that we'll do everything in our power to bring justice to the perpetrators and give everyone at the cottage a much safer and improved quality of life."

Everyone in the room nodded firmly.

"Before we continue, I want to note that I have some good friends on the Gold Coast who've heard your story and have offered substantial financial and moral support," Tina continued. "Georgia and I will get that set up over the next few days, and I'll let you know the details as things get closer to being finalised. Sister Marion, could you please give us a rundown of the situation on the cottage?"

Sister Chrissy started with the unusual changes to the cottage routines following the arrival of McGarry and O'Brien, as well as the histories and backgrounds of all the girls who'd since gone missing. The nun spent over half an hour giving an overview of all that had occurred, often referring to files and notes she'd prepared in advance. Georgia, Tina and Mike wrote copious notes. Jane and Amber chimed in with things that only the residents would know, answering questions as they went. Tina then outlined the case from a police perspective and asked many pertinent questions. The two girls and Sister Chrissy were surprised at the amount of evidence they'd already accumulated.

Tina called for a break and ordered some sandwiches and juices from downstairs. While they were waiting, her secure phone rang. Seeing it was the commissioner, she took the call but remained in the room.

She mostly just listened, making many notes in her notepad throughout the call.

"That sounds promising," she said finally. "We'll be ready when they get here."

Tina then looked at the others, particularly at Sister Chrissy.

"You mentioned Graham Larkin, a senior nurse who went missing after the murders," she said. "He just handed himself in at Day Street Police Headquarters, asking for immunity in exchange for information. Senior Constable Hanagan is bringing him to us now. They're due to arrive in twenty minutes. Let's not get our hopes up, but it's possible this might lead us towards the ringleaders. Georgia, can you start the interview with Alison? The rest of us will watch through the one-way mirror.

"Later, we can continue our discussions on where the girls may be now. Larkin might be able to help, depending on how much he knows. Failing that, we also have Jane and her special gift. We'll get there, one way or another. That's a promise."

By the time Alison arrived and brought Larkin upstairs, the others were nowhere to be seen, all sitting in the dark area adjacent to the interview room.

Alison sat Larkin down in the small, sparsely-furnished room, empty save for an off-white table, three chairs, built-in cameras and overhanging lights. On the table was a compact recording device with small microphones pointing in three directions. A water jug and three plastic glasses completed the setup.

Georgia joined them in the room and read Larkin his rights. He remembered her from her original cottage visit and presentation.

"I'm not saying anything 'til I'm guaranteed immunity," he said immediately.

Georgia responded by advising him that their ability to grant it would depend on the quality of the information he gave them, and eventually, he started to talk.

Larkin was sweating profusely when the interview began, drinking the whole jug of water they'd given him in a matter of minutes. Georgia asked him if he'd known McGarry or O'Brien prior to the cottage, and was surprised to learn they'd brought him in from a boys' home where they'd worked together previously. He named three shelters involved in the scheme: Weatherall Cottage, his previous boys' home on the Central Coast and a third girls' refuge in the Wollongong area. When asked if he knew of any other, similar operations, Larkin revealed he'd spoken to others over the years who'd been involved in the trade. Amongst them was Homeless Peoples Mission, which supposedly offered vagrants a new home and a better life. Any who accepted were never seen again.

Georgia asked him about the missing girls from Weatherall Cottage, and Larkin became vague with his answers. When asked specifically about individual girls, Sister Chrissy reacted involuntarily to Angie Murray's name.

"Angie was adopted out the week after she made an official complaint about Larkin's unwelcome advances and suggestions," said Sister Chrissy. "I remember it clearly."

A minute or so later, Georgia excused herself and Alison continued questioning him. Georgia had seen the tiny green light in the corner of the room; a signal that she was needed outside. Tina passed on what Sister Chrissy had said, and Georgia went back into the room. She sat back down and waited for her moment.

"Graham, records show that Angie Murray lodged a complaint about you the very week she went missing," she said. "Did you have anything to do with that?"

Larkin balked, looking very uncomfortable.

"I had nothing to do with it," he blurted.

"Angie's body was found last Wednesday. You may well be implicated in a murder here."

Larkin was rattled. He'd had no idea about a body.

He started to give details about the sham parents. Even though he wasn't supposed to know them, he'd run across two sets of them later in pubs and at parties and had got to know them socially.

"They all talked about some studio somewhere near Mittagong. They never said exactly where."

Georgia was on the scent.

"Does this studio have a name?" she asked.

"I remember one of them said something at a barbecue about a *Mystery* or *Misty* retreat. The others shut her up pretty quickly after she said that. I have no idea where it is."

"What would you say if I told you that McGarry and O'Brien have recently turned up dead, and it's very likely that you're next on the list?"

"That's why I came in," Larkin whined. "My landlady said Sluggo and Spud had come looking for me. They threatened her, and she rang me straight away."

"Who are Spud and Sluggo?"

"That's all I know 'em as. They've done our residents' transfers for years after each parade. I think Sluggo is a bouncer, and all I know about Spud is that he has a bad limp."

Georgia, Tina and Mike all stiffened but showed no outward signs.

*Bingo,* thought Tina.

Amber's eyes lit up. She knew where this was going.

Alison and Georgia recorded Larkin for a few more minutes before Georgia began to close out the interview.

"Graham, your life is in mortal danger. We're going to place you into witness protection, where you'll have a safe, secure place to live, with all your meals and needs organised for you until we have everyone in custody. I will talk to the superintendent about your request for immunity, but I cannot guarantee it. If you cooperate fully, however, I think your chances are good. What I *can* guarantee is that you'll live long enough to testify. We need you to sign your statement and under no circumstances are you to contact anyone—not even your own mother. Do you understand?"

"Mum's dead," Larkin replied quietly.

He slumped back in his chair, looking miserable and alone. No one watching from the next room had any sympathy for him.

"What a deadshit," said Roxy.

She looked to Sister Chrissy.

"Uh, sorry."

"I couldn't have said it any better myself," said the nun.

The girls giggled.

Soon after, Sister Chrissy, Dave, Georgia and the girls left the station. They drove out from the underground carpark, heading towards the Cahill Expressway and Harbour Bridge, and the sun was setting, reflecting a golden glow in the harbour waters as they approached the city.

"Dr. Holder, Georgia, thank you both for such an inspiring day," said Sister Chrissy. "I have no idea how you put up with this sort of thing day in and day out, but I'm really glad you're on our side. Do you think we can save the other girls?"

"I'd love to say yes, but all I can guarantee is that we'll do our best," said Georgia. "Thanks to Larkin, we now have four more pieces of the puzzle, including confirmation that Jane was spot on about something horrible going on in the Southern Highlands. Do you remember when we cleared out McGarry's and O'Brien's desks?"

The nun nodded.

"There were brochures in both for a *Misty Falls Five-Star Luxury Retreat*. By the looks of it, we're definitely on the right track. The task force is working out a surveillance plan for the retreat tonight, and we should know more within twenty-four hours. I believe we're getting close."

Georgia looked directly at Jane.

"Something else we found when we cleared out both offices was two white feathers dipped in blood. I recall seeing them once before, on the ground in the North Head clearing."

Jane lowered her head.

"Sorry," she said quietly.

"Don't be. We'd had the phones at the cottage tapped, and it was those feathers that caused McGarry to call the chief justice," said Georgia, beaming. "Thanks to that, we now have all the evidence to link it all together."

Jane instantly felt better.

"I just wanted the bastards to suffer," she said.

"Sounds like it worked," said Amber.

They spent the afternoon at the cottage, then dropped Sister Chrissy off at the monastery and headed for home. Dave suggested pizza for dinner, and all three girls accepted with pleasure.

Over dinner, Amber talked more about the garden design, which now included pavers, a large barbecue area, a bird bath and even a wood-fired pizza oven, as well as a host of colourful plants and shrubs.

"We'll know more about them after our visit to the nursery on Thursday," said Dave. "They have bird baths with fountains as well."

They sat around the fireplace in the lounge room, feeling mellow and hopeful.

"Jane," prompted Dave, "since the day we found Trish at the canal after the fire, I've been wondering about your special ability. You correctly identified the Southern Highlands as the place where Cate is being kept, you're in touch with your sister Darlene and you have contact with the ghost of an old nun at the cottage. Do you know how you're doing all this?"

"Not really. It just happens," said Jane. "I'll see or hear something and just start talking, and sometimes they talk back. They come to me, mostly."

Dave rose to his feet and turned the lights off, leaving only the glow from the fireplace to send shadows flickering around the room.

"You told me they normally come out after dark," he said. "Is anyone here with us now?"

There was a long silence. Then, Jane suddenly looked at a point just above the fireplace.

"I can see a nice old black lady poking a stick in the fire. She has a white patch of hair above her right eye. She's singing."

"Jesus, Jane," said Amber, wide-eyed. "That sounds like Gran."

"She's asking for Karrikin Bunyip."

"Oh my God," Amber shrieked. "Gran always called me that."

Tears flowed from her eyes.

"She says to stay away from the Gubba Gubba men, and to trust the gungies. She likes your Tidda Bunji," said Jane.

Amber was taken aback.

"Those are the bad people. The gungies are the police, but she didn't like them back then. 'Tidda Bunji' means female authority, and close friend—she must mean you, Georgia. I guess you made her come around."

"She's saying that you 'Yabba Yabba'. What's that?"

Amber laughed hysterically.

"She's right. I do talk too much. Please tell her I love her."

"She can see and hear you. She's nodding."

Tears continued to fall down Amber's cheeks.

All went quiet for a while.

"She's gone now, but she's very happy," said Jane.

This time, Georgia spoke up.

"Jane, can you see Cate?"

Another long pause.

"Cate's in terrible pain. She's badly burnt, and her flesh stinks."

Now they were all in tears.

"Shit, Dave. We have to do more," said Georgia.

Dave had a lump in his throat. He just nodded.

They sat in stunned silence, watching Jane as her shoulders sagged.

"I told her we're coming," she said.

There was fire in Georgia's eyes.

"Damn right we are."

# Chapter Forty-Five

Handcrafted metal lettering adorned the beautiful wrought-iron gates: *Misty Falls Retreat*. Angled sandstone walls ran in from either side along the roadway, standing tall at over three metres high, winding through the picturesque Southern Highlands hills.

Driving along Range Road towards Mount Lindsay, guests could see enchanting forests, craggy hills and slow-moving streams leading into fields of colourful tulips through the thick, green, plastic-coated wire fence surrounding the nearly two-thousand-acre resort. What they did not see were the cameras hidden in the trees every hundred metres or so, sending images back to a sophisticated security setup inside the complex gates.

Guests who entered through the sealed, one-way driveway felt very secure as they traversed an assortment of magnificent, well-kept trees and shrubs, subtly lit for ambience at night. On the approach to the stately two-storey manor, complete with turret-style attics, it could easily be mistaken for a royal's hideaway.

The main building was a marvel of architecture that blended in with the banks of the snaking Nepean River, totally out of sight. Nestled into the tranquil rainforest, the resort was a world away from the chaos of civilisation and urban life. Adorning the walls in abundance were pictures of colourful butterflies, pretty birds, local wildlife, misty waterfalls and leafy freshwater swimming holes next to weeping willows.

Misty Falls Retreat was the perfect escape for well-heeled city executives seeking cosy fireside chats and breathtaking mountain-view sunsets. The guest list boasted many well-known Australians and overseas dignitaries.

But that was only half the story.

This week's regular five-day retreat and seminar had been hastily cancelled 'due to unforeseen circumstances'. The eighteen high-profile attendees, who'd each paid $54,000 to attend, had all been notified at the last minute, and all speakers, masseuses, personal trainers and activities had been dismissed for the week.

Eleven people sat around a crackling open fire, but the mood was anything but harmonious.

"It's too soon to panic," said the now former deputy police commissioner. "As far as we know, no one is remotely aware of our existence. Our network has gone into lockdown until we're sure it's safe to recommence operations."

He appeared to be in charge of the meeting, dressed casually in a sloppy joe and tracksuit pants.

"That's alright for you. You're divorced, with no family," said a worried Dr. Salman Bohr. "I've got a large medical practice here in Bowral, a wife, three children and nineteen staff. If I go down, what happens to them?"

Dr. Bohr was a fifty-year-old former research scientist from Tel Aviv-Yafo who'd been in practice in the Southern Highlands for over twelve years. In addition to his very successful twenty-four-hour medical clinic, he had another, very different role here at the retreat.

"At least you have something to go back to when this is over. I'm ruined. I'll never see my family again," wheezed the miserable chief justice. "My entire life's work, gone."

"Stop whingeing, Larucci. You brought that arsehole Latta into the group," said Scarface Mario Savalis. "If not for that, none of this would've happened, and we'd still be on top of the world. If we get raided here, we're all dead."

"I feel very sorry for anyone who tries to get in here," said Boris Heidrach.

Bavarian-born, fit, in his mid-fifties and suntanned, he was a grandson of one of Hitler's famous generals. He'd spent much of his life as a mercenary in many theatres of warfare worldwide, and had been happy to fight for whichever side offered the most money. He'd been headhunted for Misty Falls over seven years before, where he now ran a private army of about twenty battle-hardened compatriots under the guise of 'resort security'.

"There's nowhere in Australia as well fortified as here," he claimed.

"What happens to my people if they do come?" Carol Ford almost snarled. "I'm not going to die for you bastards."

A hardened authoritarian of around sixty, Ford was the short and stocky, grey-haired and pockmarked matron from the special medical complex in the dense forest about a mile from the main area.

"No one dies," said Heidrach. "The choppers would have us out long before an army could make it through our booby traps, mines, tripwires, dogs, guards and guns. We'd be on the high seas well before they reached the door—and by the time they did, there'd be a lot of dead troops in the raiding party."

He almost licked his lips in anticipation.

The company had a multi-million dollar, four-hundred-foot winged keel mega yacht moored in Pittwater for just such an occasion. Named *Alis Volat* after the Latin phrase *alis volat propriis*, meaning *she flies with her own wings*, the power yacht was complete with eighteen luxury apartments.

"Let's have no more talk of raids or death," said Warren Hardcastle. "We have a number of contingency plans, and we're a long way from needing any of them. At this point, we have two things to work on; keeping the studio and surgery operating as usual, and working on an exit strategy for those of us caught up in the Latta tapes. We know that Weatherall Cottage and the missing girls are on their radar, but both McGarry and O'Brien have been silenced, and there's no one else who can lead them to us. There's been no sign of trouble at the other homes but both are on high alert just in case, and street patrols are on standby."

"What about that nurse, Graham Larkin? Those two brought him with them from the Central Coast boys' home," said Savalis. "He could make things hard for us. That slimy bastard can't be trusted."

"Larkin's not a threat. He knows little of our operation, and nothing about the studio," said Hardcastle. "He's gone to ground somewhere, but Sluggo and Spud are on his tail, just in case. They'll find him, and that'll be the end of it."

"You seem to forget we have orders to fill and movies to film. I've got my people ready to go, so why the hold-up?" said Norm Salzberg, the very unpopular 'studio director'.

Orchestrator of the brutal torture, pornography and filming, all in attendance knew him to be a depraved monster—perfect for the job. Prior to Misty Falls, he'd eked out a living making Z-grade porn movies in Indonesia, where life was very cheap.

"This week's retreat has been cancelled, so you can go ahead whenever you like," said Matron Ford.

Normally, filming was not allowed when guests were in the house, since the screams were sometimes loud enough to be heard in the main building.

Dr. Bohr then asked, "Does that mean my surgery is okay to proceed? I've got two kidneys and one lung to supply urgently to our Saudi friend. I'm running low on stock. Those street patrols are needed now."

Omar Hezbah, the group's Arab negotiator, had been sitting silently at the back of the room. He spoke with a deep, guttural rasp.

"We're behind in all our orders. The girl's body has not arrived as promised, and the Emir is very unhappy."

"What? It's the first I've heard of this," said Dr. Bohr. "We dispatched it exactly as promised. It was drained, chilled and sent on its way; everything went according to plan."

The doctor was getting quite spooked. Nothing was going right.

This news was also disconcerting to Nat Larucci. He'd thought the girl's body had been dispatched a week ago, under his authority. None of the previous bodies had ever been delayed or compromised, and nor had any of the donor organs. It had always gone like clockwork. Their grisly practices had been building for years; trade was brisk, and money poured in from all over the world.

The double doors to the lounge flew open, and a security guard motioned for Boris to follow him. He did, and returned soon after.

"We may have company," he said. "We're tracking two drones approaching from the western fence. They may be armed."

Everyone in the room was tense.

The doors burst open again.

"Boris, there's an unidentified chopper coming in low down the valley."

The security chief ran out of the room.

# Chapter Forty-Six

Despite the dark rings under Commissioner Palmer's eyes betraying his lack of sleep, he was in a buoyant mood as he addressed his 'A Team' around the huge circular table at police headquarters.

"We can see the light at the end of the tunnel at last," he said. "There are still a few grey areas and unknowns, but thanks to an amazing effort from each and every one of you, we can finally get to work on busting this heinous mob wide open—and hopefully purge the force of some unwanted garbage at the same time."

The tension in the air was palpable.

"The road ahead is treacherous, and we need to be at the top of our game. For the past twenty-four hours, Alan and Dick's officers have been in the Southern Highlands with drones and a large surveillance team surrounding a nearly two-thousand-acre luxury resort known as Misty Falls. They've identified a number of buildings apart from the resort complex itself, hidden away in some dense bushland. We assume that these buildings are where they carry out their twisted operations.

"There's an elaborate security system surrounding the whole property and, no doubt, throughout every part of the resort," the commissioner continued. "Mittagong police have had three recent reports of explosions in this area, but investigations have turned up nothing. Dick thinks it's possible that wombats or kangaroos may have set off landmines on the property, so we must tread carefully and plan for the worst. We have no idea how many of those poor kids are still alive in there, but this mob knows we're onto them, and we can assume they'll do anything to try and cover their tracks."

"So, what's the plan?" asked Tina. "It sounds like they're armed to the teeth. They're not going to make it easy for us. Where do we even start?"

"We're going in tomorrow night, coordinating simultaneous raids on the other two shelters in Central Coast and Wollongong," said Palmer. "Dick has decided it'd cost too many lives to try and come through the bushland—too many deadly hidden obstacles. We'll be flying in with six choppers, each carrying military troops and landing at their three helipads and three other selected sites near the main building. Our emphasis will be on rescuing those still alive, then capturing or taking out as many of their team as possible. At the same time, a separate group of us will come through the fence near the front gates and neutralise the security complex there."

Those in the room took in the enormity of the operation, the urgency required and the guarantee of the loss of life on all sides, potentially including the young girls and boys imprisoned on the site.

"I'm splitting us into seven separate groups," said the commissioner. "The six airborne units will have ten personnel each and will be headed by myself, Max, Tina, Mike, Alan and Georgia. The ground assault will be under Dick's command. I've organised for a copy of today's full surveillance report for each group. Assignments are as follows: I will be taking on the main resort, Dick will raid the front security complex, Max, the film studio, Alan, the medical complex, Tina and Mike, the staff security compound and Georgia, the prison complex. Dick is planning a precisely timed, pre-emptive missile strike on the dog kennels, the staff and security compound, the main resort and the front security building."

This came as a surprise to everybody in the room. They'd never used missiles before.

"Each group will have five experienced army commandos under their team leader, as well as four of our own personnel. We'll all meet at noon at the Sydney Skydivers School in Wilton to run simulations on models we're constructing today. We will also have a screening of the recent drone footage so that we're all familiar with the layout. The mob themselves will be aware of our surveillance and the possibility of an imminent raid, and will be well prepared. I don't have to tell you all how dangerous this mission is, but there are some innocent youngsters imprisoned in this hellhole crying out for help, and we're their only hope. Keep that in mind as we move forward."

They spent the next half-hour discussing the logistics of the raid, the missile launch and team selections before the commissioner wrapped up the meeting.

"Tonight, I recommend you spend time with your families and those closest to you. Remind them, and yourselves, the reason why you joined the force and took the Oath. We'll synchronise watches tomorrow. Sleep well, and good luck."

Palmer knew full well that most of them wouldn't sleep. He himself was extremely nervous and would not get much rest knowing he was putting his team into such a dangerous situation.

Tina, Mike, Alison and Georgia stayed behind to go over the brief, organising sandwiches to be brought in for lunch. Once they began, Alison insisted she be put on one of the teams.

"This is what I signed up for," she said fiercely. "Give me the chance to prove I'm up to it."

"You're in," said Georgia. "I'd already set aside three to go with me. You can be the fourth."

"That's settled then," Tina agreed. "So, let's go over all these surveillance notes."

They ate as they talked.

Just before leaving, Tina put some distance between her and the others and rang Rusty Nolan. After some discussion, they agreed to meet at 5.30pm—this time at Manly Wharf, where no one would take any notice of them amongst the thousands of peak-hour workers returning home. She then jumped onto the computer and sent what she had to Rusty.

Mike also made a call, organising an unscheduled meeting of the task force for 3.30pm at Chatswood.

Tina, Mike and Georgia arrived back at Chatswood just before 2.30pm and immediately got to work marshalling their chosen team members. They chased up information on available equipment, armoury and protective clothing.

At 3.30, the team assembled and were given a full briefing. Georgia picked Alison, Bruno Campbell, Brad Henderson and Brian Carey. Mike selected Graham James, Elwyn Bell, Terry Smythe and

Charlie Wake. The latter two Parramatta detectives were keen to atone for the sins of their colleague, Joe Hudson.

Tina addressed the group. "Don't forget to expect the unexpected."

Tina felt strange knowing that Mike would not be beside her in battle, as he'd always been. She chose the bureau's top marksman, Sgt. Terry McCulloch, a big lad, but great to have in a shootout. Her second choice was Senior Sgt. Charlie Martin, the bureau's fitness instructor and a former commando. She decided she'd name the others later in the day.

Tina also decided that she was up to driving, despite what her doctors might say. She drove out of police headquarters just after 4.30, arriving at Manly Wharf early. She was already sipping a hot coffee when Rusty appeared on the wharf, having caught the fast ferry catamaran from Circular Quay twenty-five minutes earlier.

Rusty ordered a coffee, then sat with Tina.

"You've got an exciting twenty-four hours ahead of you," he said.

"I'd say it's more like a terrifying twenty-four hours," said Tina. "I'm way out of my comfort zone."

She brought Rusty up to date with everything currently on the table.

"So that's why JP has been leaving me alone," he laughed. "I was surprised to hear you're using missiles. That's some serious stuff."

"We're up against an army of combat-hardened mercenaries, so I can appreciate the need … but I'm terrified they'll use the children as hostages and we'll end up doing even more damage. I can't bear the thought of them just *dying* after all they've been through."

"Well, my news won't calm you down," said Rusty. "You're dealing with some serious shit here. I was able to run the scant images you sent me through to my contacts, and they believe they've identified the registration of the chopper that flew into the retreat yesterday. They're almost certain it was the AS532 Super Puma, owned by the kingdom of Saudi Arabia. Their info says that it's usually reserved for the sole use of the royal family, and they play for keeps. If I'm right, it was the Airbus Eurocopter registered to the Royal Saudi Navy based in Riyadh."

"What would that be doing in Australia? It's way out of area," said Tina.

"Not necessarily. Prince Omar bin Dallaz's huge mega yacht, *Alis Volat*, is out here—for the annual yearling sales, we think. It's currently moored in Pittwater. It'd make sense for this chopper to be aboard the vessel," said Rusty. "The AS532 is an amazing aircraft that can fly up to twenty thousand feet high or at ground zero level, and it's very fast across the ground, with a long range of some eight hundred kilometres. It's the best of the best."

"The surveillance team are pretty sure it arrived with a full load and left quickly with the pilot alone, which means they probably brought in reinforcements," said Tina. "The body of the missing lass from Weatherall Cottage was destined for Saudi Arabia too. This is linking well."

"Sounds like it, but be very careful. These guys make up their own rules as they go, and money is no object."

"Okay. Fingers crossed. Thanks. Now, one good turn deserves another."

Tina handed Rusty a DVD.

"This is footage of the Kings Cross strip club meeting just before the bomb went off. Your name comes up, and the news is not good."

A thought occurred to her then, and she couldn't help but voice it.

"Crazy question. Would you like to be part of the raiding party? I've got two spots left on my team. I was toying with bringing a couple of ex-commandos I know, but I think they'll be a better fit for another part of the mission."

She then told Rusty the whole story about Brad and Bert, showing her hand in full.

"Well, I've taken every risk imaginable over my lifetime, but nothing like this," he said. "To hell with it. Why not? I've got the perfect person for the other seat too, if you'll trust me with it."

"I do. Consider it done," said Tina. "You both need to be at the Sydney Skydiving School tomorrow at noon. We'll be doing exercises all afternoon and then going in after dark. We'll supply the armoury and protective clothing. I'll need both your sizes."

They talked some more, then Rusty walked back along the wharf to the ferry and Tina returned to her car.

Though she was glad to be driving, the pain was giving her grief. She phoned Brad through the car and brought him up to date. He was concerned about her safety and her physical ability to lead a team on such an operation. After some discussion, they agreed that the 4G Team would set their sights on the mega yacht and the Super Puma chopper, leaving the Misty Falls raid to the police and the commandos. Brad gave her a few tips for engaging hostiles with combat experience and they wished each other luck.

Tina then rang David at home, organising dinner and a special bottle of wine. David knew just enough to realise that something big was happening, and he was concerned.

As she drove back to Chatswood, Tina made the decision to ring Catie's former editor, Bob Millman, the next day. She'd promised Catie the night before she died that if a big story was about to break, she would alert Millman as thanks for all his support in the past.

Arriving back at Chatswood a little after 7 o'clock, Tina was not surprised to find the whole team was still there, making last-minute plans for the big day. After dealing with her own messages, she walked into the control room and delivered a similar spiel to what the commissioner had given a few hours earlier. She ordered them all to head home, knowing they'd be back very early in the morning.

Just as she was leaving her office, her secure mobile vibrated. Looking at the screen, Tina saw it was from Brad and answered the call.

Brad spoke in a low tone

"Bert and I have an idea, and we think we can make it work. Are you in?"

Tina nodded firmly to herself.

"Always."

# Chapter Forty-Seven

*Unknown Caller* shone out from the screen as the mobile buzzed. The recipient answered.

"Hello?"

"That you, Spud?" said the caller.

"Who wants to know?"

"It's me. Graham, from the cottage."

Murphy sat bolt upright and put the call on speaker, motioning for his mate to listen.

"Shit, Graham. Where've you been? With all the crap that's been going on, we've been trying to find you to see if you need anything."

He winked at Sluggo.

"Where the fuck do you think I am? I'm on the run," said Larkin. "The fuckin' coppers have been looking for me everywhere. I'm in deep shit, Spud."

"We know all about it. Our boss told us to find you," said Murphy. "He's happy to put you up until we can sort it out. Where are you?"

"Nah, I'm okay. Some mates are helping me out. All I need is some dough to get me through the next few weeks."

"No worries. I can bring some over late this arvo." He smiled at Sluggo. "Just tell us how much you need and I'll bring it over."

"That's too late," said Larkin, exasperated. "We're leaving at 1 o'clock today to head south. I need two grand before I go. Your people owe me much more than that."

"Okay. I'll fix it up with Mo and get the dollars. Where do I bring 'em to?"

"Don't tell a bloody soul, but I'm in the shed behind my gran's house at Drummoyne. There's a way into the back yard from the lane behind us. I'll tie a rag or a hanky or something on the back gate. You'll see the door to the shed from there. And for Christ's sake, don't let her see you."

"Don't worry about that. No one'll see me—not a single soul." Another wink and a smirk to Sluggo. "What's the address? I can be there around 11."

"It's just behind Birkenhead Point. She lives at 498 Renwick Street, but you can come in off Ferry Lane. It's one way coming in from Day Street, about a hundred yards on the left."

The sound of Larkin rooting around in the garage came through the phone.

"Look for the red rag," he said finally.

"You just sit tight. I'll get the dough and be there around 11."

He smiled as he ended the call and gave Stokes a high-five.

"Thank Christ for that. Mo was on the warpath. Larkin is expecting me at 11 ... but it's just gone 8, so we'll be there well before 9. I can't wait to see the look on that arsehole's face."

"Where are we gonna take the body?" said Sluggo. "We could be seen in daylight."

"We're not taking it anywhere, knucklehead. We'll use silencers and leave the body in the shed. We'll be doing his grandma a favour; he's a piece of shit. We need to wear gloves and socks over our shoes. We don't want to leave any forensic crap around. And make sure you pick up all the spent shells to take with us this time."

"Aren't you going to tell Mo?"

"Not until we've got some good news. He was pissed off with us an hour ago. This'll put a smile back on his face."

Both men put their revolvers and ammunition in their backpacks, along with everything else they needed, and went into their messy garage. Murphy opened the roller doors with his remote and they left in the Toyota just after 8.15. It wasn't far to Drummoyne.

Meanwhile, back at the witness protection safe house, Detective Inspector Brad Henderson took the unregistered phone from Larkin.

"You did well," he said.

But it did little to cheer up the nurse. He realised that if things went pear-shaped, he'd just signed his own death warrant. Brad left the room and rang Georgia, who was already in situ at Drummoyne, to give her the update.

"They wanted to come over at night, but Larkin convinced them he was leaving at 1. They promised they'd be there with two thousand in cash around 11. My guess is that you can tie the red rag to the back gate now, since I reckon they'll be there much earlier, and with guns instead of money. Good luck."

"We're ready. I'll talk to you later."

At the Drummoyne residence, there were police hidden everywhere in and around the back yard, in the neighbours' yards on either side and across the back lane, plus a couple in the house. The owners were police officers, and were happy to help out.

In the shed itself, which was nicely fitted out as a granny flat, the two Parramatta Dog Squad detectives Terry Smythe and Charlie Wake waited inside with their German shepherds, ready to go at the signal. This was what they practised for every week.

Right on 8.51, the radio came alive.

"Attention all units. This is car twenty-eight. A light-green Toyota Tarago is on the approach. Two male occupants. They're travelling east along Renwick Street. Looks like they're going to drive past the front of the house first."

"Stand by, all units," said Georgia. " No one moves until they get to the shed."

"Car twenty-eight. They're turning left into Day Street. Nearly there."

All those in hiding heard the car as it drove slowly along Ferry Lane and came to a stop at the back gate with the red rag tied to a broken panel.

Both men got out of the car with revolvers cocked, out of sight. Stokes slid back the metal gate bolt quietly, opened the gate by half and nodded the all-clear to Murphy. He motioned for him to follow over to the right side of the yard, hidden from view of the house.

Approaching the shed door, both men pulled out their revolvers and Murphy lifted his leg to kick in the door. Just then, Detective Graham James came out of a small tool shed nearby. "Stop! Police! Drop your guns and get down on the ground, now!"

Both men turned instinctively towards the loud voice. Murphy panicked and threw his gun, but Stokes lifted his at Graham James and fired. Graham threw himself sideways, firing back as he did. Police appeared from everywhere. Terry Smythe jerked open the shed door, firing at Stokes just as the dogs flew past him, latching on to both men as Stokes, hit twice, fell to the ground, dead. Murphy was petrified, standing still with his arms in the air and screaming as the police dog latched on to his leg.

"On the ground!" yelled Smythe as police came racing towards him.

Realising that Graham James had been shot by Stokes, they moved to his side and Georgia called for ambulances and backup forensics. She walked quickly over to the wounded detective who was in pain, sitting against the fence.

"You won't believe it, boss," James blurted out. "It's the same bloody hand. Same as the Riley Sampson shooting. It must have a bloody target on it."

Georgia smiled.

"You never know, Graham. One day, you might get a Purple Heart."

Realising it was almost time to leave for Wilton, she ordered her team to take Murphy to Chatswood and straight into the interview room. She told the forensic team about the green Tarago and the fact that O'Brien and McGarry's bodies had been in the boot before being dumped, asking them to check the paint against the flakes that Amber had found at the scene.

"Don't let anyone touch it until you've given it a thorough once-over," she said. "It's going to be our strongest evidence."

Georgia then went over to check that Stokes was, indeed, dead before leaving quickly to get back to headquarters. As she drove out, sirens converged from every direction. Ambulances, additional police and forensic teams arrived along with early media crews looking for a scoop.

Arriving back at Chatswood, she went straight into Mike's office to report. He'd been following the news on the police radio.

"How's Graham?" he asked immediately.

"Chirpy as a parrot. It's the same hand that got hit during the Riley Sampson rescue," she said. "I think he's more distressed about missing out on tonight's raid, though. He tells me you'll need to replace him in your team. He wasn't a happy chappy, but he'll be okay."

Georgia filled Mike in on the green car, the forensic teams, the death of Stokes and the internal procedures to be followed before heading to her own office to prepare for that night. After that, it was time for her interview with Murphy. Time was very tight. Before that, she rang Dave to report that all was well so far. The whole situation had him on edge.

After entering the interview room, Georgia read Murphy his rights.

"Rohan, we've got your footprints, DNA and tyre prints from the Mt. Ku-ring-gai Chase National Park where you dumped the bodies of O'Brien and McGarry. By the end of today, we'll have the matching green paint from the tree you hit when turning the Tarago around at the scene, as well as matching shells and bullets. We've also got clear CCTV footage of you with a limp and Stokes at Sydney Airport escorting two scientists who were murdered shortly after.

"We both know Savalis wants you dead. What happens next is up to you. If you cooperate with us, we can protect you and take it into consideration at the court. Your call."

Georgia let that sink in.

Murphy looked up, defeat showing clearly in his eyes.

"What do you want to know?"

Georgia started off gently.

"Where'd you get the limp, Spud?"

"My old man kicked me. Broke my leg in five places. Came home pissed, and I tried to protect me mum."

"How old were you?"

"About eight or nine, I reckon."

An hour later, Murphy signed a complete statement giving valuable new evidence about the other two children's shelters, the sham adoption parents, the homeless street operation, the organ-smuggling trade and more about the airport killings and their contacts on the ground, which included a senior border force informant.

Georgia went back to her office and called for the team to depart. As she was leaving, her office phone rang. She tossed up whether to answer it, and decided that she'd better. It was reception downstairs, advising that a Dr. Marie Emslie was on the phone for her. Georgia immediately recognised her as Tina's friend and oncologist and took the call.

"Georgia, this is not the way I normally do things, but Tina has spoken about you often, and I'm in a jam," said Dr. Emslie. "She's not returning my calls or messages, and I must talk to her. Can you help me?"

"I hope so. She's up to her neck in the middle of a huge operation right now, and it makes sense that it's been hard to contact her. I'm due to see her south of Sydney this afternoon and will certainly pass on your message. We may not finish until very late tonight, but I guarantee I'll have her at your surgery first thing in the morning."

Dr. Emslie was very thankful. Georgia ran from the office to join her team.

As they drove south along the Hume Highway under siren, she was in a very low mood, well aware of the challenges that Tina faced and concerned for the news that the morning would bring.

# Chapter Forty-Eight

Amber and Jane knew Dr. Holder was worried when they saw him. The four of them had spent several hours around the kitchen table the night before trying to picture the outcome of the next twenty-four hours. Georgia had told them of the plan to use Larkin to sting Murphy and Stokes early, going into detail about the operation to come.

"I can't believe you're using missiles," said Dave. "What if the cottage girls get hit?"

In truth, he was more worried about Georgia and Tina's teams going up against mercenary commandos, but he didn't want to admit that.

"The ADF is behind all that. There are more of them involved than us," said Georgia. "In addition to the missile launchers and the five of them in each chopper, they'll have around two hundred troops on top of ours hidden around the perimeter to collar any escapees."

Amber asked, for the second time, "Can I *please* go with you? I'm sure I can help. I can calm the cottage girls when you rescue them."

"I'm sorry, Amber," Georgia said firmly. "I'm sure you'd be a great help, but regulations forbid you from being involved."

"Are those the same regulations that are sending peacekeepers to fight battle-hardened troops?" said Dave. "It just doesn't make sense to me."

Nothing was going to placate Dave. He thought the whole thing was too dangerous.

Jane had been very quiet, and Georgia thought she was hiding something. On a whim, she switched the lights off so that only the faint light coming in from the street entered the room.

"Jane, is anyone here?"

Jane said nothing, looking straight ahead, nodding and shaking her head at different times. She looked as if she was in some sort of trance. The other three just watched and waited in silence.

A few minutes later, Jane blinked and looked around. She seemed surprised to find they were sitting in near darkness.

"Welcome back," Georgia said softly. "You were deep in conversation. Who were you talking to?"

She switched the light back on.

"Darlene and Cate. Darlene was sad," said Jane. "She said to tell my lady police friend to 'beware of the dogs'. I don't know what she meant, but she said it was horrible. Cate is really excited. She thinks the girls can help you. Most of them are underground, but they know how to get out if the guards are distracted. She said that the fence is electrified, but the gates aren't. Apparently they could turn the fence and the alarm systems off, since the electricity board is located inside their building. She also told me they could make a crossbow somehow, but I don't know what for."

Georgia noted all that for later.

At breakfast next morning, Dave was still tense. Georgia left just after 5am, promising to ring at various intervals. Dave and the girls drove to Camperdown, arriving at the cottage in time to be greeted by Sister Chrissy before going into morning classes.

She waved to them enthusiastically.

"Have fun today. Is Georgia not going with you?"

"No. Work commitments," Dave said offhandedly.

The others said nothing, as Dave had requested.

They met up with Roxy and Trish and began going over the revamped garden design, which now included a small rotunda behind the proposed bird bath and fountain.

Roxy was the practical one.

"How do you get water to the fountain?" she asked.

Amber pointed to an 'x' marked against the nearby fence.

"That's an existing tap. All we need to do is cut into that line with a T piece and run a small underground PVC pipe into the base of the bird bath."

"Good thinking," said Dave. "You're emulating the six 'P' principle."

"What's that?" asked Trish.

"Prior Planning Prevents Piss Poor Performance," Dave grinned.

The girls all laughed.

"Good one," Roxy clapped as they headed for the car.

Not one of the four girls had ever been to a nursery the size of Swanes at Dural. Their eyes widened as they wandered through acres of plants, flowers, trees and shrubs. The roses were spectacular, and there was a huge variety of pots and garden extras. Amber fell in love with the metal bilbies.

"We had them back in Arnhem Land, only those were live ones," she giggled.

After a delicious Devonshire tea in *Café Botanica*, Dave drove them just two kilometres along to Glenhaven, where they went through the Flower Power Garden Centre.

Jane brightened up.

"Here's an idea. We can plant half a dozen of these pine trees and have one for every Christmas, replanting just one every year."

Everyone thought that was good thinking. Amber wrote it down.

Later, they crossed the Hawkesbury River on the Berowra car ferry. This was a new experience for all the girls. They soon arrived at Australian Native Landscapes, another nursery at Terry Hills. This had Amber writing furiously. She much preferred Australian flora.

Back in the car, Dave turned left off Mona Vale Road onto McCarrs Creek Road. Amber became alarmed.

"Where are we going?" she said, obviously upset.

"It's okay," said Dave. "We're going to a very special place in Broken Bay that Georgia and I come to often. It's called Akuna Bay, and it's home to one of Australia's best marinas. Why the worry?"

"This is where Mrs. O'Brien and McGarry's bodies were dumped."

She pointed to the spot as they drove past a few minutes later. Amber was spooked at first, but calmed down not long after they passed.

Arriving at Akuna Bay, the girls were stunned. Roxy had never seen anything like it. Dave parked in General San Martin Drive car park and they walked across the bridge into the d'Albora Marina complex. Monstrous yachts and powerboats for the rich and famous were moored onto a series of floating pontoons. The girls were mesmerised, their mouths open.

"Wow. Look at that!" Roxy exclaimed.

She'd spied a huge, sleek yacht named *Spirit of the Sea* at the end of one of the floating fingers, the biggest she had ever seen.

There was a fit, middle-aged lady looking resplendent in some sort of naval uniform at the top of the gangway. Dave introduced himself and gave her the girls' brief history. She smiled and introduced herself.

"Hi, girls. I'm Mia Franks. I've lived most of my life on the water. Come aboard and I'll show you around."

Half an hour later, two things were obvious: the first was that Roxy had realised a life-long ambition by climbing aboard such a magnificent vessel, and the second was that Mia had really taken a shine to the four girls, having come to see what the visit meant to them. Dave thanked Mia profusely for her valuable time and the opportunity for the girls to see the vessel. They exchanged cards and Roxy was amazed to find that Mia was actually the yacht's skipper, having thought that only men held such ranks.

The girls were excited as they ate lunch in *The Shed* café, then watched all the fish swimming under and around the boats and piers. Dave was in a more relaxed mood, having received a call from Georgia while they were on the *Spirit of the Sea* informing him of the successful outcome at Drummoyne.

"Akuna is an aboriginal word meaning *flowing water*," Dave told the girls as they strolled back to the car park.

"I'll never forget this day, ever," said Roxy.

The others nodded in agreement.

"Neither will I," said Dave. "My wife has completely forgotten that it's my birthday."

'Happy birthday, Doc!" the girls chorused.

All five of them were on a high as they drove into Weatherall Cottage car park in the mid-afternoon.

Sister Chrissy soon joined them in the common room, delighted to see the girls so excited by what they'd seen. They were talking over each other, all wanting to be the first to tell her what they'd experienced.

"These designs look like they might rival the Botanical Gardens," Sister Chrissy laughed. "But that aside, I've got some news. Father Shepherd told me earlier today that we're having a welcome-back party next Saturday evening here at the cottage. The board, our patrons and a few friends are being invited, and I was hoping that Jane and Amber could come for the night to join the others—particularly as both yourself and Georgia will be here. They're even bringing our piano back from the storage shed. It'll be a grand occasion."

"Not a problem," said Dave. "That sounds great. We've had a top day. Lots of ideas for the garden, and we now know that Roxy is destined for the high seas."

Dave said his goodbyes and walked out with Jane and Amber while Roxy raved to Sister Chrissy about the sleek yacht and Mia, the female skipper.

"I'll need to go back to the clinic to check in and finish these reports," he said. "You two can both have a look around the shops at the galleria level on the mezzanine floor. I won't be too long. After that, we can all go home and await a call from my wife."

Dave was about to leave his office as the phone rang. The receptionist advised him that Dr. B wanted to see him in the boardroom, and he made his way over.

As he walked in, Dave could see a couple with a well-dressed young lad, around eighteen or nineteen, sitting with Dr. Brinsmead.

"Hi, Dave. Perfect timing. I'm glad you came back," said the doctor. "I'd like to introduce you to Trent Jacobson and his mum and dad, Mavis and Leon. They've been referred to me by my good friend Professor Howard, Dean of NSW University. I'll let Trent here explain."

"Thanks," said the young man. "I'm in my third year of an engineering degree at uni and I'm on the Campus Arts Council. I saw some poems in this month's uni newsletter written by a Roxanne Jenkins, and Professor Howard told me it was you who submitted them."

"That's right. Roxanne is a patient of mine. She's very talented," said Dave. "I was hoping to get her work into the public arena somehow. I'm very pleased you like it, but what it is that brings you out here?"

There was a light in Trent's eye that Dave was sure he'd seen before.

"Roxy's my sister."

# Chapter Forty-Nine

A convoy of military trucks and equipment travelled south out of Sydney, arriving at the Wilton Skydiving Centre just before noon. They made for an impressive sight. Eight truckloads of special service troops, armoured personnel carriers, mobile rocket launchers and even a specialist mobile radar unit joined the six troop-carrying helicopters already on the ground.

Large marquees had been hurriedly erected over the past twenty-four hours. They were set up as catering centres and meeting areas for the separate roles. The convoy was directed to a spot near the 'temporary city' and began disgorging troops and equipment. Locals had been told it was a normal military exercise. They were used to such things on the parachute range.

Major General Damien Kennedy had arrived an hour earlier to work with the police. Kennedy had made a reputation for himself in Papua New Guinea as a tough fighter with a brilliant tactical mind. He was the perfect match for Dick Sellis, and was looking forward to what would probably be his last major combat experience, as he was retiring the following month to fulfil his long-held dream of a life in outback Queensland.

Together with those two, Commissioner Palmer, Tina and Alan McDonald made up the five people in the makeshift briefing room. The commissioner had been surprised to learn that Rusty Nolan would be in Tina's assault team. Dick was at the whiteboard showing off the plan, and Major General Kennedy was impressed with the attention to detail.

Mike, Max and their teams had arrived from Sydney just before noon and met up with Alan and the Canberra AFP crew, who'd driven in a few minutes earlier.

Georgia had phoned in to advise they were running some fifteen minutes late, but would be there before the planned briefing.

Right on 12.30, some four hundred men and women in all sorts of camouflage uniforms from across the defence and police forces crammed into the largest marquee on the site, some spilling out of the sides, having to stand under the shade of the tied-back canvas flaps erected over the open end.

There was a raised stage with nine people seated at the long table. It resembled a major corporate shareholders' annual general meeting. John Palmer moved to the lectern and whiteboard, calling for quiet. Everyone was attentive. This was new territory for some of them, and together with the more experienced troops, they were keen to listen to the briefing.

"Good afternoon all. I am John Palmer, Commissioner of the New South Wales Police Force, and I welcome you all to this very special mission. Tonight, together, we are hoping to rescue many young girls and boys who have been hidden away, imprisoned in the Southern Highlands. Many of them are already injured and suffering, trapped in the dark world of the illegal organ trade and brutal torture and sex pornography. We are their only hope, and between us, we can give some of them their lives back and put a permanent end to this massive, worldwide operation of death and mutilation.

"At exactly the same time as we move in tonight, there will be raids and arrests happening concurrently all over Australia and the rest of the world. This is an enormous operation, and we are the spearhead."

The commissioner then introduced all the team leaders at the top table, including Brigadier Grant Millar, the Kiwi electronics wiz who would be heading the missile strike. Dick Sellis and Major General Kennedy then used the whiteboard and went through a precise timing, entry and exit strategy, including various routes and operational procedures, the location of the command post and backup options in the event that some things didn't go according to plan.

All listened intently, and many took notes. They then watched a screening of drone footage of the area.

Finally, the commissioner returned to the lectern.

"I just want to wish everyone Godspeed and good luck. After lunch, we'll break into our designated groups and carry out our simulated exercises. Hopefully, everyone will get a break before we head south in smaller groups to our agreed positions," he said. "First out will be those on perimeter patrol duties, followed by the missile launchers and finally, Superintendent Sellis and his team. We're planning to be in place on the ground just after sunset. Helicopter teams will be leaving from here at 1924 hours and flying directly to the site, as we don't want an obvious build-up of personnel in the immediate vicinity.

"We need complete radio silence until the distraction flares go up and you get the command to move, which will come at precisely 1945 hours, as the missiles strike. Remember, we have two main objectives; the first is to rescue those in captivity, particularly the children, and the second is to put an end to these heinous atrocities. Where possible, take prisoners alive, but under no circumstances put your own lives at risk. Shoot to kill. Good luck to everyone. What we do here today will make the world a far safer place."

During lunch, Mike confided in Georgia that Tina was not coping well. She was noticeably tired, appeared to be in pain and was not up to her normal performance levels. Georgia told Mike about Dr. Emslie's call. They both agreed not to bring it up with her until the operation was over, but to make sure she got to the San Hospital Specialist Suites first thing the next day.

It was a hectic afternoon for all the separate groups. Makeshift buildings resembling the various Misty Falls complexes and main resort building had been hastily constructed, and practice raids were carried out from the planned chopper landing areas, or in Dick's team's case, from the bush opposite the security fence. Dick knew they had to be well out of the way until after the missile strike.

Georgia and Tina's teams worked together, as the staff and guards' complex was adjacent to the prison-style compound. Georgia briefed Tina on the new information they'd received from Larkin, watching her very carefully all the while, trying to pick up on any signs of a problem. A strong coffee, however, seemed to have picked her up, and she appeared to be ready for action.

The nine leaders met at 1630 hours to go over their final notes. They all shook hands, with a hug here and there, splitting up in time to farewell the first of the troop trucks leaving with the perimeter patrol defence force and police.

Tina, Mike, Max and Georgia then spent time going over last-minute details with their defence force team members. Tina was very impressed with Rusty's companion, whom she'd immediately recognised as well-known rugby league international Mitch Fowler, a forward nicknamed 'The Enforcer'. They shared many funny stories on the way south from Sydney, and Tina was convinced he was a great choice.

With all the trucks, missiles and ground troops gone, others began dismantling the makeshift buildings as the light began to fade with the sunset. The chopper teams ate a small meal before packing all their equipment and moving towards their aircraft. At precisely 1924 hours, the choppers all rose as one off the ground and began their flight south.

Phase one was officially underway.

# Chapter Fifty

E arlier that day, around 1.30am, leaving only half an hour before their scheduled departure time, Bert Hunter was worried. He, Brad and Bernardo had worked through the day and into the night making last-minute adjustments and cleaning and reassembling the rocket launchers. However much caution they took, he knew that when working with highly explosive limpet mines, it was very dangerous to be half-asleep. Unfortunately, they were out of time and had little choice but to use them as they were.

For the past three weeks, they'd spent many nights doing their 'after-hours' work at the 4G Factory on the Gold Coast, preparing to meet the huge Panama-registered tanker, *Atlantic Voyager*, in the middle of its voyage from the Port of Santa Marta in Colombia. Instead of its usual payload of oil, it carried a huge, concealed load of over four hundred million dollars' worth of drugs.

Three nights ago, those plans had changed.

The morning after Tina's briefing on the impending raid in the Southern Highlands, Brad and Bert had taken the first flight to Sydney to survey the area around Church Point and Scotland Island. Bert had returned late afternoon to modify the mines and their detonation mechanisms. There was a big difference between the hull of a massive tanker and that of a billionaire's super-toy, and they needed to get it right.

The news that the yacht's sleek Super Puma AS532 Eurocopter had flown in and out of the Southern Highlands retreat that afternoon threw another spanner in the works. In order to address the threat, Brad returned on the last flight to retrieve the rocket launchers they'd used on a previous mission.

"It looks like that will be their escape plan; chopper to the yacht, then sail for international waters," Brad said. "The *Alis Volat* apparently has some sort of diplomatic immunity, as it's owned by the royal family in Saudi Arabia. Tina feels the authorities will have no jurisdiction over the vessel and will be powerless to stop or search it. If that's the case, we may be the only ones who can stop the yacht, and possibly the chopper as well."

At that, Bernardo looked rather grim.

"How long have we got?" he asked.

"The raid is on Friday night. We need to be in Sydney by midday to set up. It's tight."

Bert scoffed.

"Shit, Brad. That's impossible. The odds are heavily stacked against us."

"You said the same thing that night in Panwa Village, but we pulled that off, didn't we?"

Bert shrugged his shoulders before shaking his head and walking back into the factory to get Bernardo to help him with the rocket launchers. They'd worked through the entire next day, careful not to let the other staff see what they were up to.

Around 10.30 that night, a taxi pulled up outside the 4G complex. A lone figure got out, paid the cabbie and walked up the path to the front door.

David Samuels was greeted by Brad with a bear hug and together, they walked inside. David knew he'd be a mess if he stayed waiting for news of Tina, so he offered to drive the boys down to Sydney so they could sleep on the way. He'd spent the day chartering a houseboat and chasing the diving equipment Brad had requested.

The drive south to Sydney was uneventful, aside from a stop at Port Macquarie for fuel and food as the sun rose. David drove without rest while the three boys recovered their strength. Brad then took over the wheel near Hexham and drove the rest of the way to the marina at Church Point, arriving just in time for lunch.

Bert and Bernardo drove into Mona Vale, and later Warringah Mall at Brookvale, to secure last-minute supplies and audio equipment. They returned in the late afternoon to find that Brad and David had loaded everything into the chartered houseboat. They'd also put up all the hydrogen-filled balloons, bunting and coloured lights in preparation for what looked like a great party on the water.

Bert was still laughing.

"You should've seen the look on the bloke's face at the adult shop when Bernardo bought eight blow-up dolls, including two males," he cackled. "Told him he was bisexual. The idiots' eyes were wide open."

They all chuckled as they checked everything before leaving the wharf just before sunset.

By the time the golden sun had disappeared over Church Point, the boys had blown up all the dolls and tied them to the cabin roof and the deck, allowing for a metre or so of movement. As darkness fell, David cranked the music up while Brad, Bernardo and Bert went about reassembling the rocket launcher on the back deck upstairs. Once it was operational, they covered it with canvas and tied it down just to be safe.

Brad and Bert then climbed into their wetsuits as the party boat, all noise and flashing disco lights, approached the huge mega yacht *Alis Volat* moored in the quiet waters in the lee of Scotland Island.

The lookouts on the bridge of the mega yacht frowned as the noisy bunch of drunks cruised in their direction. They mumbled between themselves and watched the men and women in the dimly-lit cabin cruiser moving to the music blasting out across the water, disturbing their night.

They didn't see Brad and Bert, their wetsuits, their self-propelled underwater vehicles or the large, bulky backpacks over their shoulders. Both divers had heavy weight belts on as they slid silently off the port side of the party boat and slipped under the dark harbour waters. Thirty minutes later, they checked their compass and some six hundred metres south, the two divers were hauled back on board unseen.

As the houseboat proceeded slowly east towards Lion Island and the open seas, Brad smiled at the others and gave them the thumbs up.

# Chapter Fifty-One

M isty Falls Retreat was far from emulating its brochure's promise of *quiet luxury relaxation and cosy open fireplace chats*. The resort had been in a state of turmoil since the sleek helicopter arrived two days before, bringing new instructions from its owners along with nine well-trained troops under the command of the infamous Major Abdullah al Bidawar. The battle-hardened explosives expert was a brute of a man with shifty eyes. Also on board the chopper had been Sheik Rahul bin Lafifa, carrying orders from The Chief.

Boris Heidrach, head of the retreat's security force, was not impressed with the attitude of the recent arrivals and had already clashed with the major on a few issues.

Sheik bin Lafifa had spent the first day in meetings with Hardcastle, Savalis and the medical complex team. Discussions became quite heated.

Warren Hardcastle pointed out that there was no need to panic, as he was in the position to know that forty-eight hours before, the authorities had no idea their organisation existed, or its location. By his assertions, it would take weeks if not months of surveillance to gain enough usable evidence before the authorities took any action. He told the sheik that there'd been no movement of any kind since the drones had been seen two days before, and therefore there was nothing to alarm any outside observers. He speculated that the local council had been active in the area since the last report of an explosion on the retreat acreage two weeks before, which had been caused by a feral pig setting off a landmine.

The sheik was not convinced. His orders came direct from Prince bin Dallaz and they were straightforward: he wanted no witnesses and a lot more organs, and considered this their opportunity to achieve both.

Carole Ford and Dr. Bohl had been very unsettled by the directive to euthanise, dissect and embalm all thirty-one people currently in the compound, including the young stars of their movies, within the two weeks requested. It had been made very clear that they had no option; they were to commence the operation within forty-eight hours and should expect more people for the operating table. Filmmaker Norm Salzberg had been distraught when ordered to dismantle all his equipment, sets and props for collection by the end of the following week, but he too knew better than to show dissent.

At the end of that day, everyone was told to report back the next day with the plans needed to meet the targets and deadlines they'd been given. Boris Heidrach was instructed to work with the major and his men to fortify the front entrance, driveways and the two other access gates and internal roads.

"We want to ensure we can repel any attacks and have time to evacuate if necessary," the sheik informed him. "Just in case."

Dinner was a sombre affair, the various groups sitting apart, discussing their own personal challenges and concerns about the new orders.

Later that evening, Hardcastle, Larucci, Savalis and Hudson sat together in Larucci's unit discussing their futures and making a plan to negotiate their immediate relocation overseas. Unbeknownst to them, their meeting was being filmed and recorded directly into the studio set up in Omar Hezbah's suite and fed back to the mega yacht in real time.

At around the same time, Sheik bin Lafifa, Hezbah and the major were finalising their own agenda.

The next day, the various groups met with the sheik to submit their plans. He'd ordered minimal movement in the open until they were sure there'd be no more drone activity. None had been sighted or recorded since late the previous morning.

Hardcastle and his cohort were not impressed with this meeting. The sheik offered no concrete plan to evacuate them in the short term, or to organise passage to Majorca for their promised relocation to Palma. They'd been guaranteed beachside apartments on the Balearic Islands in Spain's holiday mecca, but there was no evidence of a plan to follow through.

"We need to get all the equipment, organs and cadavers away first," said the sheik. "You'll be needed here to help us clear all the offices and pack everything we have to take. When all of that is satisfactorily underway, the four of you and I will be evacuated. That may take up to a week."

The group was not happy, and it showed.

The sheik spent that afternoon at the medical complex running through plans and schedules. A stressed Dr. Bohr was preparing for major surgeries to begin first thing the next day, and Matron Ford had prepared the mortuary and cold storage fridges for the influx. The first transport vehicle was set to arrive the following Monday, and a full list of organs and cadavers had been prepared. They'd had difficulty securing ongoing transport without Larucci or Judge Latta in place to approve the documentation. As a short-term solution, they therefore planned an illegal aerial operation from Goulburn. They'd need to be extra careful because of the resort's proximity to Canberra.

When the next day dawned, things were anything but normal. Away from the resort, in the secure compound, it was now the third day without filming or captives being taken to the hospital wing. Even the guards were uneasy, and many of those imprisoned wandered aimlessly around the yard. There was much more activity than normal around the resort so they too knew that something was different. The guards who'd come onto the afternoon shift the day before had seen the new troops and equipment being marshalled, and rightly assumed that defences were being fortified. None of them knew what for, and this made them especially uncomfortable.

Inside the dormitories, Cate and her fellow inmates were busy. They'd spent the morning quietly retrieving bits and pieces they'd hidden around the complex during their stay, using them to construct a mean-looking, heavy-duty metal crossbow out of strong piano forte wire and steel mesh. Amongst their hidden arsenal were five underwater spear gun harpoons they'd stolen from the film props room long before. Norm Salzberg had not been brave enough to report them missing. He knew full well the penalty for such insolence, so he'd quietly had them replaced and resolved to keep them under lock and key in future.

When Cate had told her trusted friends she'd received a 'message' saying that help was on the way, they'd been very sceptical, thinking she might be losing it. Seeing all the unusual goings-on over the past two days, however, they began to believe that something might be happening and allowed themselves to become hopeful.

Two of the girls stood guard at the windows but no patrols came near them, and most of the other inmates were locked away. Dinner the previous night and today's breakfast and lunch consisted of thawed sandwiches, and not enough for each of them. They were certain that something was amiss.

Cate told all her close associates to meet downstairs near the underground cells as soon as it was dark. She instructed a young orphan named Ben Dawson, who'd only been there a few months and was recovering from a kidney removal and other injuries, how to dismantle the electric fence and alarms when the time came, giving him the makeshift key they'd made. A few of the braver kids had used this several times over the past six months, including Cate, who'd broken out after dark to steal food and other items from the film studio and medical wing.

Just before sunset, Carole Ford delivered a list of names to the compound security room.

"I want these eight brought to the hospital for harvesting by 6 tomorrow morning," she ordered. "Make sure none of them eat anything beforehand."

As she left, the two guards on duty scowled. The matron was not a popular person in this part of the complex.

There, in the middle of the list she'd given them, was Cate's name.

Major al Bidawah sauntered into Boris Heidrach's office just after 6.

"Ah, Abdullah. How did the installations go?" Heidrach sneered.

"Your men are not accustomed to hard work, but that didn't stop us from finishing the driveway and both the side gates," said the major. "We start at dawn tomorrow and should be finished before dark." Then he ordered, "I'll need men to transport four unconscious people from the resort to the hospital at 8pm precisely."

"And who would those people be?" Heidrach enquired suspiciously.

"Ask no questions," said al Bidawah, striding out of the room.

Over at the resort, Carole Ford and the doctor complained to both Hardcastle and the sheik about the proposed workload and their shortage of staff.

"There must be no witnesses," the sheik reiterated. "By any means necessary. You will just have to cope."

There were no smiles when the four of them left to join the others at dinner as darkness enveloped the resort.

After the customary pre-dinner drinks, all twelve of the 'executives' sat at the dining table and were immediately served a delicious potato and leek soup—perfect for the cool temperatures of the Southern Highlands in spring.

More wines were poured and then finally, the new regime seemed settled. The conversations began more positively than they had the previous two evenings.

Staff cleared away the soup dishes, and some—but not all—of the diners were surprised to see four of their colleagues showing signs of distress. The sheik, the major and Omar Hezbah took little notice as Warren Hardcastle, Nat Larucci, Scarface 'Mo' Savalis and Joe Hudson began to lose consciousness.

Hardcastle and Hudson fell to the floor, while Larucci slid sideways on his seat, appearing as if he'd fallen asleep. Similarly, Savalis' head gradually came to rest on the polished wooden table.

Both Matron Ford and the doctor knew the four of them were on the list for the next day, along with the eight from the compound. They also knew to keep quiet about it.

The sheik then ordered Boris Heidrach and Salzberg to assist the staff in placing the unconscious men onto nearby lounge chairs, laughing as he insisted that someone take a photo of the four of them.

"They'll be picked up soon," he told the others, raising his glass with a smirk. "A toast, to disappearing imbeciles."

The rest of them drank nervously.

Just as the sheik's glass landed on the table, a loud crack came from outside and the darkness surrounding the resort turned a deep red.

It was precisely 7.45pm.

# Chapter Fifty-Two

Residents of the quiet Southern Highlands were oblivious to what was about to unfold. As the last of the sun's rays filtered through the tall, straight pine trees, two large military M270 Multiple Launch Rocket System vehicles slowly made their way along Bong Bong Road to their firing location, each carrying a crew of three.

Upon arrival in the bushland just past the Highlands school on the approach to Old South Road, Brigadier Grant Millar directed the proceedings. The two rigs, nearly three metres wide and almost the same height, were armed to fire off two Patriot-style PAC-3 missiles within twenty seconds of each other. After they'd fired, the plan was to leave the site immediately and proceed to assist with the perimeter surveillance along George Emery Lane, near one of two rear gates on the western side.

After the final setup and calibration of the target settings, they waited in silence in total darkness. They occasionally heard other vehicles passing, presumably to take up their positions around the perimeter fence, being careful to avoid any cameras.

On the other side of Misty Falls, Dick Sellis and his team were also at a school—the Glenquarry Public School on Tourist Road.

The teachers and pupils were long gone, replaced by police and troops unloading in the dark, readying themselves to make their way through the bush and take up their positions on Range Road opposite the retreat's main gates. They had two extra crews of three operating M252 mortars and were cleared to use them immediately after the missile strike. Inspector Sellis prayed that the missiles did not stray, but kept his thoughts to himself. Even fifty metres off line would be a disaster for him and his troops.

Light rain began to fall as they made their way quickly and quietly through the dense bushland towards their setup locations. Four of the troops carried heavy-duty wire and boltcutters, ready for action.

Meanwhile, on the troop-carrying helicopters, the aerial teams donned their bulletproof jackets and advanced combat helmets. This was the first time that any of the police crew had ever used the enhanced night vision (ENV) goggles for other than training exercises.

The ENV goggles were PSQ20s and though heavy and uncomfortable, their sensors allowed them to see in the dark and rapidly detect and engage targets. They also permitted the use of existing rifle-mounted aiming lights.

In addition, each commando carried six F1 hand grenades manufactured by Thales Australia. The ninety-six-millimetre, hand-thrown, high-explosive grenades weighed nearly half a kilo, and were attached securely to their webbing belts. Each had over four thousand tiny metal balls inside the casing, lethal within a six-metre range. They were ideal for clearing the enemy from inside buildings or behind solid objects. Their time-delay fuses could be set between four and a half and five and half seconds, which could make all the difference in situations like this.

Tina was edgy. There were so many unknowns; so many things that could go wrong. So many people depending on them. The knot in her stomach was rock solid.

"Two minutes to target," came the voice of the chopper's skipper, Captain Ron Seymour. All those on board collectively took a deep breath and did last-minute checks of their equipment.

Tina looked at Rusty, who was a picture of total concentration.

"Still glad you volunteered?" she yelled above the noise of the chopper.

"Seemed like a good idea at the time," Rusty grinned.

Tina laughed.

"One minute to target."

Looking out the front windscreen, all was dark—until a few seconds later, when things instantly took a dramatic turn.

Those on board the choppers had front-row seats to four red flares exploding in the black sky above Misty Falls Retreat, reflecting an eerie, blood-coloured glow from the low, dark clouds.

Those looking out the left side of the chopper could see two lines of orange tracers as the first two PAC-3 missiles streaked across the treetops with their deadly payloads. Seconds later, the whole sky seemed to erupt as the missiles struck—one a direct hit on the main gate security complex, the other smashing into the staff and guards' compound buildings.

A mass of debris, some burning, was thrown hundreds of feet into the night sky before stalling and starting to fall back to earth just as the second wave of missiles came in. The first struck the northern side of the main resort building, and the second landed at the southern end of the guards' compound, closer to the dog kennels this time.

The scene below looked like total chaos from the choppers as they flew through the dust and smoke towards their six chosen landing spots.

Dick Sellis galvanised into action, signalling for the mortar attack to begin as the rest of the troops raced across the road to cut holes in the fence. Once inside, they fanned out to surround what was left of the guard house. Two armed men brandishing pistols ran from the building, and both were swiftly brought down by the commandos.

Another explosion, this one unexpected, caused Dick's men to dive for cover. It seemed to come from somewhere near the resort, where the line of six choppers had come through the smoke. They were a menacing sight as they sped in low, tearing towards their landing zones. Commissioner Palmer was in the lead chopper, which landed heavily on the resort helipad. Major General Kennedy and his defence commandos hit the ground immediately, racing towards the bombed building.

A heat-seeking surface-to-air missile fired from somewhere in the bush behind them, whistling through the air and making a direct hit on the third chopper, a Black Hawk S-70 that had been heading for the film studio under the command of Superintendent Max Logan. The stricken aircraft veered left as if in slow motion, smashing sideways into the walls of the film complex and coming to rest against the building before bursting into flames, causing an instant fireball to rush upwards into the night sky. The troops who survived the blast could be seen running through the flames, half of them alight.

The other four helicopters, a mixture of the Black Hawk S-70s and CH-47F Chinooks, all made it safely to the ground.

Tina and Mike landed simultaneously adjacent to the main guards' complex and staff accommodation, and the sight that greeted them as they dismounted from the choppers at speed was one of total chaos. There were men and women on fire, some running in circles, others trying to put them out. Many staff were screaming in surrender, wanting nothing to do with the battle going on. Guards could be seen running, some into the bush and some back into the building, most of them armed and in various stages of dress.

Gunfire erupted from inside the damaged building. Someone fired a Browning M2 .50-calibre air-cooled machine-gun from the guard station at the northern end of the complex, causing everyone to race for cover.

Charlie Martin, the Chatswood HQ fitness instructor and one of the special service commandos, immediately broke cover and raced past a burning staff member, diving in behind a Besser block garden wall and crawling forward on their bellies. Martin raised his head a fraction and quickly drew fire from the machine-gunner. A few metres ahead, the commando saw where the tracer was coming from and hurled a grenade up and through the window. A split second later, an explosion and a scream filled the air, and the machine-gun went silent.

At the same time, one of the retreat guards armed with a .50-calibre M107 long range sniper rifle fired through a curtain slit from an upstairs balcony window, pinning down most of the troops. Using his ENV goggles, Marksman Terry McCulloch took careful aim with his Beretta M9 pistol and fired, landing a direct hit. The guard's rifle barrel suddenly pointed skywards and stayed there, unmoving.

This allowed the others to fan out and enter the building at both ends. As the troops moved forward throwing grenades into darkened rooms, there were two more explosions in quick succession. About half a dozen staff, too terrified to move, were screaming out from the kitchen, but a few of the security forces were still holed up and trying to make a fight of it. One giant of a man burst out of a cupboard brandishing a bayonet and ran straight at Tina, who was standing just a couple of metres away and facing in the wrong direction.

As she turned, too late to save herself, Mitch Fowler threw himself sideways and made the perfect crash-tackle into her. Just as Tina recovered, she kicked the guard's arm with such force that the bayonet smashed against the wall, falling to the ground. Rusty Nolan jumped on the man's back and in a matter of moments, they soon had cuffs on him.

"One move and you're dead!" Rusty shouted.

The man stayed very still.

Tina looked straight at Mitch.

"I owe you," she said simply.

Mitch grinned and gave her the thumbs up.

Somewhere close by, they heard the sound of ferocious dogs barking.

In the adjacent secure accommodation building, several of the young prisoners had moved very quickly the moment they heard the first missile explosions. Three of them were ready when the duty guard panicked and ran down the corridor towards the inmates' cells, failing to see the tripwire laid out across the hall. The man speared forward along the floor, losing his pistol as he hit the ground hard. The three youngsters jumped on his back and quickly bound his hands and feet as he struggled in vain to break free.

As they trussed the guard up, Cate, Ben and five of the young prisoners raced past them, Cate picking up the guard's pistol as she went. Ben ran straight to the locked cabinet, opening it and disarming both the fence and the alarms before throwing the main power switch just as Cate had instructed. He soon rejoined the others, who raced upstairs to set up the crossbow. They watched as Georgia's Chinook chopper emerged from the smoke and landed just outside the fence.

Guards began to emerge from everywhere. Two of them, guns in hand, branched off and began running up the stairs to where some of the children were imprisoned, not knowing that Cate and her friends had already taken out the patrol guard and were waiting.

As they reached the landing, their eyes opened wide as they caught sight of the gruesome crossbow's main frame. The lead guard didn't even hear the hissing as the steel harpoon shot from the prod and went right through his body, the barb showing on the other side. He felt nothing as he fell lifelessly backwards, his pistol falling onto the metal stairs.

The second guard continued his approach, and Cate pointed her pistol, closed her eyes and pulled the trigger. The bullet struck the guard in the shoulder, causing him to scream in pain. His accomplice's falling body knocked him sideways off the stairway and onto the quadrangle below, where he regained his feet and began crawling towards the gate.

After leaving the chopper, Brian Carey saw a jeep parked with the keys in the ignition.

"I'll get the gates!" he yelled, jumping into the jeep and firing up the engine before driving straight for them at speed.

There was a wrenching sound as the hinges gave way, causing the gates to burst from atop their mounts. The vehicle screeched to a halt, but not before careening into the guard that Cate had wounded.

Georgia, Alison, Brad Henderson and two of the commandos ran through the gates and headed towards Cate and the others, who they'd seen watching from the landing upstairs. Georgia yelled at them to take cover inside as Bruno Campbell and three commandos entered the right side of the downstairs corridor, firing at the guards still occupying the passageways.

Georgia was halfway up the stairs when Ben Dawson shouted and pointed at the upstairs balcony. Cate and her friends followed his line of sight and saw the guard taking aim at Georgia with a sniper rifle. Cate screamed a warning as the crossbow arched for the second time and, thankfully, struck the guard's chest just as he was pulling the trigger.

The bullet missed Georgia by just a few centimetres, ricocheting noisily off the metal railing as she stumbled against it.

Over at the main resort, John Palmer and General Kennedy realised that some of those inside the building had escaped. It looked as though they'd gone into the bush through the back door, which had been blown off in the explosion.

In reality, Abdullah al Bidawar and Sheik Lafifa had followed Boris Heidrach into a secret tunnel located behind the large library bookcase in the main lounge. The instant the first missile struck,

Heidrach had yelled at them to follow him into the lounge, where he'd pressed the hidden button to open the secret door. He'd closed it again as soon as the other two were in the tunnel, then activated the battery-run lighting system. They'd bent low as they ran down along the dimly-lit tunnel towards the camouflaged exit.

Omar Hezbah ran straight into his communications suite and began screaming down the line what little information he had about the attack—the missiles, flares, choppers and chaos—before begging for their immediate evacuation by helicopter as planned. He was advised they were on their way.

Hezbah grabbed his pistol and ran back to advise the sheik and the others that help was on the way—but instead, he ran headlong into the attackers. The last thing he saw was the flashes from the barrels of two commandos' rifles.

Meanwhile, John Palmer and Major General Kennedy had discovered the four unconscious men in the dining room. The commissioner recognised the four immediately, but their current condition was a complete mystery. They'd sustained no visible injuries from the missile explosion, which had hit three rooms away, and a quick check revealed no bullet wounds or other injuries. All four men still had a pulse. John Palmer instructed his men to handcuff and guard them while they cleared the building, then called for medical assistance.

As the strike team entered the damaged kitchen, they found the petrified staff still in the area. Two of them had been injured by flying debris. One of them had sustained a severe head wound and was covered in blood and moaning in a fetal position on the floor. The rest of the staff had their eyes wide open and their hands so high they almost touched the ceiling. Ordered to get on the floor, they obeyed instantly.

At the film studio, Norm Salzberg was rudderless. He, Carole Ford and Dr. Bohl had raced out the back door and circled around towards the medical complex in search of shelter. Hearing the gunfire, explosions and barking dogs, they saw Alan McDonald and the federal police frogmarching the remaining medical staff into the front yard, yelling at them to lie down.

Realising there was no hope, the three of them turned and ran together towards the film studio. Though it was well alight, there was no signs of police or combat troops—just the remains of a burnt-out helicopter. They found four of the staff cowering in what was left of the foyer and protected by two guards. Salzberg yelled for them to follow and all nine raced into the undergrowth, wading across Diggers Creek along a well-worn pathway towards the back gate on the western end of the property. Salzberg and the matron knew there were no landmines on the paths themselves, and that they were free to run without fear.

As they approached the gate through the dense bush, Salzberg motioned for silence. They crept towards the fence in the dark. Using the matron's master key, they unlocked the gate, silently slid the bolt and slipped quietly through, listening to the sounds of battle and chaos behind them.

Suddenly, the whole area lit up, the headlights from the two missile launchers and three other vehicles burning into their eyes.

Brigadier Millar yelled at them to drop on their knees, but instead, both the guards raised their pistols. Unaware of the nearby troops, neither of them had the chance to fire a round and they fell, mortally wounded. The others were quickly on their knees as troops appeared from the undergrowth.

The brigadier then saw a camera flash go off just behind the missile carrier.

"Bloody media!" he shouted. "Jim, Jeff, get rid of them. This is a restricted area! How in the hell did they get here so fast?"

Bob Millman's large team had been in town. They'd eaten early, not knowing what to expect but certain it'd be big. They'd sprinted to the scene as soon the explosions started. A barricade on Range Road had barred their path, so they systematically went down each of the side roads until they came across the escape attempt at the back gate and began filming.

Back at the prison compound, cries of joy rang out as the raiding party confirmed that all who were being kept in the holding cells had survived the raid. Having removed keys from the dead and captured guards, police were opening the cells one by one, instructing them to stay inside until the area was secured and declared safe.

Recovered from her tumble, Georgia realised that the kid with the crossbow had saved her life.

"Which one of you is Cate?" she asked.

Cate stepped forward.

"I am," she said, dropping the pistol.

Georgia recognised her from the photos, and went straight up to her.

"Jane told me to give you a big hug."

She did, and tears rolled down both of their faces.

Brad Henderson came up the stairs.

"We've cleared both blocks," he said. "A handful got away, but not many. We've unlocked all the cells. Most look okay, but some are unwell. There's still action at the guards' compound next door, so we'd better keep everyone inside until things settle."

Georgia turned on her radio. She heard Dick Sellis reporting that one of his team was injured, and that they had a number of dead and injured guards. Commissioner Palmer called in for medical assistance for four unconscious men, plus a number of injured staff and security guards. He, too, reported a number of deaths, but also that some of the ringleaders had managed to escape. Major General Kennedy then called in to report the downing of the third chopper and the unknown fate of Superintendent Max Logan and his team. Commissioner Palmer and the others were shattered; they'd all heard the explosion as the missile hit the chopper, but were unaware of the catastrophe that had followed.

Tina was only a hundred metres from Georgia but she couldn't see her through the chaos. She reported that they'd cleared the entire staff compound, though there were casualties on both sides. She advised that very few had escaped, and that she needed urgent medical help in the area.

With the situation deemed secure enough for the evacuation of those injured, Superintendent Dick Sellis then authorised the implementation of Code Blue, which had been set up with local authorities. It wasn't long before the Southern Highlands were full of sirens, ambulances, fire brigade, police and emergency services.

The sheik, the major and Heidrach had all escaped through the secret tunnel, which exited through a camouflaged opening be-hind the dog kennels. The three men and two of the dog handlers had spent the previous five minutes trying to settle some of the vicious Belgian Malinoises that had gone berserk during the raid. There was an evil glint in the eye of Major Abdullah al Bidawar as he and one of the handlers strapped the explosive vests on two of the dogs.

Heidrach got reports from his men that things were quietening down in the guards' complex and prison compound areas, and that the police and troops seemed to be congregating in two groups about a hundred and fifty metres from the kennels. He also noted that the film studio was ablaze from end to end.

"Well, this will give them something to really cry about," sneered the major as he grabbed his rifle and moved towards the side door of the kennels. One of the handlers and the major each had a shepherd strapped with explosives, on leashes and pulling hard. Heidrach followed them outside with the wireless detonation device and handed it to Bidawar.

The sheik looked on nervously. He was aware that a rescue helicopter was on its way, but that meant little if they couldn't take out the bulk of these troops and ensure that the chopper could get in and out safely.

Over by the broken compound gates, Tina and Mike began walking towards Georgia and her team, who were on their way out.

Suddenly, Alison Hanagan let out a desperate warning cry. Two dogs were racing silently towards them—one towards Rusty and the two teams, the other towards where Georgia and her troops were emerging. As Bidawar and Heidrach came out of the bushes, firing semi-automatic rifles and causing everyone to run for cover, Georgia and Tina simultaneously recalled Jane's warning: *beware of the dogs.*

Tina saw one of the dogs heading directly towards Rusty, Mitch, Mike and all those standing together. She tried to alert them and deliberately ran towards the dog, hoping to intercept it. The dog saw the gun in Tina's hand and immediately changed course, prioritising the armed enemy as it had been trained. The dog almost upon her, she aimed her pistol right between its eyes just as Bidawar pressed the detonator.

There was a massive blast as the dog's vest exploded, killing Tina instantly.

Bidawar looked for the second detonator button as the dog approached Georgia, who also had her gun drawn. Just as the dog bore down upon her and her team, a shot came from the secret tunnel opening behind Bidawar.

Commissioner Palmer's bullet killed Bidawar instantly, as Georgia and Terry McCulloch simultaneously fired at the dog, each shot making its mark.

Bidawar lay dead on the ground, the second detonator fallen from his hands. Heidrach ran to retrieve the dropped detonator, but Damien Kennedy emerged from the tunnel shortly after Palmer, firing a shot that killed him mid-stride.

Georgia screamed and ran towards Tina. Rusty and Mike, who'd realised that Tina had saved their lives, both picked themselves up, covered in blood, and ran towards Tina's lifeless body.

They were too late. Dr. Emslie would not have to bear the burden of breaking the bad news to Tina at the hospital the next day, and David was now a widower.

# Chapter Fifty-Three

L ights came on all over the *Alis Volat*, its crew moving efficiently from bow to stern, quietly preparing for an unexpected departure. All had been calm aboard the vessel until just before 8pm, when the radio officer had reported the urgent distress call from Misty Falls and the request for immediate evacuation. Per the captain's instructions, the Super Puma Eurocopter would be dispatched without delay.

Captain Farah al Darugh interrupted Prince Omar's dinner party to deliver the news. The prince begrudgingly left the dining room to join him out on the deck, where the captain informed him of the raid and the distress call. The prince's body language, silhouetted against the ship's dimmed lighting, showed his displeasure.

"Imbeciles! Let them rot in hell. Forget the evacuation. Prepare for immediate departure," he said. "We need to get to international waters as soon as possible. Lower the tender and get my guests back to the marina. Those fools can join us at sea if they make it that far."

Prince Omar bin Dallaz rejoined his guests, the chairman of the NSW Office of Racing, the deputy premier of NSW and their spouses. He apologised, claiming he'd received word that his ailing father had taken a turn for the worse, and so he must return to the kingdom at once. The guests understood and were soon on board the luxury speedboat, making their way back to Church Point Marina.

The prince ordered the captain of his private jet at Sydney Airport to make preparations for departure in two hours, and for the Puma AS532 to be made ready to deliver him there in ninety minutes. The staff on board immediately sprang into action to organise flight plans, customs and immigration clearances and the normal bureaucratic requirements, as well as the usual bulk luggage challenges.

As the main anchors were stowed noiselessly and the bow pointed towards Barrenjoey Lighthouse, the *Alis Volat* cruised silently and slowly north-east across the calm, sheltered waters of Pittwater. The lights around Lovett Bay and Morning Bay reflected off the surface, looking like something out of a fairy tale as Lion Island eventually came into view ahead.

On the bridge, the captain and three crew members were carefully navigating a safe passage towards the Tasman Sea. As the lights of Palm Beach and Whale Beach appeared on the starboard side, the yacht's tender caught up with the vessel, where it was quickly winched on board and lashed to the back deck.

Inside the main cabin, the prince and his entourage were glued to the television news channels, watching unfold the story of a major police and defence force operation in the prestigious Southern Highlands. There were reports of an apparent missile strike, the downing of an army helicopter, heavy casualties and gunfire. Amongst all the doom and gloom, there were also reports of a major rescue of imprisoned missing persons, including young boys and girls. Even in the absence of many details, the media was billing the event as the largest of its kind in Australia's crime-fighting history, with many unanswered questions and conspiracy theories still surrounding the circumstances.

Unaware of all this, the captain and bridge crew altered course to starboard, concentrating only on getting the floating palace safely around the Barrenjoey Headland. They took no notice of the many houseboats and pleasure craft moored off Shark Point, just past the main Palm Beach ferry terminal.

Had they looked more closely, they might have noticed the party boat that had been cruising noisily around their mooring an hour before, now completely bereft of balloons, bunting, coloured lights or revellers.

As the massive mega yacht turned seaward, the unadorned houseboat quietly moved through the other moored craft in the dark, causing a small bow wave to brush against the other vessels, rocking them gently. With minimal navigation lights, they began to follow in the wake of the *Alis Volat*, using binoculars to monitor any activity on board.

Brad was at the wheel of the houseboat, while Bert and Bernardo had moved up to the top deck to ready the missile launchers. David, manning the binoculars, alerted Brad to movement on the yacht's back deck around the chopper. Brad called Bert on the two-way, and they all watched the lights come on around the helipad and people moving towards it.

Soon after, the rotor blades began winding up as the pilot went through his pre-flight checks.

Brad veered slightly to port, moving away from the yacht's wake in the direction of the deeper waters around Lion Island. David moved astern to loosen the ropes securing the small dinghy and, as Brad cut the motors, he carefully manoeuvred the rubber craft into the water alongside the houseboat and attached it with ropes.

Brad grabbed the wireless detonator and sprinted up the ladder to join Bert and Bernardo. Timing had to be perfect for their plan to succeed.

"You know, boys, these blokes think they're untouchable with their diplomatic immunity and bureaucratic protections," said Brad. "They think they can do what they like, when they like and how they like, without repercussions. Well, tonight, they've met their match; people who are prepared to take them on at their own game. Let's be thankful for all our commando training. This one is for the likes of Catie Lanyon, Nick the Greek, Derek, Garry and the many other good people taken out by these arseholes."

Not another word was said as they waited in silence for the chopper to get airborne. After what seemed like an eternity, they heard increased revs from the motor and saw the blades beginning to rotate more quickly until the chopper began to lift off from the helipad, gracefully turning away from the mega yacht and into the night sky.

Bert was starting to sweat, his fingers tightly on the trigger mechanism. He switched on the location beam, aimed at the aircraft, heard the 'ping' and saw the red light come on.

"We're locked on target," he whispered to the others.

"Fire when ready," commanded Brad.

Bert felt the launcher kick hard as the heat-seeking missile snaked over the water, twisting and turning as it flew towards the yacht, then arcing upwards to follow the chopper.

Brad was ready. He pressed both detonator buttons at once, and they all heard and felt the dull thumps and whoosh of the limpet mines exploding. The water rose on both sides of the vessel a split second before the missile struck the helicopter about five hundred metres ahead of them.

David saw none of this. Below deck, as soon as he heard the first explosion, he reversed the bilge pumps and opened both the bilge plugs, watching the salt water gush into the houseboat.

Brad and the boys quickly joined him at the stern, stowing a few bags onto the rubber dinghy and pushing off in the dark. When they were about fifty metres away, they heard a final, very small explosion, just enough to successfully complete the scuttle of the houseboat, which quickly sank below the surface with all its equipment.

Only then did the four of them look back at the mega yacht, which had come to a complete stop in the yawning mouth of Pittwater and was beginning to list slightly to port. There was no sign of the helicopter from their vantage point, but they could imagine the debris floating in the Tasman Sea.

A few minutes later, the rubber dinghy was back amongst the hundreds of pleasure craft moored at Palm Beach.

No one took any notice, as many of those living on the moored vessels were putting out to sea to try to help those on the stricken yacht. No one knew what was happening or why, but as smoke began pouring from the yacht, they all assumed the worst.

There was also activity on land. Sirens wailed and lights flashed everywhere along Barrenjoey Road as the first responders approached in numbers.

The four boys waded ashore, lifting their rubber dinghy and carrying it to their four-wheel drive, quickly loading the rest of their gear and tying it down. They waited inside their vehicle until a number of ambulances, fire trucks and police vehicles came to a stop near the jetty about half a kilometre north, then quietly drove out as men and women ran around the marina in all directions.

As they drove south towards the city, Brad turned on the radio. They were immediately beset by news about the Southern Highlands operation, but reports about the yacht and the chopper in Pittwater were notably absent.

They were soon aware that there had been casualties down south, and all became very concerned. David began wringing his hands nervously as they turned towards his home in Epping, hoping to get a full report of their success when Tina and her team returned home later that evening.

David then rang Dave Holder and asked him to turn on the TV to the news channels.

The raid was the only story.

# Chapter Fifty-Four

D r. Holder was in the process of discovering that no number of university textbooks, graduations with honours or years of successful psychology practice were enough to prepare him for the crisis he'd been living for the past twenty-four hours.

After a wonderful day with the cottage girls at the nurseries and Akuna Bay, Dave, Jane and Amber had bought pizzas and headed home to wait for news from Georgia. Their last contact had been about the successful sting at Drummoyne around lunchtime.

After dinner, Dave produced a pack of UNO cards. Both of the girls groaned, but smiled all the same.

Jane won the first game.

"You can see what cards I'm holding, can't you?" accused Amber, aware of Jane's supernatural capabilities.

"No way," Jane laughed. "I'm just smarter than you two."

They were on their third game when Dave's phone buzzed. It was a call from David Samuels, telling him to turn on the TV news channels to see the coverage of the police raid. He was on his way home, and sounded very concerned.

An hour later, every one of them was filled with dread. The news was mind-blowing. There was talk of missile explosions, helicopter

crashes, fires, gunfire and worse. The whole area had been barri-
caded off for public safety. Dave rang David Samuels back to find
he was home alone and not coping well.

They talked for some time, trying to make sense of the unfolding
story.

It was just after 10.30pm when Dave's phone buzzed again,
and he saw Georgia's name on the screen. He quickly took the
call and the two girls watched as the blood drained from his face.
Georgia related the whole saga between sobs and obvious trauma,
promising to be home as soon as she could. She asked Dave not to
tell David Samuels yet, as the commissioner was on his way to the
unit to deliver the news in person.

Jane then called Dave into the lounge to witness the news of a
sinking mega yacht and the downing of a chopper in Pittwater.

"My God," he said. "Is this ever going to end?"

Nearly an hour later, Dave received a call from David Samuels.
He hesitated before answering; lying had never come easy to Dave.
He ended up taking the call, hoping his voice didn't give him away
when he told David he hadn't heard from Georgia, promising to
call him back as soon as he did.

By now, David was well and truly fearing the worst.

Amber and Jane stayed up with Dave, trying to distract him
from his thoughts and cheer him up.

Well after midnight, after spending two hours at the station
finalising reports with her surviving colleagues, Georgia returned
to the household. She'd managed to hold it together up until now,
but the moment she saw Dave and the girls, she could contain
herself no longer. Dave put his arms around her and squeezed tight
as she sobbed uncontrollably.

The four of them sat in the lounge while Georgia told them what had happened, and how Jane's prediction had come to a horrible reality.

"We saved every single person in that prison compound, and we're very lucky we didn't lose a lot more of our people," said Georgia. "That place was far better armed than we'd imagined. Landmines, machine-guns, electric fences, dogs, booby-traps ... they were ready, and they weren't going down without a fight."

She told them how Cate and her friends had constructed a crossbow and disarmed the fence and alarms.

"Cate saved my life," she said. "I gave her a big hug from you, as promised. She's in Mittagong Hospital but she should be okay to come home tomorrow—or later today, should I say."

They all agreed it was now safe for the two girls to go back to the cottage the next day, and Dave promised to sort out Cate's transport needs in the morning.

"Sister Chrissy will need all the help she can get for Saturday night's party. I've still got a couple of surprises up my sleeve." Dave smiled. "Can we assume there'll be others returning from Misty Falls?" he asked Georgia.

"There were five girls being sent back as I left the station. They've all given their initial statements and are free to go," said Georgia. "I gave them an update on the recent changes and they were all delighted, happy to be going back under the new management. I rang Sister Chrissy to find that she'd gone into the cottage as soon as the news broke, having worked out what was happening."

Georgia realised she needed a long, hot shower and a sleep before going back to work in a few hours. She wanted to be there well before the scheduled 10am task force debrief. She was worried about the commissioner, who'd had to give the sad news to David Samuels. Mike Broadfinger had also said that he'd go over there first thing in the morning before coming to Chatswood.

The fact that they'd successfully saved all thirty-one of those imprisoned, as well as broken up two major international crime rings, had not fully sunk in for Georgia. She'd been too caught up thinking about Tina, Max Logan and the others who'd been killed and injured to appreciate the outcome.

Over at Weatherall Cottage, everyone was still awake. Like the rest of the nation, they'd all been watching the unfolding news, not knowing that their former residents and friends were in the thick of the action until Sister Chrissy had arrived and brought them all up to date.

From then on, they'd been glued to the TV. When Georgia had informed Sister Chrissy that they'd managed to rescue all thirty-one prisoners alive, she'd been ecstatic and started to shed tears of joy—but these soon turned to ones of sorrow when she learned the fate of Tina and the others.

Georgia had advised her they'd be bringing some of the girls home later that night, and the cottage soon became a hive of activity. Some prepared rooms, beds and storage while others cooked fresh scones, pikelets and cakes for the welcome home.

Two police vehicles drove in just after midnight, and the five girls received a right royal welcome. Senior Constable Alison Hanagan, who'd accompanied them, briefed Sister Chrissy about the remaining girls. Cate and Barbara were still in hospital and the three others remained under observation. Alison stayed on for an hour, listening to the youngsters tell their stories and the horrors of their life in the prison. By the time she left, she was tired beyond belief, but happy she'd stayed.

Around 2.30am, Sister Chrissy went into her office and shut the door.

She sat down, picked up her bible, closed her eyes and began to pray.

# Chapter Fifty-Five

The mood in the task force command room at Chatswood Police HQ was desolate. A devastated Inspector Mike Broadfinger and the other surviving members of the rescue effort waited for the commissioner to finish his press conference downstairs. They could hear the ruckus from there. Mike had just come in, having spent the morning with David Samuels, trying to make sense of Tina's death and offer some solace. David had not slept a wink since the commissioner had knocked on his door at 1am to deliver the awful news.

The commissioner himself was wiped out. His face was a waxy grey, his eyes red and retreating into their sockets. The media conference was a dogfight from the start. He'd decided it was best to withhold the information about the involvement of corrupt police, including that of his senior deputy commissioner and the chief justice, until things settled down.

He'd first briefed the media on the good news that all thirty-one of the boys, girls and homeless imprisoned in the Southern Highlands had been rescued safely, though some had been sent to hospital for observation. He'd also advised them that one of the world's most horrendous and brutal pornography and paedophile rings had been dismantled from the top down, as well as the major organ and body smuggling trade that had been running in tandem.

The media were thirsty for more specific information, and the commissioner promised more details as they became available. He thanked the defence force and everyone involved in the operation for their tremendous contributions.

When quizzed on the sinking of the mega yacht and the downing of the helicopter, Commissioner Palmer told them it was far too early to connect these events to the operation in the Southern Highlands. When put on the spot as to whether one of those killed on the helicopter was a member of the Saudi Royal Family, he deflected again, saying there was not enough information and they were unable to release further details of the investigation at this time. In this, he was telling the absolute truth; his team were totally in the dark as to who'd conducted the Pittwater operation. They were certain the two cases were linked, but there'd certainly been no police or defence force involvement in the Sydney operation.

Upon being questioned on the number of casualties across both of these events, the commissioner was again very evasive, admitting there'd been deaths and injuries on both sides in the Southern Highlands operation, but reiterating that the Sydney investigation was not far enough along to comment. The media bayed for more answers, seeking to confirm or deny the conspiracy theories surrounding the events, shouting questions from all over the pack. The chaos continued to mount until the commissioner reached his boiling point, throwing his hands in the air and walking away from the podium. Flashes went off all around the room, but he had more important matters to attend to.

A few minutes later, it was a different commissioner who walked into the task force command centre and stood at the fore.

"Yesterday, we lost some of the best men and women this proud force has ever produced," he said to a hushed room. "Superintendent Samuels didn't know it, but she was about to be appointed deputy commissioner next Wednesday. Her heroic actions saved the lives of a number of you in this room, though it ultimately cost her her own. Superintendent Max Logan was not just a long-time friend of mine, but one of the most respected officers in the history of the force."

He looked around the room and saw the haunted looks on the faces of those involved. Georgia was in tears. She'd phoned Dr. Emslie earlier and learned that even before the operation, Tina wasn't long for this world, but it didn't make her feel any better.

"The world works in mysterious ways," the doctor had said.

Commissioner Palmer then gave a full list of fatalities, including the helicopter pilot, two defence force commandos and their own Detective Brett Sawyer who, along with Superintendent Logan, had all perished in the chopper crash. A number of others on board had been injured, three critically. He advised that a further three police and five defence force personnel had been injured around the compounds and subsequently hospitalised, but all were stable. This included Detective Graham James, who'd been shot in the Drummoyne drama earlier in the day.

"One thing still has us puzzled," said Palmer. "Hardcastle, Savalis, Hudson and Larucci were all found unconscious in the main resort area. We haven't been able to interview them as yet, but I'm told that three of them have regained consciousness. All four are under guard in Mittagong Hospital. I've increased security there, as I suspect that others within our ranks will be very worried about what they have to say.

"So far, we know of at least twenty-one casualties on the opposing side, including three of their key executives and sixteen armed security personnel. Two were killed by a crossbow fashioned by the young prisoners; three were neutralised at the perimeter when attempting to escape; three more in a shootout at the front security complex; one of the dog handlers; two snipers; and a machine-gunner. The rest were killed in the missile strikes on the guards' compound, the prison area and the main building.

"There were many others injured, and thirty-five captured at various points. These include the head doctor, the matron, the filmmaker and the prince's right-hand man, Sheik Lafifa. At this stage, there are still some names unaccounted for, but these may be explained by explosions heard throughout the bush, as landmines and traps were known to be present throughout the complex. We'll be doing a thorough clearing and search of the whole area over the coming days.

"I would now like to congratulate Inspector Broadfinger, his task force and Inspector Dick Sellis for an incredible result in such a short time," Palmer continued. "There were many leads, crimes and flashpoints to follow up—it was a huge operation, certainly the largest I've ever been involved in. Your attention to detail, ability to source and follow leads with punishing deadlines and see all of it through to a satisfactory conclusion will be written into textbooks for others to follow in years to come. Make no mistake, the tragic losses we've incurred would've been far greater without your brilliance. As sad as we're all feeling, the world is now a much better place thanks to your efforts and professionalism. Thirty-one people have been rescued from almost certain death or mutilation.

"By far the biggest mystery of the day is the sinking of Prince Omar's mega yacht, *Alis Volat,* and the downing of his Puma Eurocopter. From what we can determine, everyone aboard the chopper was killed, including the prince himself. We're awaiting a police diver's report from the scene for confirmation, but either way, the incident has caused diplomatic turmoil, and our political masters demand answers immediately. Unfortunately, that means there'll be no rest for us until we come up with some. Inspector Broadfinger will be setting up a new squad today, and the first briefing will be in this room at 3pm. I fully realise you are sleep deprived and in need of some downtime to process events of the past twenty-four hours—likely even some counselling—but our hands are tied. We have no option but to soldier on.

"I'd also like to add to that. As some of you know, I've been concerned for some time that a vigilante anti-corruption organisation has been at work behind the scenes. We have very little information on them, but I'm hopeful that between us, we can solve this issue quickly."

Realising that he was near collapse himself, the commissioner closed the meeting quickly to allow everyone time to regroup.

The commissioner was sitting with Mike in his office a few minutes later and Mike decided to weigh in.

"With respect, Sir, unless you get some downtime, you may well be more of a hindrance than a help to the rest of us."

"Jesus, Mike. What else can I do? We're all in the same boat. I can't just up and leave."

"Commissioner, I'm sure I speak for everyone when I say we feel and share your pain," said Mike. "But as our leader, we need you alert and clear-headed at the helm. Forgive my bluntness, Sir, but you look like shit."

John Palmer needed to make a quick decision; either to come out fighting and put Mike in his place, or accept the advice.

He slumped down in his chair.

"Get me a car," he said. "I'll go home, have a hot bath and a few hours' kip. I need you to hold the fort for a few hours. I'll be back here just after 6pm."

"Consider it done. I'll set up the new task force, call for urgent reports and have everyone reconvene at 11am tomorrow. All I need is your imprimatur before that meeting."

"Whatever you do will have my blessing, Mike. I'm well aware of your personal loss with Tina, and can't thank you enough for keeping on. Many others would've thrown in the towel."

"Believe you me, I gave that a lot of consideration at David's this morning," he said, "but we owe it to Tina to finish the job."

Mike's eyes showed the pain he was going through.

Just as he was leaving, the commissioner's phone beeped. He checked the screen. A simple message from Rusty Nolan:

*We need to talk.*

Having been through so much with Rusty over the years, he knew to take this seriously. He texted back.

*Dinner, 8pm at the club.*

He pressed the send button as he walked out, shoulders down, looking every bit his age as he made his way to the lifts.

Mike immediately sent for Georgia, who appeared in seconds.

"How are you holding up, kiddo?" said Mike as she sat down.

"I'm on autopilot and feeling very flat," she said, "but so is everyone else, I suppose."

"Any news from the cottage?"

"Yep. I haven't had the time to go myself, but Dave has been there all day. Five of the girls from Misty Falls are back already. Apparently, Sister Chrissy was like a mother hen, organising flowers, presents and extra people to set them all up. Cate is still in Mittagong Hospital, but reports suggest she'll be discharged later today. Dave is organising to pick her up. If there's one good thing to come out of this whole sorry mess, it's Weatherall Cottage."

"What's next for them?" Mike asked.

"Dave tells me they're still going ahead with their party this Saturday night, but it's now more of a 'welcome back' affair. Tina would've been so proud of what we've done. All those kids just need a start in life, someone to believe in them."

Her lips started to tremble at that thought, but she composed herself, breathing deeply, and added, "Have you heard about the other two shelters?"

Mike chuckled.

"Spud Murphy sang like a bird after Drummoyne yesterday. Long Bay gaol are putting up the 'no vacancy' sign. So far, there are nine people in remand on various charges, including accessory to murder. There are still two more persons of interest on the run, but the lads are confident we'll soon have them all. In the interim, we've put Murphy into witness protection. The so-called 'street mission' vans have been impounded and forensics are giving them the once-over. We just need more hands. There's so much to do. The commissioner is out on his feet. He's gone home for a hot bath and a nana nap and will be back at 6. I'm going to ask for more troops but I'm not confident of an affirmative result."

Mike frowned, as if he were wrestling with a dilemma.

"Georgia, can I ask you something out of left field? At Tina's home this morning, David was understandably distraught, but something he said struck me as odd. He insinuated that there were two Tinas, and both were trying to make the world a better place. I felt he wanted to open up and tell me something, but that he never quite got there. Can you make any sense of that?"

Georgia thought long and hard about how to respond. She knew her boss was good through and through, but she'd also had a few nagging thoughts. She reached into her briefcase and pulled out that day's *Daily Telegraph*, showing Mike the page two editorial under the heading, 'Two Fearless Crime Fighters'. What followed was a brilliantly written, full-page tribute by editor Bob Millman about two of the country's greatest achievers in exposing organised crime and corruption who'd both paid the ultimate price. It was written about former Walkley Award-winning journalist Catie Lanyon and her friend, Superintendent Tina Samuels.

"This was obviously written before yesterday's raid," said Georgia. "How could that be?"

# Chapter Fifty-Six

It was just after sunset as the police commissioner drove out from under Chatswood Police HQ. He was feeling fresher, even after only a five-hour break, and was very happy with the job that Mike Broadfinger had done pulling together the new task force and delegating the various roles in his absence. He'd given his full support to the extra responsibilities Mike had given to Alison Hanagan, who'd proved her worth on many occasions and was more than deserving of the accolades.

John Palmer watched the moon rise over Sydney's magnificent harbour and reflected on the fact that he'd now been a widower for over five years, since Dorothy had succumbed to cancer. He'd thought of asking Alison out to dinner on several occasions but decided against it, thinking it could compromise both of their roles.

Arriving at Eastern Suburbs Leagues Club, he went straight to the lift and up to Rusty Nolan's office and knocked. He was surprised at Rusty's demeanour as he opened the door. The usual sparkle and ready grin was gone, replaced by an almost angry scowl. This was not like his long-time friend.

"You look washed out. Are you okay?" he asked Rusty as he sat down.

"John, we go back a long way, but this week was a real turning point. I should be dead. That bloody dog was heading straight for me until Tina called out. She should be here right now, and I can't stop thinking about it."

"Rusty, Tina wouldn't have had it any other way. She knew exactly what she was doing, and it doesn't surprise me one bit. She was one in a million. One of the best."

"Yeah. That's what we need to talk about, John. I haven't slept for two days and I've decided to do a 'tell-all', which is not my usual style."

For the first time, an impish grin appeared on his face.

"There are many things I haven't told you," he said. "Call it self-preservation."

This was no surprise to the commissioner. Rusty's questionable associations and the information it afforded him had been a huge asset to his career over the years, and had made Sydney a much safer place. Still, he could imagine the risks that Rusty would have taken to make that happen, and had accepted that he'd always know more than he let on.

"Just hear me out," he said. "I'll answer any questions you have after I've told you the full story. I reckon even you won't see this coming."

Rusty then went on to explain how he and Tina had begun working more closely about nine months before when she'd approached him for some confidential assistance.

"Because of the information I gave her and the events that followed, I put two and two together and worked out that Tina was working with others to tackle those arseholes who fancied themselves above the law, mainly because they were being protected by crooked pollies or cops."

He told the commissioner that not long before the raid, Tina had opened up about how her cancer diagnosis had brought her back into contact with journalist Catie Lanyon, two ex-commandos, the Colombian, Bernardo, and others whose time was limited in one way or another. All of them had decided to band together with whatever time they had left and take out some of the untouchables.

"That's what happened to your crooked cop Jim Hegarty and that scumbag, Joe Iminez. Others, too. In many cases, I was the one who supplied her with the intel necessary to take them out. Most recently, I worked with her on Judge Jim Latta and the Kings Cross bombing. All of the intelligence on Misty Falls came from Latta's computer, which her team got to first, and an informant of mine helped get into the system. This week, they took out the mega yacht and downed the prince's helicopter all on their own. They've been very busy, and very successful. There are a lot fewer evil mongrels out there today thanks to their efforts."

John Palmer was gobsmacked. In his mind, Tina was the last person in the world who'd break the law, no matter how good the reason. He could feel his jaw sagging, but said nothing.

"John, I want you to look at the recording of the Kings Cross meeting that Tina's team took before they sent it sky-high."

Rusty turned his computer screen to face Palmer and pressed play.

The commissioner watched and listened, in awe of the names and details being discussed. He blanched when Rusty's name came up under the suggestion that he was the commissioner's 'puppet', and at the $100,000 contract offered for taking him out.

"Tina gave me these two weeks ago, and I've been on edge ever since. These bastards play for keeps, John. I've got to make some major changes if I'm gonna survive. Thanks to Tina, I've got a fighting chance. You can keep the DVD and this photo that the mob have of Tina's team at the Cross. All I ask is that you take into consideration all the good they've done. Without them, you wouldn't have had any of your recent successes on the world stage."

Rusty was well aware that John Palmer was as straight a person as you could find, and that he wouldn't ordinarily turn a blind eye to this information—it just wasn't in his nature.

The two men later went downstairs to the club's restaurant, *Olive and Oak*. Rusty had booked a table at the far end, enabling him to have his back to the wall with a good view of the front entrance.

The men ordered drinks amid a handful of other late diners.

"Scotch, on the rocks," said the commissioner. "Make it a double."

Rusty ordered a schooner.

After scrutinising the menu, Rusty went for a big boss chicken schnitzel burger. Palmer ordered the smoked salmon and avocado salad.

The two men talked in hushed tones over their meal. Rusty continued to impart information about Tina's team's role in uncovering the vital links between Weatherall Cottage, the organ-smuggling operation and the paedophile ring.

"I know it goes against your ethics, but you have to face reality," said Nolan. "Without Tina's team, you'd have had none of those amazing breaks over the past year."

John Palmer was deep in thought. He wondered who else was involved, and was very uncomfortable with the thought that other good people might be caught in the crossfire if he exposed the information that Rusty had just given him. In all his years on the force, he'd never imagined he'd be faced with such a difficult dilemma.

Suddenly, Rusty's face froze. Two men barged into the restaurant and he immediately recognised them: Cisco Polanski, Morabito's top hit man since Wipeout's demise, and Karl Zebberman, 'Killer Karl'. Both men pulled pistols from inside their jackets, pushing over a waiter as they advanced. Focused solely on Rusty, they didn't notice two nearby diners, Rusty's 'minders', rising from their seats with pistols in hand.

Rusty threw himself across John Palmer as the thugs' guns erupted a split second before the minders', taking both of the killers out. People screamed as Rusty's men walked away from the mayhem and into the foyer, others running about everywhere.

The commissioner had felt the bullets thump into Rusty's flying body as he'd knocked him from his seat. By the time he pushed his way back up, both the killers were lying dead on the floor, and he saw the backs of two men disappearing out the front door.

He looked down at the lifeless body of the friend who'd just saved his life, tears streaking down his face.

# Chapter Fifty-Seven

With only thirty-three hours to go before the big 'welcome back' party, Sister Chrissy was not impressed to see three Channel 7 TV vehicles pulling into the cottage car park at 9am on a Friday. Considering Weatherall Cottage's relationship to the Misty Falls raid, she'd expected something like this eventually, but she didn't need it right now. It showed on her face as she strode out to confront them.

She was stopped in her tracks by the cheerful voice of Dr. Holder, greeting her as he came up the stairs with a tall, fit and pleasant lady.

"Morning, Sister Chrissy," he said, beaming. "This is Johanna Griggs from *Better Homes and Gardens* and her colleagues Adam, Graham, Charlie and Ed. Between Channel 7, our team and Tina's good friends the Peterson's, Amber's magical garden and landscaping design will be fully up and running before our big night tomorrow, with water flowing from the fountains and a special cook-up for the party."

Sister Chrissy was totally unprepared for this generosity but she soon brightened as she recognised the famous TV family. She welcomed everyone, invited them inside and went looking for the four girls involved in the project.

Within an hour, the whole yard and gardens were a hive of activity. "Fast Ed" Halmagyi charmed all the girls in the kitchen as he set about organising the catering for the team and preparing some special treats for the party. The girls happily played up to the TV cameras, which were following the progress inside and out.

Charlie Albone, himself a multi-award-winning designer, was very impressed with Amber's plans and attention to detail.

"It made our quantity surveying and ordering an easy task," he told her.

Amber was very pleased with herself and happy to be involved in the labouring alongside Roxy, Trish and Graham Ross in the garden areas.

At first break, Johanna and Ed took Jane aside for a chat. Dave had told them of her knowledge about the Manly and North Head National Park areas and the story of her survival.

Ed asked her if she knew of Bear Cottage Children's Hospice.

"I saw it from the old St. Patrick's Monastery grounds on Darley Road," she said.

"I spend a lot of time there," he said. "It's another very special cottage, just as this one is. I'd love to show you the place one day."

He explained how Bear Cottage operated and how successful it'd been. Jane relished any excuse to be back on the headland. She told them about Brokenfoot, the ageing, long-nosed bandicoot.

"Would he come out if we were there?" asked Johanna.

"As long as I'm with you, yeah."

"Let's do it. It'd make for some great footage."

Ed noted that it was Bear Cottage's twenty-first birthday in March, and that he was planning a trip there the next day to discuss the catering. They organised to pick Jane up at 8am.

"Can Amber come?" she asked.

"If she can tear herself away from the garden project, sure."

By lunchtime, the gardens were already taking shape. All the formwork was set, the watering system and fountain pipes were in situ and the fountain was ready to be set into a concrete base. All the materials were ready for the rotunda, and the turf had been ordered for

3pm. A number of teams worked busily outside, moving with practised efficiency.

Inside the cottage, Sister Chrissy and her staff gladly accepted the extra hands for putting up the party decorations, the small mobile stage, and the sound system and lighting they'd arranged for the day. They manoeuvred the old piano nearby, finally free from the storage shed.

Late that afternoon, Dave returned and sat with Sister Chrissy in her office. He told her of Georgia's struggle and the attempt on the commissioner's life the previous night.

"I don't think any of them imagined what a sick world we live in when they signed on," he lamented. "Georgia is still hoping to be here tomorrow, at least. She was delighted to hear about the garden project and can't wait to see it, but she's heavily involved organising Tina's funeral, and it'll be hard for her to step away. It's looking like it'll be on Tuesday at North Sydney Crematorium."

"This whole macabre situation is playing on the minds of all involved," said the nun. "Look at the damage done to Jane. She's held onto those horrid fears for such a long time, and not without reason. Young Cate is so pleased to be back here, yet you can see she is still terrified. You'll have your work cut out with a number of our girls for quite a while yet.

"In brighter news, I've invited that lovely Johanna and her team along for tomorrow. They really seem to be enjoying this. I can't wait to see the look on Father John's face when he arrives. I haven't told him the good news yet, so it'll be a complete surprise."

"I've also taken the liberty of inviting *Spirit of the Sea*'s captain along with its owner, Ross Ardblaster," Dave said. "Apparently, Ross recently sold off his printing empire and he's keen to use the proceeds to help kids like Roxy. They were so good to us on Wednesday. There may be three others too, if that's okay."

"That won't be a problem. That TV chef, Ed, has been cooking way too much food. It'll be a feast to remember," she laughed. "What a character."

The two of them went outside to talk to Johanna and the project team who, by now, had laid all the turf and were already tidying up.

"We're almost done for the day. We'll be back tomorrow to complete the rotunda roof and fit-out, then plant all the bushes and vines," said Johanna. "It'll be a picture by tomorrow's party. Ed and I are taking Jane and Amber to North Head in the morning, but we'll be back by lunchtime to finish the job. We've been talking to a number of the girls here, and our team are amazed at what some of these youngsters have had to overcome. They're a wonderful bunch, and we want to do them and you proud with this programme."

Johanna had formed a close bond with Sister Chrissy, and was very keen to make this whole project a great success.

"We'll all be done for the day in less than an hour. See you to-morrow morning. I'll apologise in advance, since we'll be starting at first light."

Dave received a text message from Georgia before he left. He read it inquisitively.

*Tina was right—expect the unexpected. Tell you later. We have a dinner date with the commissioner at 7pm. We need to leave home at 6.30. Be there.*

This was a very unusual message from Georgia. He replied, saying he'd be there, then went to make a phone call. He looked up his contacts, found Trent Jacobson and pressed dial.

Meanwhile, back inside the cottage, the girls were all grouped around Cate in the dining room. Knife in hand, she carved her name into the top of the wooden table.

"I didn't think I'd ever get to do this," she laughed.

Everyone cheered.

# Chapter Fifty-Eight

P olice Commissioner John Palmer felt calm for the first time in days. He'd made up his mind around mid-morning and was at peace with his momentous decision—one he never imagined he'd have to make.

Watching Rusty's body being loaded into an ambulance the previous night had been gut-wrenching for the commissioner. He'd already been trying to process the loss of Tina and Max, and now Rusty, all in just twenty-four hours. On top of it all was the unseen twist that Tina and her associates had been waging their own war against evil outside of the law, and the information on the Kings Cross footage. It was a lot to take in.

Having remained in his office until well after midnight writing all the necessary reports and setting up an internal investigation, he'd eventually returned home, but without much hope for sleep, and with little drive to eat.

He'd formulated his plan for moving forward both personally and professionally into the small hours of the morning, knowing he'd have to make some fast decisions in all areas. He'd written furiously, laying out the various approaches available to him. He'd sent out a number of emails requesting meetings in the morning, plus a full meeting with most of the force's top echelon at 3pm. By then, he hoped he'd have made up his mind. He'd also fired off an email to newspaper editor Bob Millman, asking him for a 5pm meeting at Day Street Police Headquarters. Finally, he'd fallen into bed at 3.30am, his alarm set for 6.30.

The commissioner had arrived at his office right on 8, beginning with a series of meetings with those closest to him, trying to glean who knew what and to piece together everything that was happening. He eventually concluded that Tina had probably been working on her own, as far as the force was concerned. She must have avoided involving anyone else in her clandestine activities very carefully and cleverly, using Rusty to get all the evidence and intelligence she obtained into the police system.

*I take my hat off to you*, he thought to himself, looking towards the heavens. *You done good.*

When lunchtime arrived, he was finally feeling hungry, with a new vision for the force's future firmly in his mind.

Meanwhile, both Mike and Georgia were speculating as to the purpose of the 3pm meeting they'd been summoned to attend at Day Street. They drove together, arriving about twenty minutes early and proceeding to the main operations room. They soon realised that all the force's top brass and many of their colleagues and task force members had been invited. Some thirty or more were already there, including the AFP Commissioner Alan McDonald, Major General Damien Kennedy and Superintendent Sellis.

Everyone was aware of the attempt on the commissioner's life the night before and the death of his close friend, Rusty Nolan. The mystery surrounding the sinking of the mega yacht and the downing of the Saudi Royal helicopter was still at the forefront of everyone's minds, and they all wondered if they were about to get some answers. Many questions remained as John Palmer took up his position at the lectern, speaking in a slow, strong and deliberate tone.

"Good afternoon, ladies and gentlemen. I don't have to tell any of you it's been a rough couple of days. Thanks to the efforts of many in this room, we've been able to piece together what we believe to be an accurate assessment of events over the past few weeks. Some of what I'm about to impart may seem somewhat speculative, and I'm not at liberty to discuss names or sources of some of these facts at this time, but rest assured that time will prove these theories to be accurate.

"You may remember I spoke earlier this week of my concern that we may have a group of vigilantes operating here in Sydney. I'm now able to confirm that another organisation was responsible for the death of Judge Latta and the unearthing of all this evidence, along with the Kings Cross bombing, the sinking of the mega yacht and the downing of the chopper. The identity of this group is now known to me, and I'll be in a position to say more at a later stage. What I can say is that despite their highly illegal methods, it turns out they've been responsible for a good deal of our most critical intelligence over the past year, somehow working it into our system through the proper channels."

This started a buzz of conversation and speculation around the room, causing the commissioner to rap the lectern for silence.

"I'm aware that you're all keen to know more, but I'm sure you're familiar with the damage that making announcements prematurely can cause. In the meantime, we have some very big shoes to fill as a result of our losses, and today, I want to single out two of our team who have performed over and above throughout this whole saga."

John Palmer then picked up a small box and looked out into the room.

"I am proud to call Superintendent Mike Broadfinger and Inspector Georgia McHenry-Holder forward to receive their new badges of rank and merit certificates."

The whole room erupted with instant applause and acclamation as a bewildered Mike and Georgia stood and walked forward.

"Tina would be very proud of you two. I'm sure she's watching from somewhere up there," said Palmer. "Consider this a well-deserved recognition of your professionalism, dedication and success."

Those in the room continued to clap and call out encouragement as the commissioner pinned on their new badges and ranks.

"That will be all for today, but there will be more to say over the next few days. Again, my thanks to everyone for making the world a better place. I have asked Commissioner McDonald and Major General Kennedy to pass on our thanks and congratulations to those from the AFP and defence forces involved in making this operation a success."

As everyone started to clear the room, the commissioner turned to Mike and Georgia.

"I know this is late notice, but I've booked the three of us a table for dinner, as there's more for us to discuss. Georgia, considering your husband's role in all of this, I'd also like for him to attend. Is 7 o'clock at the Rose Bay pier okay?"

"I'll get hold of Dave. It should be fine," said Georgia. "Thank you, Sir. For everything. We know what you're going through more than most."

Georgia teared up as they left the room. On the way out, she and Mike ran into Alison Hanagan, and they all decided to go for a quick coffee.

"Something's happened," said Alison. "I've never seen the boss change so quickly in such a short time. Yesterday, he was completely washed out, but after narrowly avoiding death last night, his whole demeanour has changed. His body language, his attitude ... suddenly, he's calmer and stronger than ever. I'd love to know what's changed."

Intrigued, the three of them went their separate ways.

Later, when Dave arrived from the cottage, Georgia quickly picked up her new insignia and handed it to him.

"Check this out. No need to bow," she teased.

Dave hadn't seen her smile for a few days and reacted immediately.

"Congrats. Well deserved, if I may say so."

Georgia gave him a rundown on the commissioner's report as they both made ready and departed right on 6.30. When they arrived at the pier, Mike was already seated at a table set for five booked under the commissioner's name. Georgia and Dave sat down, ordering drinks.

Dave immediately proposed a toast.

"To the new super and inspector. Long may they serve."

The three of them touched glasses and drank. They chatted away about the current situation until John Palmer arrived some fifteen minutes later. The three of them were very surprised by his guest. He was accompanied by David Samuels, who still looked distraught but a lot better than when Mike had left him yesterday.

Unable to find the words to say, Georgia gave him a huge bear hug. She was very fond of David, and shared in his grief. Dave, too gave him a hug, and then they all took their seats. They spoke about life without Tina and the events of the past few days.

John Palmer ordered a red and a white wine for the table, and the waiter explained the daily fresh specials. The five of them decided to share a large baked snapper, caught that morning, with all the trimmings—the house special, along with an entrée of fresh mixed seafood.

After a glowing report from Dave on the return of the seven girls to Weatherall Cottage and the *Better Homes and Gardens* project, which would be completed in time for the party the following night, the food began to arrive at the table. Everyone tucked in.

Their conversation flowed easily. Even David chimed in with a few light-hearted stories until the commissioner took the floor, talking quietly so as not to be overheard.

"I've spent the past couple of hours with David going over some information that Rusty gave me just before he was killed," he said. "Before I begin, I'd like to recognise that everyone at this table, and none more so than myself, holds Tina in the highest regard, and rightly so. With David's blessing, I'm about to deliver some news that may surprise the three of you—however, I don't intend to go into specifics, as the knowledge could complicate your futures unnecessarily.

"Earlier today, David spoke with Tina's friend and oncologist, Dr. Marie Emslie, who reported that Tina's condition was far worse than any of us imagined. She was about to be advised to resign immediately and to get her affairs in order, and though she was never given the news, David here suspects she'd been expecting it. As you may know, Tina's diagnosis a few months ago brought her back in touch with an old friend of hers, journalist Catie Lanyon. Through their relationship and shared diagnosis, they encountered others who wanted to make the world a better place with the time they had left—and together, they decided to take matters into their own hands. David knew of this decision, but she made sure never to involve him.

"Without going into detail, the group that formed around them has provided the force with a wealth of intelligence over the past twelve months that we never would've obtained otherwise, resulting in unimaginable successes in the fight against organised crime worldwide. My good friend and confidant, Rusty Nolan, worked closely with Tina and her friends, and he too worked tirelessly to make our world a safer place to bring up our kids. I've also spoken with Catie Lanyon's old boss, editor Bob Millman. He and I go back a long way. Bob was able to provide the final pieces to a number of these unfinished puzzles, and is announcing his retirement on Wednesday. Though I can say no more, let it be known that they all deserve our praise.

"Regardless of the group's success, however, their methods were far out of alignment with the laws of this country," Palmer continued. "As Police Commissioner, I am amongst those chiefly responsible for upholding those laws. If I remain in the role, I will be duty-bound to open an investigation that will have serious consequences for a number of good people still with us, and dishonour the legacy of those who have passed. After a long, sleepless night, I've arrived at my decision, and I'm at peace with it.

"I am the only person with all the knowledge and evidence to establish a successful inquiry into these matters. Without me, there can be no follow-ups or retributions. As such, I will be making a statement at Tina's funeral on Tuesday and then disappearing into the sunset a very happy man, knowing that my tenure in this role has been extremely successful and that justice has been served.

"I don't propose to discuss any of this any further for obvious reasons—I just wanted to finish us off with a toast to Tina, Rusty, their friends and all they accomplished for the good of humanity."

He raised his glass.

Mike, Georgia and Dave were completely blindsided, but David Samuels joined the commissioner in raising his glass.

"To the most beautiful person I've ever met," he said simply.

They drank.

# Chapter Fifty-Nine

J ohanna, Fast Ed and the Channel 7 crew couldn't believe their luck. The sight of old Brokenfoot limping out of the scrub and running straight up onto Jane's lap was terrific, unique footage. Even better, with Scarface now behind bars, Jane had felt safe enough to finally recount her nightmare. As far as the network's producers were concerned, this was as good as it got.

Jane's eyes had been opened an hour earlier when Fast Ed had taken them through Bear Cottage Children's Hospice, just down the road in the grounds of the original St. Patrick's Monastery.

"You never stop to think there are so many people worse off than you," Jane told Johanna, almost embarrassed. "We've all been on a journey, one way or another."

They'd arrived back at Weatherall Cottage just before 1pm, in time to see the last of the plants, shrubs and garden furniture being placed into position in the landscaping project. The rotunda looked sensational; in fact, the whole project was beyond every-one's expectations.

Right on 3 o'clock, all the girls and Sister Chrissy were asked out-side for the 'turning on' ceremony. They all clapped and cheered as the fountain came to life, water cascading down the rocks like a waterfall and into the birdbath, completing the dream.

"We'll get some more shots tonight when the lights come on," said Johanna. "Should be an amazing sight. Is it okay if we shoot a few bits of the party?"

Sister Chrissy was happy to oblige. She couldn't wait to see the look on the chairman's face when he arrived, due sometime after 6.

Once inside, they found the workers putting the final touches on the main lounge and the entry foyer and staircase. The setup looked incredibly welcoming, all the girls were excited.

Dave and Georgia drove into the yard just before 6 with Mia Franks, captain of *Spirit of the Sea,* and the yacht's owner, Ross Ardblaster, in tow.

Sister Chrissy gushed as they climbed the front stairs.

"What do you think?" she said, pointing at the gardens.

Even Dave, who'd been there for some of the early work the day before, couldn't believe the transformation.

"Wow, and wow again," he said. "This is unbelievable."

Georgia and the others were equally impressed as Dave did his best to convey to Ross and Mia what it had looked like just two days before.

Jane and Cate then came out from the cottage, and both immediately made a beeline for Georgia. Cate hadn't seen her since the turmoil of the Misty Falls operation, and both she and Georgia thanked each other tearily as they hugged. It was a heart-warming sight.

The chairman and three of the board members were next to arrive, and the looks on their faces said it all.

Sister Chrissy laughed.

"Fear not, Father John, for the costs have all been covered by sponsorship."

Father John chuckled, shaking his head in disbelief.

The group then walked inside to join all of the others, who were already getting into party mode as Ed's tasty hors d'oeuvres were being handed around. Sister Chrissy watched like a hawk to ensure that no one under eighteen partook of the champagne cocktails. A few of the girls gave her pleading looks, but the old nun firmly shook her head.

Dave walked over to where Mia and Ross were in conversation with Roxy and Amber.

"Congratulations, Amber," he said. "Did you ever imagine you could pull this off?"

"No way. I just thought it'd be a good idea—something for us all to look forward to," she said. "I never thought it'd get this big. I have to keep pinching myself."

Jane introduced the *Better Homes* team to the girls. It seemed that every girl was starstruck and keen to tell their stories. The team was just as interested in them. The TV crew had never heard so many heart-wrenching tales from just one location. They were in awe of the perilous journeys that most of these youngsters had endured.

As night fell, the DJ cranked up the volume and the party started in earnest.

After much dancing and merriment, Dave Holder took to the stage at around 7.30. There was a drop in the boisterous noise levels.

"Good evening, folks. I don't think I have to ask if you're all having a good time," he said cheerfully. "Before we really get underway, I'd like everyone to move out onto the veranda for the turning on of our new garden lights."

Everyone shuffled out through the front doors. Sister Chrissy systematically switched off all the veranda and porch lights, aiming to give the new ones maximum effect.

Father John was given the honours. He flicked the switch and immediately, a dazzling kaleidoscope of colours blazed into life, emerging from under hedges, shrubs and bushes everywhere, some even shining down from the old acorn tree nestled up against the wall. The fairy lights in the rotunda made everyone gasp. Water spurted forth from the fountain, changing colours every few seconds, from vivid greens, deep purples, blood reds and sky blues. 'Oohs' and 'ahhs' escaped from all who watched, the cameras capturing it all.

Once they returned inside, Dave was back on the mic, urging everybody to settle down. He then introduced the chairman, Father John Shepherd, who took the microphone.

"Who'd believe what a difference a month could make in all of our lives," the father began. "When I think of the dire straits we were in such a short time ago, and then I look at all the recent changes, I can hardly believe it. To be able to welcome back seven of our girls to see the transformation of our drab old courtyard into this magnificent garden warms the heart more than I can say. I don't want to say much; I'll let the obvious smiles, laughter and good spirits tell the story. Before I go, I just want to single out two wonderful human beings who have made these transformations possible: Sister Chrissy and Dr. Dave."

The room clapped, cheered and roared with approval.

"I now call upon our CEO, Sister Chrissy Marion, to say a few words."

More thunderous applause erupted from the crowd as Sister Chrissy stepped onto the stage.

"Good evening, everyone. Just twenty-three days ago, I was packing my bags, excommunicated from Weatherall Cottage and thrown onto the ageing scrapheap. I was in tears, knowing what was happening and realising what we had unintentionally inflicted upon so many beautiful souls. Tonight, I am the happiest nun in the world. Even Saint Mary MacKillop, my own personal hero, would be proud."

Sister Chrissy paused for a moment, looking solemn.

"Let us not forget, however, that the price of our jubilation and euphoria has been high—very high indeed. We should never forget what all of these kind and generous people have sacrificed and undertaken to get us to this stage. For me, the turning point was the day Dr. Holder brought in his beautiful wife, Georgia, to address the girls and give them some inspiration. We got way more than we bargained for. Our thanks to Georgia who, as of yesterday, is now a detective inspector—the youngest ever to be sworn into the New South Wales Police Force."

More loud encouragement from the audience.

"To Georgia's colleagues and the defence force personnel, some of whom gave their lives for our one chance to have a wonderful future, we can never repay you. What I can promise is that, for whatever time I have left on this earth, I will take what you've given us and work tirelessly to improve the opportunities for those around me in the hope that, in some small way, it will justify your sacrifice and support."

She started choking up as everyone rose as one, clapping and cheering.

When they settled, Sister Chrissy went on.

"The one thing I know for sure is that the girls in this cottage just need a start—a leg up, and someone to believe they can go out and succeed in this big, wide, wonderful world. Your talents are endless, and I know all of you can do it."

The applause and encouragement reached a fever pitch.

"In closing, I want to thank Amber for her creative genius and the efforts of all involved for our beautiful new gardens and surrounds. I also want to thank Father John and his new board for the faith and trust they have put in us. We will deliver. Finally, I wish to endorse the chairman's remarks. Our greatest blessing was the day Dr. Holder walked up these stairs and into our lives. We will be forever grateful. I now hand back to the good doctor. May God bless you all."

There were tears, cheers and happiness all around as Dave returned to the stand.

"Thank you, Father John and Sister Chrissy. You've just about said it all. Georgia and I consider it an honour and a privilege to be counted amongst your friends. I agree that we have an endless pool of talent in this room. On that note, about two months ago, a few of us heard a poem written by one of our very own. A few weeks later, we heard a second poem of hers, recited in the bushes on Sydney's North Head. I was so impressed that I sent her work to some friends at university for their assessment, and I'm delighted to announce tonight that our very own poet laureate, Roxanne

Jenkins, has penned another masterpiece. This one is dedicated to the life of her friend, and yours—Jamie Bennet."

There were some looks of confusion around the room.

"You know her as Jane Dee, but she is anonymous no more. She has asked that we call her by her real name, Jamie. Without further ado, please give a big hand for Roxanne!"

Roxy climbed onto the stage very sheepishly, breathed deeply and began to recite.

"*Fly Free, Special Angel*, by Roxanne Jenkins.

Secrets abound

Some rosy, some sad

Hiding a past

Entwined in raw grief

Dreaming of good times

Hope lingers around

Tears falling so gently

Splash onto the ground

Sing, mummy, sing

So soothing, so strong

Tears down your cheeks

Fear is so wrong

The end, far too soon

Now, precious angel

Fly free and fly high

Cradle your heart

Leaves whistling, they sigh

Minds, seeking answers

Hearts burning numb

Missing thy love

Your freedom a blessing

In a world far above

Sleep well, precious angel

Weather the storms

Sunflowers and laughter

Nightmares not norms

Tempests pass, hope springs eternal

Fly free.

"Thank you."

The only noise in the room was the quiet motors of the TV cameras.

There was a long pause as Roxy finished—time enough for tears to reach the ground before a burst of spontaneous applause. Roxy reddened and looked at Jamie, who was in tears but smiling broadly and clapping enthusiastically.

As the noise died down, Roxy noticed three unfamiliar people, a middle-aged couple and a fine-looking young man, standing near the side of the stage.

"Well done, sis," shouted the young man. "That was brilliant!"

Roxy immediately recognised his voice.

Roxy shrieked.

"Trent? Trent!"

Racing down off the stage, she threw herself at her missing brother, wrapping herself around him. Those in the room watched in amazement as the rough, tough Roxy they knew melted before their eyes, reunited with her brother after so many years apart.

Dave just held Georgia tightly, tears of happiness rolling down both of their cheeks.

"Job done," he said, looking into her eyes.

Sister Chrissy, a frustrated jazz virtuoso, sat on a stool beside local pianist Owen Reynolds, leading the merry singers in a number of old favourites like *You Are My Sunshine*, *Ain't Misbehaving* and *That Old Black Magic*. No one in attendance would ever forget that night.

As Tina Samuels had often said:

*Expect the unexpected.*

# Chapter Sixty

Sydney turned on a bleak, miserable day for Tina's funeral. Despite this, a huge crowd crammed into the North Sydney Crematorium's largest chapel, with hundreds more waiting outside in the light rain. The service was also being live streamed to the rest of the world.

David Samuels stood in the front pew surrounded by Tina's siblings, their spouses and their ageing mother.

The commissioner sat directly behind David next to Dr. Emslie, and gave one of the most powerful and heartfelt eulogies ever heard by the congregation. He paid tribute to Tina's bravery, tenacity, loyalty, ability and above all, her decency. He spoke of her love for David and her many great successes against organised crime and corruption over a long and distinguished career. He did not mention, as some had anticipated, his own pending retirement or plans for the future.

Brad, Bert, Bernardo and Garth were tucked away in the back corner of the chapel, taking it all in.

The minister had known Tina personally, and had also done his homework with David and the family. He, too, delivered a warm and meaningful sermon, pointing out the wonderful legacy that Tina had left behind for others to learn from and follow.

There were many dignitaries from all walks of life in the chapel, including the New South Wales Premier, Prime Minister Isla Rose, Commissioner Alan McDonald from the AFP, Major General Kennedy and General David Ambleside, chief of the Australian Defence Forces. Many of Tina's other senior colleagues formed part of a large police guard of honour outside the chapel prior to the casket being brought in.

Mike, Georgia and Dave sat with Sister Chrissy and many of the task force members around the middle pews, with editor Bob Millman and some of his executives nearby.

Just before the final prayers, Commissioner John Palmer left his seat and walked purposefully up to Tina's casket, removing his badges, rank insignia and tie and placing them in his cap. He left it all sitting on the head of the casket and there was a moment of silence as everyone tried to make sense of the gesture.

Reverend Max Court rose up and stood in front of the altar, facing those seated.

"I ask you all to stand."

He held both hands high.

"I am the resurrection and the life, saith the Lord," he recited solemnly. "They that believeth in me, though they were dead; yet shall they live, and whoever liveth and believeth in me shall never die."

Reverend Court continued as the casket rolled towards its final destination: the furnace, heated between eight hundred and one thousand degrees Celsius, awaiting the casket and all its adornments.

"In the name of our Lord Jesus Christ, crucified and risen, we commend to God's merciful care Tina Elizabeth Samuels. Earth to earth, dust to dust, ashes to ashes. Blessed are the dead."

He dropped his arms to his sides.

And then there were four.

Brad, Bert, Bernardo and Garth slipped quietly out of the side door, standing at the rear of the mourners as the bulk of them filed out of the main chapel vestibule.

They were surprised when, minutes later, the commissioner sidled over to them.

"I'm sorry for your loss," he said. "She was a wonderful human being. We had a common enemy."

He disappeared into the sea of people, leaving the boys speechless.

Everyone watched as the final members of the family, close friends and colleagues made their way down the two chapel steps onto the white, crushed marble walkway.

No one noticed the commissioner slip out the back of the crowd, sit on a bench under a huge eucalyptus tree, take out a flask and wash down two bright red pills. It wasn't until he fell sideways off the bench a minute or so later and hit the ground that people saw him and started running towards him.

As promised, Commissioner John Palmer had made his statement.

# Epilogue

Twelve months after Tina's funeral, Georgia put the last of the veggies in the oven in preparation for Dave's birthday celebration. Being that it shared a date with the Drummoyne shootout, the Misty Falls raid and Tina's death—just a few small things that had taken up her attention a year before—she'd completely forgotten about his last birthday. Dave had laughed it off, but she was determined to make up for it, starting by inviting Amber and Roxy to take part in the celebration.

Milling about the kitchen, Georgia reflected on their good fortune. Dave's partnership at the clinic was going from strength to strength; this year, their first-ever partnership profit dividend was eye-watering. The only problem was the tax challenge it created.

Dave had also been made chairman of the Weatherall Cottage board in December after Father John had accepted an overseas missionary posting. Under his direction, the cottage was thriving more than ever before. Sister Chrissy was tiring, but still leading by example. She'd instituted a very successful adoption and fostering programme and, with the help of Cate, started a miniature employment service, which had found gainful careers for a number of the girls.

The healthy sponsorship of Dr. Brinsmead's practice and the Peterson family had allowed them to install state-of-the-art IT equipment and training facilities, which made them national leaders in their educational pursuits. On top of this, their new outdoor landscaping design project had won three major industry awards throughout the last year. The positive publicity, particularly their regular segments on *Better Homes and Gardens*, had lifted their profile to an all-time high.

Of all the things that Georgia and Dave had achieved during the year, the highlight had been the purchase of Tina and David's holiday paradise down south at Mossy Point. David had suggested it one night when he came over for dinner. He'd been keen to get out of Sydney and set up a new life somewhere else, and they soon agreed on a deal. Georgia and Dave had been down there to stay three times already, and were utterly enamoured by it.

On David's advice, they often called into the Braidwood bakery, left gifts for Pooh Bear on the Clyde Mountain and became regulars at the *Mossy Point Boat Ramp Café*, where they watched the friendly giant stingrays, local birds and wildlife. They were particularly taken with the Birdland Wildlife Sanctuary at Batemans Bay, and even attended the organisation's fiftieth anniversary party.

David Samuels had not been seen by, or in contact with, any of his close friends or associates for the past six months. Some thought he'd gone to sea on a round-the-world yacht trip; others heard he'd relocated to Tasmania. Interestingly, a man resembling David, save for his hair colour, style and the presence of a droopy moustache, had signed on at the 4G Factory on the Gold Coast, and was keeping a very low profile.

Roxy had been a real success story. She'd been formally adopted by Mavis and Leon Jacobson, Trent's parents, whom she now lived with very happily. They'd hit it off from the start at the Weatherall Cottage party night, where it had been obvious how close the two siblings were. On top of this, she'd started working full time under Captain Mia Franks on Ross Ardblaster's luxury yacht, *Spirit Of The Sea,* and had immediately taken to it. Roxy was coming directly from the yacht to dinner at Georgia and Dave's.

Amber was Georgia's pride and joy. Following the force's response to her forensic and tracking capabilities during the previous year's events, Amber had jumped at the offer to enlist, graduating as dux of her squad at Goulburn Police Academy the previous month ahead of sixty-two others. The passing-out parade had been the best day of her life. She now worked under Alison Hanagan at Day Street HQ, making great strides and amazing her senior colleagues at every turn.

Amber had been delighted with all the awards for her garden design at the cottage. She'd become a mini celebrity after all the TV coverage, and had secured the means to move into a two-bedroom apartment with her cousin Maryanne at Alexandria. They were a good match for each other and loved their life together.

Back at Chatswood, things had finally settled down. Mike had been promoted into Tina's old role, with Georgia as his 2IC. They worked well together, enjoying continuing success against the mobs. They occasionally had discussions in private about Tina's so-called 'other side', but agreed never to investigate further. Tina was still the pin-up girl of the New South Wales Police Public Relations Unit, and they thought it only fitting she stay that way.

Georgia was sad that Jamie couldn't make it to their dinner but was proud of how well she was doing at university in Melbourne. She was nearing the end of her first year of a psychology degree, which Dave had facilitated. She was also in love, having fallen for a fellow student, Barry Constance. They were both smitten. Barry had come up to Sydney with Jamie for the past two holidays, as Jamie still had her own room at Dave and Georgia's. Barry had bunked on the lounge, and both Dave and Georgia thought he was a fabulous guy. They struck the pair as perfectly suited, and saw a bright future ahead of them. Georgia had received Jamie's present and birthday card for Dave some time ago, and would give them to him tonight.

After 'Scarface' had confessed and led police to where the remains of Jamie's family had been buried, she'd finally had the chance to put them to rest, giving her closure at last.

Amber was the first to arrive, a few minutes before 6. She was excited, as she'd made her first solo arrest that afternoon. She told Georgia all about it.

Dave came home in the mood to party, carrying a couple of special wines and a slab of his favourite orange cake.

Roxy seemed to be running late and Georgia was surprised that she hadn't called ahead. While they waited for her to arrive, Georgia gave Dave Jamie's present and card. He opened the gift first—a number eight jumper of his favourite team, the Eastern Suburbs Roosters. They all laughed, as Jamie had always given him grief on behalf of her beloved Manly team.

He opened the card and read it aloud.

*Dear Doctor Dave,*

*I can't imagine where I'd be or what would've become of me had you not walked into my life. I know I wasn't always the easiest person to counsel, and I can't express my gratitude for your persistence and guidance or Georgia's unbelievable support and encouragement enough. I may never be able to repay you, but I'll do my very best to make you proud of me.*

*I'm sorry I can't be there to celebrate with you tonight, but I'm there in spirit. Please have a wonderful birthday and an even better year ahead.*

*Love always,*

*Jamie.*

*P.S. DROP DEAD!*

They all roared with laughter.

Amber tried to get hold of Roxy on her mobile, but had no luck. She left a message.

A few minutes later, there was a rap on the front door. Georgia opened it to find two uniformed police standing by the entrance.

"Georgia Holder?"

"Yes, that's me. What's the matter?"

"I'm very sorry to have to tell you, but ... there's been an accident."

# Also By

**LANCE COLBERT SMITH**

THE BRIGHTER SIDE OF A DEATH THREAT.
Autobiography. 2020 www.lancecolbertsmith.com

DEEDS OF SALVATION.
Fiction. 2020. www.deedsofsalvation.com

# Acknowledgments

Once again, what a fabulous journey it's been, and another top team effort. Without Helen, Gail Tagarro, Tyrone Couch and Jim, we'd have no engine room—and our creative friend Patrick has covered us in style, as usual.

In particular, I want to thank Cousin Pam and the Court-ney-O'Connors for their faith in this project, and all their assistance in making our dreams come true.

This story may be a work of fiction, but it's a good yarn, and it deserves its place on bookshelves and big screens everywhere. All of the above people's efforts and support have made that a possibility.

Let's see what happens, eh?

# About The Author

Lance came into this life on Raglan St, Mosman, in 1943. His school years in Broken Hill, Bathurst, Cootamundra and Coffs Harbour taught him many valuable lessons and gave him a solid launching platform to leave Australia, aged 17, to travel the world on his own.

His late teens found him working in Piraeus, Greece; Delft, Holland; Berlin, Germany; and Paris, France before returning to the UK. There, he joined the London Fire Brigade and was able to follow his other passions, playing rugby and pranks in equal measure.

Transferring home to the New South Wales Fire Brigade, he was stationed at Kings Cross for a few years before heading north to work on Queensland's Daydream Island over 50 years ago, where he met and married his soulmate, Helen.

Together, they reared three great kids in beautiful Batemans Bay on the picturesque New South Wales South Coast. There, Helen and Lance found time to run their motel, develop and open a wildlife park and establish Merinda River Cruises. Lance became President of the Lions Club and Chamber of Commerce before becoming a Councillor, then Shire President of Eurobodalla Shire Council. Along the way, Lance was admitted to the George Bass Surfboat Marathon Hall Of Fame. Together with Normie Rowe and Dr. Victor Chang, he was also the recipient of the Bicentennial Advance Australia award in 1988 before being appointed Benefactor of the Camperdown Children's Hospital a year later.

In 2009, Lance was awarded an Order Of Australia (AM) for his work with Bear Cottage Children's Hospice in Manly, then later became the first ever lifetime member of the Outback Queensland Tourism Association. He was also awarded the 2012 Vince Evett award for the most outstanding contribution by an individual for his work in Longreach and the bush.

Now living in a retirement community on the beachfront at sleepy Hastings Point in northern New South Wales, Lance enjoys his daily river swim, a relaxed lifestyle and writing books.

His latest novel, *P.S. Drop Dead*, is a sequel to *Deeds of Salvation*, published in 2020. He is already hard at work planning the third book of the trilogy.

Look forward to it!